"We Know What's Going To Happen In November."

Joe wasn't sure what Lazard was getting at. He raised an eyebrow, and Lazard continued: "American politics is a reasonably predictable process. It is extraordinarily foolish not to plan ahead when one can."

"What are you planning?"

"We're gonna do what we've wanted to do for twenty years."

"What is it?" asked Joe impatiently.

"Put someone in the White House."

"Why bother?" asked Joe. "Why take the risk? You guys get most of what you want, most of the time."

Lazard fixed Joe with a look of uncalculated anger and astonishment. "I'm afraid you don't understand, Joe," he said slowly. "We want the whole loaf."

GAME OF HONOR

TOM LEWIS

CHARTER BOOKS, NEW YORK

First published as *Billy's Army* by Nicolas Babcock.

"Silver in the Stubble," words and music by Sidney Carter.
© Copyright 1970 TRO Essex Music Ltd., London, England.
TRO-Essex Music, Inc., New York, controls all publication rights for
the U.S.A. and Canada. Used by permission.

This Charter book contains the complete
text of the original hardcover edition.
It has been completely reset in a typeface
designed for easy reading, and was printed
from new film.

GAME OF HONOR

A Charter Book / published by arrangement with
Atheneum Publishers

PRINTING HISTORY
Atheneum edition / July 1982
Charter edition / January 1986

ISBN: 0-441-27316-5

Charter Books are published by The Berkley Publishing Group,
200 Madison Avenue, New York, New York 10016.
PRINTED IN THE UNITED STATES OF AMERICA

For EWL and PFL

PART   1

"*Never forget that the most profound force in the world is love.*"
Nelson Rockefeller to Henry Kissinger

ONE ═══════════════════

THE CEMETERY WAS quiet, but it was not a peaceful place for him, and he was glad to leave. He had paid his annual visit to the graves of his wife and daughter, and now he could go. He hated the place. The slopes of short green grass were cared for like a golf course. The trees were ten-foot whips held upright by ugly wires and stakes, and they were planted at precise, regular intervals. The stones were in perfect order, each in one of the four approved colors and styles—a boneyard of gray or black granite, or pink or white marble, heavy in design, carved by machine. Under the smooth grass were tons of mahogany and brass caskets encased in hermetically sealed crypts of lead and concrete. There was none of the consolation of a graveyard in this place, only the glare of painful memories.

The stones he had chosen for Mary and Ellen were the best he could do: gray granite with their names and dates of birth and death. A few lines of poetry from Donne and Yeats were engraved on the stones—he had pondered the choices for days. He wished he could have buried them in a rural cemetery in New England or his own Wisconsin, where their graves would have been surrounded by eroded limestone and hand-carved

3

granite, shaded by huge oaks, maples, and tall cedars.

But his wife and daughter were not present in the graves before him, he reminded himself. Their bodies were dead and therefore did not exist, and their souls had fled through the low door of death to somewhere he could not imagine, a place out of all human experience. He was not sad for them, but he was miserable for himself. He missed them terribly. When they died, one after the other, they left a wound in his life he could not heal.

He turned and walked down the broad slope to his car. He passed fresh graves covered with sod and heaps of flowers. He passed open holes with neat piles of sod nearby, and heaps of clay and marl under green tarpaulins.

These sights hurt him. He yearned for the close-packed disorder of old graveyards near churches; their unkempt paths and dark ivy, with the tattered little flags and weathered bronze medallions marking the passage of veterans of the Grand Old Army, or the Spanish-American War in Cuba and the Philippines, or the American Expeditionary Force. He thought of young men from little towns crippled from bad doctoring, food poisoning, and tropical diseases, or dying lingering deaths in veterans' hospitals from gas damage to their lungs. Young men picked up, carried away, and struck down. He could have been one of them but he had survived the most recent war and returned. The ones he left at home were struck down instead. He came close to wishing they had lived and he had died, but he couldn't bring himself to give in to the thought.

The bare grounds under the hot Potomac sun were awful. He was sorry he hadn't parked closer to the graves. He prayed for Mary and Ellen as he walked across the grass, and for Billy and himself. It was the only time he prayed—when he came here—and this time he wept, too. It wasn't the aesthetics of the ugly, bare-assed cemetery that bothered him—it was the awful loss of Mary and Ellen, and Billy's loneliness, and his own unending isolation.

That was the morning. The afternoon was worse. Near Bethesda Naval Hospital on his way back into the city from the cemetery, he decided he was hungry. Confronted with a choice between McDonald's and Howard Johnson's he chose a restaurant called

Shanghai Garden. It was a mistake. They gave him wonton soup that tasted canned, and a bowl of greasy lo mein. He drank Coke to cut the grease, and two pots of tea. They charged him for the second pot of tea, which annoyed him, so he went back to his table and picked up the tip. The waiter made a waterfront comment in Chinese. He turned on the waiter and told him, in a passable Shanghai dialect, why he had picked up the tip and where the waiter could stick the second pot of tea.

On the sidewalk, he stopped by his car to light a cigar, one of the cheap Filipino cigars he bought by mail from a tobacco shop in Cambridge, Mass., on Harvard Square. He had discovered the place years before when he was invited to a private seminar on Southeast Asia held by a joint committee of scholars from Harvard and MIT—academic cold warriors, some of the most ambitious men he'd ever encountered. Now they were in power or about to be. Half of them were at State or Defense, and the other half were working for the Bush or Reagan campaigns. Joe knew more about Southeast Asia than all of them together, and he was out of work.

He looked back up the street at the blue Ford Fairmont that had picked him up at noon as he drove out of the cemetery. The two men inside looked blankly back at him for a minute, then the driver started the car, and they waited for him to get into his car and drive away. They no doubt knew where he was going.

He had some time to kill, so he stood on the sidewalk in the sun, puffing his cigar. He debated playing a game with them. But he wasn't sure who they were, and he was sure they knew the back streets of the District as well as he did, and he knew it wasn't smart to make any sudden moves now; so he got into his car and drove straight down Wisconsin Avenue to the public garage at Albemarle Street, where he sat in his car with the engine running and the air conditioning on low until it was time for his appointment.

The garage was dim and gray like a basement, with stalactites of lime hanging from the concrete ceiling along the drip lines. The walls were open. He had parked against a railing, so he could see the building across Wisconsin Avenue where he was about to go. It was a nondescript five-floor office building—the tallest in the area—of the dirty red brick with steel casement windows. It was postwar Washington architecture of the most utilitarian kind.

All he could see in the windows were fluorescent lights, the backs of metal filing cabinets, a woman watering potted plants, a few men standing over their desks. Most of the windows were blanked by venetian blinds, lowered against the afternoon sun. It didn't have the look of a government building, but a thicket of complicated radio and TV antennas was guyed to the flat roof. A mast held an array of microwave dishes aimed in different directions.

He shut the engine off, locked his car, and walked down the long winding ramp from the third level to the street. He wanted another look at the two men. They were parked tail-in a few slots from the entrance, where they had a clear view of all the ways out, and a quick U-turn to the exit. He got a good look. Old, puffy, and worn-out. They were the taxi squad, retired DC cops or FBI agents picking up a few bucks on the side. They weren't a tail; they were a convoy. He wondered who sent them. He had been here before, but never with an escort.

He crossed Wisconsin Avenue. The men stayed in their car. Several blocks of shops ran north along the avenue. To the south down the slope toward downtown were large houses and a church. Farther down Albemarle toward Connecticut Avenue was a residential neighborhood that seemed from his angle as he walked toward it to be nothing but trees, shaded and inviting.

He wanted to keep walking, but he turned into the lobby of the office building. It was functional and bare. A boy and girl from Woodrow Wilson High School stood necking in the corner of the lobby, out of sight of the street. The sweet smell of pot hung in the air. The school was a block away. The nearby streets were crowded with students hanging out, cutting classes or loitering during their lunch period. He thought of Billy and wondered if he had gone to school today.

The couple was oblivious to his presence as he waited for the elevator. The girl leaned back against the wall and the boy leaned against her. They explored each other's mouths with their tongues and moved slowly and lightly against each other. The boy's hand was buried down the back of the girl's jeans. Her hands stroked his back under his T-shirt.

The elevator came and he rode it up to the third floor, feeling sexually aroused for the first time in days. He could not remember what it had been like at that age. Maybe he had never known. The needs had always been the same but the new rules were very different.

There were five doors on the hall. Three were blank. One was marked MEN. The last said SECURITY ASSOCIATES, INC. He entered it after knocking lightly. The receptionist was a pretty black woman in a smart blue uniform with a square gold badge. She sat behind a desk facing the door.

The reception area was small. Two doors led into inner offices. There were a couple of worn chairs behind a cheap coffee table littered with worn magazines. It was like a doctor's shabby waiting room, except that the large mirror behind the receptionist was a one-way mirror with a video camera behind it, and the room was miked. Joe knew they would tape his every word and do an immediate stress analysis on his first few remarks, to try to get the edge on him before he went inside.

"Yes?" said the young woman.

"Joe Ball," he said. "I have a two o'clock appointment."

She looked at a short list next to her paperback book and nodded. She offered him a ball-point pen. She took a triplicate form from a drawer and pushed it toward him. "Fill this out and sign it," she said. "And press hard." She waved him to a chair and opened her book.

He bent over the coffee table, put the form on the back of a magazine, and filled it out. He printed where it said PLEASE PRINT, and signed where it said PLEASE SIGN YOUR FULL NAME. They wanted updated information about his marital status and job, and a sample of his writing. It was part of the drill. He passed the completed form to the guard. She disappeared through the door to the right.

He sat down again and leafed through an old *Reader's Digest*. He let the words on the pages blur before his eyes. He concentrated on his breath rate and let his mind drift until his inner eye locked on a familiar object—a small, intricately carved jade fish, resting for the moment in an embroidered cloth purse in the breast pocket of his suit jacket. For the next two hours, he would have to struggle to keep the beautiful fish in the center of his attention.

For a few minutes before the guard returned to get him, he

felt the sadness and rage of the morning lift away. He visualized the sadness as a heavy, dark rain cloud, and managed to send it down the outer hall and out an open window into the air over the trees along Albemarle Street, but he could not rid himself completely of the corrosive rage. He tried to localize it in the center of his stomach, where he would be aware of it. He knew he would be exhausted and nearly ill after a two-hour effort to keep it there, but it would not betray him at a touchy moment.

The guard jerked the door open and said brusquely, "Mr. Kavenaugh will see you now, Mr. Ball." She stood back to let him pass. As he walked by her, he inhaled. She smelled warm and clean. His arousal had not diminished. That was useful. If his mind wearied of the jade fish, and the rage began to rise out of his belly, he could think of the gold chain against the dark brown skin in the hollow of the woman's neck, in the vee of the open collar of the light blue shirt.

He said, "Thank you."

She went back to her desk and her book. There was a faint click as the electric lock in the door snapped shut.

When he and the other surplus warlords were fired, they all went their separate ways as fast as they could, even though they vowed to stay in touch. They joked about forming their own private 40 Committee, their own government-in-exile. It was a form of gray-black politics they were adept at—and none more than Joe. He had been one of the senior warlords, the one whose experiences were turned into classified case studies and taught in the training schools, not to beginners but to the middle-level operators brought back for advanced work. "OK," said the instructors. "Pay attention. This is how it's really done."

When they were fired, the last act of the Office of Security was to warn them to check in twice a year for a quick interview and a flutter on the box, just to be sure they stayed kosher. Today was Joe's day.

Joe knew Kavenaugh—a thin, nervous man in his forties, with jet black hair and pale Irish skin covered with freckles. He was the ace on the box, their best interrogator, and he always had been, from the day he started. He had a natural talent. They used him for the hard jobs.

They used him on Powers, when the U-2 pilot came back in the trade for Colonel Abel, and they used him on defectors: Anatoli Golitsin, code-named STONE; and the most difficult and enigmatic defector of all, Yuri Nosenko, the KGB executive who told fairy tales about Lee Harvey Oswald's days in Minsk and Moscow. It was said that Kavenaugh had done Oswald himself when Oswald returned to the US in 1962, but there couldn't have been more than half a dozen people alive who knew the truth of that, and Joe wasn't one of them.

Joe had met Kavenaugh and heard the stories, but had never faced him in a duel on the box. There had never been a reason. Now, as Joe sat down in a hard wooden chair facing the plain white wall of the interrogation room, he brought to mind the image of the jade fish. He enlarged it in the lens of his mind's eye and projected it against the blank wall, where the image floated as if on a movie screen.

Kavenaugh bustled around, murmuring pleasantries, fastening the electrodes to Joe's palms, the blood-pressure cuff to the upper arm, and the corrugated plastic expansion tube around Joe's chest to measure his rate of respiration. Then Joe heard the scrape of Kavenaugh's wooden stool as the interrogator sat down behind Joe, out of Joe's sight for the rest of the session.

The room was soundproof, and warm but not uncomfortable. The air seemed quite dry. After a few minutes, Joe could feel his nasal passages drying out. "Blood pressure OK?" asked Joe. "This is the only time I bother to get it checked."

There was no immediate answer. Joe could hear the faint click of toggle switches and the even fainter rasp as the intricate graph paper began to unroll beneath the recording pens. He sensed Kavenaugh peering at the digital readout that showed systolic over diastolic blood pressure.

"One-thirty-five over eighty-eight," said Kavenaugh. "I'm no doctor, Joe, but that's marginally high." Joe heard the rustle of paper. "It's your highest so far," said Kavenaugh. "You ought to see an MD."

"They used to bring one to these things," said Joe.

"Budget cuts," murmured Kavenaugh. "Same old shit."

"Right."

They were silent for a moment as Kavenaugh adjusted the machine.

"I have to pee," said Joe.

"You'll have to wait." Kavenaugh's voice was nearly inaudible. The scratch of recording pens on the rolling paper sounded like insects in dry leaves. Joe's eyes closed and he watched the jade fish swimming before an ornate cloud chariot in which rode an ageless, beautiful Chinese goddess. He could have gone to sleep. He remembered that he had seen the goddess on a calendar over the cash register at the Shanghai Garden. The fish in his pocket, the fish in his mind, and the fish on the calendar were all the same fish. He opened his eyes and jerked the muscles of his abdomen tight, as though he was doing sit-ups.

"Stop twitching," whispered Kavenaugh. "Or I'll tell the girl to take another blood sample."

The nurse who took the blood sample was inept and rough. She had left a nasty bruise in the crook of Joe's right arm. The needle she used was as dull as a knitting needle.

"No thanks," said Joe. "Where'd you find her?"

"On the street," said Kavenaugh sarcastically. "She used to work in one of those storefront clinics where they pay winos and other victims of hepatitis twenty-five bucks for a quart of their blood."

"Same old shit," said Joe.

"Umm."

"You still under a cloud?" asked Joe.

"No. I've been promoted."

Kavenaugh had masterminded the hostile interrogation of Nosenko, after which the Soviet Union Division and James Jesus Angleton's counterintelligence gang had concluded for the second time that Nosenko was a KGB plant, a disinformation agent trying to muddy the waters of US intelligence after the Kennedy assassination. It was an unpopular conclusion in the inner circle of the Nixon administration; the reasons for the distaste were as confused as everything else at the time, but seemed to have something to do with J. Edgar Hoover's insistence on believing Nosenko, who more or less confirmed Hoover's 1963 advice to the Warren Commission that Oswald had acted alone.

Kavenaugh was almost the only one of Angleton's protégés who was not fired by William Colby when Colby became Director of Central Intelligence in 1974. Kavenaugh was too good to lose, so his performance was excused on the grounds that he was a technician and not a policymaker, and therefore not responsible for any part of the attempt to discredit Nosenko, who was now settled in North Carolina with a CIA pension and a new identity. But Kavenaugh's wrist was slapped by shuffling him from counterintelligence into Security, where his career was put on hold and he was consigned to the boredom of routine cases.

"Promoted to what?" asked Joe nicely.

"Your case officer," murmured Kavenaugh.

The jake fish faded and shrank, and the ball of rage expanded like a helium balloon in Joe's belly. At that moment, Kavenaugh asked his first question.

"When did you meet your wife, Mary?"

"1959," choked Joe. "You sonofabitch. You knew I went to the cemetery this morning."

"No, no," whispered Kavenaugh. "I'm sorry."

The fish disappeared. The rage rose in Joe's throat like vomit. He struggled to see the thin gold chain against the woman's dark skin. "You fuckers had a tail on me all day."

Kavenaugh said nothing. Joe sensed him listening to someone talking into the earphone plugged into his right ear. The pale pink plastic plug, wired to a jack in the console of the machine, made Kavenaugh look like an anchorman or a Secret Service agent. The door opened and someone walked in. Kavenaugh's breathing was audible. There was a rustle of papers.

"Don't turn around, Joe," said Kavenaugh.

The door closed, but whoever entered remained in the room. A man I don't know, thought Joe. He swallowed the ball of rage by physically swallowing over and over as though a large pill had stuck in his throat. He dismissed the image of the woman's soft skin and called up the image of the pale green fish. It was a carp, beautifully formed, with a swirling tail and an open, somehow expectant look.

Joe had its twin, carved in rose jade and even more lovely, but the twin was in the safe deposit box in the bank, and the green jade fish was in his jacket pocket. The jacket hung on a hook on the back of the door behind Joe's right shoulder, the door the stranger had entered. It was much easier to visualize the green jade fish than the rose jade fish or the woman's gold chain.

"OK," said Kavenaugh briskly, in a clear voice. "We'll start over."

The momentary confusion in the little room vanished. The morning's convoy was forgotten. The translucent image of the green jade fish shimmered as large as a dolphin on the white wall.

Kavenaugh went through a series of biographical questions at a fast pace, establishing a baseline, then went back through them again, starting with the question about Mary. Then he began the variations, throwing curve balls, sinkers, sliders, and a few change-ups. He inserted new questions into the routine, sometimes repeating one several times, then dropping it, then repeating it again ten minutes later. A trickle of sweat started down Joe's sides, a few itchy drops turning in a few minutes to a river. The extremely dry air in the room made him more conscious of his sweat, and made the machine more sensitive to the changes in perspiration.

"Aspirin is the only drug I ever take," lied Joe. He heard himself tell the harmless lie twice more as Kavenaugh went through the routine. It was the same lie Joe had repeated every year to the doctors during the annual physical. And to the flutterers. Their dials and recording pens always jumped a bit when he said it, but his little lies drew his own baseline—the maximums and minimums on the graph, the peaks and valleys drawn by the bright-colored inks of the recording pens that outlined the limits of his adherence to the truth.

There was a whole history of little lies about how much he drank, about his sexual fidelity, about his money habits. Over the years, he varied the lies a bit, always avoiding anything too dramatic that would make the pens jump too quick. He was especially inventive and thoughtful about his lies during the surprise flutters when the boys from Security showed up while your dinner was being served in Bangkok, or you were working late at night in your Langley office. They hooked you up on the spot and sweated you as hard as they could. Each time, Joe's white lies broadened the baseline, and a bit more innocent confusion and bad memory crept into the transcripts.

The Security boys were skilled but not subtle, trained to follow leads like bloodhounds—straight through the cornfields and into the woods. The outright torture of an American citizen had been disallowed after a few ugly incidents in the early fifties; hard questions in isolation were the worst they could do. If they sniffed the spoor, they went after you as hard and fast as they could. If they didn't bore right in or come back at you in the second, or third, or fourth round, you were probably OK.

Kavenaugh was different. He understood the game as well as Joe. Kavenaugh had recovered from his confusion about the convoy, and in the process had lit a warning light in Joe's mind. But Joe had managed to swallow his rage and project his green fish back up on the screen. They were evenly matched. It was going to be a long afternoon. It was, after all, a matter of more or less—there was no such thing as absolute truth that could be measured on a black box—and the game of more or less was one Joe had played all his adult life, with more or less success.

"What time is it?" asked Joe. They had taken his watch.

"Sorry, Joe," murmured Kavenaugh. "I don't know." There was a rustle of paper behind Joe's right ear as the third man in the room turned his wrist to look at his watch. The man was holding a sheaf of papers in his left hand, thought Joe. There was a faint odor of cigars in the room. Kavenaugh didn't smoke.

Kavenaugh's lie was a polite one, but it was a mistake. Joe had done his share of interrogations and had learned long ago the oldest rule in the book: Never lie to the subject about anything. Your lie legitimizes his.

Now Joe knew he had an infinitesimal edge on Kavenaugh. And Kavenaugh knew he had made a mistake. He came on very strong. The presence of the third man in the room must be bothering him. It was the most unpleasant and hostile interrogation Joe had ever endured. Kavenaugh went at him in the old fifties manner of *Are you now or have you ever been?*

"Have you been contacted by any foreign intelligence agencies or officials since the last time you were here?"

"No." It was the truth, although Joe was now wondering who the two hoods in the blue Ford worked for.

"For any reason whatsoever, have you been in touch with any former colleague from the CIA?"

"No." It was a lie.

"Has any present member of this agency contacted you outside channels?"

"No." It was another lie. He had been contacted yesterday

by a man he hadn't seen or heard from in twelve years. They were meeting for lunch the next day.

Years of such inquisitions, years of wearing the cuffs and electrodes, had taught Joe how to lie to the box. Like most good agents, he had taught himself a crude technique for bio-feedback. He kept his physiological reactions—pulse, breath rate, and skin moisture—within the broad band established by his years of white lies. He had deliberately let himself sweat like a river early in the session, to minimize wide swings in the galvanic reaction to changes in skin moisture later in the session when it got tough.

So when he lied about being contacted, the pens barely twitched on the graph paper unrolling slowly beneath them. It was brinkmanship, but there were no follow-up questions, and Joe took that as a good sign, more or less.

Richard Helms once testified to the Congress that it was pointless to use lie detectors on Eastern Europeans and Soviet nationals because they lived in a political culture where lying was an accepted norm. What Helms didn't tell the credulous congressmen, and what they would not have understood, was that the purges inside the CIA during the sixties and seventies had created a Slavic political culture in the Agency that made it nearly impossible to interrogate the Agency's most sophisticated employees for the purposes of internal security. They had gotten too good at lying—to each other, to their bosses, to themselves.

Kavenaugh's questions showed that he knew everything the file had to say on the subject of Joe nmn BALL (the acronym *nmn* stood for "no middle name"). Kavenaugh knew, for example, that a dozen times a year Joe took five milligrams of Valium to control outbursts of rage. The targets had usually been Mary or one of the kids. When he was overseas, Joe didn't need the Valium because he had targets for the rage, and weapons to use on them.

Kavenaugh knew the Agency's hired shrinks had assured Joe that his anger was the inevitable sort that builds up inside the pressure cooker of the normal American nuclear family. Kavenaugh knew, because the shrinks had recorded their opinion, that Joe chose to believe this nonsense. Joe's choice was taken as a sign of his stability because it was a measure of his attachment to his family; therefore, in the twisted logic of hired shrinks working for an intelligence agency, Joe was not a candidate for defection to the Soviet Union.

And the docs and inquisitors knew, because Joe once told them, that a handful of times a year he would smoke a joint, or rather, share one with Mary. It was a pleasant minor vice they had acquired during his one year in Mexico in the early sixties, fresh out of training, before the long tours in Asia. He was mildly allergic to marijuana—it made him cough painfully—but it had an aphrodsiac effect he enjoyed and sometimes needed.

Joe would smile as he said this, and the docs and inquisitors would nod, offer solemn smiles, and take more notes for his file. They had a pathetic faith in the box, and in the crude norms and statistics of their academic psychology. For them and their bosses, the box was a management technique, not an intelligence technique. It was a way to keep order in the ranks, not a way to dig out double agents or ferret out information.

The Agency had confused efficient management and good intelligence for so long that it no longer knew the difference. That was why Joe and his cohorts among the secret warlords were fired: because they knew the difference. And that was why Kavenaugh had been exiled to Security: because he knew the difference too. As the interrogation wound down toward the end of the long afternoon, Joe inventoried what he knew about Kavenaugh, and wondered who the other man was.

The door closed sharply. The other man had left the room. Switches clicked softly. The paper stopped rolling. Kavenaugh scraped back his stool and stood up to stretch.

"What time is it?" asked Joe.

"Four o'clock," murmured Kavenaugh, as he came around to unfasten Joe.

Joe sat erect in the chair, mentally feeling himself all over, like a man who has lived through an auto wreck. It was the longest session he had ever been subject to, and he thought it wouldn't be long before they called him back for another one, or dropped in on him late one night at home. He hoped, perversely, that he would get Kavenaugh again. Having a strong adversary made the entropic fear and waste of energy endurable.

"Hurry the hell up," said Joe. "Get me out of this harness before I piss in my pants."

TWO ===============================

HE HAD A headache when he woke up, but he wasn't hung over. Just to be sure, he lay unmoving in bed for a few moments, and decided that the light pain at the base of his skull was the headache he suffered when he was tense. It would go away when he got up and started moving around. Two aspirins would help.

He turned his head tentatively and looked at the green numbers on the face of the clock radio, 11:03 AM. Ten hours of sleep. It was too much sleep, a familiar sign of depression, and there were long, tangled skeins of dreams he couldn't remember.

Too much alcohol screwed up his dream life. Then the dreams about Mary and Ellen turned into nightmares—agonizing dreams that woke him up shouting, sometimes bringing Billy from the next room with a glass of milk, wanting to comfort his father, but alarmed and worried, too. Billy had a child's respect for nightmares; Joe, the respect of a man who had lived for years with the tribal people of Asian jungles, whose animist beliefs and fears had intermingled with his own half-remembered Catholic orthodoxy. Joe's dream life was important to him. Dreams were his only way to remember the

17

living faces of his dead wife and daughter. So he normally drank very little.

Joe stood up stiffly and walked around the room, stretching and scratching. He pulled a robe on and opened the heavy floor-length drapes that covered the sliding glass door leading to the deck outside the bedroom. He made the bed. It was an antique double bed, not much larger than a modern twin bed. There were two pillows, but the other side of the bed was unslept in. It had been unslept in for two and a half years, and even now Joe slept only on his side of the bed.

He unlocked the sliding door and went out. Under the late morning sun, the wide boards were too hot for bare feet. He crossed to the grass. It needed cutting. The hot sun felt good on his back. He toured the yard slowly, thinking about the day before and the afternoon to come. He stopped in the dense shade of a large mulberry tree.

The fruit was beginning to form on the tree. Later, when the fruit had ripened, he would get purple feet from walking through the litter of fallen berries on the lawn. It was always a mess. Birds flocked to the tree, but the fruit was cathartic, and the neighbors complained about purple stains on their clean laundry.

Once, he threatened to cut the tree down for firewood after a neighbor's angry complaint, but the kids claimed the tree for a hideout and built themselves a tree house. They built it to last forever. The solid platform was still there, wedged and nailed in a crotch of heavy branches about fifteen feet off the ground. The structure was now nearly invisible—stained and mossy. The weathered tree house had become a camouflaged part of the living tree.

He stood staring up at the tree, clinging to the fading images of the dream as long as he could, but soon he stood alone in the peace and quiet of his own backyard, with no ghosts in his mind. He could hear nothing but the faint noises of the neighborhood—a car starting, a vacuum cleaner in the next house, a barking dog.

Not so many years before, all of them—mother, father, girl and boy—would sit comfortably around a blanket on the large platform, enjoying a picnic in the cool shade of a summer evening. The memory struck him like a high wind. Joe turned away from the tree and fled from the garden into his house.

The family's peaceful happiness had been destroyed as though on purpose. Only weeks after the first pains and the first diagnosis, Mary died of cancer. Three months later, Ellen was killed in a violent auto accident. She was fifteen. The boy driving her home after a summer party was drunk. He survived, hardly touched. The lovely girl was crushed and burned beyond recognition, like a victim of war. In Joe's mind, it was murder.

Three months after that, Joe was fired. Bam, bam, bam. First Mary, then Ellen, then the private ceremony in the Director's office, and the gold medal no one would ever see because the citation was classified TOP SECRET, NO FORN. Not that Joe's life was not the subject of extensive files in half a dozen computers around the world.

Billy remained, now sixteen, drifting and uninterested. He was alive to his father, and they were close, but the boy had few friends and no school life. Other than Joe, the only real force in Billy's life was a young parish priest—a friendship founded on basketball, not religion.

Joe stood in the bathroom. His head throbbed. He rubbed his agitated stomach high up under the ribs. The aspirin would make his stomach worse as it made his head feel better. His hand touched the odd tingle of the scar on his left side under his arm. It was the scar of an old wound from his first tour. It was jagged and ridged.

A large, red-hot rocket fragment had hit him as he led a patrol of Laotian Hmungs toward an NVA transportation camp just inside the southwest corner of North Vietnam. His men carried him away, all the way to their village—a two-day nonstop jog. Then they carried him out to a rendezvous with a Special Forces helicopter. They were pursued every step of the way by an NVA patrol.

The Hmungs had wrapped the wound with leaves from some plant. The first time Joe peered at the wound in a mirror, he expected to see the foliate impression of the leaves on the ugly scar. At the Special Forces hospital on Okinawa, the docs told Joe the leaves had saved him. The wound was a severe burn. The heat had cauterized the blood vessels, and the wet leaves had prevented infection in the burned tissue. "You're lucky," they said, but Joe knew it wasn't luck. The Hmungs knew what they were doing. Three weeks later, he was back with them in the Laotian jungle.

He thought about eating a banana with milk for breakfast. It would be easy on his stomach, but he couldn't remember if there were any bananas left. He couldn't remember if he had gone shopping yesterday, or if Billy had. He couldn't remember anything recent when he wanted to; but the events of two, five, and fifteen years ago were as clear as water in his memory, and flooded in unbidden and unwelcome.

He looked out of the bathroom at the clock radio. He had to get moving. He rinsed his face in hot water, soaped it, and lathered up. As he shaved, stretching the skin of his cheeks and neck taut with his fingers and pulling the blade along, he decided things weren't so bad.

If I took better care of my head. The rest of me's OK. I run twenty miles a week. I'm not overweight. I don't smoke. I'm not funny-looking. I'm not afraid to walk down a dark alley at night when I have to.

His hair was cut short, almost military, but without shape and without white sidewalls above the ears. It grew in motley patches more gray than brown. He laughed out loud at his image.

He rinsed his razor and looked down at his body with familiar interest. Like the rest of him, it was a month over forty-two. He laughed again. The 40 Committee! Christ, he hadn't forgotten that loony business, even though there were more important things he couldn't remember.

All the others who were fired with him were near the age of forty, plus or minus a few years—field hands and Agency warlords who'd been burned out one way or another in Southeast Asia and brought back to Langley with nothing to do. None of them were management material, in the august opinion of management. It was Langley dogma at the time that good field hands made poor analysts or executives.

So a dozen of the best were fired, and hundreds more from the lower ranks. The dozen best had twenty years experience apiece in running secret armies, from the tops of the Himalayas to the jungles of Colombia and Peru. One of them had spent twenty years in South Korea, running couriers and escape and evasion networks that spanned all of North Asia, from the Urals and the frozen wastes of Arctic Siberia to the subtropics of South China.

These men were declared fit for nothing in the new American intelligence service being touted on the pages of the press and in the halls of Congress—a press that had willingly collaborated with the CIA in the bad old days, and a Congress that had happily looked the other way. No more criminality! No more brushfire wars! The cries of moral outrage rose from the White House staff in their tiny offices in the basement of the West Wing.

Henceforth this would be an intelligence service under the law and the Constitution, an *American* service. Knowing too much and fit for nothing, the old hands were unspiked cannons rolling around on the deck in the storm. Joe and the other loose cannons were shoved overboard.

But of course it wasn't a matter of morality; it was a matter of power. Carter's men in the White House were trying to establish control over the heaviest and loosest cannon of all— the CIA—which they had belatedly learned was not really an intelligence-gathering agency. It was primarily an agency for clandestine intervention in the affairs of other nations, and for surreptitious entry into the political life of citizens at home.

Watergate had briefly shown, with the brilliant clarity of a magnesium flare, that the CIA was an organization for secret politics, no more and no less, and it was an instrument of the President only to the extent that the President understood its role and could exercise control.

Understanding this, as Joe and the others did, made it easier to share their bitter private joke about the 40 Committee-in-Exile. The real committee, the overlord of U.S. intelligence operations, was disbanded by Carter's people and reconstituted under a new name. New members were nominated who were loyal to the new regime. It was an act in the best tradition of the corrupt old European services, thought Joe.

The wits in the color-coded halls of Langley quickly gave the name of Chekists to the few survivors of the old committee, after the original members of Lenin's secret police who survived the later purges and name changes under Stalin: GPU, OGPU, NKVD, MVD.

In America, thought Joe, we've had the Special Committee,

then the 303 Committee in 1965, then the 40 Committee after
February 1970. Now it's something else. He racked his brain.
He couldn't remember. Shit. *Shit.*

"SHIT!" he roared at his face in the mirror.

How *had* he and Billy survived these two years? In the
darkness of Joe's mind as he stood naked before his mirror, in
a fury with no object and no outlet, with one foot in the un-
redeeming past and one foot in the hostile future, he decided
he and Billy had to do more than just survive. Survival wasn't
enough; it was an animal instinct, not a human aspiration.

Joe suddenly felt as though he had been writing memos to
himself for months, making fine distinctions that would mean
nothing when the time came to act. It was time to act *now.* He
wasn't a bureaucrat. He had been a gunslinger all his adult life.
He would do what he had to do for himself and Billy. There
weren't many choices to make, really. He had already made
most of the choices allotted to one man's life.

He didn't pursue the thought. He turned the shower on as
hot as he could stand and stepped into the water. He was soon
singing a fine Irish tune with the voice of a man who has made
up his mind.

> *Early in the mornin',*
> *Hear the razor roar.*
> *The silver's in the stubble,*
> *And it wasn't there before.*
>
> *For the leaves are gettin' greener,*
> *And spring is on the way,*
> *And girls are gettin' prettier,*
> *And younger every day.*

He had a vigorous voice, a surprisingly fine baritone, and
the faintest trace of a brogue from somewhere. Mary had loved
his singing. This was the first time he had sung a line of any
song since the day she died.

A dark, lightweight suit over a white shirt with French cuffs—
he was always a careful, conservative dresser. But he left the
knot of his tie loose and carried his jacket by the collar. The

house was warm and humid, even with central air conditioning.

Along the hall, he stopped and listened for a moment by a door, knocked lightly, and opened it. Billy was asleep in a tangle of sheets. The room looked like it hadn't been cleaned in a year. The cleaning lady was forbidden to enter because Billy was supposed to clean his own room. The stale air smelled of dirty clothes and pot.

Joe kicked the boy's bed gently. "No school today?"

Billy stirred and grunted, hoarse and sleepy. He was big and good-looking, with a broad, open face and fair skin tanned dark from hours playing basketball on the school playground. Forehead, ears, and neck were covered with unruly dark brown hair.

"What'll you do, Billy, when the Brothers kick you out of school?"

Grunt.

Joe turned and went out, closing the door softly. Here was one the Marines would have to straighten out, like Joe was straightened out when he was Billy's age and lied about it to enlist. It was like the goddamn fifties—the Church failed, the family failed, and the sons went off to the Marines to mature in the pseudo-peace of the Cold War. The daughters got married, or went to college and then got married.

His rage rose and grabbed his throat again. He slumped against the hallway wall, breathing hard, and forcibly drove the memories from his mind. He thought about the living. "Let me live with the living," he breathed. He thought about Billy.

No, it was something else now. It wasn't the Cold War anymore, and it wasn't Cold War Two. It was the eighties, and there was no name for it, only a sense of dread and menace. It was nameless, and no one knew what the hell was going on. Joe sure didn't know, and he'd be damned if he'd send Billy unarmed and unprepared into the void. Sending Billy meek and mild into the eighties would be a death sentence. It would be like sending him into outer space. Joe wanted to keep Billy at home. The two of them would stick together. They would figure something out together.

Joe pushed himself off the wall and walked to the kitchen. This rage was like grand mal—the attacks were unpredictable and severe, and sometimes like blackouts. They left him deeply unsettled and weak, but he sought no help. There was no drug made to cure him. There was no drug to bring back his wife and daughter.

The portable black and white TV buzzed and rattled at him when he entered the kitchen. It must have been on all night. The tiny speaker vibrated with the noise of a hysterical young woman hugging a grinning MC.

"Trash," hissed Joe. "Shit. Weakness. Rot."

He snapped it off in real irritation. He hated the daytime game shows and soaps. He hated the mindlessness and petty corruption.

He waited for the rage to come up in his throat again, but it wasn't there. Instead, there was just a dry, dull hunger. The TV set rested in the middle of the counter. He unplugged it and pushed it out of the way, turning it to wrap the line cord around the little hooks on the back. Then the rage boiled over. He almost threw the set to the floor.

Through the holes in the back of the set, he had seen the glint of brushed aluminum, and the sight triggered this rage that nearly drove him to his knees. He knew what it was without looking. It was a repeater, a small transmitter hooked into the power circuit of the TV set. It was a small transceiver, repeating and amplifying the signals from small, battery-operated bugs placed around the house. Their signal was too weak to travel more than a few hundred yards, but this repeater—and there were probably several others—could boost the signals from the bugs to a level that would carry several miles. Someone had bugged his house.

Without thinking, he reached into a drawer for a Phillips screwdriver and took the back off the set. Carefully, in cold fury, he disconnected the repeater. It was about the size of a pack of 100-mm cigarettes. The letter *B* was lightly scratched into the side of the aluminum case. He took two screws out and opened the case. A circuit board rested inside with a handful of tiny transistors, resistors, and other parts soldered into little holes or onto silver intersections on the surface of the plastic board. It looked organic, like the insides of a weird parasite that had hooked onto a larger organism. It looked brand-new.

Joe's fury sank, replaced by avid curiosity. Billy was out when Joe came home late the night before, convoyed by the two hoods in the blue Ford. With nothing but good intentions, Joe had wanted to be home in time to take Billy out to dinner, but had eaten by himself in Georgetown. The two passive men in the car had made no attempt to hide, and he had made no attempt to ditch them.

The TV was on in the kitchen when Joe got home. He had made himself a sandwich and a last drink—the evidence was in the sink—and had gone to bed, drunk just enough to believe Billy could take care of himself on the streets of Washington late at night. He had no idea where Billy had been. Billy rarely stayed out so late, and almost never without leaving a note.

"I should have left the damn thing in place," said Joe softly to himself, staring at the repeater. He dropped the thing in a drawer and cleaned up the kitchen quickly. Then he made his breakfast—orange juice, a vitamin pill, a bowl of banana slices in milk, and tea with milk. The food settled his stomach.

He ate standing at the kitchen counter, looking through a window into the backyard. They'll come back, he thought. They'll have to replace the repeater. Then I'll know who it is. It was starting all over again, and he had done absolutely nothing to set it in motion. Passive choices, he thought. By doing nothing, I've made passive choices. I've consented to receive, he thought, remembering the words of a priest from long ago.

The yard looked good through the kitchen window. It had never looked better. Billy was a natural gardener. He liked working in the yard better than going to school. Joe wrote a note and propped it against the coffee canister: "Billy, Please cut the grass. I'll be home by six. I'll do the shopping. Love, Joe."

At exactly noon he started his car and backed down the driveway. He drove slowly down the street. The sidewalks were full of little kids walking home from school for lunch. Some of them waved, and he waved back. The always unpredictable rage rose and subsided, and a wave of deep sadness flooded through him, carrying something else he was condemned to remember without wanting to. He had missed the years when Ellen and Billy were small, the long years he spent in Laos and Vietnam.

This was a prosperous neighborhood of expensive, older houses; they were large, mostly two floors, with tile and slate roofs and weathered copper flashing. At night, through lighted windows, there were glimpses of fine furniture and paintings in well-proportioned rooms, and smart people in good clothes. They were upper-echelon civil servants, lawyers, congressional aides—the permanent mandarinate—nearly all government people, with a few from the private sector. There were cocktail parties and food co-ops and an active neighborhood association, all of which Joe avoided most of the time. There were quite a few working wives, many with professional jobs similar to those of their husbands.

The private sector. Joe laughed out loud to himself, remembering Mary's jokes about the mysterious, shadowy private sector. She knew it well. She had been a CPA in a partnership with two men, and in the last few years had earned considerably more money than Joe.

She claimed that saying "private sector" to a government official was like flashing a crucifix at a vampire—they reeled back in a horrified fascination. Drunk one summer night at a neighbor's party, she went around the yard hissing "private sector" and other curses and seductions into the ears of deputy secretaries and special assistants until she had them all screaming with laughter under the dim light of the Japanese lanterns.

But when she was sober and serious she often said, "The New Deal is dead, Joe. The ideals you and I grew up with are bankrupt, as fine as they were. The private sector is where the real power lies now. Soon they'll take over the government, and it'll be a major shift in the way this country is governed."

"It's just the old battle of right versus left," Joe would say.

"It's more than that," she would answer. "It's private power and wealth against public ideals."

Joe knew she was right. She was never wrong. He was one of the hottest gunslingers in the free world, running the secret wars of the permanent government, and he knew very well how public power had corrupted the old ideals, and how secrecy had turned that power into a tool for the ambitions of a handful of men.

He wasn't a general, but he was a warlord, a manager of wars, and the generals deferred to him. He knew about power, all right. He and his colleagues greased whole Third World countries. They paid off every little shit who had a hand to hold out and a pocket to put it in. And if the gang in office didn't cooperate, he bulldozed them into the nearest ditch and put a new gang in power. If nothing else worked, they just blew them all away—like Laos, like Cambodia, like Vietnam. She wanted him to resign, but he couldn't. He was more than a true believer—he was a worker. Once set onto a task, he had to finish it, or have it ended for him.

Tears for Mary choked him, and rage for his own fate rose and choked him too. He breathed hard in the car, trying to blink away the tears, breathing like a runner at the end of five hard miles. They ended it for him, all right. They fired his ass.

She was right, thought Joe. She was never wrong. He gasped with the effort of maintaining control. I wish she was here, he thought. The private sector is where I am now. And I'm in deep water. I wish to God she was here.

He turned off Nebraska Avenue onto Connecticut and headed downtown, slowing in the heavier traffic. He watched his mirrors carefully. The two goons in the blue Ford weren't there this morning, and no replacements, either. It looked clean behind him. He *felt* clean. He slowed down. He had plenty of time.

It was ten after twelve, and the PBS broadcaster was still carrying on about the hostages in Iran. Joe pounded the steering wheel with his hand. "Shit," he said viciously. "Those fairies. We should have gone in there right away."

The rest of the news was about primaries and inflation. Kennedy was bumbling and Carter was sleep-walking. The voters were angry and afraid—those who would bother to vote. The issues were Iran and a faltering economy. At least, those were the overt issues. The real issue, Joe knew, was the political process itself. It had stopped working.

It was going to be Reagan against Carter, Joe was sure, and the election was Reagan's to win or lose. Even a rescue for the hostages couldn't help Carter—the revulsion for the man was so deep. Joe would bet on Reagan right now, but there was no one to bet with. Billy hated politics and ignored it. Mary and Ellen were the bookies in the family, the newspaper readers, the TV watchers.

Tour buses and yellow school buses filled the downtown streets. The sidewalks were crowded with high school kids on their annual pilgrimage to the shrines of the capital. They wandered in a daze, terribly young, led by teachers as ignorant of government as their pupils. They stood in long lines to get into the White House—the graceful manor house their president lived in.

Men with automatic weapons sat behind the locked front door of the classic portico facing Pennsylvania Avenue. The lovely lawns and gardens were full of buried electronic sensing devices and hidden remote-control video cameras. The lower branches of the huge old trees held powerful floodlights. When they flashed on at night, triggered by automatic sensors, the lawn was brighter than a football stadium. There were no shadows, and there was nowhere to hide. Clear fields of fire swept every angle of every approach.

Deeply preoccupied, Joe drove slowly past the White House, detailing the interior layout in his mind: the warren of offices, passages, stairs, and private rooms. It was an old habit, born of a mild fixation with the trappings of office. In Joe's own priestly service in the jungles, his trappings were often no more than a rice bowl, a short wave radio, a .45, and a captured AK-47.

He turned south past the Treasury toward the bridges over the river. He tuned along the radio dial for classical music. Finding none, he listened for a weather report. The prediction was dismal: hot and humid for the rest of the week. Finding nothing but talk shows, easy-listening, and the noon-hour babble of public broadcasting, he snapped the radio off. It was 12:30.

He crossed the Potomac into Virginia. A few small boats cruised downstream under the bridge. The water looked like gelatin. Smoking jets dropped into National Airport or lined up to take off. Heat shimmered from the roads and rose above the runways like the air over a desert.

He turned onto a highway that ran through a long shopping strip. It was as ugly as sin, lined with banks, real estate offices, junk food franchises, discount stereo warehouses, gas stations, jean boutiques, and all the rest of the fast-turnover retail circus. The newer the structures, the more garish and shabby they were. Hundreds of cars cruised the highway, and thousands more were parked on dozens of acres of asphalt baking under the sun.

Not one but several enormous shopping centers rose like

unfinished ziggurats from the fields of black asphalt. The structures were fully enclosed and air-conditioned, each drawing enough electricity to power a county seat. These sights sickened Joe, who knew they were built on land where dairy farms and apple orchards had once produced wholesome food. To the man who had once been a Wisconsin farm boy, building shopping centers on farmland was no better than spraying herbicides on rice paddies in the Plain of Jars, which he had tried to prevent. His jungle wars had been against political leaders, their generals, and their troops, not against the helpless peasants who were swept back and forth like insects. But he could not expiate his past. He was part of a war machine that had obliterated whole cultures. The scene along the highway reminded him and fed his voracious anger.

Plunked down at irregular intervals along the strip were small office buildings of two or three floors. Their flat roofs made them appear shrunken, and their walls of bronzed glass reflected a surreal vision of temporary permanence. They were surrounded by unkempt commercial landscaping—browned-out evergreens and small parking lots full of windblown litter. There was no commerce here, no solid investment; nothing more than speculation, write-offs, tax shelters, and fast amortization. Greed and the paper games of accountants, thought Joe. Mary wasn't greedy, but she knew the rules of all the games. I wish she was here. I don't know enough to do what I have to do.

None of the office buildings were fully occupied. The tenants were lawyers with no clients, software hustlers, and public relations consultants whose work required only a few pieces of used office furniture, a rented electric typewriter, and two telephones with three lines each and a red hold button.

And a working air conditioner, he thought. One of the offices was his, in the buildings just ahead. He had picked it because it was the only building on the strip with green-tinted glass and windows that opened.

The DC phone number was an answering service. There were no associates. It was an unincorporated one-man show. What Joe knew about big-time public relations could be poured in a teacup, but Joe Ball Associates was not a PR shop. It was a laundry.

Joe was laying a foundation, drawing a baseline, building

JOE BALL ASSOCIATES

Public Relations Consultants

Box 1940,
Olde Towne Station
Alexandria, Virginia 22313   (202) 666-1629

a track record, putting points on the board. He was following a plan worked out by Mary five years before. With Joe Ball Associates, he was careful to do enough business of an appropriate kind to justify his existence to IRS.

When he was ready, he would set up two offshore companies, one in the Bahamas and one in Bermuda. They would become clients of Joe Ball Associates, paying substantial retainers and fees for the services of the firm. Both companies would also do considerable business on their own as venture-capital investors, most likely in small high-technology companies and US real estate.

Joe's plan was Mary's plan, but he was now uncertain of it. The financial and organizational side of it was Mary's part of the show, but the laws changed constantly, and he himself knew little about offshore money movement. It was an aspect of spook life he had no experience with. All he ever did was yell into the radio, "Hey, this is Chop-Chop to Fat Cat. I need fifty AKs, five hundred grenades, and fifty thou in small gold bars." And Air America delivered the load on the next up-country milk run.

Mary was the brains, and he was the mechanic. Now, just as he had to be both mother and father to a lonely boy, he had to be both CPA and gunslinger. It's a hostile economic universe out there, thought Joe as he drove along the awful commercial strip, and I'm damn sure gonna take care of that boy before I do anything else.

He cruised in the right lane at moderate speed, braking for turning cars and stopping at lights. On a long stretch without lights he moved left, moved back to the right, moved left again and stayed in the lane. He watched his mirrors. He stopped suddenly, waiting for a break in oncoming traffic, then swooped left into a Burger King, circled the lot fast, and turned back onto the road in the opposite direction.

Now he drove faster, well over the speed limit, cutting from lane to lane, intent on the mirrors, hoping his Fuzzbuster would protect him to the front. For the first time since they handed him the pink slip there was reason for someone to be watching him.

The day before yesterday there had been a rare message at his answering service: "Call Billy at four. Don't forget." Joe recognized the old work name and word code. At 3:30 he called his service again. The second message read, "Dad, call the school. 442-5983."

From a pay phone near his office Joe dialed 259-4483. A woman's voice asked, in the proper nasal tone, "Your number plee-az." He read off the number of his pay phone backward, hesitating automatically between the third and fourth digits as he read. These were old habits, unforgettable, like riding a bike. A moment later his pay phone rang, loud in the closed booth. A voice he recognized from years before, like a voice from the bottom of a well, said, "Dad, this is Billy. Can you be at the school Thursday at two fifteen?"

"Sure. Be glad to." And that was it. A meeting with a man Joe hadn't seen in a dozen years was set for Wednesday at 1:15. It was a simple code, idiot-proof. Now Joe was on his way to begin his education in up-to-date scams.

Joe turned off the highway and drove down through the side streets of Alexandria toward the Potomac waterfront. He wished he had a scanning CB in the car, and a hi-lo public service scanner. Good surveillance teams used all three sets of frequencies—the high and low public service bands reserved for law enforcement agencies, and the CB band reserved for the public.

The watchers would jump around from channel to channel in prearranged patterns, often using audibles to change the pattern, like a quarterback at the line of scrimmage. But some-

times they got careless or lazy and stayed on one or two channels, and sometimes the well-equipped rabbit got lucky on one
of his scanners.

Joe hadn't been a rabbit in a long time. The goons in the
Fairmont yesterday were the first since he had been fired.
Although he was pretty sure no one was tailing him today, he
was a bit anxious. Most of his work life had been on the side
of the hunters.

Shit! he thought. What if they got into the garage last night
and stuck a homing transmitter under the car? But there was
nothing he could do now, short of using a good frequency
sweep, which he didn't have, or crawling under the car
with a flashlight. Piss on it, he thought. It's too late to worry. I'm
back in the game.

Down near the waterfront, the smell of mud flats was rank
and strong, mixed with the dense, sharp smell of jet exhaust
from the planes at National a couple of miles north up the
river. He drove slowly down a street next to the river. The
cobblestones were patched with asphalt. Old frame houses and
decrepit small businesses lined the street. He parked in a dirt
lot between two small buildings that seemed abandoned. He
was right on time.

He tightened his tie, checking the knot in the rearview mirror. The jet noise nearly deafened him when he got out of the
car. He was under the exit flight path out of National. He
wondered if the low, large planes climbing in different directions might deflect and flutter the signal from a small homing
transmitter. He decided they might, and then decided again not
to worry about something he could do nothing about.

Half his adult life had been spent waiting in airports of all
descriptions. This was the noise of travel, action, and work.
It was familiar and comforting. He shrugged on his suit jacket
and looked around. Nothing was changed, except the scrubby
sumac and locust trees in the vacant lots had grown larger. The
buildings were the same. They would look the same until they
fell down.

Across the street, on the river side of the road, was the most
substantial structure in the neighborhood. It was a large, old
stone building, more deep than wide, with a peaked tin roof
like a hay barn. The roof was painted with aluminum paint to
reflect the sun's heat. It glared in the high sun like a mirror.

Long front porches ran the width of the first and second floors.

It was an old waterfront tavern that had been standing when the British burned Washington in 1814; but closely looked at, it was in good repair. The mortar between the stones had been recently repointed. New screens covered the upstairs windows. A wooden plank door and a screen door opened from the upstairs center hall to the upstairs porch, where a few wooden chairs stood in a semicircle. It looked like a home for war vets.

The wood trim needed painting everywhere. The lower halves of the front windows on the first floor were painted dark green; the upper halves were too dirty to see through. An American flag decal was stuck in the upper corner of one window. A strip of yellow plastic surveyor's tape was tied around one of the porch supports in front of the center entrance. The double wooden doors were glazed with milk glass. Faded black lettering on the glass read THE POTOMAC HOTEL.

Half the first floor was a bar, the other half a dining room, little used, and there were rooms for rent upstairs, unadvertised. Joe had never heard anyone call the place the Potomac Hotel. It was known as Mike's Place. He hadn't been here for a long time.

Joe lit a cigar and took a quick look up and down. The street was deserted. He crossed and mounted the porch, his heels sounding loud on the boards. The hollow noise made him feel like a character in an old black and white Western movie.

The porch door slammed loudly behind him. The interior was cool and dim. A staircase led up from the back of the long, narrow center hall. The dining room to the right was set up but smelled hot and dusty. A heavy swinging door to the left led to the bar. Cool, air-conditioned air leaked around the edges of the door and hit Joe with a rush when he pushed it open.

The barroom was narrow and deep, dimly lit, paneled in a dark wainscoting. An ancient zinc-topped bar ran along the right, a heavy shelf at elbow height along the left. In back was a large cavelike room with a dozen booths and large tables.

Anyone entering the bar was silhouetted in front of the dingy windows for a moment as he looked down the long room, getting his bearings in the smoky darkness.

There was a moment of nearly audible tension, then the bartender said, "Hi, Joe."

"Mike," said Joe in a flat, low voice. All he could see clearly in the dim light behind the bar was the bright splash of the bartender's white Filipino shirt.

Anyone walking into Mike's Place who didn't belong would have been a fool not to turn right around and go out.

THREE ========================

A GROUP OF big, battered men in their forties and fifties stood
at the bar. They watched Joe with lethargic curiosity. They
wore a kind of uniform: loose Mexican or Hawaiian shirts, or
golf shirts, and khaki pants. Their shoes were spit-shined black
or brown oxfords.

The men looked both hard and soft, like the retired front
line of some pre-expansion NFL team, maybe the old New
York Giants. They weren't past their prime or gone to seed so
much as fallen into disuse. It struck Joe as he looked at them
that this afternoon had the aspect of a reunion. He knew them
all.

They weren't ex-jocks or off-duty cops, which is what a
stranger might have thought. They were retired hard men, re-
dundant Agency hoods, retired like Joe—given a large lump
sum in cash from one of the Agency's off-the-books investment
trusts, supplemented by an inadequate but overt monthly pension.

Joe walked slowly by them, slapping arms and backs, touching hands, saying, "Philly. Kurt. Pete. Volko. Harry."

They were glad to see him, and he to see them. They had

35

been the senior NCOs of the spook wars of three decades: hard workers, steady, competent, and loyal. Joe had been a colonel, or the Agency's civilian equivalent, and like the Army itself, it was the colonels and NCOs who ran things day in and day out. Joe stopped for a few minutes, chatting. He bought them a round. He got a rush of sentimental pleasure at the intense familiarity of the place and the men.

The walls were crowded with photographs—black and white pictures of men who looked like the men at the bar, standing still a moment for the camera, in jungles mostly; but there were forested hills and high mountain passes, and the open sweep of desert and steppe with empty sky in the background and a bare, straight horizon.

The dim light filtering through the gray windows made it hard to see the photos clearly, but Joe had seen most of them before. He was in a few of them, and knew most of the other figures. There were faded shots of men in suits and trench coats, posed in front of pockmarked building façades in the bombed-out streets of Europe in 1945. There were a few men who looked like diplomats or journalists, but most wore the battle dress of three wars spread over forty years. The history hung on the walls was crude and incomplete, but it was closer to the truth than the history in a lot of books. It was the history of KILROY WAS HERE.

The less faded photos showed tall whites and American blacks in soft hats and jungle fatigues, carrying guns of all kinds, sometimes talking into the handset of a radio-telephone strapped onto someone else's back. The Americans were usually surrounded by shorter men with tan, brown, or yellow skins in uniforms that looked too big for them. In the backgrounds were rice paddies or jungle tree lines, or villages, or airfields, or columns of smoke. There were few machines in these photos—the most common were armored personnel carriers and helicopters. This was Kilroy's recent history.

Over the big mirror behind the bar hung a flag of Brigade 2506, and hanging from the ceiling at the end of the bar was a tattered white banner with the letters ELLS painted on it in Greek characters. There were several Viet Cong flags, and others. Street signs were tacked to the walls, overlapped the way farmers nail up old license plates in the barn. The street signs were in German, Russian, Spanish, Chinese, Arabic, and a dozen other languages, from places forbidden to Americans at the time the signs were snatched. Joe knew there was a rule: For a street sign to be mounted on the walls of this place, it must have been taken by an American citizen, not merely brought out by some local native agent.

There was one pair of panties—tiny, white lace bikinis, with BARNARD 1969 printed on them in broad, red felt-tip pen. These were framed and matted under glass, like a large tropical butterfly.

Dangling from a nail in the mirror's heavy oak frame was a string of human ears that looked like dusty dried figs. Around the rim of the mirror were also a few berets and scarves—black, red, green—and a pair of shrapnel-shredded GI jungle boots. There was a tattered and bloody white shirt said to have been worn by Ngo Dinh Diem the day he was executed in the rear of an APC in Saigon in 1963.

The provenance of this bloodstained rag was authentic, Joe knew. The man he was here to meet was a witness to the shooting. Some said the man had pulled the trigger himself when Diem's own bodyguard refused, but Joe had never asked. Some said the man was acting on orders of Attorney General Robert F. Kennedy, but Joe had never asked about that, either.

Above the cash register, in a place of dubious honor, was an autographed photo of President John F. Kennedy accepting a green beret in a ceremony at Fort Bragg. The glass in the frame was shattered, and the photo was torn and stained, as though some object, perhaps a bottle of beer, had been thrown at the holy ikon.

Joe bought another round for the retired hoods and walked into the back room. Two men were playing bumper pool. "Joe," they said, as if he had only gone out for a walk and come back with a fresh cigar.

He hadn't been in the place for twelve years, not since he last saw the man he was here to meet. The man waited in a back booth. He was a large, heavy man with short black hair brushed back in the manner of a European. His face was clean-shaven and ruddy, but swollen and puffy—a drinker's face. The man looked awful, but he always had. The antique word *apoplexy* came to Joe's mind.

The man was eating a big platter of steak and potatoes with ferocious concentration, washing the food down with gulps from a tall glass of whiskey and soda. A TV hung from brackets in the corner above the booth. The sound was broken. It rasped loudly, like a gang of mutant insects at a game show. It made a terrible noise.

"Joe," said the man through a mouthful of food. He motioned with a piece of meat speared on the fork in his left hand. Joe hung his coat carefully on a hook and sat down. They shook hands with the perfunctory ritual of the French.

"*Ça va?*"

"*Oui, ça va.*"

Ça va for twelve fucking years, thought Joe. Half my adult life.

The man wore a checked tan suit of the sort of polyester supposed to be wrinkle-proof, but his bulk and sweat had defeated the fabric. His wrinkled blue shirt was dark with sweat, even in the cool of the air-conditioned bar. His loud, wide tie was stained with the souvenirs of many meals. Joe loosened his own tie and collar a fraction in deference to his host.

On the wall of the booth was a small bronze plaque that read THIS BOOTH RESERVED FOR FRANCIS GARY POWERS. Above hung a framed photo of a man wearing an unmarked high-altitude pressure suit. He had one foot on a ladder to the cockpit of a long, thin silver plane, also unmarked, with wings so long and thin that the tips sagged to the runway. An inscription read, "To my pals at Mike's, F-U-2. Gary. 31 Dec 58."

Set in the wainscoting below the plaque was a doorbell button. Joe's host poked the button with a heavy finger. A moment later an attractive Vietnamese woman—Joe guessed she was in her mid-thirties—pushed through the swinging door from the kitchen. She wore black pants and tunic—the "black pajamas" of Vietnam—and thick rubber flip-flops. Her hair was pulled severely back in a bun and covered with an American bandanna.

"*M'sieur?*" Her voice was mocking and light, like a girl's.

"What'll ya have, Joe? Mary's the best cook around."

"What is there?"

She listed a menu of Asian food—Chinese, Thai, and Vietnamese—and added, in nearly unaccented English, "Plus your usual NCO Club bill of fare—steaks and chops—very bad for your heart and liver."

"Oh, oh, j'ai mal au foie," groaned the man with comic exaggeration, placing his heavy hand over the pit of his distended belly; but his face was as unchanging as the face on a statue of Buddha.

The woman smiled. Joe laughed. He ordered fish-ball soup, a bowl of noodles and pork, and a pot of black tea. He thought of the pun in French on the words for liver and faith, *le foie* and *la foi*, and then he thought, *Mary*. She must be a Catholic from the north, and she looks half-European.

In Vietnamese, he asked her where she came from. She named a provincial capital in the Red River delta, one of those anomalous towns in Catholic Vietnam where the local church spire lifted into the gray skies of the rainy season over a flat landscape of canals and diked fields not unlike the North Sea coast of Europe.

"Is Mary your given name?" he asked.

"Marie," she said. "My father was French." She smiled, not unkindly, and turned abruptly back into the kitchen.

"She even cooks *cous-cous* once in a while," the man said. He was not truly obese or immobile, but very heavy, with the deliberate gestures and manner of authority that some heavy men have, as though they were born to sit in chairs, receive petitioners and messengers, and give orders.

"Paul," said Joe. "It's nice to see you."

"Likewise, Joe. Reach up and turn the sound on the TV up just a bit, if you don't mind."

Joe obliged. The French accent was still there, but not as strong as in 1968. Joe was on his way to Saigon then, one of the young hotshots, and Paul was back from fifteen years in Asia. The clear purpose of the meeting then was to let Paul size up Joe. Joe apparently passed the test, because his career got kicked over into the inside lane of the fast track.

Joe later heard that Paul had gone back to Saigon in 1972 and was very close to Thieu right to the end. Joe heard that Paul might even have been the cut-out between Nixon, Kissinger, and Haig in Washington, on the one hand, and Thieu in Saigon—but that was unverified hearsay, some of it from reporters Joe knew, who often seemed in those days to know more about what was going on inside the Agency than those inside.

Joe had also heard—hearsay again—that Paul had been back in the States since 1975, spending most of his time in

New York, but doing what, Joe did not know. Their paths had not crossed. Political stuff, some political fixing maybe, but it was stories and rumors Joe was hearing, nothing reliable. It was flotsam and jetsam.

Paul rapped sharply on the table with the bottom of his empty glass. Mike appeared. "Another bourbon and soda. Make it darker this time. And something for Joe."

Mike looked at Joe. "A Bud," said Joe. Mike left.

Joe said to Paul, "What's on your mind?"

"1984."

"The book or the year?"

"The election."

Joe waited.

"We're worried," said Paul.

"Who's *we?*"

"Who the hell do you think?"

"Langley?"

"Yes."

"I wasn't sure," said Joe. "I thought it might have been the royal *we,* or the papal *we.*"

Mike returned with the drinks. He poured the beer. "It's on the house, Joe. Welcome back."

Joe raised his glass to Mike. "Thanks, Mike. It's nice to be here."

Mike walked into the kitchen. Paul looked annoyed. He said, "Actually, it's the Republican *we.*"

"I didn't know Langley, or Paul Lazard, identified so closely with the Grand Old Party."

"Where've you been since 1968?"

"Is that a serious question?"

"No."

Lazard was testy, and Joe was beginning to feel a little testy too. He asked, "Aren't you guys a little premature? Isn't 1984 contingent on what happens in November 1980?"

"We know what's going to happen in November." Lazard mopped his plate with a piece of bread. He spoke slowly in the condescending tones of a French pedant addressing a stupid schoolboy. "American politics is a reasonably predictable process. Unlike most other countries who bother with elections, voting here is done on a statutory, regular basis. Officials serve fixed terms. Even the parliamentary democracies cannot manage as much as this. It is extraordinarily foolish not to plan ahead when one can."

"What are you planning?"

"We're gonna do what we've wanted to do for twenty years." The sentence was spoken with the same ferocious intensity aimed at the food on the table.

"What is it?" asked Joe impatiently.

"Put someone in the White House."

"Staff? This is hot news? Or is it the Oval Office you're after?" Lazard frowned at the sarcasm.

"Why bother?" asked Joe. "Why take the risk? You guys get most of what you want, most of the time."

Lazard fixed Joe with a look of uncalculated anger and astonishment, then shoved his clean plate out of the way and started eating a large chef's salad mounded with dressing and coated with an almost solid layer of freshly ground black pepper. After a few mouthfuls Lazard said, "We want the whole loaf. We've lost enormous ground. NSA now consumes eighty percent of the appropriated intelligence budget. DOD gets more than half the rest. We're picking up crumbs."

"I wouldn't know," said Joe. "Not being a member of the management team on the top floor, with the wide view of things."

"The reason they threw you out is what I'm talking about. There wasn't enough to go around."

"Bullshit," said Joe bitterly. "To the guys on the top floor, I was just one of the roughnecks, one of the hired guns like those guys out there at the front of the bar. I never ran an army that blocked traffic on the main channels of the Ho Chi Minh Trail for three months. I never tied down two NVA divisions for a year. I never ran a deep recon mission into Haiphong that brought out mug shots of every crew member on every Chinese and Soviet ship in the fucking harbor. No, no, it wasn't me who did those things. It was some fucking *ghost*."

"They kept you on for two years after you came back."

"Yeah, that was generous. And before that they left me in Laos for six months after the fall of Saigon, with no support, telling me every night over the fucking radio to organize massive guerilla resistance to the new regime. Half the fucking NVA was chasing me."

Thoughtfully, Lazard leaned forward an inch and said,

"You're probably the only one of us who knows what it must have been like to be in the Viet Minh in the old days against the French."

"Yeah, terrific. I'll do some oral history tapes for you."

"When you got back, they put you in charge of US labor contacts. That's important."

"Yeah, and then they said I was too aggressive. They said, 'Take it easy, Joe. This isn't a war anymore.'" Joe's voice rose in a mocking falsetto.

"That was the White House talking, not Langley. Jimmy Carter was mad at George Meany. Meany liked you, Joe."

"I didn't hear the bad news from the White House. I heard it from the top floor at Langley." Joe paused. He watched Lazard load food into his mouth. Lazard wouldn't look at him. Joe said, "You know? It's funny. I always assumed you got rewarded for the work you did, not kicked in the head when you were down."

"You took Mary's death pretty hard, I hear."

"You're goddamn right!" It was a snarl.

"You're bitter," observed Lazard with his pedantic detachment. He still did not look up.

"Goddamn right!"

"Do you know why you were fired?"

"Apparently not."

"We had nowhere to put you, but now we do."

The rage roared around inside Joe's head like surf. There had been no reason to fire any of them. Kick them out and see who lands on his feet. Then use him again as long as he stays upright. When he wavers, shove him overboard again.

"You're doing all right, aren't you?" Lazard still hadn't looked up from his salad. He ate like a machine.

"Jes' fine," drawled Joe.

Now Lazard looked up from his food. "Maybe you have a little nut squirreled away for a rainy day?"

"I wish I'd been that smart." The lie came without effort. Talking to Lazard was like talking to the lie detector.

"What did you gross last year?" Not that Lazard didn't already know.

"Thirty-eight thousand." It was the figure on his tax returns.

"Mortgage?"

"Mary's life insurance paid it off when she died."

"You're in good shape then."

"I could always use a little more."

Lazard nodded into his salad bowl, his mouth full. Joe thought, That's the first step.

Are you available for some dirty work?

Yes, for a price.

Good, because we've been looking you over, and you're our first choice.

Lazard cleaned his salad bowl with a piece of bread. He pushed the bowl away and pulled a fourteen-inch wooden salad bowl into position in front of him. It was filled with a fancy tossed salad, garnished with chopped hard-boiled eggs, crumbled tuna, chopped scallions, and artichoke hearts. Into a pint Mason jar filled to the three-quarters mark with olive oil, red wine vinegar, dry mustard, and chopped garlic, Lazard ground about a quarter-inch of black pepper. He screwed the top on the jar and shook it vigorously, then poured it over the salad, tossed it, and started eating, his fork in one hand and a large piece of French bread in the other.

"It's my only meal of the day," said Lazard. "I call here and order in advance, usually the day before, so Mary has time to get what I want."

"You come here often?"

"Not very."

Joe said, "I understand why you guys want the White House, but why wait? Why not this year?"

"Because Reagan's got it in the bag."

"Is he in bed with you?"

"Not really, but he's no problem, either. It's the next time we're worried about. Bush is weak."

Lazard's evasiveness was normal for this step in the seduction of an agent. Joe felt a shock and twist in his upper stomach. After nearly two decades on the other side, he was now going to be someone's agent. This is very interesting, thought Joe. He asked, "What if Carter turns the economy around, or gets the hostages out?"

"He won't. He can't. The economy is like a supertanker. It'll take two or three years to turn around, and besides, there are a lotta folks doin' jes' fine as it is. Reagan isn't gonna turn any economies around. He's gonna accelerate it in the direction it's going."

"What direction is that?"

"Them that has, gits."

Joe caught the note of mockery. "The hostages?" he asked.

Lazard looked up at him again. "Carter's gonna try at the end of this week with Sea Knights and C-130s, but *mon ami*, there is no way he's gonna make it."

"How do you know?"

"We have almost nothing to do with it. We don't want another Bay of Pigs on our record. This is strictly the Joint Chiefs and DOD. The old 'Can Do' boys are at it again. They stuck their necks way out. We advised against it, although we're piggybacking a little resupply op as far as their first stop in the desert. That's where we get off. Carter'll be lucky if they *don't* make it the rest of the way to Teheran. If they do, the militants'll slaughter the hostages. And that could lead to the first presidential lynching in history."

"Does that bother you?"

"Not in the immediate case, but it would be a bad precedent."

"And that's a bad pun," said Joe, as Mary arrived with his lunch on a tray. The mood lightened. Lazard was silent while Joe ate, except for rapping his glass on the table to order another round. Joe ate slowly. The irritating rasp of the TV overhead was the only sound in the place, masking the murmured conversation at the bar. This is exactly what I wanted, thought Joe.

He asked, "You don't suppose the Joint Chiefs have decided to write off a few men and choppers in the Iranian desert to embarrass the President in an election year? It would be the coup de grace for this jerk."

"I haven't heard any talk like that," said Lazard without looking up. With no pause, he said, "You're just the guy we need, Joe. You're a self-starter, a real survivor."

And you're the sonofabitch who fired me, thought Joe. To see if I'd land right side up, to see if I'd keep my nose clean, to see how well I'd lie to the box.

"Why me?" asked Joe. "Why me in particular? There are a dozen other guys like me at loose ends."

"Because you're savvy, smooth, cultured, well-dressed, hard-working, invisible in a crowd, and hungry. You understand that politics is a hard, rough game. You don't pick your nose at the wrong time, you won't fuck another man's wife, and you're full of enormous rage."

That was all true, and the rage rose up on cue. Joe sipped his soup calmly from the porcelain soup spoon in his right hand, but the fingernails of his left hand pinched the inside of his right thigh hard enough to leave a blood blister.

"We're gonna give you a target for your rage."

"Who?"

"The next Democratic presidential candidate."

"Carter?" Joe's surprise was plain.

"No, no. Mister 1984, whoever it is."

"I'm not a hit man."

"Oh, no. No. No," said Lazard, holding up his hands palms out, pushing the thought away. "That's not what I'm talking about. That's not what we want."

"What do you want?"

"Information and influence."

Joe finished his soup: fish balls with spinach in rich chicken broth. It was delicious. He picked at the pork and noodles with his chopsticks. It was oily and salty-sweet, a Peking dish made with fermented black beans in brown sauce. The noodles were whole wheat, freshly made.

This was how they must have done it in 1972 when they wanted their own guys in the White House, when Nixon was barrel-assing downrange out of control. They put them in ahead of time through the campaign apparatus. Retired guys. Friends of friends. Look around and see who's on the beach, and who can still walk and talk.

In a moment of historical reflection, Joe thought, with sudden wonder, That means they didn't already have guys in there before '72! Which means they didn't put anybody into Nixon's campaign in '68! Which means they thought they didn't need to! They thought they had Nixon by the balls, and they didn't. I missed all that, thought Joe, while I was fighting their fucking war.

"Will you do it?" asked Lazard without preamble.

"Yes." The answer was not premeditated. Joe had been prepared to say no to a weak offer. This was too good to refuse.

"Good. We want you in place before the convention."

"Detroit or New York?"

"New York, Joe. August." Lazard's tone was mock-exasperation. "I didn't say anything about the Republicans."

"You said a lot about them."

This was pure Washington, thought Joe. The high drama of assholes fighting over power and money. An all-male world; no emotions beyond fear, greed, and anger. A life of negatives. Not acquiring power, but avoiding power's loss, avoiding failure. These people, whoever this *we* was, already had power. Use it or lose it. That was all they believed. The rest was blue smoke and mirrors.

Joe had been a Democrat of the old Adlai Stevenson variety, one of the old CIA lefties. Asia made him a righty. Then a little more Asia turned him to political Jell-O. Mary's death ended his emotional life. Joe knew he wasn't really helping Billy. He was just trying to avoid losing him. Joe sensed he fit right into Lazard's scheme, and Joe decided he was content to wait and see what the scheme was.

Mary returned, bringing apple pie and ice cream for Lazard, and hot tea and almond cookies for Joe. When she left, Joe asked, "How old is she?"

"I dunno. Younger than you and me, that's for sure. Maybe thirty-five."

"How'd she get here?"

"Somebody knew her and told Mike about her. He sponsored her out of a refugee center in California. Widow of an ARVN colonel. She was cooking in the embassy in 1975 and somebody threw her on a helicopter at the last minute. She's a hell of a cook. Too good to leave behind."

Joe thought of all those left behind and his stomach churned and knotted.

"She lives in one of the rooms upstairs." Lazard looked up from his food. "You interested?"

"Christ, no. Just curious."

"You ever fuck a Vietnamese?"

"No."

"All those years?"

"I was married."

"That's why we like you. You think about this job for a few days, Joe. Don't rush it. Think about how you're gonna do it."

Joe nodded.

Lazard pointed his fork at Joe and said, "You'll be traveling

all the time. What about your boy? Can he get along? And
think about who you know, about where your résumé won't
raise eyebrows. You know what I mean? Maybe one of those
labor movement guys you worked with the last few years you
were at Langley. They liked you."

"Have you spoken to them?"

"Christ, no."

"Don't speak to anybody. Let me do this my way."

"That's what we want, Joe. That's what we want." Lazard's
tone was placating. It annoyed Joe. Lazard asked, "Maybe one
of your PR clients on the Hill can help. Didn't you do some
work for that young Democratic congressman from Long
Island?"

"Yeah, but he knows about my Agency background. It didn't
matter to him because he was getting me cheap. I think it
turned him on. But he'd think twice about sponsoring me for
a job with the Democratic party, or somebody's campaign."

"Nobody gives a shit anymore. That's all done with. And
you *did* get fired, after all."

Joe kept silent.

Lazard said, "I don't want to write a legend for you, Joe.
Too many people know you. It wouldn't work. And I don't
want to provide cover for you either."

"Why not?" asked Joe jokingly. "You gave Howard Hunt a
wig."

Lazard looked up with pure fury on his face. "That dumb
bastard! Forget Howard Hunt!" Then, more calmly, "Things
have changed, Joe, even in the past couple of years. Now, a
cover operation inside US limits has to be approved by Justice
and the chairman of the Senate and House Intelligence
Committees." Lizard's face held a look of amazement and
profound distaste.

"You tell them everything, do you?" asked Joe.

"Of course not, but this is too close to the bone. No one
knows about this. The fewer people on my own team who
know about this, the better."

I know all this shit, thought Joe. Who's he talking to?

"Who's paying me?" asked Joe.

"Be here next week at the same time and we'll talk brass
tacks," said Lazard. "You should plan to work your way from
the campaign into the Democratic National Committee after

the election in November. That's gonna be the key place to be after Carter gets his clock cleaned, because the DNC is gonna have to pick up the pieces, *n'est-ce pas?*"

"I'm sure you're right," said Joe.

"We're rarely wrong."

Joe snorted.

Lazard looked offended.

"How can I reach you?" asked Joe.

Lazard fished in his shirt pocket and handed him a business card.

PAUL PERRIEUX, PRES.

PERRIEUX & CIE.

TWO WORLD TRADE CENTER   212/888-4223

NEW YORK, N.Y. 10048   CABLE : RAISIN

"Raisin?"

"I'm in the wine business. Ask for Paul Perrieux."

Joe looked at the card for another moment and said, "Very good cover, Paul. I always thought a good raisin d'être was better than bona fides."

Lazard roared with laughter. He slapped Joe on the arm. "You're a hell of a guy, Joe. It's good to have you back among the living."

Later, they stood at the bar drinking coffee and cognac. The hoods had paid up and gone. Mike was in the kitchen. The TV in the back corner was off. The place was quiet, cool, and dark.

"Yeah, you're right," Lazard was saying. "It's gonna be a

hell of a joke on everybody when Reagan wins. The sweetheart
of the lunatic fringe is gonna bring back to Washington all the
old Republican fat cats from New York, all those Eastern
Establishment blue bloods the right-wingers love to hate so
much. What'd Roosevelt used to call 'em?"

"Black Republicans."

"Black Republicans. I like that. That's what he always called
Bill Donovan. I knew an old New Dealer like you would remember that."

"I'm not that old."

"But you know *history*, my friend." Lazard pronounced the
word like a benediction. He was a little drunk, thought Joe,
and slipping into a verbal disguise. The French accent was
completely gone, replaced by the language and manner of a
tough American politician.

"Sonofabitch," slurred Lazard. "It *is* a joke. Reagan's gonna
bring back the old Rockefeller gang. Helms and Laxalt an' the
other redneck barons in the Senate are gonna shit bricks."

Joe watched Lazard in the mirror. The heavy man had hoisted
himself onto a bar stool. He sat in placid stillness, studying
the inside of his glass carefully, then licking it clean.

"That gang from New York hasn't been in direct power
since the end of the Eisenhower years," observed Joe to his
own glass. Joe ran his fingers over the nicks and dents in the
zinc bar.

"That's true. They even got closer to Kennedy than they
did to Johnson and Nixon. They buzzed around, but Nixon
never liked 'em much. Didn't trust 'em. Kept 'em at arm's
length when he could. Finally told 'em to go take a jump.
That's when they blew him right outta the water." Lazard lifted
his bulk off his stool and walked around behind the bar. He
poured two more glasses of cognac and made two pencil marks
on a bar chit.

"What about Kissinger?" asked Joe. "He was Rocky's pro-
tégé."

"That was different. That was a deal, pure and simple. When
Rocky realized he wasn't gonna make it in '68, he told Nixon
he'd support him if Nixon would put ol' Henry in the basement
of the White House and let him run foreign policy. They told
Nixon they'd look the other way on Nixon's other stuff—Bebe
Rebozo and all that. Least that's what people say."

Lazard had been talking to the mirror. Now he turned to face Joe. Lazard wasn't drunk. He was angry. "We almost had it," he said. He slammed his big fist on the bar. "We were that close." He held up his thumb and forefinger an inch apart.

"Almost had what?"

"The whole loaf."

"When was this?"

"'74."

"When Nixon resigned?"

"Yup."

After a moment's pause, Joe asked, "How did Rocky really die?"

The question was like a blow to Lazard's big belly. Lazard's face changed color and shape, like soft metal under heat, then rearranged itself into its mask.

"Doin' what he loved doin' the most," said Lazard softly. "Lookin' at his etchings in his office." It was an unguarded moment, and Lazard corrected himself quickly. "Least that's what the papers said at the time." Lazard drained his glass. His tongue darted around the rim.

He's a chameleon, thought Joe. And he's a sponge for accents and mannerisms. Joe had always heard that Lazard had a gift for disguise. Lazard was said to have attended the annual meeting—two weeks long—of the Polish Central Committee one year in the early fifties, disguised as a Deputy Minister of the Interior. The actual minister had defected without notice only two days before the meeting, giving Lazard almost no time for briefing and preparation.

Lazard's reward for the coup was the Intelligence Medal, awarded by Allen Dulles himself *in camera* at a ceremony in the CIA compound in Frankfurt. It was the first award of the medal to a naturalized citizen. And on the spot, Dulles promoted Lazard to Chief of Station in Saigon.

"Were you close to Rocky?" asked Joe.

"Naw, hardly knew him. Met him once years ago when he was Ike's special assistant. A real backslapper."

Until Nelson Rockefeller died of a heart attack in January 1979, Joe followed the stories about him closely. Rockefeller had always personified to Joe the enormous sweep and power of the permanent government, but dead was dead, and Joe had lost interest.

Lazard was staring at him. There was a pinched coldness

in his face that Joe had not seen before. It was odd—they had
met twice in their lives at a twelve-year interval, for maybe
six hours altogether, but they seemed to know each other very
well.

There was a honk from the street. Lazard's taxi had arrived.
"Lunch is on me," he said. "It's been a business doin' pleasure
with ya."

They shook hands over the bar, the firm grip and hard pump
of a congressman running for reelection. "Tune in next week,"
said Lazard, and exited.

His Rotarian manner, thought Joe, is his least attractive and
most peculiar, not chameleon-like at all, but something labo-
riously learned. It struck Joe that Lazard was under considerable
stress, a bit out of control, slipping from one disguise to another. The politician's mask suggested to Joe that Lazard had
recently spent a lot of time around some of the rednecks in the
Congress.

Joe was, himself, a survivor. Over the years he had acquired
great skill at reading the layers of other people's personalities,
and the crosscurrents of behavior. As Joe sat alone in the silent
bar in the lengthening afternoon, he tallied the behavior of Paul
Lazard and concluded that Lazard was possibly lying about
working for the Agency, and that Lazard had been close to
Nelson Rockefeller.

Meditating about the current state of the Republican Party,
Joe concluded further that it was really two parties: the party
preferred by the Eastern Establishment because it reflected their
goals most directly, and the party of the power brokers of the
new Sunbelt. That was oil, land, and banking. That's funny,
thought Joe. That's what the boys in New York are interested
in, too. There must be a hell of a struggle going on under the
surface of Reagan's campaign.

But at that point, Joe would have bet, if he had anyone to
bet with, that Lazard was working for the Agency and free-
lancing for some gang of Sunbelt Republicans. Factions, thought
Joe. Anybody who thinks it's one big happy family at the top
is nuts. All the bastards do is quarrel over the spoils, and the
rest of us fight over what's left.

I should call somebody at Langley and find out what Lazard's
status is, thought Joe. But no, there's no point in stirring the
pot yet. I'll wait.

•   •   •

After a while, Mike came out of the kitchen. He had been a young mess orderly at an Army Officers' Club in Manila in 1941. When the Japanese invaded, he stayed behind as a coast watcher. He spent four years hiding and radioing Japanese ship movements. He was rewarded with a job as a waiter, then manager, at the Fort Myer Officers' Club outside Washington. How he came to own a watering hole that was the closest thing to a private club for CIA hoods had never been explained to Joe, and he had never asked.

"Another drink, Joe?"

"No, thanks. I've got to go."

Mike began straightening the bottles along the back of the bar.

"Mike, are any of your upstairs rooms free?"

"There's one in the back, a nice one. Overlooks the water."

"Can I rent it?"

"Sure. Fifty dollars a week. Shower and bath down the hall."

"OK." Joe put fifty dollars on the bar. "Do I need a key?"

Mike nodded. He opened a drawer in the back bar under the cash register and pulled out a Redskins key ring with two keys on it. "Outside door," he said, holding one up. "And this is the room key. Meals are separate. Kitchen opens at eight AM and closes at midnight. Help yourself to booze if I'm not here, but leave a chit."

"OK."

"And no outsiders, Joe, but I know I don't need to worry about that with you."

"No, you don't," said Joe. "Can you keep this under your hat?"

"I'm not a talker," said Mike, "but someone's gonna see you sooner or later."

"That's all right, as long as it's later."

Mike folded the money and put it in his pocket. He ran a rag along the clean bar. "Are you in trouble, Joe?"

"Not yet."

FOUR ═══════════════

"SHIRTS OR SKINS?" asked the priest.

"Heads," said Billy.

The bottle cap spun off the priest's thumb into the air. It landed with a click and a bounce. ROLLING ROCK, said the cap.

"Classy beer," said the priest. "The color of the cap matches the broken glass we just swept up."

"We're skins," said Billy. "You get first outs."

The priest took the ball. He stepped back under the basket, bouncing the ball with two hands, until he was out of bounds, then he flicked it in a high arc to one of the two kids on his team. The kid shot the ball back to the priest in a hard bounce pass under Billy's arm. The priest stepped once and dropped the ball into the net with a soft hook shot.

"Suckers," laughed the priest. "That's two for us."

"That's *all* for you," said Billy. He grabbed the ball and stepped back under the net.

They played half-court basketball in the schoolyard for the next hour. Except for their game, the large yard of St. Joseph's Church and School was deserted in the late afternoon. Everyone else had gone home for supper. Billy and the others had hung

53

around, hoping Father Kelly would show up. When he did, they played three on three.

The priest was an assistant pastor at the church, an English teacher in the high school, and the CYO basketball coach. "A basketball priest," said Joe contemptuously, when Billy started hanging around the church gym and playground, but Joe apologized to Billy later for the comment. The priest had helped keep Billy on his feet and out of trouble since Mary died.

Kelly didn't look like a priest on the bare asphalt of the playground, and the kids didn't defer to him in the game, but he had an adult presence that wasn't diminished by his worn sneakers and the faded gym shorts and T-shirt from Fordham University.

He stood at the top of the slot, took a short pass from outside, feinted to his right, pivoted left, and drove hard for the basket, switching to his right hand. Blocked by Billy, who was taller, the priest stopped and went up for a jump shot. Billy slapped at the ball and knocked it loose. It hit the priest's foot and rolled out of bounds under the basket.

"Foul," cried the priest. "You hit my wrist."

"Did not," cried Billy. "I didn't touch you. It's our out."

The priest glared hotly at Billy for a moment, then turned and stalked toward the water fountain. "Time out," he said. "I need a drink."

Billy shouted at his back, "This isn't a league game, goddammit. You want a ref, you got to play on a wooden floor."

The priest flapped his hand in irritation.

"He's mad because he's losing," said Billy to the others. One of the kids flipped him the ball. Billy took a little drop step and bounced up off his toes in an effortless jump shot, his body straight, his hands high, the ball arcing high off the fingertips. It dropped through the net. *"Swish,"* said Billy.

"How come you never played varsity for Saint Joseph's?" asked one of the others. "You're better than anyone. You'd make League All-Star for sure."

"Bad grades," said Billy. "Besides, I like CYO. If Father coached varsity, I might play."

"How come you and him are so thick?" asked the other boy, pressing his advantage. Billy rarely talked about himself. He was an enigma to the other kids: He was acknowledged to be bright, but it was known that Father Kelly and Billy's own

father had to plead with the high school principal to promote
Billy into junior year.

Billy shrugged, spinning the ball on his first finger. "I dunno.
He helped me."

Kelly walked back onto the court. He looked at Billy and
motioned for the ball. Billy bounced it at him. "You're right,
Father. I hit your wrist."

"And watch your language when you're on this playground," said the priest.

"Sorry," said Billy.

"It wasn't me you cursed. It was God."

Billy shrugged. In that instant, the priest tried to pass hard
over Billy from out of bounds, but the boy jumped and deflected
the ball high overhead, then jumped again and snatched it down.

"Take it back," shouted one of his teammates, who leapt
for the back court. Billy passed over his shoulder in the direction of the shout, without looking, and cut hard for the basket.
The other boy whipped the ball back to Billy, who jumped and
roled the ball off his fingers into the hoop in an easy lay-up.

"Game," shouted Billy. "Twenty-one, sixteen. All *right!*"
He pranced around, slapping the outstretched hands of his teammates.

"Nice," grumbled the priest. "Good game, fellas."

'See you tomorrow, Father?" asked one of the boys.

"Absolutely," said the priest. "Can I speak to you, Billy?"
The boy nodded. The others wandered off.

"You didn't go to school today," stated the priest. "Father
Evans called me. He's gonna throw you out if you do this much
more."

Billy shrugged. It was a characteristic gesture, but Father
Kelly had learned it bespoke confusion, not reluctance to answer.

"Go home and clean up, then come back and have dinner
with me at the rectory," said the priest.

"My father left a note. He said he'd go shopping and be
home by six."

"Well, call me if he doesn't show up. I wasn't going to eat
until late anyway."

"OK, I'll call you."

"Please," said the priest.

He watched as the boy wandered away across the empty

playground, pulling his sweat shirt on, turning to wave, then loping off at a run and disappearing into the background of shrubbery, trees, and houses in the neighborhood that bordered the large grounds of the church and school. The late afternoon sun turned the yellow bricks of the church to red-orange and cast dark shadows between the distant houses. A breeze stirred the dust on the softball field.

The priest had never known a boy so self-possessed and warm but so vulnerable and lonely. The boy loved his father and feared losing him. The father was a decent man, but distant and wary with everyone but Billy. He was said to be a lapsed Catholic and a lapsed CIA man. There was no one else. Father Kelly thought the boy was too young to trust himself to survive without help.

Feeling a bland menace in the quiet evening, and suddenly moved to fear for the boy, Father Kelly cast up a silent prayer for Billy's safety, and turned and went inside the rectory.

Tatters of a garish orange sunset hung in the sky when Joe drove into the parking lot next to his office. In the dusk turning to darkness, the lights along the strip were imitation Las Vegas— hot and bright—but there were patches of dark where stores and offices had closed for the night.

Joe sat in his car for a minute, scanning the lot. There was one other car, which he recognized as having been parked in the lot every day for the past week. He knew its owner. Joe locked his own car with heavy deliberation and stood by it for a long time, watching the flow of traffic along the highway.

Standing only fifty yards from the highway, he nonetheless had a sense of peaceful, almost bucolic isolation. He walked around to the front of the building. The large ground-floor office was lit; every other office in the building was dark. Light glared out of the lit office. The blinds were open in the large plateglass windows. The room inside was big, maybe thirty yards on a side.

In the far corner of the room were a desk, chair, telephone, and wastebasket. The rest of the office was bare. Scuff marks on the tan floor tiles showed where other desks and chairs had rested recently. A lone, darkly bearded man in a three-piece suit sat at the desk patiently working through a stack of forms, turning them slowly with one hand while the fingers of his right hand flew over the keys of an electronic calculator. It was the knack of experienced bookkeepers and accountants. Mary had had it.

A continuous long loop of tape unrolled across the floor toward the window. Joe knocked on the window as he passed, and waved. The man looked up, recognized Joe, smiled, and bent his head back over his forms. The matter-of-fact loneliness of the scene reminded Joe of some of the paintings of Edward Hopper.

Until late the night of April 15th, there had been scores of people in the office—clients and workers. The office was the temporary quarters of a fly-by-night tax accountant who installed a dozen desks, phones, and calculators, and two shifts of assistants. The clients were processed by the numbers, like Medicaid patients who could not understand the bewildering forms they had to sign at the bottom.

The morning of April 16th, the phone company disconnected all but one phone. Some men in a large rental van took away all the furniture but the one desk, chair, and wastebasket. The personnel all disappeared but this one young man. Every day at about noon he showed up in his suit, sat down without taking off his jacket, and went to work on a fresh pile of forms. It might have been a task assigned to the hero of a fairy tale. He and Joe smiled and waved to each other each time Joe came and went.

The front entrance was locked. There was no night watchman. He had been fired a month ago to save money, according to the landlord. Joe fished out his keys and entered. He took the elevator up to three, the top floor, and walked along the crimson rug to his office door. The interior decor of the building reminded him of a hot-sheets motel. He was the only remaining tenant on the floor. The owner was emptying the building, trying to sell it.

Joe locked his door behind him and walked through the small outer office without switching on the lights. The green-tinted glass in the wall of outer windows darkened what faint light was left in the western sky and gave the large inner office the feeling of an aquarium. The room was stuffy. He swung one of the windows open.

The noise of cars on the highway below struck him like a

light blow. He instinctively held his breath for a second, expecting the foul smell of exhaust, but the air was fresh. It smelled of warm earth, as though it had blown over newly plowed fields in the last few acres of farmland west of Alexandria and Arlington.

Still in darkness, he went to his desk and called his answering service. A message from Billy said, "Eating with Father Kelly. Home at ten."

There was a half-size refrigerator in the outer office. He hung his suit jacket over the back of a chair and took out a can of beer. He wished he had some potato chips to eat with it. The muffled pop of the can as he opened it sounded like a shot fired from a silenced .22. Over the noise of traffic and the low whine of the little refrigerator, he heard the heavy electrical hum of the elevator. It rose to his floor, and the doors opened and closed. There were no footsteps, but he held his breath and listened for a long time.

Two hours later he sat in his shirt-sleeves at a battered oak rolltop desk in his bedroom. The desk was marked and stained by years of use. It was from his father's farm. The desk had been his father's office, where the old man had sweated over four decades of bills and payments. It was the only piece of furniture Joe saved when his father died. The rest was sold at auction. Joe hauled the desk back to Washington in the back of his father's old pickup, then sold the truck. He cleaned the desk but didn't bother to refinish it. One drawer still held the smell of pipes and chewing tobacco.

That was the drawer where Joe kept his gun, an old double-action Colt .38 revolver with a five-shot cylinder and a four-inch barrel. He had bought it years before in a gun shop outside the gates of the Marine base at Quantico, and taught Mary how to shoot it. This was when they were first married, before the kids were born, and he wanted her to have the protection when he was away.

She kept it in the drawer of her bed table for the rest of her life, never needing it. Now and then, when he was home, Joe remembered to reload it with fresh ammunition, and he wondered absently now if he had checked it recently. He couldn't

remember, but the flash of irritation at his forgetfulness failed
to ignite his incendiary rage. He was too absorbed in the object
before him.

He sat hunched over into a pool of bright white light from
a drafting lamp that lit every nook and cranny of the desk but
left the rest of the room in darkness. The house was quiet.
Billy wasn't home yet. He was late again.

A large, rough-cut emerald lay on a small square of black
velvet on the green blotter. Joe picked the stone up and squinted
at it through a jeweler's loupe mounted on a headband. Joe knew
little about gems, other than liking them and knowing his were
worth a great deal of money, far more than he had paid for
them. They had a talismanic quality that attracted him, as well
as their practical qualities of small size, portability, and liq-
uidity.

Last night after the exhausting session with Kavenaugh, Joe
had gone to his bank to put the jade fish back in the safe deposit
box. On impulse, he had cleaned out the box, dropping the
two bags of gems in his jacket pocket and slipping the velvet
jewelry case into the inside breast pocket with his notebook.

Then, tonight, he had cleaned out his office of essential
personal items, including a passport and twenty thousand dollars in one-thousand-dollar bills in a sealed refrigerator bag
hidden in the air conditioner. He hadn't liked the eerie silence
of the third floor after the elevator doors opened and closed
for nobody. It was time to consolidate and redistribute his loot,
and relocate his escape hatches.

He raised his head and listened carefully. The dark house
was breathing at him, but he heard nothing, and he had searched
the house with meticulous attention when he got home. Without
benefit of electronic equipment he found one more repeater
and three bugs. He was sure there were more. But as long as
he wasn't talking, no one was listening. Does a tree make a
noise when it falls in the forest and no one is there to hear it?
All they knew, whoever they were, was that he was home and
in his bedroom; and that he had searched the house. And had
opened two beers and peed twice. And had let the phone ring
on two occasions without answering it.

Joe reached into a cloth bag and pulled out a larger emerald.
He easily understood the magic and superstition that attached

to gems over the centuries. This green stone was said to come from north Burma. It was the first stone he bought and sent home to Mary.

He bought it as a gift, but it gave rise to their plan to build a nest egg for themselves. It was the first of many gemstones, some rough, some finished, and a few valuable antiques like the carved jade fishes. Their plan grew slowly over several years as Joe bought several hundred thousand dollars' worth of gems on the Asian black market and sent them home from Bangkok, Vientiane, Tokyo, Saigon, Hong Kong, or wherever he happened to be.

He never had the stones appraised in the US, but he knew their value was far more than what he had paid—he guessed they were now worth a million dollars. And there was more.

There were bars of gold in a bank vault in the New Union Bank of the Bahamas.

It had begun on a small scale, and like other decisions he had made, it began in anger. During his last few years in Asia, his anger grew to bursting at the monumental stupidity and corruption around him. And the handwriting on the wall told him that the Nixon-Kissinger policy of Vietnamization meant the end of the spook wars in the highlands. He guessed that Langley would bring him home and kick him out, after a decent interval. His anger gave him the excuse he needed to join the heroin trade in a small way.

It was easy. All he did was buy one of the other Agency warlords a drink one night in a bar in Vientiane. The other guy said, "Hell yes, I'll help you. There's nothing to it. We thought you'd never ask."

Joe was nervous about letting anyone else in the Agency know what he was up to, but part of the other end of the heroin trade lay in China, and he didn't want to risk a future accusation that he had been doing business on his own with the Red Chinese. He decided he was better off to begin by skimming profits out of a group operation with people he knew, even if it meant an entry in his file.

The idea was to build a small off-the-books retirement fund for him and Mary, but the astonishing profits ballooned into something else. He concealed his profits by pulling out of the group operation after a short time, saying it was too hot for him, and he was too busy fighting his wars up-country. This was made credible by his reputation as a straight arrow. Then he went into business on his own. After making a killing on two large shipments, he pulled out for good.

From an initial investment of $5,000 in raw heroin, he bought 2,000 ounces of the soft yellow gold common to Asia. The gold was now worth nearly $1.5 million, although it looked like the price was going to drop back down to somewhere around $550 or $500 an ounce. He didn't care. He had bought it for under $50 an ounce, and paid a little more to air-freight it to the Bahamas from Vientiane via Bangkok and Hong Kong.

Then he bought more gems in small lots and mailed them back. When one fine emerald arrived home, Mary's comment in a letter was, "You may not know much about handling money, Joe, but you sure have good luck and good taste."

And there was still more: $100,000 in US dollars, and another $100,000 in Swiss francs, mailed back at intervals to Mary and hidden in the house along with several sets of passports. Now Mary was gone. She was the wizard. He was the mechanic. Now his task was to set up a long-term scheme for Billy, so he could transfer the stuff to the boy without getting them both in trouble.

Joe's most pressing problem was deciding when to tell Billy about the loot, and what to tell him. It was not only the origins of the loot that made it dangerous, but the amount. The bounty hunters, Joe knew, would love to know about all the stuff, or any part of it.

That was Langley's hold on him. Just today, Lazard had given a good hard jerk on the line. They knew he had a little nest egg, but they had no idea what or how much. If they ever found out, and he got out of line, they'd let the dogs off the leash after him. The bounty hunters weren't Agency employees. They worked on contracts, and they were allowed to keep whatever they got their hands on when they found you. It was their reward for efficiency.

Two or two and a half million dollars' worth of assets. It was a real treasure. Only Joe knew where it all was. It was like pirates' loot. Joe smiled to himself. Half of it was offshore, just like the old pirate days, buried in a bank on an island off the coast. If anybody ever found out, there would be quite a chase.

Billy was the big problem. He was just a kid. Somehow

Joe had to make a kind of map for Billy, so if anything happened, Billy could save himself and get his hands on the treasure.

Under the loupe, the stone in Joe's hand glittered on the surfaces of its angular facets, but the inside of the stone held a soft green light that seemed to have no limit. Looking into the stone was like looking down rows of apple trees in a big orchard at the height of summer—green was laminated on green, translucent, from sunlight to dark shade. Or the endless greens of the jungle.

> *Meanwhile the mind, from pleasure less,*
> *Withdraws into its happiness:*
> *The mind, that ocean where each kind*
> *Does straight its own resemblance find;*
> *Yet it creates, transcending these,*
> *Far other worlds and other seas;*
> *Annihilating all that's made*
> *To a green thought in a green shade.*

He did not know how long he was mesmerized by the stone, but when he looked up, he knew he had been holding his breath a long time, as though he was coming up from a deep dive. He had heard something. The house was lifeless, not like the jungle where there was never stillness or silence. He closed his eyes to concentrate. Now he heard nothing.

When he opened his eyes, a black man in a blue Adidas warm-up suit stood in the doorway of the bedroom, holding a gun. Joe's left hand clutched the stone. His right hand swung at the desk lamp and smashed it with a crash and a brilliant blue flash from the exploding bulb. He heard the soft beer can sound of a silenced gun and saw the orange-white flower of the muzzle flash. The bullet smacked the side of the heavy desk.

Joe jerked open the middle drawer on the right of the desk and yanked out his .38. The silenced gun popped again. The bullet smacked the wall. Joe fired twice into the pitch-black rectangle of the open doorway, aiming slightly above and right of the muzzle flashes. There was a groan and a thump, then a sliding noise as the man slumped against the hall wall and sank to the floor.

"Don't move," said Joe. "Don't make a sound."

There was a grunt of effort. Joe fired and lunged off the chair onto the floor. He fired again. The .22 popped again, but the bullet hit the ceiling. Joe waited. Now the only sound was the awful wet suck of a man trying to breathe through a hole in his chest.

"Shit," said Joe. His own breath sounded like a high wind in his ears.

There was just enough light from the outside through the sliding door to make out shapes. The man in the warm-up suit lay against the hallway wall. The noisy suck of his breathing was hard and labored. The man's body was tense. He drew his knees up and flattened both hands on the floor as though trying to push himself back up the wall to a standing position. His gun lay on the floor between his legs. It was a .22 automatic with a fat four-inch silencer screwed into the muzzle.

Joe scrambled across the floor and lifted the .22 away by putting his finger through the trigger guard like a stick. There was no other sound in the house but the man's breathing. Joe laid the .22 on the desk. He stood up slowly and walked to the sliding door. He opened it a few inches and stood by the screen door listening. He stood for a long time. Outside, the central air conditioner for the house hummed loudly, hidden in shrubbery off to one side, but there was nothing else. Everyone in the neighborhood had their air conditioner on tonight. Joe could have set off a bomb without alarming anyone. He closed the door and drew the drapes across.

He turned on the light by the bed. When he looked at the man, he could see the man was dying. "Shit," whispered Joe. "Who did this?"

Then, pointing his gun at the man's face, Joe asked in a loud voice, "Who sent you?"

There was no answer but the suck of air.

"Are you alone?"

"Yes," whispered the man with a sibilant hiss.

"Who sent you?"

The man watched him.

Joe picked the .22 off the desk, checked the load, cocked it, and aimed it at the man's head. The man stared back. Joe squeezed the trigger. *Pop!* A small black hole, less than a quarter of an inch in diameter, appeared in the white wall an inch from the man's left ear. The man winced.

Joe moved the muzzle a fraction. "I'm aiming at your ear," he said. "Who sent you?"

The man closed his eyes. He whispered, with ghastly sibilance, "I'm gonna die. Please don't dump me somewhere. Bury me right."

"OK. I'll bury you right. Who sent you?"

"New York."

"Mayor Koch?"

The man laughed quickly, suddenly, with an involuntary spasm of his face and chest. Then his whole body stiffened. There was a bubbling whistle from the center of his chest just below his neck.

"Who in New York?" shouted Joe. "Who, goddammit?"

The man's head jerked and slumped forward.

Joe lunged at him, grabbed him by the hair, and yelled into his face, *"Who?"*

The answer was a whisper as faint as wind in the top of a pine tree. "Jerry. Julie. Somethin' like that. Gold watch. Gold cuff links. Armor . . ." The wind faded away.

"Armor?" said Joe to the dead face he held by the hair. "Armor? What the hell does that mean?"

FIVE

NOW JOE WAITED. He searched the house. It was empty. The dead man had entered through the garage and from the garage into the kitchen. Ordinary household locks were no deterrent to a professional. Joe was not surprised that the man got in, but he wondered why the man was there at all.

Joe's conclusion was disturbing. Whoever sent this guy was not the same group who put the bugs in the house. The buggers would have known Joe was home. This was the first wave of the bounty hunters. So there were two groups watching him—the buggers and the bounty hunters. Someone, somehow, had gotten a whiff of Joe's loot. This guy had been careless, hadn't cased the house carefully, had walked in cold on Joe.

Joe had been careless too. He should have swept the whole house as soon as he found the repeater in the back of the TV set. If there was another repeater somewhere in the house, and all the bugs had been installed properly, the listeners had just gotten an earful. If they wanted to screw him, all they had to do was call the cops.

But there was no rising and falling warble in the quiet night; no slammed car doors, no loud knocks and loud voices. Joe opened the kitchen door. There was nothing more than a distant radio from someone's back window, and the sound of a breeze in the big mulberry tree. Joe waited patiently in the night stillness, listening like an animal in his hole, but there was no sign that anyone was responding to the shooting.

Now the bad part—he had to get rid of the body. First, he searched the man. He found car keys plus forty-eight dollars and change in a zippered pants pocket; auto registration and driver's license in a jacket pocket. On a long chain around the man's neck, like dog tags, hung a set of the finely made picks and rakes used by professionals to open ordinary locks, and two plastic credit cards—one stiff and thick, the other thin and flexible. It was all the guy needed. There might be a gym bag outside the house in the bushes with heavier burglar's tools that hadn't been needed, or the tools might be in the guy's car, if Joe could find it nearby.

A professional, Joe concluded, but careless. He had been surprised to find Joe at home. He hadn't gone all the way around the house, hadn't seen the lone light in the back bedroom. Under his warm-up jacket the man wore a light shoulder holster, custom-made from nylon webbing and Cordura cloth. An extra clip of ammo for the .22 was taped to the holster. Thinking about it, Joe concluded the guy was alone. If Joe had done this job, he would have done it alone, and bounty hunters tended to work alone. There were fewer to divide up the loot.

If this guy had found anything, he would have kept most of it for himself, gone back to New York, and told Jerry or Julie or whoever the hell it was, "Hey, you sent me down to DC for nothing. This is all there was." He would have dropped a handful of cash and a few small stones on the table, and that would have been the end of the joke. Joe would have been another crime statistic in one of Washington's better neighborhoods, and Billy would have been an orphan.

Joe got three large black trash bags from the kitchen. He pulled one down over the man's head and pulled one up over the man's feet. He slit the third bag open at the bottom and slid it down over the man's head to his middle. He taped the construction together with plastic packing tape, leaving some slack in the bags so they wouldn't break when the body was lifted or twisted. He turned out the light, ready to drag the body through the house into the garage.

Light, tentative footsteps hit the wooden deck outside the bedroom. Joe whirled, jerking the .38 out of his waistband, mentally counting the number of rounds left in the cylinder. One empty chamber, four rounds fired, none left. Shit! He was careless, too.

The screen door slid slowly back. Joe tossed the .38 onto the bed and snatched the .22 off the desk. A dark shape stepped into the room. Joe held the gun on the center of the shape's torso and began to squeeze the trigger.

"Dad?"

"Billy?"

"Dad, are you OK?"

"Don't move," hissed Joe. "Are you alone?"

"Yeah." Billy's voice was loud. He was frightened and querulous.

"Close the door behind you. Pull the drapes."

"Can't you turn on a light?"

"Do what I tell you, goddammit."

The boy obeyed. "Dad?" he said. "What happened? Are you OK? I thought I heard shooting." He was badly scared.

"Don't move," said Joe. His voice was harsh. This was the worst thing that could have happened.

"Daddy?" screamed the boy.

Joe snapped on the bedside light.

The boy's face turned ashen. His father was pointing a gun at him.

Joe looked down at the gun. "Christ! Jesus Christ, I'm sorry. I didn't know who you were. Then I thought someone might be holding a gun in your back."

"Daddy, what happened?"

"Don't touch anything. I just shot an intruder. I thought he might be a burglar."

"Is he dead?" The boy was staring at the homemade body bag.

"Yes."

Billy looked at the side of the old desk. "He shot at you."

"Yes," said Joe. "Where were you?"

"He missed."

Joe asked again, more gently, " Where were you?"

"In the tree house."

"Did you see anyone?"

"No."

"Hear any cars?"

"No."

"Did you know I was here?"

Billy looked back and forth at the .38, a dull gleam of blue-gray and walnut brown on the white bedspread, and the .22 in Joe's hand. The silencer was the size of a frozen orange juice can. "Are those both your guns?"

"The .38 is mine. I gave it to your mother years ago. The .22 came with the guy in the bag."

"I didn't know you had a gun in the house."

"Lots of people keep guns."

"I didn't know you had one," insisted Billy.

"Did you know I was here?" asked Joe again. He could see that Billy was struggling hard in his mind to connect his father to guns, to the shooting, to the dead man hidden in the bags.

"I could see you from the tree house," said Billy, his tone flat. He hadn't moved an inch from where he stood.

"Were you there when I got home?"

"Yes."

"Doing what?"

"Nothing. Just sitting."

"Smoking?"

"A little."

"Grass?"

"Half a joint." Billy looked straight at Joe.

"I wish you wouldn't."

Billy shrugged. "I don't, very much."

"Why didn't you come in?"

"I liked watching you sitting at your desk."

Then tension suddenly flowed out of Joe and he softened and relaxed. "OK, kiddo. I don't mind." Joe took a box of .38 ammunition out of his desk and reloaded his gun. He checked the load in the .22 and put it on safety.

"What kind of gun is that?" asked Billy.

"An old Colt Woodsman. They haven't been manufactured for several years, but they're sentimental favorites with a lot of shooters. Ruger makes a .22 auto that's probably a better gun."

"Is it hot?"

"No. It's cold."

"Huh?"

"A hot gun is hot because it's stolen. A cold gun is a gun that's been worked on to disguise its origins. That's significant in itself." Joe turned the gun around in his hand. "The serial number was ground off. The place where the number was, they struck over with a blank die to alter the underlying metallurgical fingerprint of the original die. It would be impossible to trace the history of this gun."

"Why would anybody go to the trouble?"

Joe shrugged. "To cover their tracks. By itself, a hot gun doesn't mean much. There are millions of 'em floating around. But you can still trace them."

"Did you use cold guns in the CIA?"

"I never did. They rarely went to the trouble of preparing a gun like this." Joe watched Billy closely, and Billy watched back. Joe said, "When they had a messy job to do, they rarely used their own employees. They used contract agents. Sometimes they gave them a hot gun they bought off the streets, usually from a mob connection. The mob is the best cover the Agency has for its dirty work."

"What's the significance of this gun? You said a cold gun signifies something."

Joe thought for a moment, watching the boy, then said, "They tend to use them when the gun has to cross a border between two countries. But there are other countries, Billy, and most of them do nasty things too. There are whole networks of agents and couriers all over Europe and Asia who exist only to pass stuff like this along the pipeline—guns, money, false identification, stuff like that. People, sometimes, who have to be moved."

"What about this guy?" asked Billy. "Is he a Russian?"

Joe laughed. "No. He was a Washington, DC, burglar who walked into the wrong house."

Billy pointed at the chain Joe had removed from the man's neck. "What's that?"

"Lock picks," said Joe. "This guy was a professional burglar."

"Can I have the gun?"

"No," said Joe. "We have to get rid of it. And we have to get rid of the body."

"You should call the police."

"No," said Joe. "Help me look for something outside, then we've got a long night ahead of us."

"I don't know," said Billy. "I don't like this. It's wrong not to call the police."

"Help me," said Joe. "Then I'll tell you a few things you need to know. You're old enough."

"Well, all right," said Billy slowly. "What are we looking for?"

"Get the flashlight from the kitchen cabinet. We're looking for a gym bag or briefcase with burglar tools in it. It might be in the bushes by the side of the house next to the garage."

"Old enough for what?" asked Billy.

"Huh?"

"You said I was old enough."

Joe snapped back, "When I was your age, I dropped out of high school and lied to enlist in the Marines for two years. Then I finished high school and went to Princeton. Then I went back into the Marines as an officer for four years because the Navy gave me a scholarship to go to Princeton, and I had an obligation to them."

The boy's face was blank.

"An obligation," repeated Joe. The boy didn't understand, but that was all right. He would, soon enough. Joe's mind focused on a more immediate problem.

Billy led the way outside.

Fifteen minutes later, they were standing at the kitchen counter, talking in very low whispers into each other's ears, looking down at a large black fiberglass briefcase lying open before them.

Poking around in the briefcase, Billy said, "Geez, Dad, this is like a little electronics lab, full of little tools and instruments." He held up a brushed aluminum box the size and shape of a walkie-talkie. On its face were a couple of switches and knobs, a small meter, and a digital readout. "What's this?"

"I'll show you. We'll start in my bedroom." Joe took a small screwdriver from the array of tools in fitted Styrofoam niches.

He positioned Billy in the center of the bedroom. "Now pull out the antenna. Turn on the little red toggle switch. Turn the black knob to LOW. Now turn slowly in a circle, sweeping the room with the point of the antenna. If the needle jumps, you've found a bug, and the readout will tell you what frequency it's transmitting on."

"Geez," said Billy.

"Turn slowly."

The boy turned slowly, dipping and raising the antenna toward floor and ceiling.

"It looks like you've been doing this all your life," said Joe.

"Look," whispered Billy. "It jumped."

Joe looked. The needle on the strength meter barely flickered. "Good. The battery in the bug must be dying. That means it's not strong enough to transmit out of this room."

"Is that why this man was here?"

"I don't think so. I don't think he had anything to do with anything that's already in the house."

"You mean there's like two groups?" Billy's whisper quavered with excitement and fear.

"Yes, I guess so, but I don't really know. Now, turn the knob to HIGH. The signal is so weak it won't register on the readout, so you have to amplify it inside the sweep, but you don't want to do that unless you have to, because you'll drain the sweep's own battery."

"One-oh-eight point six," said Billy. The blue numbers glowed feebly under the plastic face of the device, then faded when Billy switched back to LOW.

"Right off the high end of the FM band on an unused local frequency. I'm surprised the neighbors haven't heard me talking in my sleep." Joe's tone of voice was normal.

"*Shh,*" hissed Billy. "They'll hear you."

"The neighbors?"

Billy nodded. "What if someone was tuning along the dial on their radio?"

"I was kidding, but anyway these things are too sophisticated. It's probably transmitting on one of the sidebands. It takes a special circuit in the receiver to reconstitute the signal. Without that, all you can hear is garbled duck-talk."

"What about the others?"

"The guys who put the bug in? What about them?"

"Can they hears us?"

"I found a repeater in the back of the TV in the kitchen this morning and took it out. I found another one in the garage tonight. These little bugs can only transmit a few yards. The repeater picks up the weak signal, amplifies it, cleans it, and sends it out again. Sometimes to a receiver in a nearby van or house, sometimes to a larger repeater that can send a signal for miles." Joe knelt down and felt all around and under the table next to the bed. He pulled out the drawer and felt under it, then turned it over, dumping its contents out on the bed. "There it is."

"It's tiny," said Billy. The bug was a flat aluminum box the size of a couple of large postage stamps glued to the bottom of the drawer. Two thin wires led an inch to a round, thin battery the size of a quarter, also glued to the wood. Joe stuck the tip of the screwdriver under the two pieces and popped them off.

"I don't get it," said Billy. "What if there's another repeater in the house?"

"If there was another repeater on this frequency," said Joe, "the signal on the sweep would have been much stronger, and it would have been strongest when the tip of the antenna was pointing in the direction of the repeater, not the bug."

"Oh."

"We've got ourselves one bug," said Joe. "There's probably a box of these scattered around the house. "We'll do the same thing in every room."

Billy rolled his eyes at the black plastic bundle on the floor.

"That's next," said Joe. "I promised him I'd give him a decent Christian burial. We'll have to do it at sea."

They found five more bugs, all dead or dying, and no more repeaters. They verified that there were no taps on the phone lines, which Joe checked with equipment he found in the briefcase. When they finished, they returned to the bedroom. It was one o'clock in the morning. They hadn't spoken a word for nearly an hour.

"We're clean," said Joe. "You do good work, kid."

"What about him?" asked Billy. His face was beginning to show signs of real strain.

"I have to find a boat."

Billy's face glazed over with fear. "Is this guy from the CIA?"

"I don't think so."

"Don't you know?"

"No"

"Are you still working for them?"

"No." But I should say, thought Joe, *I don't know.*

"Is someone watching the house right now?"

"No." *No, I don't think so.*

"If they are, they know something happened to this man."

"That's a problem."

"Then what are we going to do?"

Billy's "we" rang in Joe's ears. Joe said, "They won't rush in here looking for him."

"This is like shirts and skins," said Billy.

"Huh?"

"You know. Basketball."

"Oh, yeah. I haven't played for twenty years."

"Dad, are you shirts or skins?"

"I dunno." Joe smiled. "I can't say I've thought about it. Shirts, I guess."

"Are you captain of the shirts?"

"I guess so. By default."

"Then I'm shirts too," said Billy.

"You wanna be on my team?"

"Yep."

"Ok, kiddo, you're my first pick."

Billy grabbed Joe and hugged him like a little boy who hasn't seen his father for a long time.

As they stood in the embrace, Joe began to weep, then sob.

Billy held his father hard, with the strength of a grown man. "What's wrong, Dad?"

"Nothing. Nothing." Joe breathed deeply to control himself. "It's just that I never realized how much you've grown. You're bigger than me. You're not a kid anymore."

"No," said Billy. "I'm not." But then his voice altered slightly in tone, and there were haunting undertones of a little boy afraid of the dark. "Now can we get rid of the body, Dad?"

They put the body in the trunk of Joe's Chevy, a large, dark blue, four-door sedan, and covered the cargo in its black plastic with a layer of saltwater fishing equipment and clothing. Joe crawled under the car with the frequency sweep, finding nothing. From under the car, on his back on the greasy concrete of the garage floor, he asked Billy to start the car in case their adversaries had attached an electronic hitchhiker to the car's electrical system, operating only when the car's ignition was on. There was nothing. Joe was surprised. He would not have neglected to do it, were he on the other side.

It also made him more alert to the possibilities for a tail, since the other side might be counting on physical surveillance rather than electronics. Joe sent Billy to bed for a few hours of sleep, and worked for three hours repairing, patching, and painting to cover the scars of the brief gun battle in the bedroom. He hid his gemstones in a temporary hiding place in the furnace ducts in the basement.

At the faintest sign of first light, long before dawn, when the stars nearest the eastern horizon began to fade, he went out for a fast run around the neighborhood. The .22, *sans* silencer, was strapped in the nylon shoulder harness under his sweat shirt. Outside, he encountered his neighbor's dog, an agile, friendly young beagle, and invited her along for the run. The dog accepted. They encountered no strange vans or cars parked along their route, which covered every street and intersection with access to Joe's block, and the dog discovered no strangers hiding in bushes or behind trees along the way. Joe thanked the dog for her help.

He woke Billy, and after quick showers and a fast breakfast, they were on their way as dawn broke and the eastern sky turned from dark blue to rose and near-white, a white as hot as the fire of a huge furnace. It was an ancient sight.

"I'm sorry we're not already on the water," said Joe. "I love the dawn. There's no other time like it."

"We could have left earlier," said Billy.

"No, I didn't want to haul this load out in the dark. At this hour, there's enough light to see up and down the streets, but it's too early for much traffic. It's the perfect time of day to move a hot load."

"How dangerous is this?" Billy was both excited and calm.

"Not at all. We're clean. We're a father and son going fishing. No one's gonna stop us or ever look twice."

Billy laughed. "I guess I'm good cover. Isn't that what you call it?"

"Yeah." Joe was laughing too. "You're the best cover I ever had." He touched Billy's arm, then he touched the hard edge of the .22 under his own arm like a hitter touching a holy medal around his neck before stepping into the batter's box.

They took the same route Joe had taken the morning before, down Connecticut Avenue into town, past the White House—looking at this hour more than ever like a closed museum. Across the Potomac in Virginia, Joe stopped at the first public phone.

A sleepy voice came on the line.

"Mike?" asked Joe.

"Yeah." The gravel of sleep remained in the voice but the tone was instantly alert.

"Joe."

"You in trouble, Joe?" There was real concern in Mike's voice.

"No. Should I be? You keep asking."

"No, Joe. It just worries me to see you back in bed with your old pals, that's all." There was no hint of warning or menace in Mike's voice.

"I appreciate that, Mike. Listen. I need a favor."

"Shoot."

"Do you still keep that boat in the marina down the road from your place?"

"Sure. But it's newer and bigger than the old one. It's a thirty-two-foot Hatteras with twin diesels and a flying bridge. It'll go anywhere."

"I'm impressed."

"I always liked boats."

"Can I borrow it? I wanna take my boy fishing this morning."

"Sure. With a crew, it'll cost you five hundred a day. Bareboat, and since it's you, I'll do it for a hundred."

"Done."

"Come by and get the keys. I'll be down in the kitchen."

"OK. Fifteen minutes?"

"So close? Where are you?"

"On the highway."

"I'll give you breakfast."

• • •

Mike walked out on the porch with them as they left after breakfast. He looked up and down the ramshackle street with the expansive good humor of a farmer surveying his land. He said quietly to Joe, "You've got a nice kid there."

"Thanks."

"He's all you've got left."

"Yeah."

"Take good care of him, Joe. Don't get him involved in any foolishness."

Joe touched Mike on the elbow. "I won't, Mike. Thanks for your concern."

"Paul Lazard is a bad guy, Joe."

"Do you know something I don't know?"

"No, but I don't like him. I never have. I've always liked you, Joe, and so do a lot of other guys—those guys at the bar yesterday, to name a few. We'd hate to see something happen to you, Joe. And your boy. Who'd take care of him if something happened to you?"

"I don't know. I haven't thought about it."

"Maybe you better."

"What's bugging you, Mike?"

"I don't know. Just a feeling. Just vibes, that's all."

"Nothing's gonna happen, Mike. I'll have your boat back at the dock before nightfall, OK?"

"OK. Come back here with the keys. I'll tell Mary to expect you and Billy for dinner."

"We'll bring some fresh fish."

"You bring me some fish or I'll make you pay for dinner."

It was high noon before the rites for the private burial at sea were ready to begin. Getting the body on the boat had been easy, or lucky. On the weekday morning, the marina, which had slips for maybe forty boats, was deserted except for a sleeping night watchman, who was encouraged by a ten-dollar gift from Joe to run back to Mike's Place for a Thermos of coffee for the two fishermen. The body was then moved in perfect privacy.

The boat was a dream—new and perfectly maintained. Joe ran the bilge fans for a few moments to clear fuel vapors out of the engine compartment and bilges, then started the engines.

They ran smoothly and easily. He turned on the maritime radio. The double row of little red lights on the scanner ran back and forth in rapid sequence across the maritime frequencies. There was no radio traffic and nothing moving on the water. He backed slowly out of the slip and ran out into the channel of the Potomac, heading downstream. The sun was blazing hot and the humidity was high. The day began as an idyll.

They ran slowly downriver, while Joe gave Billy brief instructions in running the boat, and pointed out some of the waterfront landmarks on both sides of the river. The noise of airplanes overhead was loud, nearly constant, but as they moved farther downstream the jet noise lessened, and they could talk without shouting at each other.

"I want to be well out in Chesapeake Bay," said Joe, "before we drop off our friend. It'll take about three hours. You might as well go down and get some sleep."

But Billy was too excited. "I wanna stay up here with you, Dad."

It occurred to Joe that Billy was afraid of the bundle in the forward bunk, tied with ropes against the rolls and pitches of the boat when it met the choppy surface of the bay. Six concrete blocks and six lengths of heavy nylon rope were set on the floor of the forward cabin.

Joe said, "Then open a pack of that frozen smelt and put it in the baitwell, and rig the rods. We told Mike we were going fishing, and we'd better bring him back some fish."

At noon, they were in Virginia waters at a point roughly between the tip of Northumberland County on the western shore and Tangier Island to the east. There were eight decent-sized striped bass in the livewell, courtesy of a large school they had encountered moving across the mouth of the Yeocomico River below Sandy Point, on the Virginia shore of the Potomac estuary. Joe had told Billy he had fished there once before, years ago, and it had been a good spot. After twenty minutes of excitement, Billy agreed.

He wanted to fish all day, but Joe climbed up to the flying bridge, taking binoculars with him, and pushed the throttles forward to full speed. The heavy boat surged out toward the mouth of the Potomac and the center of Chesapeake Bay. Billy went below, at Joe's order, and brought the rope and blocks up the ladder from the forward cabin to the main cabin. Then he sat facing the stern for a long time, watching the wake boil up behind and the gulls following, until the engines slowed suddenly and the boat rose and fell on the high roll of the wake.

Joe came quickly down the ladder from the high bridge. "Here," he said. "This is the spot. Let's do it fast. There's not another boat in sight."

They dragged the body up from the cabin. The boat idled slowly in a southerly direction, just fast enough to maintain headway against the wind chop. They tied the blocks to the man's arms and legs, pulling them out through slits in the plastic garbage bags. They tied two blocks close around the body's middle. They hoisted the body and the blocks up onto the wide transom of the boat, taking care not to mar the finish of the wood and fiberglass with the rough blocks.

"Take your hat off," said Joe.

Billy took his battered old Little League cap in his hands.

Joe pulled a sheet of paper out of his trousers and unfolded it. There was handwriting on both sides. He dropped his hat onto the deck, out of the breeze. "I couldn't find a Mass for the Dead at Sea, and I don't know what religion this man was. I don't even know his name. So I took a prayer from the English *Book of Common Prayer*, for the burial of the dead at sea, and another from the old Daily Missal your mother used years ago."

Joe began to read. "Absolve, O Lord, we beseech Thee, the soul of Thy servant John Doe, from every bond of sin, that he may be raised up in the glory of the resurrection and live amongst Thy Saints and Elect. Through our Lord Jesus Christ, Thy Son, who liveth and reigneth with Thee in the unity of the Holy Ghost, world without end. Amen."

Billy mumbled, "Amen."

The paper in Joe's hands rattled in the breeze. Joe turned it over. He said, "That was the Catholic part. This is the Protestant part. If this guy was Jewish or Moslem he came to the wrong funeral parlor."

Billy couldn't smile or laugh.

Joe read, "Unto Almighty God we commend the soul of our brother departed, and we commit his body to the deep; in sure and certain hope of the Resurrection unto eternal life, through our Lord Jesus Christ; at whose coming in glorious majesty to judge the world, the sea shall give up her dead; and the corruptible bodies of those who sleep in him shall be changed, and made like unto his glorious body; according to the mighty working whereby he is able to subdue all things unto himself."

"Amen," said Billy, with a firm, loud voice, moved and stirred by the prayers.

Joe dropped the page of paper over the stern, where it fluttered for a moment and fell to the water. A gull swooped at it and pulled up sharply. "Roll him over," cried Joe.

With Joe at the shoulders and Billy at the feet, the dead man was rolled and shoved in one hard motion over the stern. The body sank fast, pulled down by the weight of the heavy blocks. In three seconds it was gone in the bottle-green darkness of the cold water. A few gulls circled and swooped and cried. Air bubbles rose from the sinking body and disappeared in the wake.

"Let's turn around and head back," said Joe, his arm on Billy's shoulders. "We'll have the tide and currents against us going back upriver. We've done what we came to do."

"Yeah," said Billy. "We caught some fish and we fed some."

Joe dropped his arm from his son's back and turned away. He put on his hat. "I've done something no father should ever do to his son. I've got you mixed up in a crime. You're an accomplice to a felony."

"You didn't murder the man," cried out Billy. "You killed him in self-defense."

"I didn't report the shooting to the police, and the disposal of a body is a crime in itself."

"Who was this guy?" asked Billy with angry urgency. "He wasn't any burglar!"

"I'll tell you," said Joe. "There's a lot I have to tell you now. Take this card." Joe took a calling card out of his shirt pocket. "Put it in your wallet."

Billy looked at it carefully. "Who's Paul Perrieux?" He pronounced it "Perr-ux."

"His real name is Paul Lazard. If anything happens to me, give this card to Lazard. Tell him about last night and today, and everything else I'm about to tell you now. Tell him everything, you understand?"

Billy nodded. He looked frightened.

"Let's have a little fun first," said Joe. He turned and went below, returning with some empty soft-drink bottles and cans, and the .22 pistol.

"This guy had some extra ammo with him. I'll show you

how to shoot this thing, then we'll toss it overboard." Joe flipped a can over the stern into the wake. The can bobbed away. He raised the gun and fired. The can, now almost invisible in the water, jumped.

"Good shot, Dad!" Billy's voice was excited.

"You sound surprised."

"You hit that little can from a moving boat!"

"It's not as hard as it looks. I'll show you." For fifteen minutes, he showed Billy how to load and operate the gun. With three rounds in the clip, he told Billy to aim into the middle distance and squeeze them off. "Most of the pressure in your grip should come from your thumb and middle finger. Your third and fourth fingers are more for balance. Don't wrap your index finger all the way around the trigger. You'll jerk the muzzle slightly to the left when you fire. Put the ball of the finger on the trigger and pull it straight back."

Joe threw another can into the water. "Slap this clip in there and shoot the can."

Billy's third shot hit the can. He shouted and jumped. Joe's hand clamped down hard over Billy's on the gun. Billy winced.

"That's a gun, goddammit, not a toy. Point that thing downrange at all times. Never, never wave it around, and never point a gun at someone unless you intend to kill them."

They looked at each other for a moment. Billy asked, "What do you do then?"

"Aim at the center of the torso. It's the biggest target. Don't try for the head. It's too small and hard. Never shoot to wound. Aim at the guy's breastbone and empty your gun into him."

When they ran out of targets and ammunition, Joe said, "I'm gonna go below and clean up down there. Toss the gun over and clean up the brass." He gestured at the litter of small brass cartridges on the deck. "Make sure you get all of them."

As Joe turned his back, Billy stuffed the gun down inside his jeans and pulled his sweat shirt down over it. The metal was uncomfortable against the skin and the blade of the front sight gouged his leg, but in that moment Billy decided he had never seen anything he coveted so much.

A moment later, Joe returned. He threw some stuff over the stern. "All done?" he asked Billy.

Billy grunted and shrugged.

"Go up on the bridge," said Joe. "Make a slow, wide one

hundred and eighty degree turn. Then push the throttles up to full speed. Make sure the RPMs on the two tachometers are the same. I'll bring us up a couple of cold Cokes."

Billy turned the boat in a slow half-circle, feeling it roll under him as it came broadside to the swell. He felt powerful and free in the wind on the upper bridge, with his hands on the wheel and throttles, with the weight of the pistol in his waistband. He steered the boat into its own wake so they were heading back along their outward course. He pushed the twin throttles forward as he had seen his father do, with a firm, smooth motion. He felt the powerful boat surge up on the choppy water and settle down as if it were running along a smooth road on rubber tires. He turned and watched the wake boil out behind, and heard the throaty rumble of the engines. It gave him an extraordinary sense of well-being and self-possession. It made him feel older. As his father came up to the bridge, Billy matched the RPMs on the two tachs, and headed the boat a couple of degrees to port, as if to set his own course, slightly off the course his father had ordered.

Then for several hours in the wind and hot sun, Joe told Billy stories—war stories about a decade and a half of fighting in the jungles of Southeast Asia. It was the story of Joe's life, but it was a story Billy could never have imagined for himself because Joe's adult life was an official government secret. Billy never had more than the vaguest idea of what his father did for a living, and now Joe told him just about everything. In an earlier time, it would have been a wonderful adventure story, and Joe told it that way, but there was no hiding the underlying horror of a terrible war inflicted on millions of innocent people, the victims of the mechanized terror of the Americans and the political terror of the radical Communists who filled the vacuum left by the retreating losers.

But there was some of the story Joe simply couldn't tell his son—the web of connections that made sense of the actual history of the decisions and motives that drove the engine of secret history forward at hideous speed. It was forbidden fruit, this knowledge, and it would have endangered Billy to know it because there was always someone else who wanted to know it too, and didn't care how he found out.

So in the end, Joe realized that he had only succeeded in romanticizing Billy's image of his father, without making Billy understand that although Joe had been a powerful warlord, he was only one of many in the service of others far more powerful than himself, for whom Joe's whole career was no more than a couple of revolutions of a high-speed reel of magnetic tape on a computer.

To compensate for this, Joe did something he had not planned to do—he told Billy a little about the loot, simply that there were a bit of gold and a handful of jewels hidden away against a rainy day. It would help pay for Billy's college education and maybe buy them their own fishing boat someday. That was all. He didn't tell Billy there was maybe two and a half million dollars' worth of assets awaiting Joe's decisions for investment and use, or that nearly half of it was stashed in the house at the present moment.

They were well up the Potomac River, past the birthplaces of George Washington, Robert E. Lee, and James Monroe, when Joe ran out of stories to tell. He knew he had pulled the boy into something that boys of Billy's age hadn't had to face since the end of wooden ships and the Pony Express: the necessity of physical survival at an early age, learning to be a man at fourteen or sixteen.

Billy sat silent for a long time then, turning the wheel slowly to keep the boat on its steady course up the center of the curving channel. He was fully confident with the powerful boat. He passed close to the right of another boat idling slowly downstream and waved jauntily to the men on board. Joe recognized a senator and a lawyer-lobbyist for one of the oil companies. They waved back. Joe looked away.

Billy asked, "Would you have told me all this if Mom had lived?"

"Probably not. There would have been no need until you were much older. None of this would have taken place."

"It's unbelievable," said Billy. "It's like *Treasure Island*. Gold, pirates, and all."

PART 2

"Back home, we'd run him for office.... You can't go wrong in politics going from no place to nothing."
William Faulkner on Ronald Reagan in 1945

SIX ════════════════════════════════

JOE STOOD BY the stone railing of the great open belvedere at the top of the terraced stairs leading to the west façade of the Capitol. He looked up the Mall and Pennsylvania Avenue in the perfect dusk. Traffic lights flashed green, yellow, red in the translucent evening air. Taillights and brake lights glowed and flashed on the few buses and cars in the light evening traffic. Pale orange and mercury-silver streetlights marked the boulevards radiating in all directions out from the monumental buildings and markers of government.

Joe glanced at his watch. It was nearly eight o'clock. On the dot, he would start down the stairs, holding the briefcase in the left hand, the afternoon *Star* folded in half under his left arm, and the novel with the bright blue jacket in his right. The jets rose and fell out of and into National Airport off to his left. Their incessant noise drowned out the bright music of the befrogged and red-uniformed USMC Band at the bottom of the steps, which formed a natural bandshell projecting the music out toward the crowd on the grass.

The crowd was surprisingly large. Joe searched it, looking for his contact, someone he had never seen before, a young

woman wearing tailored khaki slacks, an olive-drab silk blouse
with elbow-length sleeves, and a large enameled silver clasp
at the neck of the blouse. Dark hair. Blue and white running
shoes. A large shoulder bag of carved leather.

"And a briefcase, newspaper, and novel just like yours. And
a nice smile. They showed me your photo and you look like
a nice man. I hope you are," she said over the phone. "I'm
tired of dealing with jerks and creeps and assholes."

"I'm none of those," Joe had said, and hung up abruptly.
She sounded like a flake, but he had a professional lifetime of
dealing with flakes. He had given up complaining long ago.

He was at the roof level of the city. It was a flat landscape,
he thought. The long lawns were green, and the stone of the
Washington Monument was pale tan in the half-light. The gravel
paths of the Mall were the same color. It was lovely. Across
the leafy treetops and buildings he could see the distant
Georgetown ridge.

The façade of the Capitol, one of America's grand buildings,
was a bit dingy up close, with heavy cross-braced beams holding it together. It's all fortress and bunker, he thought; Victorian
forts and modern bunkers. Even this old building. The Capitol
was lackluster gray in the setting sun. Black maids stood in
the lighted windows, looking out over the huge federal plan-
tation they worked on.

The Smithsonian was in an old fort. All the other government buildings looked like ministry buildings in Central Europe. Hapsburg, he thought. That's what it is. *Fin de siècle*
Vienna. The observation satisfied him. The glowing embers of
a burned-out culture. He had no particular reason to be thinking
such apocalyptic thoughts, but he was angry and bored. Two
months of hectic work, endless travel, and long hours at the
Democratic National Committee were taking a toll.

A black and white sheepdog played at the edge of the crowd,
barking at something. It was looked at severely by a number
of the audience, who could only hear half the music anyway,
due to the jets. It grew darker. Joe watched the endless arrival
and departure of the planes. He had thoughts like a kid: Where
do they all go? And how do they stay up in the air?

All around, seemingly from every direction, came the faint
snap, crackle, and pop of police walkie-talkies. You couldn't
go to a concert or a museum, or any public place, without

some damn guard standing near you with one of those things going *"brsst-zzzttt."* The smell of pot rose in whiffs on the breeze from the crowd below. People smoked it everywhere. A very handsome young policewoman stood at the railing a few yards to Joe's right. She was black, dressed in the tan uniform of the Capitol police. Her walkie-talkie lay on the limestone railing. It made fuzzy noises. She jingled the change in her pocket. There was a faint smell of sewage on the air from the Potomac River less than a mile away. She wrinkled her nose, looked at Joe as if he had farted, and looked away. She reminded him of the guard in Kavenaugh's office on Albemarle Street.

Joe picked up his briefcase and started down the stairs, down the broad flight to his right, walking slowly down an imaginary line in the center of the stairs. He was counting in his own mind: "One thousand. Two thousand." Et cetera. It was the counting sequence for jumping out of an airplane. When he got to twenty thousand, he stopped. If he had waited this long to pull his rip cord, he would be dead.

He was dead center in the stairs, with no one near him. Someone with opera glasses could have seen him clearly from the top of the Washington Monument. He transferred the briefcase to his left hand, jammed the paper up under his left armpit, cursing the damn greasy newsprint smearing his hands and suit, and brandished the blue-jacketed book in his right.

At that same instant, the young woman started up the staircase on a collision course toward him. She matched his pace. They met on the second landing. She looked startled. She had green eyes the color of the sea where it is deep and cold, far offshore in the early part of the year. But when they kissed like old friends, she smelled sweaty and musky, not cool and fresh as he had expected only a split-second before.

"We're reading the same book," she said brightly, as they walked slowly down the stairs together. "I love the photo of the author on the back."

He hadn't looked. It was a head and shoulders close-up of a man with a salt and pepper beard and windblown hair staring intensely at the camera. "He looks like he's playing pocket pool," said Joe.

She giggled.

"What shall I call you?" Joe asked quietly.

"Diane," she said, in a near-whisper.

"Why are we whispering?"

"I don't know," she said, transferring all her items to her right hand and shoulder, taking his right arm in her left hand, steering him toward an empty spot on the grass in the middle of the crowd.

"Let's sit down and listen to the band for a while," he offered.

"That's what I had in mind," she said. She was a bit distracted.

"Something wrong?"

"No."

"Is there a convoy?"

"No."

"Here," she said, and her hand directed him to sit immediately. Her grip was firm. She held him as though she had him in polite custody in a dignified white-collar proceeding before a federal judge. As they pivoted and sat in the crowd facing the band, Joe heard the rapid buzz and click of a 35-mm camera with an automatic winder.

"Open your paper," she said. "There's a news photographer panning the crowd from your left."

Joe did as he was told. "Shall we take in a movie?" he asked.

"I'm working," she said. "Be nice."

"How long do we have to sit here?" His tone was official and bored. He felt exposed. The photographer was walking slowly through the crowd toward them, taking candid shots with a short lens as he went. He wore press badges on a chain around his neck.

"No longer than we have to," she said curtly.

"Goddammit," he said loudly. "You told me you wanted to go to a movie. I'm going now, and you can come with me or stay here."

He got up quickly, pivoting away from the camera, snatching up her briefcase, realizing in that instant how good she was at what they were doing, and walking away from her and the photographer as fast as he could move through the seated, lolling crowd. He was followed by a wake of hostile looks and comments, including one loud and clear, "Motherfucker." It was her voice, but he didn't think the guy she brought with her had gotten a clear shot of them together.

At the edge of the crowd, he turned slightly and glanced back, holding the novel up to shield his face. The photographer was frantically changing to a long lens. Joe smiled at Diane and discreetly held up the middle finger of his right hand along the spine of the book. She looked furious, but she had his briefcase firmly in hand and appeared to be about to get up to leave. He waved with his fingertips, and called loudly, "Ta, ta."

At Maryland Avenue he flagged a cab. He told the driver to veer right on Constitution Avenue. At the first public phone, he told the driver to wait. He went into the phone, called a number in Maryland, and gave the man who answered a curt message for Paul Perrieux, asking for a meeting the next day.

Then Joe told the driver to take him home. He sat in the back of the cab, pissed-off at the woman but glad to have a chance to eat dinner with Billy. In the last two months, Joe had spent more time in New York than Washington, and when he was in Washington, he worked late every night.

The meeting was set for New York. Lazard was still using the old word code. The message at Joe's answering service read "Saturday at 0900," which meant Friday at 0800. It was the Fourth of July weekend. Friday was a holiday, and travel would to tough. Joe cursed when he got the message. Lazard liked to keep the screws tight.

Billy took two steaks out of the freezer and built a charcoal fire in the grill on the deck. Joe made himself a vodka martini, dropped a sharp, salty Salonika pepper in it, and sipped the drink on the deck while Billy worked. The backyard looked beautiful. Billy kept it in perfect shape. School was over. Billy had managed to get his act together during the last couple of months of school, and had passed his junior year. Father Kelly had simply taken over. Joe wondered how much the priest knew—the priest was Billy's confessor, and the boy occasionally went to confession when he was deeply troubled by something. It was a habit Billy had learned from his mother.

Now, Billy spent the days working as a summer gardener for half the people in the neighborhood, well paid in cash. Billy had no trouble grasping the utility of off-the-books employment. He spent his evenings playing basketball, or in the company of Father Kelly, who had put Billy on a rigorous summer reading schedule.

"Why?" Joe had asked.

Billy's response was, "He said it's time I learned serious things in a serious way."

It was Joe's turn to shrug. He was troubled by his inability to spend time with the boy, although Billy didn't seem bothered by it. This in itself bothered Joe. It was as though, having been drawn close together by the conspiracy on the boat in Chesapeake Bay, they were now drifting apart again. Joe was helpless to do anything different.

The phone rang. Joe went into his bedroom to answer it.

It was Diane, but she didn't bother identifying herself. "You'll be picked up at seven Saturday morning. Transportation to the meeting is being provided."

"OK," he said, but the line was already clicking. She had hung up.

They're coming out of the closet, he thought. It was the first time she was involved in making arrangements, although Lazard had told him at the beginning that she was the desk officer at Langley for the operation. "Very sharp," Lazard had said. It was interesting, Joe thought. Something was developing. He had gotten closer to the center of the action at the DNC than he would have thought possible in so short a time. He was now one of the DNC's senior advance men for the Carter-Mondale campaign. He knew the Secret Service had gotten a look at a sanitized version of his 201 file, but it didn't bother anyone that he was ex-Agency. He was very good at his job, and he quickly learned that despite the intense competition for jobs and access to the top in a political campaign, talent was in short supply and great demand. Once on board, he was quickly signaled out and pulled into the center. Lazard was "as happy as a pig in shit," as he said when he was in one of his tiresome redneck personae.

Joe went to the sliding door and called out to Billy, "Pick some of your lettuce and spinach. I'll make the salad. Do you want bacon in the dressing?"

"Sure."

"I don't have to leave tonight. They're picking me up at six tomorrow morning."

Billy's face lit up. It was all Joe needed to recover his good spirits. He stepped out to the deck to get his drink and carried it into the bathroom, where he ran a steaming hot shower. Soon Billy heard him singing part of a song he hadn't sung in Billy's hearing in years, since Mary died.

> Summer's in the meadow.
> Winter's in the wood.
> O fare thee well, you wicked world,
> I'm going to be good.
>
> For the leaves are gettin' greener,
> And spring is on the way,
> And girls are gettin' prettier,
> And younger every day.

As soon as the Eastern shuttle leveled off somewhere above the Atlantic coast of Maryland, Diane dropped the tray from the back of the seat in front of her and opened two Styrofoam cups of coffee she had been carrying in a brown paper bag. "I got you regular," she said. "Not knowing what you usually drink."

"Tea," he said, without looking up from his *Post*.

She looked out the window at the green-gold-blue mosaic below. When she turned back, she said, "I'm going to have to teach myself to be patient with you. It'll be sort of like being a nurse to a handicapped war vet. I'll have to get used to all your little moods and habits."

"You don't have to do anything," he said. "Besides carrying my bags through the airport to the limo."

"Sweetheart," she said softly, below the level of the hum and vibration of the rear-mounted jet engines.

Joe looked at her curiously. She was leaning away from him into the corner between her seat and the cabin wall, but she was turned toward him, facing him, and her blouse was loose. Through the neck of her blouse, he saw the dip and rise of the top of her right breast. She wore a maroon blouse and a purple bra. For the first time, he became conscious of her age and sex. She was in her early thirties, attractive, and sexual. That is, thought Joe, her sexuality was not so much a part of her private life as part of her public personality.

"I'm your new case officer." She said it so softly that he couldn't really hear it above the engine noise. He was reading her lips. Louder, she said, "You should be carrying my bags. Isn't that the way they used to do it in the old days?"

He turned back to his paper.

She leaned toward him. She was angry and flushed. "I'm sorry you got jerked around yesterday, and I know how you felt, but you better get used to it."

"There's a right way, and a wrong way. And there's *our* way. Is that it?" He spoke without looking at her.

"That's it."

He turned toward her and put his right hand gently on her left arm. Her skin was warm and dry. He said, "No more pictures. None of that entrapment bullshit." The back of his hand brushed her left breast. It was heavy and firm. "And no sex on the job."

Her face flushed, not the light pink of excitement, but the mottled red of anger. "No problem," she said, and poured his cup of coffee in his lap.

The car that met them at the Eastern terminal at La Guardia had a radio-telephone. Joe got into the front seat on the passenger side. Diane sat in the back seat with the newspapers. The driver looked curiously at the large dark stain in the crotch of Joe's trousers. Joe's suit was light tan.

"I couldn't hold it," said Joe. He picked up the phone and handed it to the driver. The car was already speeding along the Grand Central Parkway toward the Triborough Bridge and Manhattan. "Call in, and tell Perrieux we'll be an hour late for the meeting."

The driver looked at Diane in the mirror. She nodded. The driver made the call. Joe directed him to West 55th Street, and told them to wait.

There was a dry cleaner on West 55the between Fifth and Sixth avenues, on the south side of the street about halfway down the block from Fifth, which was where traffic entered the block because it was a one-way street. Joe remembered the place from years before, and was agreeably pleased to find it was still there, and was open.

Inside, Joe agreed to pay ten dollars for immediate service, plus five-fifty for cleaning and pressing. In addition, Joe advanced the presser a five-dollar tip for smiling service. The job took twenty minutes, and Joe waited on a stool in a curtained-off area at the rear of the shop while they cleaned his pants and underpants.

At the car, he dropped his newspaper through the open window onto the back seat and said, "Now we're all going to have some breakfast. We said we'd be an hour late, and I don't want to call in again. I'm buying."

He escorted them both into a coffee shop a few doors down the street toward Sixth. As they ate, Joe held out his hand to the driver and asked for the car keys. "I want to get my paper," said Joe. "There's something in it I want to show you."

The driver looked at Diane. She nodded. Five minutes later, the driver and Diane were standing on the corner of 55th and Fifth, frantically trying to hail a downtown taxi in the slow, early-holiday-morning traffic. Joe was already crossing West 34th Street on Ninth Avenue, speeding downtown to his meeting with Paul Lazard. The phone under the dash buzzed and the incoming-call light flashed all the way down to the World Trade Center. The light was still flashing as Joe drove down the ramp into the basement parking garage reserved for official cars and VIPs.

"The stuff you gave us at the drop yesterday," said Lazard, "was good. It's the kind of stuff we want from you all the time—internal drafts of issues papers, memos, phone logs, private correspondence, schedules. Especially the draft schedules. That's important."

Lazard bent forward and poured hot tea into Joe's cup. They were drinking out of French porcelain cups, with an eighteenth-century English silver service set on an inlaid walnut eighteenth-century English serving table. Lazard's office was furnished entirely in antiques. The interior of the huge corner office contrasted sharply with the two-sided view of a sweep of New York Harbor from Governor's Island and South Brooklyn to Hoboken. They were on the eighty-eighth floor.

"When it's clear," said Lazard, "You can almost see Philadelphia."

"Who would want to?" asked Joe.

"Ha, ha," said Lazard, imitating a laugh. "You're still quite the clown, Joe. I'm sure Diane won't get over your little joke for weeks.

"They want to be executives," said Lazard. "They want to be field hands. They want training. They want mentors. They want to be protégés. But they don't want to be humiliated. They don't want to be threatened. They don't like physical violence. They want to be successful. But they don't like guns. They aren't like you and me, Joe. They never will be. You and I have been humiliated, intimidated, beat up, shot at, and forced to wait in line."

"Yes," observed Joe. "And we even liked it."

"Oh, ha, ha, Joe. Dry. Very dry wit, Joe."

Lazard was in an English country gentleman mood. It's better than the redneck, thought Joe.

"What we're missing from you," said Lazard, "is where the money's coming from."

"That's not part of anything I can get my hands on. They've got that walled off from the rest of the operation, compartmentalized."

"No doubt, but we need it."

"I can't get it."

"Try."

Joe was silent.

"Joe?"

"No black bag stuff, Paul. It's not worth the risk."

"Oh, no, no. I perfectly agree. No Watergates. But what about Brother Billy and the Libyans?"

"All I know is what I read in Jack Anderson."

"Come, come, Joe. Exercise a little imagination."

"That's not what you're paying me for. Facts are what you're paying for."

"Oh, Joe. I'm disappointed. Where's your sense of fun? *Gossip is fun!*"

"Gossip is bullshit," said Joe, irritated. "And there's no gossip around there about money."

"Who's handling it?"

"The finance committee."

"That's public record, Joe. Don't play with me."

"I don't know, Paul. I'm not part of the money games."

"Well, get a part. That's what we're after."

"Who's 'we,' Paul?"

"You've asked me that before, and I told you."

"You told me bullshit."

"Are Kirbo and Bert Lance involved?"

"I'm sure they are, but you couldn't prove it by me."

"I wanna know."

"You and who else?"

Lazard said nothing.

"Come, come, Paul," mocked Joe.

"We," said Paul, "are Langley."

Joe reached into his shirt pocket and pulled out a piece of computer printout folded four times. When it was opened, it measured 8½ by 14 inches, with the perforations along the edges that mark pages that have been torn off accordion-fold paper, the kind that feeds through high-speed computer printers. The paper was a faint gray, and the printing was in a light blue ink that would not show up in a photocopy. The paper was dense with thousands of words in very fine print.

Lazard recognized it immediately. He could have sputtered, *Where did you get this?* And Joe would have answered, *I've still got a few buddies down there*. But Lazard only held his hand out in silence.

Joe re-folded the paper and stuck it back in his shirt pocket. "It says Paul Lazard resigned with prejudice in 1979 and was refused contract status when he approached the Agency in early 1980. It says any employee must report any direct or indirect contact with you immediately. You're on their shit list, Paul. What did you do?"

"What else is on there?"

"Your whole career."

"In detail?"

"Yes."

"Then you know what I did."

"Yes."

"What did I do?"

"You pilfered the complete files on two men."

"Who were they?"

"Jimmy Carter and Ronald Reagan."

"And what did I do with them?"

"It doesn't say. The printouts you took overnight were returned the next morning and everything was hushed up immediately, with very damn good reason."

"Yes, I cleaned out my desk and left in an hour."

"You mean they cleaned it out for you."

"Yes, of course."

"Now what?"

"This doesn't alter our relationship, Joe. You're still working for me and I still want to know where Jimmy Carter is getting his money."

"I just resigned," said Joe.

There was a long silence. A small high-wing Cessna flew slowly past the windows, out over the Hudson River, yawing slightly in the morning wind. Large jets landed and took off at Newark Airport in the middle distance out in New Jersey. The sky was watercolor pale blue.

Lazard picked up a telephone. "Patch that open line in here," he said. He motioned for Joe to pick up a phone next to him.

Joe did so. He heard a click and buzz and another click, then a choking sound. "Daddy?" said the voice of his son.

Lazard pressed a button on his phone and the line went dead. "We won't hurt the boy," he said. "But I want you to understand, Joe, that you're in this little game for the long haul."

Joe's eyes were closed. He tried to call up the image of the green jade fish. He couldn't. But neither did the awful rage come boiling up out of his stomach. It was as though something was dead inside him, something that had been alive only a moment before. Something had been cauterized with one terrible white-hot burst of pain, leaving nothing but a ragged cicatrix and the lingering smell in Joe's mind, or memory, of burning flesh. It was a smell he remembered from the jungles.

He opened his eyes. Diane stood next to Lazard, her hand on the back of Lazard's chair in a familiar, proprietary way. She was smiling. Lazard was smiling too.

"How long is the long haul?" asked Joe.

"Oh, I don't know," said Lazard calmly. "It shouldn't be more than four more years."

"1984," said Joe. In his own ears, his voice didn't sound like his voice.

"More or less," said Diane.

"What do you want from me?" asked Joe.

"I'd like you to have lunch with us today," said Lazard.

"Who do you work for?"

"You'll meet him at lunch," said Diane. She looked down at Lazard, or rather, talked down at him. He didn't look up. She said, "I made a reservation for four at the Italian Pavilion."

Lazard nodded. He was watching Joe.

"That's on West 55th Street, just down the street from where we were this morning," said Joe.

"Yes," said Diane. She gave a bright smile, as if rewarding a prize pupil, and looking Joe full in the face, gave him a broad wink.

Deliberately, with no trace of his bygone anger, Joe leaned forward, picked up the delicate china cups, and broke them apart in his two hands, dropping the pieces in the two saucers.

Diane gasped. "They're worth hundreds of dollars apiece!"

Lazard smiled. "That's why we like him, dear girl. And he won't fuck anyone but his wife."

SEVEN

"PICK US UP at three-thirty," said Lazard to his driver. The car drove off fast, east on West 34th Street. Lazard shepherded Joe and Diane across the intersection to the northwest corner of Eighth Avenue and 34th, where he hailed a cab. The lower edge of the garment district was deserted on the holiday.

"Why are we here?" Joe asked Diane.

"He has to run some errands."

"He couldn't drive us five more minutes uptown?"

"No."

"Is this tradecraft or stagecraft?" asked Joe.

Diane snickered.

In the cab, a new Peugeot diesel, Joe and Diane sat in the back while Lazard squeezed his bulk into the front seat next to the driver, a talkative Israeli. Lazard told him to shut up. The Israeli immediately shut off the air conditioning and rolled down his window. Diane was laughing quietly. Lazard's face and neck were flushed with anger. Joe couldn't figure out what was going on.

"Who are we meeting?" he asked.

"My *consigliere*," answered Lazard loudly. "Therefore, be nice to him."

Diane's hand slipped under Joe's right thigh and withdrew.
She was looking out the window on her side. Joe felt under
his leg and found a folded slip of paper. He palmed it into his
pants pocket without looking at it.

"Paul?" asked Joe.

"Umh?"

"I hope my boy wasn't hurt."

"Ah," breathed Lazard. He turned around in his seat to face
Joe. "There's the rub. There we've got you. He was hurt a bit.
But the next time, if a next time there must be, he will get
hurt far worse."

The Israeli's eyes were flipping around crazily from Lazard's
face to the mirror.

"Watch where you're going," said Lazard. "It would be a
serious mistake to have even a little accident."

Billy woke up on his side, curled in a tight fetal ball on the
concrete floor of the basement of his own house, but he couldn't
remember how he got there. He had the worst headache of his
life. His chest and side ached with pain. His ankle hurt where
the man had kicked him several times, laughing and saying,
"Take a jump shot on that, you little faggot."

The memory of the man's voice brought the rest of it back—
anger, fear, and humiliation. It was as though anyone who
wanted could walk into the house, shoot at Joe, beat up Billy,
do anything they damn pleased. Billy felt violated, and he felt
a fiery anger he had never felt before. The heat of it stirred
him and made his body begin to uncurl.

He rolled onto his back and stretched out on the cool floor,
breathing in and out with deeper and deeper breaths until he
was sure nothing was cracked or broken in his rib cage. He
had played enough rough playground basketball to know what
he was doing.

He was sure his face was a mess. It felt swollen and bruised.
He sat up.

Then the whole scene came back. He was sitting on his bed
reading *David Copperfield*, trying to finish it in time for a
discussion this evening with Father Kelly. He was reading about
Micawber's intention to return to Canterbury; and David's reaf-
firmation of his love for little Dora, "a favorite child of nature."

He had read about David's learning the skills of a court and parliamentary stenographer. Father Kelly had told Billy this was how the young Charles Dickens had made his living, and Billy was realizing as he read that hidden under the tragicomedy of this long novel was the autobiography of a great writer. Billy had arrived at Mr. Spenlow's discovery of David's letters to Spenlow's daughter, Dora; and Mr. Spenlow's death.

Billy was lost in the story. He felt himself in the room with Mr. Tiffey in Spenlow's office in the Commons, as Mr. Tiffey, David, and Mr. Jorkins searched for a will among Spenlow's papers. Billy read, in David Copperfield's words:

> It appeared a wonderful thing to me, but it turned out that there *was* no will. He [Spenlow, the father of the foolish, beloved little Dora] had never so much as thought of making one, so far as his papers afforded any evidence; for there was no kind of hint, sketch, or memorandum of any testimentary intention whatever. What was scarcely less astonishing to me was, that his affairs were in a most disordered state. It was extremely difficult, I heard, to make out what he owed, or what he had paid, or of what he died possessed. It was considered likely that for years he could have had no clear opinion on these subjects himself. . . . and Tiffey told me, little thinking how interested I was in the story, that, paying all the just debts of the deceased, and deducting his share of outstanding bad and doubtful debts due to the firm, he wouldn't give a thousand pounds for all the assets remaining.

Billy began to think of the story his father had told him on the boat. The boy remembered his father's dependence on Mary's financial judgment. Billy now began to wonder, as he read, how his father earned enought money for them to live on, and about the "bit" of gold and the "handful" of jewels hidden away, and what would happen to Billy if Joe died and Billy couldn't find the loot.

Billy had arrived at the point, all unknown to Father Kelly, but the point every good teacher tries to drive his students toward, where the connections between literature and life begin to be revealed, and where it is seen clearly, suddenly, for the first time, that great books have great power.

He was absolutely lost in this, and reading as hard and fast as he could, thinking about his father and the loot at the same time, when the tall, hard man with eyes like silver-blue glass appeared in the doorway to the bedroom from the hall. Somehow he had gotten into the house without a sound.

And without a sound, the man walked two strides over to Billy and slapped a hand over the boy's mouth. Billy's book flew into the air and fell to the floor as Billy struggled, but Billy was helpless. He had never encountered a stronger man. The man was no bigger than Joe, but he was hard. There was no give in his grip.

Resistance was futile, but Billy tried. As the man dragged him from the bedroom to the kitchen, Billy twisted around and slammed his elbow into the man's crotch. The man grunted but was otherwise unmoved. He tied Billy into a kitchen chair with electric cord.

Then he said, "That'll cost yuh." Standing very close to Billy, he put his forefinger across under Billy's nose and forced the boy's head back as far as it would go, holding it for long minutes as tears ran down Billy's face.

"The first rule they teach yuh in hand-to-hand is soft to hard, hard to soft. So yuh use yer boot on the guy's balls, not yer elbow. And the heel of yer hand on the nose. Like this!"

He gave a light pop with the heel of his hand to the base of Billy's nose. It was very painful. More tears ran down Billy's face. The man's hand was like a boot heel.

"If yuh really pop it hard, yuh kin drive a man's nose right up into his brain. Splinters of bone. It'll kill him. Remember that, kid, the next time yer in a bar brawl."

The man laughed. He had a high, whistling voice—incongruous in the freakishly strong body. He pulled another chair around to face Billy and dragged the telephone across the counter within easy reach. He sat down.

The man was very close. His breath smelled oddly sweet. His pupils were slightly dilated. He stared directly at Billy with the indifferent intensity of a television camera. His violence was so natural and instinctive, and so imaginative, that Billy was completely terrified. Billy knew the man was not there to kill him, but to hurt him. Billy was already prepared to do the man's will. It was an experience of total humiliation.

The man said, "Now we wait. When that phone rings, yer

gonna get hurt some. Not before. Then yer gonna talk to yer Dad—a word or two—then we're gonna hang up on him. Then yer gonna get hurt some more and I'm gonna leave. If yuh tell anyone, I'm gonna be back. Yer daddy knows—that's the whole point of the exercise—but there's nuthin' he kin do."

Billy felt sick. The man smiled for an instant, as if the corners of his thin mouth were pulled back by a bridle and quickly released. The man had a lean face, tanned dark but with a fresh burn. It was the face of a ranch hand or farmer. He wore Levi's, faded and worn, the kind that have buttons instead of a zipper, and a cotton work shirt, thin and worn. The sleeves were rolled up over forearms that looked like six-inch Manila hawsers, corded and braided, the ropes used to moor ships. He wore cowboy boots, not fancy but well made and well-worn. His belt was elaborately tooled. The leather looked new, but the silver buckle looked old.

The man's hands were scarred and misshapen. If Billy had recognized the signs, he might have known the man had once been a professional rodeo cowboy. Nearly every bone in the man's hands had been broken at one time or another. Nor did Billy recognize the man's accent as the flat drawl of the high plains; or the long silences as the laconic quiet of someone who grew up working in the vast solitudes of a Montana cattle ranch; or the easy violence as the mark of a man who spent some years in prison.

They waited. It was the silence that frightened Billy the most. Billy was wearing only cut-off jeans and a T-shirt, and he felt exposed. The shirt was soaked with sweat even though the central air conditioning was on high. The first time the boy tried to speak, the man kicked him hard in the ankle and held his finger to his lips in an odd, almost feminine gesture, saying, "Shh. Shh. There's nuthin' to talk about."

They waited nearly two hours. The man sat motionless and silent, staring at Billy most of the time. When the phone rang, it startled Billy, but the man picked it up before the end of the first ring.

"Yuh," said the man after a brief murmur from the phone receiver. Billy heard a woman's voice at the other end, but he couldn't hear what she said.

"Yuh," said the man again, and set the receiver down on

the counter without hanging up. Billy's flesh tingled and crawled, and in that instant of anticipation, the man slapped Billy across the back of the head with a blow that made Billy's ears ring. For another minute or two, he slugged and slapped and kicked the boy. Billy sobbed and choked with pain. Then the man grabbed Billy by the hair, slammed the phone against the boy's ear, and said, "Say hello to yer pop."

Billy said, "Daddy?"

The man hung up.

Billy spit a gob of blood out onto the kitchen floor and said in a hoarse whisper, "Cocksucker."

A kind of distant rage flickered across the man's face like heat lightning and he beat Billy unconscious. When Billy came to, he was sitting upright, untied, on the kitchen chair in the middle of the basement. Then the man beat him unconscious again.

From his sitting position, Billy decided to try to stand up. He rolled over on to his hands and knees, probing with his mind every muscle, joint, and bone. He had a fat lip, he discovered, but his nose was intact. His ear hurt. There was real soreness in his ankle and in the muscles of his chest and stomach. He couldn't raise his left arm without pain.

He stood up. Too fast. The gray film spread and darkened across his vision again and he dropped into the kitchen chair, forcing his head down between his knees until the faintness passed. He wondered if he had a concussion, but there was no nausea and he had no trouble focusing his eyes. His head hurt terribly, but he decided he was OK. A few aspirins, a few days of ice packs, then a few days of heat, and he would heal.

He looked around. In the dim light of the basement, the only object out of place was the chair. Nothing seemed disturbed. The house was silent. Billy strained to hear, but the only noises were the quiet, distant sounds of the neighborhood—a car passing by, a lawnmower, a dog barking. He wondered what time it was. He didn't think much time had passed, but then again, it might be the next afternoon. He knew instinctively that the man was gone, but he was afraid to go upstairs to the kitchen because he was afraid the man would be sitting there waiting for him in perfect, patient silence.

Setting his face in stoic disregard for his aches and pains, Billy walked the few feet over to the furnace. It was relatively new, a four-foot cube of green sheet metal with copper pipes and galvanized sheet-metal ducts leading in and out. The furnace was off for the summer, but the central air conditioner was running, pushing chilled air through the ducts.

Back in April he had found a section of one duct where the sheet-metal screws were finger-loose and could be removed without a screwdriver. This section of the duct was level, at head height. Inside that duct he had hidden the .22, wrapped carefully in plastic refrigerator bags to protect the gun from dust. Since hiding the gun, he had not disturbed it but he had added a box of ammunition he managed to buy at a suburban sporting goods store.

He wanted to get out of the basement. It felt like a prison cell, despite the comforting familiarity of workbench and tools, old toys, fishing equipment, old furniture—the detritus of the life of a family that was no longer a family.

Billy shivered. The familiar was no longer a comfort. He would free himself from the basement. He would creep up the stairs with the gun. He was surprised to find that some small part of him was hoping the man was waiting in the kitchen. Five shots into the body. And when the man lay helpless on the linoleum floor, Billy would carefully, deliberately, shoot out each of the ball-bearing eyes.

He took out the screws and freed the side panel of the duct, lifting it silently away and setting it on top of the furnace. Cold air blew out around his face. It smelled dry and metallic. He reached inside as far as he could, thinking for a panicky moment that he had forgotten where he put the pistol, or that someone had found it. Then he touched the edge of a plastic bag.

He pulled it out. It felt light. It was not the gun. It was a blue velvet jewelry case the size of a hardbound book. When he was little, he used to poke through his mother's dresser looking for treasures. This case was one of them. It was wrapped in a clear refrigerator bag and sealed tightly with Scotch tape. He set it on top of the duct and picked up a flashlight from the floor next to the furnace where his father left it in case of emergency.

He shined the light up the duct. There was his gun, undisturbed, and another package in a large Baggie—this one a five-

by-five Manila envelope. He pulled it out and opened it. Inside
were twenty crisp one-thousand-dollar bills and two US passports, one new and one somewhat worn.

He opened the new one. It was in the name of William
Benjamin Moore and contained Billy's most recent school pho-
tograph. There were no stamps on the visa pages. It had never
been used.

The other passport had a photo of his father taken maybe a
year earlier. The visa pages carried entry and exit stamps for
Bermuda, the Bahamas, England, and Mexico, with dates in
a sequence of six days in early June. Billy was stunned. That
was a week his father was supposed to be in New York all
week. The name in the passport was Joseph Andrew Moore.

Billy opened the jewelry case. Even with his nose full of
dust and cold air, he could smell his mother's smell. In a hinged
tray that opened with the lid were two intricately carved jade
fish—one green, the other pink. They were the most beautiful
objects Billy had ever seen. Under the tray was a layer of black
velvet cloth covering a number of large lumps. He knew they
were stones.

Under the cloth were twenty or twenty-five diamonds cut
in round or square shapes. Two were shaped like fat teardrops.
None was smaller than his thumbnail.

He closed the case. He unwrapped the gun, checked the
load, and cocked it. With the money, passports, and jewels in
one hand, and the gun in the other, he ran up the stairs in his
bare feet and burst into the kitchen. There was no one there.
The man with the fists like bricks was gone.

It was early afternoon. Sliding the loot and the gun into a
kitchen drawer, Billy went to the bathroom and took a shower.
He forced himself to make a sandwich and eat it. He drank a
bottle of Coke. Then he began to search the house. He started
at the front door and searched each room clockwise, ceiling to
floor, wall by wall, each piece of furniture, every square foot
of floor—exactly the way his father had done the night they
swept the house for bugs. Only this time Billy worked in cold,
disciplined fury. His father had betrayed him for the last time.

The cab stopped with a sharp lurch. Lazard scowled at the
driver. "Go back where you came from," said Lazard.

"I'm happy to see you out of my taxi," said the driver.

"We're here," said Diane brightly. She pushed some folded bills into the driver's hand.

As they gathered on the sidewalk in front of the restaurant, a white Rolls-Royce pulled up in the street. From the back seat emerged a man wearing a white planter's suit, a white shirt with a pale yellow tie, white buck shoes that had never stepped in a mud puddle, and gold-rimmed sunglasses with the lenses tinted light gray. The effect was not so much designer chic as the weekend costume of a *padrone*.

The man's face and hands were the red-brown color of mahogany, the deep tan of a leisured man accustomed to the special qualities of sun available only at expensive resorts, not at ordinary beaches. His head was hatless. His bald dome was covered with scabby sun blisters. He had bulbous eyes and a bulbous nose. His forehead was high and prominent. There was a light touch of eyebrow pencil in the eyebrows.

This was not a good-looking man, thought Joe, or a pleasant man, but the face was animated and surprisingly open, with a direct display of curiosity as he turned toward Joe. Joe had never met him but knew who he was. This was a new ball game.

"Julius Gold," said the man, and held out his hand for Joe to shake. The grip was firm and dry.

"Joe Ball," said Joe.

"Yes, I know, I've heard about you. Let's go in out of the hot sun and have a cold drink. Mad dogs and Englishmen, and all that . . . "

Gold turned to Diane and displayed his powdered and barbered cheek.

"Julie," crooned Diane, pecking him loudly on the upturned target. She was an inch or two taller than he.

"Julius," said Lazard with hearty good fellowship. "How nice to see you."

Gold did not offer his hand. Instead, with an impatient tone, he asked, "Did you remember to make reservations with Pietro, as I asked?"

"Yes, yes," responded Lazard with the same loud, impervious, hearty fellowship. "The table you wanted."

"Booth."

"Yes. Booth. Of course."

"Of course," said Diane. "Shall we get off the street?"

Gold held his arms out and shepherded them into the restaurant with the air of a man who owned it.

It was a holiday noon, and the restaurant was empty. The paused for a moment inside the doors, waiting for the captain. Gold took out a white handkerchief and wiped every square inch of exposed skin—head, face, neck, hands. He glistened with sweat. "Air conditioning," he said, "is the greatest contribution of America to the stability of the free world."

"Why is that?" asked Joe.

"Because without air conditioning, there would be no Houston."

Joe laughed. "So what?"

"No Sunbelt, and we would all still be under the thumb of the Wall Street WASPs. The emergence of new centers of power is the most important thing since the FDR landslide in 1932. That's why Reagan is going to win this fall."

"That's why Reagan is a candidate," said Joe, "but not why he's going to win."

"Touché," said Gold. He turned to Diane. "I knew I was going to like him."

She, in turn, smiled at Lazard, who was scowling like the Red Queen.

Just go with the flow, thought Joe.

The captain appeared from the kitchen. He was in his holiday shirt-sleeves, smiling and pleased to see them. He greeted them each by name, except Joe. He pointed to the booth afforded the most privacy.

The dining room was a few steps down from the entrance. There were several booths along one wall, tables in the center, and banquettes along the opposite wall. Large windows of tinted glass lined the wall along the street. They were covered by gauzy white summer drapes. Potted ferns and painted murals of the Italian Riviera lined the other walls and surrounded the kitchen doors.

Gold hesitated in mock indecision. He pointed to a table in the center. "How about that one instead, Pietro?"

"Of course, *signore*. Whatever you wish."

Gold directed Joe to sit on his left, Diane on his right, and exiled Lazard to the opposite side. Pietro took their orders for drinks and went to the small side bar to mix them himself. In the empty room, the tinkle of glasses and ice was a pleasant sound, the sound of summer, thought Joe, like crickets in August.

There was no small talk. Gold began immediately to review with Joe the material Joe had turned over to Diane the evening before on the grassy lawn before the Capitol. Gold was neither complimentary nor critical, but interested in the details of their acquisition, their authorship, and their use. Gold proved in just a few moments that he had an astonishing range of knowledge of political history and life. Joe knew he was in the presence of a master.

Gold was a well-known lawyer with a long history of involvement as a fund-raiser and behind-the-scenes strategist in the conservative—some would say reactionary—wing of the Republican Party. He had a reputation as a willing and ruthless litigator. Journalists feared him with good reason.

Joe had been prepared to dislike him, but found him charming and smart, very quick and focused. Joe found himself more confused and puzzled than enlightened by the talk. It was not clear what Gold was after, and not at all clear what the relationships at the table were. Gold was neither boss nor counselor to Lazard, and Gold seemed to treat Lazard and Diane as separate but equal. Just as it became clear to Joe that each of them thought they were the senior body here, it became equally clear that there was no direct chain of command. Joe wondered who the real boss was.

The dark greens and muted reds of the restaurant, and the flowing white drapes across the windows on the street, gave the large room a timeless quality—the somnolence of summer afternoons. A few more parties came in and were seated at a discreet distance. Gold asked what Joe's plans were for obtaining financial information about the Carter campaign. Joe said he had none. Diane smiled like the Mona Lisa. The waiter brought fresh drinks and took their orders. Lazard, surprisingly, ordered a light lunch, veal *piccata* with a green salad. The others ordered fish. Gold ordered two different white wines, both Italian.

Gold observed that the greatest damage to Carter was done early in his term by the loss of the services of Bert Lance, Carter's Georgia banker and confidant.

"It was Lance," said Gold, "who put Carter in the White House."

Joe understood what Gold was getting at, but he asked Gold, "How?"

"The Pennsylvania primary. Everyone was broke. The unions fell apart under Jackson. No one else had any money. That was the big watershed for the unions. After that, everyone knew the unions couldn't deliver any votes from their own rank and file.

"Lance came up with the money for Carter to run a TV blitz at the last minute, and Carter won. It's that simple. A few Democratic voters, *a handful*, put Carter over the top in Pennsylvania, and into the White House. It was a great performance on Lance's part. He understood one of the basic principles of politics."

Gold paused to sip his wine. He nodded to the waiter, who poured for the rest. Diane covered her glass with her hand.

Joe politely asked, "What's that?"

"There is no tomorrow," said Gold.

The waiter brought chilled *consommé,* bread, and salads. He made the rounds with a pepper grinder the size of a softball bat.

Gold said, "Lance understood that there are critical moments when you have to risk everything. When the time came, Lance was ready. He may have shuffled some money around a few Georgia banks—nothing that doesn't happen every day in the banks in New York, Boston, Chicago, Denver, Dallas, and LA. At any rate, when Carter held his hand out, Lance slipped in the bread. Carter wasn't the quarterback. It was Lance. Carter was a running back, and when he took that quick drop step and headed for the hole, Lance counted—one, two—and spun right. He slapped that old money ball right into Carter's skinny gut and stepped the hell out of the way."

"Carter sure was a lightweight heavyweight," said Diane.

"Is," said Gold, smiling at her. He tasted his soup. He had the superficial mannerisms of a man who enjoys eating, but Joe had the impression that Gold had no taste buds, that Gold could have been eating unheated Campbell's soup out of the can.

Joe said, "The real loss was in not having Lance running OMB."

"Right," said Gold, looking up from his soup and wiping his mouth. "It's one thing to have an outsider like Carter in

the White House. We could have all lived with that. But it's
something else to have an outsider in the basement writing all
the checks. Lance was the only one of that whole gang who
really understood money."

"What about Kirbo?" asked Joe.

"Kirbo's smart, but he wants to be liked. Lance was smart
and didn't give a shit. He was a fast learner, too. He wouldn't
have taken any crap from the Democrats on the Hill. He would've
taught that dumb Tip O'Neill a thing or two, and fast.

"The thing about the Democrats," said Gold, "is money.
Democratic voters aren't rich like Republicans. Democrats can't
raise enough money for their campaigns. They're always broke.
So they spend the taxpayer's money instead. You know what
I mean?" Gold looked at Joe.

Joe nodded.

Gold said, "You've a quick study, too. I like you better and
better. You tell me the rest."

Joe said, "With Lance running the Office of Management
and Budget, Carter would have been in complete control of
the Democratic Party, even as an outsider, because every
Democrat in Congress and every Democratic governor would
have had to kiss Carter's ass to get funds for their favorite
programs. Lance would have known exactly how to whip those
boys and girls around."

Gold nodded.

"Without Lance," said Joe, "and with the distractions of
having to defend himself against journalistic charges of corruption and illegal campaign tactics in the first months of his
administration, Carter was lost, right at the start. He never
really took control of the federal fisc, which is the biggest
checkwriting machine in one place in the world, and the only
real weapon the President has in his battles against the Congress."

"Nice work," said Gold, nodding to Diane. To Joe, he said,
"All the rest follows from the loss of Lance. Of course, there
are always events one has no control over, and sometimes those
events enable one to recover from past mistakes, but Carter is
too rigid and narrow to take advantage of such opportunities.
Witness the hostage situation. He snatched defeat out of the
jaws of opportunity."

"So what are you after?" asked Joe, aware that he had passed some kind of preliminary test by Gold.

"No matter how successful the Republican Party is," said Gold, talking in a low voice, making Joe lean toward him to hear, "it's always going to be smaller than the Democrats, because the Republican Party is the party of the rich, and there are fewer of us than them."

"It's just that simple?"

"Yes. By the end of the century, there will be as many as twenty to fifty million Hispanics in this country. It'll be the largest unassimilated voting bloc. With very few exceptions, they're not gonna vote for a party whose only ideology is *white* and *more*."

Joe laughed. "I've never heard it better put."

"So one way to hamstring the Democratic Party is to know where their money's coming from. We're not so concerned with this year as 1982 and 1984. It's always nice to have another source, and anything you can bring us this year is useful, but what we really want is a mole in the DNC who's gonna be in the absolute center of the action two years and four years down the road."

"You know what happens to moles?" asked Joe. "Nobody likes them much, especially their owners."

"You've spent too much time around the Company," laughed Gold. "You'll find us much nicer to deal with. We don't forget our friends."

"What's the deal?"

"You've passed the tests. You've brought us some shit with your fingerprints all over it, and you're smart."

"And," said Lazard in a low murmur, speaking for the first time, "we have a hostage."

"Mutt and Jeff," said Joe.

Lazard smiled. Gold shrugged. Diane smiled. In that instant, it was clear to Joe that she was the boss here.

Gold said, "Joe, we know you've got some loot stashed away. Just how much, we don't know, but we think it's a lot. We assume you want to launder and invest it. We assume you want to go fishing and your son wants to go to college, although his grades aren't so hot at the moment. You work for us—all the way—and we'll pay you a hundred thousand a year in cash, off the books, in an unbreakable trust fund for your kid. We'll find a few absolutely clean no-show clients for your little

PR shop to give you some reportable income. And we'll help you invest your loot, onshore or offshore, however you want it."

They were all looking at him.

"Deal?" asked Gold.

"Deal," said Joe.

The talk veered to gossip about New York. The waiter brought the main course. Gold refilled their glasses. They ate and drank, chatting like old friends or business associates who have decided to stay in town for a quiet holiday weekend rather than join the pell-mell rush to the Hamptons. Gold was an inexhaustible source of hard-core gossip, scurrilous information on sexual habits, backbiting, deals, monetary problems. Lazard contributed little.

Diane's role, it seemed, was to sift and record. She was a walking aide-mémoire. Both Lazard and Gold were homosexual. They were polite and attentive to her, but her sexuality held no interest for them, and since her apparent willingness to manipulate was overtly sexual, they seemed immune to her games. She was relaxed and pleasant, quite natural, playing the part of a color commentator and making little jokes. She was funny and attractive. Joe thought, if she was the boss, who was her boss?

Joe was passive. It was what the others seemed to expect, and Joe was used to playing to the expectations of others—it was one of the customary roles of the secret life, or the life of the secret bureaucracies. At the same time, he sensed in himself the deeper passivity of the permanent spectator.

His anger was gone, surgically excised by the choking terror in Billy's voice over the telephone. Joe felt numbed, or lobotomized, or—perhaps more to the point, he thought—neutered. I'm a eunuch, he thought, an official in a Byzantine court, a secret Byzantine court inside the shell of public democracy. There are too damn many secrets, he thought further, for anyone to ever understand what really happens, and why.

Diane stirred restlessly across from him. She was watching him.

What *are* these guys after? wondered Joe. There was no more parry and counter-thrust in the talk around the table. Lazard and Gold had made their minds up about Joe, had made him one of them. What the *hell* is going on? thought Joe, but it was a thought without anger. He was puzzled and curious, but no more. Worse, he had put Billy out of mind.

Joe slid his hand into his pants pocket and felt to see if his balls were still attached. His fingers found the folded slip of paper. With sudden urgency he got up from the table, excusing himself to go to the men's room.

"What about dessert?" asked Lazard, as if he couldn't understand any human act taking precedence over ordering dessert.

"Rum cake and coffee," said Joe over his shoulder.

In the men's room, he unfolded the paper. It said: "Have dinner with me. Eight o'clock. 20 Waterside Plaza. 25K. Bring red wine. R.S.V.P."

Cute, the thought, and flushed the note down the toilet.

Near the entrance to the restaurant was a pay phone in an old-fashioned wooden booth built into the wall. Joe made a collect call to Billy at home. There was no answer. He tried a second time, in case he'd dialed the wrong number. No answer.

After a moment's thought, he called Father Kelly. The housekeeper at the rectory said the priest was out for a while. Joe left a message asking the priest to check on Billy at home, saying the request was urgent, but no emergency.

Back at the table, Joe said, "There's no answer at my house. Do you suppose something went wrong with your finely tuned plans? Did your torturers fuck up?"

He asked this in a loud voice. Several people at other tables looked up suddenly, then went back to their meals, as if they couldn't believe what they had heard.

Lazard's answer was the merest murmur, almost embarrassed. "Nothing is wrong, I'm sure. there were the strictest instructions, and the help is expert. I'm sure the lad is on the basketball courts by now."

Joe didn't respond. He held the silence over the table for a long time. Finally, Gold began to tell a story about a well-known tennis star and her sexual preferences, which were plural.

Joe interrupted as if Gold wasn't there. "After lunch," Joe said, "is always a good time to renegotiate a contract. Everybody's feeling good. There's a general sense of goodwill." He nodded around the table. "I'll do my part, but I want you to understand clearly that there's no hostage." He lowered his voice. "In this business, as I'm sure you all know, no one makes idle threats, and I'm not making one now." He lowered his voice more. The others leaned toward him to hear.

"If anyone, no matter who it is, whether it's your gorillas or not, goes near my boy again, or near my house, the three of you will be the hostages. Do I make myself clear?"

Gold sat up straight, adjusting the perfect knot in his tie, and shooting his cuffs, folding his hands on the table in front of him. "We don't like threats," he said.

Joe saw the cuff links and the watch. He had been watching them all during the meal. The cuff links were balls of gold the size of marbles. The watch was a Rolex in a gold case with a gold band. In his mind, Joe heard a voice in a whisper as faint as wind in the top of a pine tree. *"Jerry. Julie. Somethin' like that. Gold watch. Gold cuff links. Armor . . ."*

"You don't have to like threats," said Joe. "Just remember them."

Into the resulting silence, Gold threw more gossip. He waved for more coffee and asked for anisette. Five thousand dollars' worth of jewelry glittered on his tanned, hairy wrists.

Joe said, "I think I'll stay in town tonight. Is there a nice waterside restaurant I can visit?"

Gold eagerly described a new restaurant on the Brooklyn waterfront, called the River Cafe. "I know the owners," he said. "I'll call them. They'll take good care of you."

"Fine," said Joe. "Thank you. I'll make a reservation for eight o'clock."

Gold looked at his watch. "I have to go," he said. "I have a date at the Armory." He waved to the waiter and made a little scribbling motion with his hand. "Sign the check for me, will you, Paul?" Gold stood up, nodded to Diane, patted Joe on the shoulder, made a little circle sign of perfection with his fingers in the direction of Pietro, and left.

"Armory?" said Joe to Lazard. "What's he talking about?"

"Don't you know? The Seventh Regiment? Up on Park Avenue?"

Joe shrugged.

Diane said, "It's an architectural treasure. You should get Julie to show you around some time. He knows the history of every object in the place."

EIGHT ══════════════════════

JOE WALKED. HE walked up Sixth Avenue to Central Park. He walked into the park along the short curving drive just west of the Pond, past the statues of José Martí and José de San Martín on their triumphal pedestals and rearing horses. He reflected on the amazing nineteenth-century romantic impulse to build public monuments in New York City to Latin American liberators. When they start building monuments, watch out, he thought. The next step is the Marines.

At the edge of the park, some people were working hard to liberate themselves. They were chanting, whispering, even singing, "Ganja. Ganja. Ganja." Or, "Joints and bags. Bags and joints."

In the unmoving, thick humidity of mid-afternoon, it smelled like there were a lot of customers for the products of people's capitalism. Joe reflected mildly, without judgment, on the evolution of the spirit of free-market enterprise.

He cut through the trees and grass behind Wollman Memorial Rink and, walking faster now, past the chess and checkers pavilion and the odd gingerbread building called the Dairy. Instead of taking the footpath leading from the Dairy across the transverse drive to the Center Drive, he turned sharply past the building onto a broad ledge above the transverse, which was in a rock-walled trench below the level of the park. Buses and cabs rushed by below him. He was in a stretch of ragged underbrush and trampled bare earth that from the smell and look of it was used as an outhouse.

No one was in sight, and Joe did as many others did. He stopped, unzipped, and aimed at the roots of a bush, looking back the way he came. As he finished, an elderly man in a light tan suit, carrying his jacket over his arm, wearing a light beard, stepped around the corner.

"Oh, sorry," he said in a faint British accent. "Had the same idea myself. Damn public rest rooms are locked up. Wouldn't go in 'em if I could."

"I know what you mean," said Joe, zipping up and walking quickly across the footbridge. There were no cabs going uptown on the East Drive. Since it was a holiday, the park's interior roads were closed to traffic. This was going to be real hare and hounds, thought Joe. The look on the man's face was unmistakable.

He had spotted the spry old bastard as soon as they had left the restaurant, as he made his good-byes on the sidewalk to Diane and Lazard. He wondered how many others there were. For a private-sector operation, these people had resources. Then again, he thought, I can't assume there are fewer than two sets of hoods interested in me.

He turned quickly to watch the old man. There was no sign of a small walkie-talkie or sleeve mike. Joe stepped up his pace. It was too hot for this, but he didn't want to take his jacket off just yet.

He crossed the East Drive through a flock of cyclists and runners and marched straight up the center of the Mall, past the statues of Shakespeare and Walter Scott, leaving Columbus and Robert Burns to port. The wide walkway of the Mall was dappled with shade under the long alley of huge trees. Here the smell of burning herb was disguised by the smell of burning meat. Half the illegal immigrants in New York must sell char-broiled horsemeat to each other in this park on weekends, he thought. He had eaten all kinds of stuff over the years, but his comfortably full stomach rolled at the thought of what was being offered along here.

He stopped and bought an Italian ice. As the grainy, pale yellow mush melted in the little paper cup in his hand, he spotted number two. This was a not-bad-looking middle-aged woman in a light shirtwaist dress. She had salt-and-pepper hair and looked to be about fifty, medium height, the skinny build of a runner, and, in fact, wearing a pair of expensive blue and white running shoes with the low-cut athletic socks that have little pom-poms behind the ankles.

Spotting her and losing her were two different things. He wished she had been in the A position when he had stopped beside the Dairy. It would have been a true test of her presence of mind, although she looked as if she might have passed it easily.

He sucked his ice and looked past her down the Mall, toward the other side of the walkway. The Mall was fairly crowded, but most of the crowd was young and casually dressed, at best. Partly dressed was more like it. And much of the crowd was on wheels—skates, bikes, and skateboards—or looked as if it ought to be.

He decided the team on his tail had been told to dress "midtown, upscale" or something like that. Not even the KGB had the resources to put four or five teams on the street for one rabbit, each team dressed for any contingency—upscale, downscale, middle-polyester, dope dealer, whatever. He spotted number three. She was trailing number two by twenty yards and off to the side. She was blond, mid-thirties, pretty, dressed in cotton pants, cotton blouse, good walking sandals on her feet, aviator sunglasses on her face, and a light shoulder bag. She had the radio, if they had one.

Number one was way back, but watching carefully, openly. Both women looked tenacious. Burning them wouldn't be enough. He had to lose them. They looked ready to follow him for the next week. He decided this was Lazard's style. He wanted to intimidate Joe, tie him down, not simply gather the list of places and times on Joe's itinerary.

Joe dropped his crumpled cup in a basket and set off briskly up the Mall again. At the first water fountain, he rinsed his hands. He threaded his way through the seats in front of the band shell, ran quickly down the steps to Bethesda Fountain past more dealers, and set off around the Lake. He was disappointed that there were no little kids sailing boats. He guessed

they were all out in real boats on Long Island Sound with their
daddies. He wished he and Billy were out on the water somewhere in a boat of their own, going somewhere and never
coming back.

Then he remembered that the kids sailed their model boats
on Conservatory Lake, farther east in the park, just off Fifth
Avenue. This lake was the Lake, where rowboats could be
rented. The Lake was full of people in rowboats—kids fooling
around or couples drifting slowly over the garbage-strewn
water.

He walked directly into the boat concession and rented a
dirty, leaky, gray rowboat. He set off slowly across the water.
Both women, keeping twenty or thirty yards apart, the younger
behind, followed slowly along the shore. Joe had counted on
their good sense, sure they would not try to rent a boat and
row along after him.

He was seized with a stunning sense of guilt and shame on
Billy's account. But the anger was dead and gone. That was a
relief in a way, but deeply disturbing, too. It was as though he
had lost a limb.

He dawdled and drifted under the footbridge. This was the
test. If one of the women crossed the footbridge, he had wasted
his time. The Lake was no more than half a mile end to end,
a rough L-shape, and narrow, no more than a stone's throw
across at the widest. If one of them crossed the footbridge,
they would have both sides of the Lake covered and still be
able to keep sight of each other.

Joe was in luck. As soon as he rowed a few yards past the
little bridge, he saw why. Both ends of the bridge were boarded
up to keep people off. With no attempt to preserve the charade,
he rowed faster. The women walked faster, the older glancing
quickly back at the younger.

He turned suddenly, cutting across the bow of a dreamy
couple of black teenagers with an enormous suitcase radio
blasting from the seat next to the girl. Joe pulled hard. The
couple didn't notice him until their boat rocked slightly from
his little wake. The girl gave him a look that would have frozen
Medusa.

No one talks anymore about liberation, he thought, pulling
as hard as he could straight for the muddy shore on the other
side, but they think it. And when it breaks out, it's gonna

be something. When it does, I hope Billy and I are far, far away.

The two women were running fast around the Lake, but it was too late. The square prow of his little boat smacked into the slimy mud and slid two or three feet up on shore. He leapt from the boat and scrambled up a steep, rocky slope. When he reached the top of the little mount, he crashed through some overgrown weeds and underbrush, startling a homosexual couple in each other's arms.

He ran hard now, and took off his jacket as he ran. He had it made. He stopped, doubled back, and headed for the foot-bridge. He jumped the low barrier like a hurdler and thundered over the bridge, jumping gaps left by missing planks. He vaulted the barrier at the other end. He sprinted along the edge of the water and up onto a path covered by thick grape vines on an arbor.

A police car cruising down the West Drive slowed as Joe neared the roadway. The driver held up his hand for Joe to stop.

Joe shouted, "My wife! Caught me in the wrong part of the park!"

The cops looked and, sure enough, a woman was running hard after Joe, her dress lifting over her knees, a look of intense anger on her face. She was fifty yards behind.

The driver laughed and dropped his hand. The other cop had a look of disgust on his face. Joe sprinted across the road and up the grassy slope toward Central Park West and the noise of traffic.

Joe took the first uptown taxi he saw. In another moment, he was out of sight of the woman. "Go up to the 96th Street Transverse," he told the driver, and leaned back. He was breathing hard. He took his pulse. One fifty. A minute later, he took it again. One twenty. That was fine. In fact, it was very fine, considering he had a full stomach and a moderate amount of alcohol in his blood. He wondered what the woman's pulse was, and wondered what Lazard's blood pressure was going to be.

Twenty minutes later, Joe was in a men's room in the Metropolitan Museum. He washed his hands, splashed his face, and combed his hair. He had half an hour before the museum closed—time enough to lose himself in the contemplation of a couple of his favorite paintings—Breughel's *Harvesters,* for one.

Then he had a few hours to kill, making sure his back was absolutely clean before he showed up at Diane's. He was curious about this tryst, curious enough to swallow his fears for Billy. He had betrayed Billy, he knew, but he still felt, or wanted to feel, that he had no choice. It would have been a larger betrayal to sit on two and a half million dollars without making provision to give it to Billy somehow.

Standing in the littered men's room, alone for a moment in the crowded museum, Joe thought for the first time that he was sorry he had the goddamn gold, and jewels, and money. He and Billy would have been better off without it. But Joe hadn't known it would grow to be worth so much, and he didn't know, when he accumulated the stuff, that Mary was going to die, and their plans with her, and Ellen, too.

He put his face in his hands and wept, racking with sobs. He couldn't stop.

A man opened the door of the men's room, said "Christ, mister, I'm sorry. I didn't realize..." and backed out quickly.

Joe wept until he could hardly breathe, and then the sobs stopped as suddenly as they began. He washed his face with cold water again and stepped out of the room. The man was waiting patiently, a look of real concern on his face.

"I'm sorry too," said Joe. "Thanks for waiting outside."

"I hope you're OK," said the stranger. "I hope it's nothing serious."

"I do too," said Joe.

In facing the painting, Joe learned something that he later thought might have been useful to have known twenty years earlier. First, there was no foreground in the painting, a fact he had never noticed before. Breughel had moved the middle distance to the bottom of the canvas, as though the painter or the viewer himself were standing with his feet in the foreground; and every thrust of line in the painting carried the eye out to the valley and the bay in the distance, or right out of the painting.

Second, there was considerable feeling in the painting—in the subject, the harvesters themselves, working or lolling beneath the tree—and in the oddly localized grandeur of the landscape, a scene familiar to the painter, perhaps; certainly seen with affectionate familiarity.

This was an idyll—not the mythology of aristocrats, but a moment in the lives of ordinary people enjoying the hard work of a rich harvest, and the implied peace and security of enough food for the coming winter. Breughel's great compositional skill drew Joe into the painting so that it became less an object to be isolated in the mind, an object of meditation like the jade fish, than a kind of surrounding landscape of yellows and greens, drawing Joe away from where he was, transporting him to another time and place. The painting drew him out of himself.

He was driven away from the painting by a museum guard holding a squawking walkie-talkie in her hand like a nightstick. She was a young woman, handsome and officious in her steel-blue uniform. He was apparently the last person upstairs in the museum, and she hurried him before her down the broad stairs to the entrance hall. A few stragglers like himself converged on the exit from downstairs galleries, each driven by his own guard.

Outside, Joe paused at the head of the great broad flight of stone steps leading from the museum doors down to the museum plaza on Fifth Avenue. He heard the doors lock behind him. He stood in the afternoon shadow under the large, colorful banners announcing the exhibition inside, but the opposite side of Fifth Avenue was still bright with midsummer sunlight, and the air was hot and still.

The banners above his head hung limp. The buildings across the street glared pale gold, with the sun on their faces of glass and masonry. East 82nd Street led straight away before him, a narrow canyon illuminated by slowly shifting light and shadow, like the chiaroscuro in the nave of a cathedral.

He felt like a figure in the timeless suspension of the painting. It was a kind of death, like his experience before *The Harvesters;* and like his weeping in the clammy men's room; and his gelding that morning in Lazard's office when he heard Billy's voice choke on the one word, "Daddy." He remembered other recent little deaths; the heart-stopping fright and violence when the man in the blue warm-up suit appeared in his bedroom door, and the long afternoon interrogation at the hands of Kavenaugh.

He knew he was not suffering any mid-life crisis on the threshold of his forties of the sort recorded in the endless flood of self-help and self-analysis offered by the media. Three-quarters of the journalists and writers he knew were rapidly approaching forty or just past it, and it was all they could think or write about.

This was something else. He was experiencing a *metanoia*— a complete change of direction and attitude, something like a religious conversion. It had nothing to do with age or stage of life. In the few moments at the top of the steps, as he was released from the grip of the painting into the grip of the city and the momentum of events he knew he couldn't control, Joe understood that he had passed into a new landscape, not un-familiar, but made new by his own changing.

It wasn't long before the little plaza below him emptied completely, leaving only a few walkers passing along the side-walk. The vendors folded their umbrellas and pushed their carts away. The litter left behind fluttered in the slack breeze pulled along by a passing bus. At the top of the broad stairs, with the locked doors and bland face of the cultural palace behind him, Joe was entirely alone, more isolated and exposed than ever in his life. He felt oddly relaxed and energized. He looked at his watch. It was five-thirty.

It was five-thirty when Father Kelly got the message to check on Billy. The priest was due to celebrate a mass in the living room of the rectory for a handful of men and women who came there daily after work. He tried to find the housekeeper to ask her to call Billy's house, but she had gone out somewhere. The priest hurried into the living room, apologizing for his lateness, and sat down in a chair behind a small table to begin the mass.

One of the others had already laid out the bread and wine in a plain pottery plate and chalice, with water in a small glass cruet, and a lit candle. The missal and lectionary were open.

"We thought you weren't coming, Thomas," said one of the others, a nun who lived in a communal house nearby in the neighborhood with several other nuns—teachers and nurses from different orders.

"Sorry," said the priest. "A hurried pastoral visit." He put his finger at the beginning of the ordinary to mark the place, and looked around the room at the others. "Today is Independence Day, my friends."

They smiled at him, wondering what was coming. He said, "I was reading a brief biographical note this morning on the great Renaissance painter Piero della Francesca. In the mid-fifteenth century he painted a picture of the flagellation of Christ. As Christ is tied to a column in the background and flogged, three men stand in the foreground. They are frozen in princely conversation, ignoring entirely the official crime taking place inside the temple at their backs."

The priest's voice was hot with emotion. "The writer of the note I read this morning says words to this effect: No one knows what the painter meant to say in his painting, but no one who has any understanding of the history of the last fifty years in this century can have missed this point—that for every three men who are free to stand in public argument and conversation beneath the open sky, a fourth man somewhere is being tortured."

The priest looked around the small circle of people. These were friends whom he saw here nearly every day.

He said, "Let us pray today, not for our country, but for our people, that we may find the wisdom in this election year to choose leaders in the pursuit of freedom, not in the pursuit of nothing more than material security. Of course, it is important to be free of want, and we know that the poorest people are the most oppressed, but we must pray for the courage to pursue freedom wherever it leads us. Not license, but the freedom to believe, and dispute, and worship.

"Forty years after the Holocaust, Jews are still threatened in their homes and synagogues, not only in Europe and Russia, but in Brooklyn and Queens in New York. They are threatened in their homeland in Israel. Jews and Christians alike are persecuted and imprisoned in the Soviet Union. And these examples from other places do not blind us to the terrors of poverty and discrimination in our own land—malnutrition, arson, unemployment, helplessness, ignorance, violence. Let us pray for the courage of our own people to free themselves from the myths of the past and find new wisdom to guide us in the future."

Then he raised his right hand and began the blessing that began the mass. The others followed the motion of his hand with the shape of the cross over their own breasts.

At six-thirty, the priest drew his car up in the driveway of Billy's house. There was no answer to the doorbell. After walking around the house, he found the sliding door into Joe's bedroom in the back. It was unlocked. He slid it gingerly along its rails. He had never entered someone's house unbidden, but he gathered his cassock—he hadn't bothered to change—and stepped into the room.

"Billy?" he called loudly. "Billy?" It's me, Father Tom Kelly."

From the hall outside the bedroom, he heard a gasp. "Father? Was that you in front?"

Billy stepped into the room, his face ashen with tension and fear. In his hand he held a .22 automatic pistol, the long barrel pointing at the floor. For a moment his face worked violently, as though he was going to cry, but then he smiled and put the gun on safety, as though he had handled guns all his life.

"I'm glad you're here, Father. Come in. I've got some coffee on the stove. I found some stuff I want you to look at."

"Are you all right?" The priest's voice cracked. He was incredulous.

"Yeah, sure. I'm fine. But I'm glad you're here. I was going to call you anyway. I need your advice. Come in." He motioned toward the interior of the house with the gun, then stuck it in his waistband and stood back to let the priest pass in front of him.

The priest's mind started when he saw what Billy had spread out on the kitchen counter—there was an open jewelry case holding two dozen large cut diamonds and two breathtaking pieces of carved jade. Two passports lay on top of a thin stack of thousand-dollar bills. A handful of other passports rested next to a large pile of hundred-dollar bills in wrappers. A smaller pile of Swiss bank notes was next—the colorful notes were held together in stacks by pins through the upper left-hand corners.

"Where . . . ?" asked the priest.

Billy shrugged and waved his arms around, indicating the whole house. "It was all over the place."

He picked up the top stack of Swiss notes. "There are about a hundred thousand dollars in Swiss francs here, if I understand the exchange rate. I had to get it from the paper. The banks are closed today and I couldn't call."

He said this apologetically, as if he was sorry he couldn't quote the exact history of the rate for the past thirty days.

"There are one hundred thousand dollars in this other pile, in used hundred-dollar bills. The Swiss money is used too. The twenty thousand in this little stack with the two passports is in new thousand-dollar bills, but the serial numbers are out of sequence, and they're not all exactly brand-new."

Father Kelly picked up the passports and examined them. Of the two new ones Billy had found in the duct, he said, "Amazing." Of the older ones lying next to the larger amounts of money, he had no comment—there were passports for Mary and Ellen, in both their own names and pseudonyms, as well as similar passports for Billy and his father.

Billy picked up a small plastic pill bottle with a child-proof cap on it. He took the cap off and spilled the small yellow pills out on the counter. "Valium," he said. With his finger, he fished out the prescription label inside. "Take a look at this."

The priest turned it over and over in his hands. "What am I looking for?

Impatiently, Billy said, "Look at the initials in black ball-point in the lower corner. Turn it over and look at the number on the back."

The initials were "NUB." The number, written in the same black ballpoint, was "A01777."

"So?" said the priest.

"I know what it is."

"What?"

"The code number for a secret bank account." Billy was excited, almost jubilant.

"Nonsense," scoffed Father Kelly.

"No, no. I know it's true." Billy's excitement had an edge of anger and frustration.

"How do you know?"

"My father told me."

"Told you?"

"He told me he had a little money put aside for a rainy day in an overseas bank."

"This is more than a little money, Billy."

"That's right. Two hundred and twenty thousand in cash, ten passports, and those diamonds. They must be worth hundreds of thousands. And this bank account."

"Put it all back where you found it."

"No."

"Yes. Right now."

"Why?"

"It's not yours."

"Some of it is."

"How do you know?"

"My father told me."

"When?"

"That day on the boat when we dumped the body in the bay."

"I'm sure he told you that he would give you *some* of it *someday.*"

"Well, yes."

"Then put it back where you found it until he makes his own decision. Until then, it's his to dispose of as he wishes, when he wishes."

"He got all this in Vietnam and Laos," said Billy.

"Stop right there." The priest held his hand up. "I don't want to know any more."

Billy looked disappointed.

"I'm sure your father told you many things that day in confidence. You very properly confessed to me your role in the disposal of that body. Would you like me to betray that sacramental confidence?"

"No."

"You father's confidence in you isn't sacramental, but it has the bond of love and kinship. Respect it."

Billy nodded, then burst out, "But he lied to me!"

"What do you mean?"

"He told me he had a little money saved for us to go fishing with, and for my college. But this is more than a little. And he had these passports. What do they mean?"

"You tell me," said the priest.

"That we were going to leave the country. And hide. He put false names in the passports. That's illegal."

"I'm sure," said Father Kelly, "that all of this is illegal— illegal in the taking and illegal in the keeping. Now put it back where you found it, exactly as it was, and put that gun back, too."

"It's mine," said Billy, touching it in his waistband. "I need it."

"Billy, listen to me. That's the gun the man tried to kill your father with, isn't it?"

Billy nodded.

"And you were supposed to drop it in the bay, weren't you?" Another nod.

"Put it away now. I'm not going to tell you how to dispose of a murder weapon, or at any rate, a weapon that was used in a crime. That's not what priests are for. But I am going to tell you to put it away and start thinking about why a boy your age needs to carry a gun, and to think about how you're going to disentangle yourself from this violence."

"I can't."

"Can't what?"

"Get away from it."

"Get away from what?"

"The violence."

"I don't understand."

"I haven't told you everything that happened today." Billy slumped back against the counter. He was crying. He put his face in his hands and cried like a little kid who lost his mommy and daddy at the country fair.

Father Kelly put his arm around the boy, and with his other hand lifted the gun from the boy's waistband. He laid it on the counter. "I'm not sure what to tell you, Billy. You tell me what happened and I'll try to help you. I don't want to know where your father hides his loot. You put all this stuff back where you found it, and we'll go back to the rectory and have dinner and talk."

"What if somebody takes these things?"

"That's not your problem, Billy. It's your father's problem. You never had these things, so it won't be a loss to you if they're taken."

Billy stood up straight and took a few deep breaths. "Ok.

I'll put it back, but it's not as simple as you think."

"I don't think it's simple. I think it's dangerous for you."
The priest looked at the boy's fat lips and swollen ear. "You
got beat up today, and your father somehow put you in this
spot. Now we have to figure out a way to get you out of this
spot without hurting your father and without hurting you. Do
you agree?"

The boy nodded, then shrugged. "I guess."

Lord, thought the priest, this foolish world. *Lord,* he prayed
silently, *you made it. Give us the strength to live in it. That's
the least you can do.*

The large, square-cut emerald glowed in Diane's navel. She
stood naked by the large window in the living room of her
apartment. She talked compulsively and restlessly. She had
the mannerisms, Joe thought, of a self-contained and self-
controlled but very lonely person.

The living room was dark, but her body was lit by the red
and blue glow of a huge sign across the East River where the
mouth of Newtown Creek divides Brooklyn from Queens. It
was like the dim glow of colored lights in some shabby after-
hours bar. She had one of the most erotic bodies Joe had ever
seen—full, firm breasts, slender neck and shoulders, slim almost boyish hips, and an almost hairless pubic mound. It was
a woman's body, inhabited by a self-conscious, ambitious, smart
woman, but it was reminiscent of a young girl's body, a quality
Diane was well aware of.

She had been sitting on the broad windowsill, hugging her
knees, or walking around the room from window to window,
talking all the while, but now she stood leaning against the
edge of the window bay with her arms folded across her breasts.
She talked about what she saw—the flat plain of the outer
boroughs at midnight, an endless horizon of streetlights shimmering in the windless summer heat.

An occasional plane landed or took off from La Guardia
Airport, at the edge of Queens to the north, or from JFK, far
out below the horizon to the southeast, on the edge of the
Atlantic Ocean. There were two vast cities out there—Queens
and Brooklyn—the size of Philadelphia and Los Angeles, but
each borough only a part of the vast, ungovernable web of

streets, tunnels, and islands called New York City.

She talked about this, how she loved living in the city, how at night from her windows she could see it all strung together by strings of streetlights like pearls. Now and then, she touched the glowing stone in her navel as if it gave her energy and strength.

"Yeah, it's nice," said Joe, "from high up and far away. But in about half of what you see out there, it's not so nice down at street level."

She fell silent. Finally, she said, "I wouldn't know. I've never lived in that half."

A plane sank slowly toward JKF, its lights blinking and shimmering like stars.

"We're taking a little trip in an airplane tomorrow," she said. "There's someone you have to meet."

"Who?"

She laughed, an almost girlish giggle. "I call him Senator Shogun. He's a very powerful western senator. He's spending the weekend out in the Hamptons, incognito. We're spending the weekend there too. I think you'll enjoy yourself, and find him interesting."

"There's too damn much mystery in all this," he said. His voice was sleepy.

"All in due course," she said.

He was naked too, sitting in an easy chair turned to face the window, his feet up on a pillow on the windowsill, a glass of ice-cold Russian vodka on his stomach. He was stretched out, half-asleep, his head raised high enough on the back of the chair to see the lights of the waterfront on the other side of the river.

He watched a large container ship loading at a dock on the Brooklyn side of Newtown Creek. The shipboard cranes lifted one container after another in a slow rhythm, fitting them carefully into the pile of containers on deck. At a distance, the cables and booms looked like delicate webs. Brilliant arc lights outlined the boat against the dark docks. There were no men to be seen, only the slow movement of the booms and the play of the lights.

"I've met the first man in the chain," he said. "That's Lazard. Today at lunch, I met the second man. That's Gold. Who's the third man? Is it this senator?"

She didn't answer.

"I'll bet I know who this Senator Shogun is."

She sat on the sill and stretched her legs across his, saying nothing. He looked at the emerald. It was probably worth thirty thousand dollars, maybe more. He could only guess. He should have them appraised. He didn't regret giving it to her, but he didn't know why he had done it.

When he had arrived at her apartment, tense and nervous from keeping an eye on his back for three hours, they had a drink and talked a bit. She was angry at him for losing the two women.

"They work for me," she said. "They were for your own protection."

"How the hell was I supposed to know?" But the old anger just wasn't there. "Ah," he said, "I just don't care."

"Don't you want to know who the old gent was?" she asked, mocking.

"I know. I never saw him in the flesh before, but I've seen him in surveillance movies and stills. George Stewart. He was the Brits' street boss in New York for forty years. He worked out of their UN mission. Whoever put him on me knows their way around. He's retired, still wired to the Brits, but free-lancing, too. What do you make of him?"

"You burned him nice," she said. "My girls were impressed. And mad as hornets when you ditched them. Where did you go?"

"The Met."

"I wouldn't have guessed," she said. "That's good."

"What do you make of old George?" he repeated.

"He'd done some work for Julie Gold in the past couple of years."

"Julie Gold?"

"Julie keeps a lot of balls in the air at once, so to speak."

Her attempt at a light witticism was lost on Joe. He stared at her.

"I don't get it," he said. "What the hell is going on?"

She shrugged. Her breasts bounced under her blouse. She wasn't wearing her purple bra.

"Fuck me," she said. "Right now, on the floor."

"No."

"You're gonna fuck me and like it," she said. "Then we'll have dinner and talk."

They made love on the floor, on a Chinese rug, in bright light and a tangle of clothing. She gasped when she felt his scar. It excited her. He was surprised at his own eagerness and pleasure. Then they got half-dressed—she wore his shirt and he wore her kimono—and ate dinner by candlelight. Her cooking was as good as the restaurant that afternoon. She gave him chicken Florentine, rice, and salad, and a nice Italian wine.

Then she turned out every light in her apartment and they made love on the bed in her room, in darkness, high above the river, with the city's noises in the background like static.

Her apartment was filled with polished, dark antique furniture and shining silver, much of it old and valuable. He got up and walked around the whole place in the dark, the furniture and silver glowing and glistening in the dim light of the night sky through the large windows.

She followed him around, describing each piece. The walls were hung with Navaho rugs and antique quilts. There was no art on the walls, but there were dozens of framed family photographs that bespoke a background of wealth and culture in the New York suburbs.

"I can't afford the art I like," she explained.

When he asked about the photos, she said simply, "Greenwich. My father was a banker."

"Which bank?"

"Morgan Guaranty."

"President?"

"Vice president."

They made love on a chair. They went back to bed, where he fell asleep. She woke him up half an hour later, saying, "No fair."

Like a sleepwalker, he got out of bed and fished the emerald out of his pants pocket. He unwrapped it from its cloth and fitted it into her belly button. Her eyes widened when she realized what it was.

"No one has ever given me anything like this before." She plucked it out and held it under the reading lamp by the bed. "God, it's beautiful. Are you sure it's real?"

He snorted.

"Oh, I'm sorry. Of course it's real." She snapped off the light and stuck the stone back in her belly button. "How did you know I've got a big innie?"

He was amused, not caring what he had done, burying all the past with one offhand gesture.

"I love it," she said. "You're really something, Joe. You're a nice surprise." She pulled him toward her. "Now let's do it again before I forget how."

She rolled on top of him. She was swollen open and so wet that he slipped inside her without moving. She began to come almost at once. It took him longer. He could feel the rim of her diaphragm, but she sat up straight and began rocking back and forth instead of up and down. All he could feel now was the wetness. She was gasping and crying out. She couldn't look at him. When he came, he lifted her off the bed with his hips. She slid and slipped off him onto her side, mumbled something, and fell into a light sleep.

A few minutes later, she woke up and said she wanted a Coke. He poured himself a glass of vodka from a bottle in her freezer, and they moved into the dark living room, where their clothes were still strewn on the furniture and floor. She turned off the air conditioning and opened the windows, as she had earlier in the bedroom.

"I hate sleeping in air conditioning," she said. "I like the heat when it's late at night and the air's clean. I love to stay up reading or watching TV on nights like this. I wish it was always like this."

Listening to her restless talk about the city and herself— she talked without revealing much—Joe wondered about Billy. He had wanted to call him at odd intervals during the evening, but dismissed the urge each time. He didn't know why, but something had snapped and broken during the day. Joe wondered if it could ever be repaired.

She asked him where he got the scar on his side, and he told her, and told her a little about himself, matching the little she had given him. He watched the ship loading itself across the river, and watched Diane's body with the same distant curiosity. He wondered what it was like to be a woman, and to be this particular woman, and to live inside this particular body. He wondered what it felt like to be fucked. He felt his penis stir and begin to stiffen, but he dismissed the thought and willed himself limp.

She was talking now about her work, and Lazard, and Julie Gold, and he wanted her to keep talking. This was what he was here for, and why he had made love to her, he guessed, and why he gave her the emerald. He was sleepwalking now.

"You understand now, don't you?" she said.

"What?"

"That I don't work for Lazard and Gold. They work for me."

"You're the third man," he said.

"Yes," she said. "But this isn't Vienna and this isn't 1946."

"What is it?"

"The World Series, Charlie. It's the ninth inning, with two outs, a tie game, and you're at bat. And you better not strike out."

"I'm gonna meet the pitcher tomorrow?"

"For lunch."

"We better go to bed," said Joe. "I need some sleep."

NINE ═══════════════════════

AT MIDNIGHT THAT night, Billy sat in the tree house. He imagined himself as the night helmsman on the bridge of a ship at sea. In the wind-rustled leaves of the tree, he heard the waves against the hull. The few lights he could see in other houses nearby were other ships anchored in a broad roadstead.

That was it—they were at anchor. He was on a supertanker in the Persian Gulf, waiting its turn to load. The helmsman sat cross-legged on the bridge, staring at the darkened shores on either side, the entire ship asleep below him. He took a last drag on the joint he'd rolled from North African ganja—it was his last from the bag he'd bought on their last voyage—he'd have to buy some more in the morning from the Arab traders who came alongside every day in their dhows, offering fruits and vegetables, ganja, hashish, opium, cocaine, heroin, silver, gold, boys, girls, frankincense, and myrrh.

He cupped the roach in his hand as he inhaled—to hide the glow from the captain, who had a habit of prowling the deck and the bridge at odd hours of the night. But then he remembered that the captain was not on board tonight—he was sleeping ashore somewhere—no one knew exactly where, and the damn captain never left messages anymore for the crew.

Billy snuffed the roach out on the deck of the bridge and shredded the remains between his fingers. He let the shreds drift overboard on the light breezes of the gulf. His aches and pains from the beating of the morning in the brig were fading in and out. He fingered the trigger of the gun resting in his lap—the night watch was always issued a pistol from the gun locker to keep thieves from coming over the side in the middle of the night.

There were money and jewels in the captain's safe some-where below—only Billy and the captain knew—and a secret map showing where gold could be found. Only it wasn't really a map—it was numbers and initials. NUB A01777. Billy didn't need the map. He had it in his head. But he didn't know what it meant. He would have to think about the code in the morning, when he was more alert. He would have to find the key to the map.

Billy's mind oscillated slowly back and forth between the captain's loot and a desire for revenge on the man who had beaten him that morning. In his mind, Billy called the man Cowboy. It seemed logical. The man wore western clothes. Billy could see the heavy, worn silver belt buckle only inches from his face and feel the white heat of the anger and humil-iation rush through his veins and muscles as the man unbuckled the belt.

The rush of anger broke the grip of the hallucination induced by the mild marijuana in the remnants of the joint Billy had just smoked. It was only half a joint, old and stale, and he had spent a long time rooting around in his room to find it before climbing up to the tree house earlier. How much earlier? Billy guessed it was now one in the morning. The neighborhood was dark. A bathroom light glowed a few houses down the street, and the shifting blue light of a TV in someone's back bedroom. Air conditioners rattled and hummed in every house.

He was barely high. In fact, he wasn't high at all. He fingered the .22. He thought of shooting Cowboy in the eyes, one by one, then the kneecaps. Father Kelly had warned him to leave the gun alone, but Billy was afraid. He knew he couldn't carry it on the street during the day, and he wondered what he was going to do about his fear in the morning.

• • •

Father Kelly had exorcised—not literally, but figuratively—
much of Billy's shame and guilt at having suffered a beating.
The brutality had only returned to Billy's memory as he sat at
dinner with the priest and tried to describe in detail what Cowboy had done to him. The priest said Billy had no share of
guilt in the act. It was like an accident—inexplicable, but not
directed in any way at a particular victim.

"He didn't beat you because you're Billy," said the priest,
"but because he's a depraved, vicious man for whom gratifi-
cation is an act of rage and violence. If you had been a dog
tied to that chair, he would have done the same. Do you understand?"

Billy said hotly, "Yes, I do understand. But I still want to
kill him."

"That would be a great sin for you and a great mistake in
every other way. And it's foolish for you to continue thinking
like this. I won't tell you to put the whole thing out of your
mind, because I know you can't, and you probably shouldn't.
But I will tell you, Billy, to put thoughts of revenge out of
your mind and to think instead about what you have to do to
regain your confidence in your father, and to help him to regain
his own senses. That's the best thing you can do for your own
future."

Billy nodded. "I know you're right, Father, but I don't know
if I can."

"Try."

"I will."

Billy had great trust in the priest, and the priest's words
took hold in the boy and stuck. Billy sat for a long time at the
table, picking at his food.

"But what about my father?" he asked. "I can't force him
to do anything. What if he goes on doing what he's doing now?
He acts as if I'm not even here."

"Your father," said the priest, "is doing what he thinks is
best for you under the circumstances. He is obviously wrong,
although I'm very reluctant to say that. You're old enough,
and you know enough about the peculiar world he lives in, to
help him see just how wrong. You have to take that responsibility for yourself. Do you understand?"

"Yes. Yes."

Against the priest's wishes, Billy had returned to his own house for the night. "I have to be there. What if someone tries to break in again?"

"It's up to you," said the priest.

Time passed. Through a gap in the dense leaves of the mulberry, Billy could see the edge of the Big Dipper. It hadn't been there earlier. He guessed it was two in the morning. It was damp. He was tired and chilled. He drifted back into the fantasy about the night watch on board the ship. He drifted in and out of sleep. The ship's radio spluttered and squawked, then fell suddenly silent.

Billy opened his eyes, instantly alert and fully awake. Radio? There was no radio in the tree house. He saw a dark figure by the sliding door into Joe's bedroom, less than fifteen yards from Billy's position. The figure was dressed in a dark uniform of some kind. A walkie-talkie with a short stubby antenna stuck out of the man's hip pocket.

It was a security guard's uniform. The man was short and compact. Billy peered at the figure as it straightened and pulled the door open. Breasts curved under the shirt. The man was a woman! A black woman wearing a uniform and square gold badge of a private security service.

Billy raised his gun and opened his mouth to shout, but hesitated when she pulled the walkie-talkie from her pocket and put it to her mouth. He heard her say, "Two Kay to One Three. Clear."

She repeated it and stuck the radio back in her pocket. Billy waited. She waited. In a moment, a lightly bearded man wearing a tan suit walked openly and brazenly around the side of the house as if he lived there. The two disappeared into the house. In a moment more, lights were on inside, as if the owner had come home. First the bathroom, then the kitchen, then Billy's room, then Joe's. Light flooded the backyard.

"Shit," whispered Billy. "This is my house."

He slowly and carefully unwound himself, ignoring the numbness and stiffness in his legs, and lowered himself down the back of the tree to the ground, in the shadow of the broad trunk. He ran to the side of the house and around front. There was a car parked in the driveway, a dark sedan marked SE-

CURITY ASSOCIATES, INC. There was no one in sight. He knew he had to move fast.

He stepped into the darkness of the garage, avoiding coiled hoses, a wheelbarrow, and his bike. He edged around his father's car to the door from the garage into the kitchen. With the gun in one hand, the silencer screwed firmly on, he felt for the door key hidden on an exposed spreader above the door frame. He put his ear to the door, listened for a moment, and opened the door.

The kitchen was empty, but the door to the basement was open and the basement lights were on. One of them was down there. He could hear the other going through the medicine cabinet in Joe's bathroom.

Billy calculated quickly. The person in the basement was trapped anyway. Billy stepped lightly down the hall from the kitchen. He could hear the pills being emptied into the sink.

As he stepped into the bedroom, the man in the bathroom glanced over his shoulder. With the quickest of movements, with a hand like a magician's, the man turned. Like something in a mirror, a gun like Billy's whirled toward Billy. The boy shot twice. The man jerked twice and fell without firing.

His gun clattered loose onto the floor. He looked at Billy with an odd smile, almost approvingly. His eyes were watery and ginger-colored, red-rimmed with fatigue. His hair was pale, thin, and ginger going to gray. His skin was fair and slightly burned above the neckline in his shirt as if he had been in the sun all day. He closed his eyes and died.

Billy picked the gun off the floor. The woman was running up the basement stairs. He went to the kitchen to meet her. She reached the head of the stairs. In one hand, she held the packets of money. In the other, she held a gun. She fired first. There was a huge noise and a little flash of orange flame. A bullet whizzed by Billy's left leg. The silenced sound of his shots was lost in the explosion of her second shot. He did what his father had said. He emptied the gun at her. She fell back down the stairs.

He jumped down the stairs. She was gasping on the basement floor. "You killed my husband," she wheezed. "Here in this house."

He scooped up the loot.

"How?" he asked.

"Your daddy."

"No," he said, "I mean, how did you find this stuff?"

"This house is bugged. We heard you talking to the priest."

"Who are you?"

She didn't answer.

"Who's the man upstairs?"

"George Stewart," she breathed.

"We buried your husband at sea. It was what he wanted," he whispered close to her ear, afraid the house full of bugs would hear. But she didn't hear. She was dead.

He knew the police would come this time. He ran to the workbench, pulled out a drawer, and pulled out two large packages of money in plastic bags taped to a shelf behind the drawer. He ran upstairs to the bathroom, found the Valium bottle on the shelf, and spilled the pills into the sink with all the others. He took the prescription label out of the bottle.

He ran to his room, found his old backpack, dumped last year's school junk out of it, and stuffed the loot in. He took the clip out of Stewart's gun and slapped it into his, putting his empty clip in Stewart's gun. He dropped his gun in the backpack and zipped it shut. He ran back to his father's bedroom, tossed Stewart's gun into the bathroom with a clatter, and ran out the sliding doors.

He ran through the backyard. A distant siren rose and fell on the night air. Lights came on in nearby houses. He went over the back fence like a raccoon, with hundreds of thousands of dollars in cash, jewelry, and false passports in a climber's day pack strapped firmly to his back. The pack was also weighted by a pistol that had now been used to kill two people, and maybe many more. The cold gun was now a hot gun.

Billy knew every backyard in the neighborhood as well as his own. He climbed fences, dodged toys, and avoided lawn furniture with the speed and agility of a steeplechase runner. He crept past houses with barking dogs. He darted across streets like a shadow. He ran into a new string of backyards he had never scouted before, but he had the instincts of a good second-story man, and made no false steps in the unfamiliar terrain of miniature meadows and forests booby-trapped with contraptions of aluminum and vinyl.

The police never had a chance. They were slow and awkward, and bound to their cars. By the time they arrived at his house, Billy had slipped into the safe darkness of the side entrance of St. Joseph's Church. He knew where the priests hid the keys in a magnetic box under the wrought-iron railing on the stoop. Inside, he slid into a front pew and knelt for a minute as he always did, only breathing hard this time. He said a quick prayer for his mother and sister, and added a query about his father.

"Dear Father," he breathed. "Do you know where my father is?" He knew he had asked an incomplete question, but he was too exhausted to reformulate it. He lay down in the pew with his head on the lumpy backpack. Father Kelly said mass every morning at five-thirty. No one ever came. This morning there would be a congregation of one.

Joe missed his morning run. He had missed it for several days. He was never much of an athlete or a gamesman, but he had a hard, well-used body that had withstood years of ill treatment, partly due to luck and partly due to the old habits of an ex-Marine Corps jock. He rarely ran less than twenty miles a week. He figured he lost an average of two days a week to early-morning appointments, or late-afternoon appointments, or bad weather, or hangovers, or the odd morning like this morning when he didn't have his running shoes with him.

He felt grubby, too. There was nothing worse than taking a shower and putting on yesterday's clothes. Diane promised to buy him some clean clothes when they got where they were going, but she was in no hurry to start.

She pulled him back into bed after his shower; then, while he took another shower, she made a huge breakfast; then took a long shower herself; then took her time getting dressed; then got on the telephone and made a dozen calls. Joe wandered around the apartment, feeling useless. He read the *Times* word for word, but it was a thin day for news. He tried the crossword puzzle and gave up. Finally, he stripped down to his shorts and sat in the hot morning sun in front of an open window, reading back issues of *Antiques* magazine.

"What the hell are you doing?" Diane emerged from the bedroom and marched over to his chair. "It's ten-thirty and we have to go right now. The plane's waiting and you aren't even dressed."

Her shadow fell across his midriff. Her voice dived at him out of the sun. He squinted up at her. He had fallen asleep.

"Getting a tan."

"Come on." Her voice was scratchy and annoyed.

"What's eating you?" He began to stretch slowly and rouse himself. He felt drugged and groggy. "You sure took your own sweet time on the damn telephone."

"That was work," she snapped.

"What's got into you?"

"It sure isn't you. Now, let's go."

He rose and dressed, stuffing his tie in the breast pocket of his suit jacket like a handkerchief. He was unmoved by her irritation, but curious about its source. He felt like a swimmer groping through the ruins of a giant sunken ship in the twilight of deep water, the only sound the hiss of air from his tank. All around him were familiar structures made unrecognizable by corrosion and the overgrowth of barnacles and weed. Nothing looked like what it was. Schools of small fish drifted by, then scattered in a flash when he moved. Larger fish in larger schools hunted the smaller fish. The big predators swam alone, turning slowly for a view of the other loners, sizing each other up, and moving off slowly or edging in a little closer.

They were in their element; Joe was out of his. He was used to the open violence of war, with maps and troops. This trail led here, that one there. This village was friendly, that one hostile. Planes flew in the dry season, or they were grounded during the wet season. The radio worked or it didn't work. A runner was sent. There was enough food and ammo or there wasn't. Lines on maps measured specific distances. Lines between men measured specific loyalties.

In the mountain tribes he fought with, kinship and village ties were so strong and definite that they could be charted, like the wiring diagrams of organizations worshipped by the planners in Saigon and Washington. What went on in the hearts and minds of men mattered a great deal, but it was reduced to essences in jungle warfare. If a man shot at you, he was not your friend.

However, you might be able to buy him or rent him for a while; then he wouldn't necessarily be your friend, but he probably wouldn't shoot you either. There were subtleties, but not very many. It was mostly a matter of letting people know where you stood, and figuring out where they stood; then deciding what to do about it, if anything. "If it ain't broke, don't fix it." If Joe had a motto, that was it, a quote from Bert Lance.

As they went down in the elevator to the lobby, Joe sang. His voice was clear and light.

> Time to t'ink of heaven,
> Time to t'ink of hell,
> Time to go to church on Sundays,
> Hark, I hear the bells.
>
> For the leaves are getting greener,
> And spring is on the way,
> And girls are gettin' prettier,
> And younger every day.

He repeated the refrain in a quieter voice as they walked through the lobby and across the plaza. Out on the footbridge that crossed the FDR Drive, Diane hooked her arm through his.

"I'm sorry I was so cranky," she said. "I like your voice and I like you, and it's a lovely Saturday summertime morning, and after this blankety-blank blitzin' meeting, we're gonna rent us a car and enjoy a weekend on the beach. How's that?"

"That's fine," said Joe. "I sure don't know what's going on, but I'm just gonna go with the flow and find out. Is that OK with you, Diane?"

"That's fine."

He realized it was the first time he had called her by her given name. She felt gay and free on his arm, and she looked happy and pretty. He decided not to look for significance in insignificant things, and to stay relaxed and alert. The political wars were not like the jungle wars. There were no maps and no trails that could be measured in yards or kilometers. Here, what went on in hearts and minds was everything, and it was essentially unknowable. The shrewdest observer could only guess.

Joe knew this much: Power was the slipperiest stuff in the world, and the most desirable. But there was no way to measure it except by the fear it inspired. If it could be quantified—measured and counted—there would be a futures market for it on Wall Street. People would buy and sell hedges against future gains or losses of power, and against the general rise and fall of the level of power in the world. Men in shirt-sleeves would meet each morning in London and Zurich and Chicago and set the morning's price of power, and other men would make decisions to buy or sell.

But this didn't happen, although it was tempting to think there were centers of power where certain favored men gathered and dispensed power. What really happened, Joe thought, was that men *grasped* for power. It was an appetite, not something tangible and hard. It was a belief. People who wanted power believed it existed, and struggled to grab and hold onto it. They believed they had it for a while, and were crushed and broken when they believed they had lost it, or when they thought someone had taken it away. But what had they lost?

Joe wasn't sure. He thought he might find out today, when they got wherever they were going. The first step was to find a cab going uptown on First Avenue, then to La Guardia, where a plane was waiting. That was as much as he knew at the moment, and what he didn't know didn't bother him at all.

Billy woke up when Father Kelly unlocked the side door of the church.

"I guess it's better than a park bench," said the priest, looking down at the reclining boy in the first pew. "We'll talk after mass. Do you want to serve?"

The priest vested himself and at the dot of five-thirty began the first mass of the day, with Billy kneeling at the side of the altar, his backpack stowed under an ornate chair in the corner of the apse behind the altar.

There was no one else. When the mass was ended, Father Kelly closed the church and locked it, and took Billy back to the rectory for breakfast. Billy's fluorescent orange backpack was strapped firmly to his back for the thirty-yard walk. At the table, he kept the pack in his lap.

After breakfast, when the housekeeper had cleared the dishes and the other priest had left the room, Father Kelly asked, "Billy, what's in the pack?"

"I'll tell you after I make a confession."

"Examine your conscience," said the priest sharply, thinking

Billy had stolen some of his father's spoils. "Are you making a confession merely because you want to ensure my secrecy, or because you want to confess your sins to God?"

"To God," said Billy.

By way of confession, Billy described, in as much detail as he could manage, all the events of the night before. Father Kelly questioned him closely, and when he was finished, absolved Billy. But he said, "Absolution is one thing, a grand jury is another. Why don't you stay here this morning while I keep some appointments, and while I try to think of some ways to help you. I've never seen a boy in such trouble. I hope you believe that you've come to the right place."

Billy nodded and shrugged. His fatigue made his confusion worse. The food made his eyes heavy, and he asked for a place to sleep for a few hours. The priest sent Billy up to his own room, and left the rectory for a meeting downtown.

The cab sped up First Avenue in the light traffic of a holiday Saturday morning, dipping into the underpass in front of the UN, turning left on 57th Street, then a quick right onto the ramp for the Queensboro Bridge.

Diane sat quietly in the comfortable back seat of the new Peugeot cab. "It's nice to find a driver who knows where he's going, for a change." She smiled at Joe. "And nice to be with a decent guy, for a change."

Joe grunted. "Where are we going, Diane? This driver knows more than I do."

"Patience, patience."

"I'm running out."

"You'll enjoy yourself. I know you like a challenge."

"Yes," he said. "I try to rise to the occasion."

She grimaced. "To the Marine Air Terminal at La Guardia, then East Hampton Airport, then a house on the beach. We'll stop at a shop to buy you some clothes. OK?"

"OK."

On the bridge, the steel grates hummed loudly under the taxi's tires. The structure of the bridge looked like turn-of-the-century battleship towers welded together. Joe observed that it was the ugliest bridge he'd ever seen. It was a mass of intri-

cately welded and riveted girders and bars and grates and rail-
ings, like a bridge designed by a child with a massive Erector
Set.

Diane said, "They say the architect never saw it while it
was being built. When they brought him to the ribbon-cutting,
he said that if he'd seen it while it was going up, he'd have
scrapped it and started over. He said he didn't know they'd
have to use so much metal."

The driver snorted. "I never heard that one, lady, but I'll
tell ya another one."

"What's that?"

"They say it's gonna fall down."

"Why are we on it?" asked Dianne.

"Because there's no toll, and it's the fastest way to get where
ya wanna go."

"New York," she said. "I love it."

"Just like the governor," said the driver. "He loves it too.
He says so every day."

"Carey?"

"Yeah. Mr. 'I Love New York.'"

"It's going to make a lot of dust when it falls over," said
Joe, bemused by the preposterous idea.

"The governor?" asked the driver.

"No, the bridge," said Joe.

"Yeah," said the driver happily. "The bigger they are, the
harder they fall."

"Yes," said Diane. She whispered it, patting Joe's hand on
the seat between them. "The bigger they are, the harder they
fall." She and the driver both seemed pleased at the possibility.

On the way back to the rectory at the end of the morning,
Father Kelly acted on a hunch he'd had since breakfast and
stopped at the Bahamian embassy on New Hampshire Avenue.
He asked to speak to the commercial attaché, and after a few
pleasantries, asked for a list of banks where he might do business.

"Are you being sent there, Father?" asked the attaché.

"Possibly, Mr. Mitchell," said the priest, wincing slightly
at the little lie, and amused that it bothered him.

The attaché produced a two-page printed list of banks, mainly in Nassau and Freeport, with a summary of the country's bank secrecy laws.

"If you need any help, come back again," offered the polite attaché.

Father Kelly thanked him and left. In the car, he ran his finger down the list. He stopped at one called the New Union Bank. He folded the list, stuck it in his pocket, and drove back to the rectory for lunch with Billy.

Billy was gone. A note on the priest's desk in his room explained that Billy had tried to locate his father by telephone and couldn't. The answering service didn't know where he was and hadn't heard from him for several days. Billy was going to find him. The note continued:

> I've left some things for you to take care of for me. I know I can trust you. They're in the top drawer of your desk. I'll call you when I find my Dad. If he calls you, ask him to call his answering service. Thanks for everything. Billy.

The drawer held the jewelry case, the stacks of American and Swiss currency, the older passports, and the prescription slip. The two new passports were gone, along with the gun.

Father Kelly opened the jewelry case. None of the contents seemed to be missing, but he wasn't sure how many stones the case originally held. In the stack of American money, the twenty thousand-dollar bills had replaced ten thousand dollars in worn hundreds.

That left the boy with ten thousand dollars, two false passports, and an assassin's gun. Father Kelly closed the drawer, put his head in his hands, and prayed for the boy's safe return, for the safety of the boy's father, and for guidance.

Then he picked up his phone and called an old friend who had left the priesthood and now worked for a Washington bank.

"Peter? It's Thomas. Have you had lunch yet? . . . You just got up? . . . Well, come over and have some lunch with me, on the house. . . . Bring some wine if you want. . . . Sure, it's a holiday. Nothing going on here. . . . Sure, you can bring a friend. No wonder you just got up. . . . No, it's nothing urgent, just

something I need to know. I'm sure you can enlighten me. . . .
Well, it's about offshore banks. . . . No, it's not for me. It's for
a friend. . . . I need to know how to make a transfer from one
bank to another. . . . Good. I knew you'd know. Bring two
bottles if there'll be three of us. . . . Yeah, see you in an hour."

TEN ════════════════

THE MARINE AIR Terminal at La Guardia contained murals painted by artists of the WPA during the thirties. They ranged around the clerestory of the mock-basilica interior of the terminal building, which had somehow missed being improved since it was built half a century before. The murals were painted in the muscular muralistic style of those times, modeled after the work of the Mexicans Rivera and Orozco. The works of man were depicted in a manner that managed to distort and glorify them at the same time, in the name of progress; or more accurately, thought Joe, in the name of the idea of history as progress. Some of the murals had been painted over recently with a coat of whitewash.

"They want to restore them," said Diane. "They paint over them to protect them." She held Joe's hand like a girl on her first date. "But there's no money. There's money for all kinds of other crap, though."

"Like your job."

"This is the private sector, Joe. I'm not on the public tit."

"Why can't the private sector restore these murals?"

"What a dumb question. Come on. There's the pilot waiting for us by the door."

Joe disengaged his hand. "I think I'd rather just stay here this morning, studying these murals, what's left of them."

"Fine," said Diane in a loud voice. They were the only ones in the main terminal. The pilot was in a second waiting room reserved for the passengers of private planes serviced by Butler Aviation. "You do that. I didn't know you were such an art historian."

"If I had it to do all over again, that's exactly what I'd be—I'd spend my life in dim buildings looking at half-dead paintings, and in darkened rooms showing slides to half-dead students. It would be a wonderful life."

"You sound as if you mean it." Her voice rose, amplified by the domed ceiling.

"I do." He looked up at the painted history of aviation, whitewashed over. The airplanes looked like the airplanes he drew on his school tablets when he was a kid—Boeing Clippers and Douglas DC-3s. They were simple planes. DC-3s were the most durable and reliable planes ever built. Some of them were still flying around South Asia and the Caribbean—most of them by smugglers, who appreciated simplicity and durability.

She turned toward the Butler lobby. "Come on, Joe. Quit screwing around. We're late. You're gonna enjoy this, you'll see. Trust me."

He felt confused. He was too old to let himself be led around like this. He stood in the center of the unlit waiting room and stared out into the glare of the sun. The waiting plane was a twin-engine Beechcraft King Air. The pilot stood by the rear door. Joe had seen this scene, or some variation of it, five hundred times.

He decided for the tenth time in two days to continue to allow himself to be led. Sooner or later, he would find out what was going on, and who was jerking whose strings. This was all for Billy.

Billy!

"Pay phone," blurted Joe.

"Now?"

"Where are they?"

Diane pointed into a corner of the waiting room.

There was no answer at Father Kelly's rectory. Joe stood at the phone booth and thought for a minute.

"Come on," said Diane.

He called Mike's Place. Mary answered. "Is Mike there?" he asked.

"Joe? He's been trying to reach you all morning."

"Why?"

"Let me get him."

Joe waited. Mike came on the phone and said, "You're in the news, Joe."

"Whaddya mean?" Joe turned his back to Diane, who stood nearby. He leaned into the wall booth and shielded the mouthpiece with his hand.

Mike said, "The cops found two bodies in your house this morning, about three-thirty. Report of a shooting."

Joe's heart felt like it was the size of a basketball. "Billy?"

"Disappeared. The cops are a little confused because they had to get all their information from neighbors. I've got one of my guys following this pretty close, Joe. Where's Billy?"

"I don't know."

There was a brief silence on the other end of the phone. "Where are you, Joe?"

"New York."

"Stay there. Stay in touch. I'll handle this down here. There's gonna be a bulletin out for you pretty soon."

"Who were the bodies?"

"A woman. Black. Security guard working for Security Associates. It's a front. And a guy named George Stewart. Retired Brit. Know him?"

"Yeah, at least I know who he was. I happened to bump into him yesterday up here."

"When?"

"Early afternoon."

"Joe? Was there anything in your house?"

"Yeah."

"Want us to look?"

"Yeah." Joe listed the loot in the house. "Mike, can you arrange for the cops to decide that Billy and I are on vacation for a few days?"

"I think so."

"Maybe they can decide this was a break-in and a falling-out among thieves. Tell the guy in charge that I'll be back in a week."

"OK."

"And find Billy. Try St. Joseph's Church. Ask for Father Kelly. He's a friend of Billy's."

"OK."

"Mike? What's your interest in this?"

"You, Joe. I'm worried about you. Call me back in a couple hours."

"Yeah." Joe hung up.

"Jesus, *come on*," said Diane.

They ran for the plane. In less than five minutes the plane was rising over Riker's Island in the East River, then over the South Bronx, bouncing slightly in the updrafts from the hot rooftops and streets, and turning slowly east as it gained altitude. Westchester County was green, dotted with blue swimming pools. The door to the cockpit was open, but the pilot and co-pilot wore earphones, and there was no sound from the radios. After a few more minutes the plane began to level off. The co-pilot came back, stooping under the low ceiling of the cabin, and handed Diane a Thermos.

"On the ground in about forty-five minutes," he said. "Perfect weather. No traffic." He withdrew to the cockpit and shut the door behind him. The engine noise dropped slightly.

Diane poured them both some coffee. "If you keep your hands to yourself this time, I won't pour it in your lap."

They sat next to each other, facing forward, separated by an aisle of about a foot and a half. Joe sipped his coffee. "How long is this meeting?" he asked.

"Maybe two hours. It's lunch. We should be out by three or four."

"Good. I'm going to Washington when it's over. Can you get me to Islip-MacArthur?"

"I'll go with you."

"This is personal."

"I know."

"What do you mean."

"That's why I was on the phone all morning."

"You knew?" Now he wanted his old anger to rise in his

stomach like a knife, tearing and ripping at his guts. He wanted the anger to come up so he could tear the plane apart. But the anger wasn't there.

He said, "Tell me exactly what you know and how you found out."

"Lazard knows."

"You mean everybody but me knew until fifteen minutes ago? You mean I'm just a fucking fifth wheel in all this? *Tell me what happened!*" He was acting, pretending anger.

"A security guard who worked for Security Associates, which used to be an Agency front but is now a spin-off, and George Stewart, broke into your house early this morning, apparently looking for something. They were shot. At first, the cops decided the woman was shot with Stewart's gun, a .22 automatic, but then they realized he'd been shot with the same gun. She had a .38 and fired a couple shots into your kitchen with it. Your bathroom sink was full of pills that had been emptied out of the bottles in your medicine chest. Part of the duct in your basement was disassembled. The woman was at the foot of the basement stairs with a chest full of twenty-twos, and Stewart was in the bathroom with two shots in him. Billy's gone. Whoever did it was damn good because Stewart was good, as you know."

"What are the cops looking for?"

"You."

"Why didn't you tell me?"

"I'll tell you exactly why," she said, looking directly at him. "It has nothing to do with all this." She waved her hand around in a little circle. "It's because I can't decide for you how you're going to handle Billy. You could have called him last night, but you didn't. You left him unprotected down there for reasons of your own, Joe, and there's nothing I can do or say that can help you with that."

She stopped and waited for him to say something, but he didn't. The plane yawed and bounced gently as it headed east over Long Island Sound.

She went on, "Billy's your responsibility, Joe. This operation is mine, and I want to keep it on track and on time. After this meeting, you'll know why."

Joe still said nothing.

"You're not a fifth wheel, Joe. You're the key to the whole thing."

"And the key to Joe," said Joe, "is Billy."

After a swim in the ocean from the beach at the end of the lawn, and a dip in the pool to get the salt off, Joe changed into his new slacks and alligator shirt, but he left his new tennis shoes off so he could feel the grass under his bare feet.

Lunch was served at a picnic table on a fine lawn the consistency of a golf green. The table was set in a small grove of oak trees, but the leaves on the trees resembled small bits of fine green lace.

"I refuse to move the table," said the hostess. "The gypsy moth caterpillars shit all over the table and the benches. It's no fun to eat lunch like that." She smiled at the other three. "So I found a sail maker out here who made me an awning that shelters the table and fits between the trees."

It was an elegant solution to a small problem in the life of a wealthy woman. It required about ten minutes on the telephone out of the busy morning of her social secretary, and the subsequent visit of a young man for ten minutes of instructions and the choice of colors.

"I was going to match the spinnaker on Robbie's boat, but I decided on this nice tan. It looks like an old canvas sail, but this new nylon or whatever it is lets light through."

Joe wondered who Robbie was. Perhaps it was her son. It certainly wasn't the senator.

Diane asked, "What do you do about the droppings?" It was the sort of practical question traded between the practical rich.

"Oh, we hose the awning off in the morning and vacuum the grass with one of those industrial vacuum cleaners they use in shopping malls. It's easy."

Easy, thought Joe. He sipped his lemon Coke. He was too tired to want a drink. He could go to sleep on the grass. The awning rippled in the breeze. It was cut in a parabolic shape and tied between the trees. It looked like a wing. It was an efficient shape. It made Joe think about angels. When he was a kid, and believed in them, he always thought of them as larger than men, but graceful and beautiful. They must be aerodynamically perfect, he thought.

"Joe?"

"Yes, ma'am." He came to his senses.

"What do you do?" It was his hostess addressing him. She was about forty, with skin like leather and the body of an aging dancer. She was the senator's East Coast mistress. She was an heiress, often in the society columns, but never linked with the senator's name. The senator's wife was old and ill, but he couldn't divorce her. He left her in an exclusive nursing home back home.

"I do free-lance public relations and political consulting."

"Who do you think is going to win this year?"

"Reagan."

"See? Daniel? You've got nothing to worry about."

The senator smiled at her. "Of course not, Charlotte. Everything's in the bag. Our fortunes are safe." Hers was textiles. His was oil, and politics. "Although our candidate isn't even nominated yet, and neither is Carter, and in politics anything can go wrong and often does. Isn't that right, Joe?"

"Yes."

Dan McCagg was the acknowledged master of the right wing of the Republican party, once a candidate for President who had failed to get his campaign off the convention floor, but who was now one of the barons of the Senate. He was the senior Republican on the Senate Armed Forces Committee and the Intelligence Committee—he would be chairman of one of them if the Republicans took control of the Senate.

He was relaxed and smooth, obviously familiar with Diane. He treated Joe with the polite respect of a man who appreciates someone who has come highly touted to the table.

Charlotte was smart and powerful in her own sphere—the world of society, gossip, and arts patronage, interlaced with politics but far removed from the back rooms. Joe might have been a visitor from another planet, or another universe—light years and time-warps away.

Lunch was served. It was fish and pasta and salad, all cold and beautifully prepared. It was an Italian summer among the rich, thought Joe. After espresso and a very light Italian cheesecake, Charlotte stood and said, "I think I'll leave you folks to your talk. I've got a book to read. It was lovely having you."

Joe rose. Diane thanked her from her chair on the terrace where they had moved for dessert. Charlotte disappeared into the enormous modern house that sat on the edge of the huge Atlantic Ocean like a sculpture—assertive, luxurious, and somehow vulnerable. Joe thought of hurricanes. Maybe that's how they think of politics, he thought, like a natural disaster that could sweep all this away. No wonder they're so frightened beneath all their contempt for the rest of us.

My loot, he thought, couldn't buy this house.

A servant brought fresh coffee. McCagg got right to the point.

"Joe, you were an asset to us yesterday. Solid gold, in the right place at the right time. But today, you're not. You're up to your ears in shit. Somebody's tryin' to do ya bad. What were they looking for in your house?"

That trace of redneck, Joe thought. Lazard's been hanging around this guy a lot. "I don't know," said Joe.

"Well, it's probably none of my business," said McCagg, "but where's your boy? I understand you have a boy named Billy."

"I don't know," said Joe. "With a friend, I think."

McCagg looked at Diane. "Not very candid, is he?"

"Help him out, Joe," she said.

"I think it's time for somebody to help me out," said Joe. He got up and walked to the edge of the terrace. The sea was calm. A small trawler worked back and forth far offshore.

"This is how I read it," Joe said, turning back to them. "Somebody's trying to do a Watergate on Carter. That's what I was hired to do. That's Lazard, you, and you." He nodded at Diane and McCagg. "I understand that," he said. "That's hardball politics. But there's more. There're too damn many free-lance hardballs involved. There's Gold." Joe held up his hand and bent one finger down. "There's George Stewart, who probably worked for Gold. There's this black gal who worked for Security Associates."

"And her husband," said McCagg. "That's another one."

Joe looked at him.

"The guy you shot in your house a few months ago."

"I don't know what you're talking about," said Joe.

"You're smart not to admit it," said McCagg, "but I'm guilty right now of suborning a felony, so you don't have to worry about me. I'll never tell." McCagg smiled at Joe with the transparent charm of the lifelong politician putting a man at ease.

And there's Kavenaugh, thought Joe, and whoever was in the room with him that afternoon. That black woman worked for Kavenaugh, and her husband worked for Gold. That links Kavenaugh and Gold. I give up.

"I give up," said Joe. "I thought I understood this stuff, but I don't."

"Joe, there's a lot of deception in politics. A lot of people say our intelligence system has infiltrated and contaminated our political system, but it would be more accurate to say it's the other way around. Politics was the purpose of our intelligence system from the beginning, or maybe the purpose of most of the influential men who set up and ran our intelligence system.

"So there's nothing new about this Watergate stuff. There's just a lot at stake. Thirty years ago, the number of people involved in both politics and intelligence was smaller, and it was easier to keep things close to the vest. And the press was shut out. Now there's too damn many reporters around with too damn many sources. But we're gonna do something about that next year.

"Also, there's a hell of a lot of free-lance hardballs, as you call 'em. I'm an old right-winger, by God, but I'll be the first to say that the lunatic fringe sure attracts its share of lunatics. And every one of these sons-of-bitches has his own private agenda. There's too goddamn many private agendas floatin' around. We're gonna do somethin' about that *this* year, by God. Right, Diane darlin'?"

"Absolutely, Senator."

There's too much fine tuning here, thought Joe. How do they keep it all straight? All the little nods and winks, the body language. All the little deals. Wheels within wheels. Deals within deals.

The senator lit a cigar. "Joe, politics is the alchemy that turns money into power and back to money. There are dozens of definitions of power. It's different here than it is in Europe or Asia, and different now than it was in FDR's time, or Bismarck's. And it's different for me than it is for, say, Henry Ford Two, or the Democratic chairman of Brooklyn, or the head of the Auto Workers. But speaking very loosely, and of the here and now, I'd say it's the ability to command broad influence on key issues.

"There are a lotta guys who can write a tax law or influence a purchasing decision at the Pentagon, and those things can mean millions of bucks for certain people, but that's not power. That's leverage. You know what I mean?"

Joe nodded, wondering where this was going.

"All of this is more defined by personality than most people think. Take Hitler. I'm no fan, but I hafta say he had an acute grasp of power. A lot of power depends on grasping the possibilities, you know? It's a matter of belief. He marched into the Ruhr with a couple of battalions. The French had the troops to blow him away, but they didn't do it, and he knew they wouldn't. So if you have power and you don't use it, you don't have it. Savvy?"

Joe nodded. He asked the senator for a cigar, and took it and lit it carefully. He puffed it slowly while the senator talked.

"For example, the current Speaker of the House, Tip O'Neill, is a good guy, a nice guy to have a drink with and play a round of golf with. But he's weak, and it's not just the fault of changing times and circumstances, the way the *Times* would have you believe. It's his own damn fault. He's just not as good at the game as he should be. But you know all this, Joe."

"It's useful to hear it from you, Senator."

"Well, that sort of proves my point, huh?" asked McCagg. "I've got a little power, and it's useful for you to know how I look at it, right?"

Joe nodded.

McCagg said, "I'll tell you what's on the table this year. After Rocky died, we had to move fast to bring the right-wingers and the WASPs back together in the party. Looking at the polls, and looking at the candidates we had, we had to move fast. I hafta say, it's been a lot harder than I thought. The right-wingers are a bunch of kamikazes and the WASPs want it all for themselves. They're a selfish bunch of bastards, they really are. There's nothing worse than a damn banker. Hell, they've got most of it for themselves already. Man, I tell you it's been *hard*. Rocky was the impediment, though, the real bottleneck. Once he was gone, it got easier. That mulish bastard wanted it all for himself, and I mean *all*."

"What do you need me for?" asked Joe. The cigar smoke rose around his head. He saw in his mind's eye the image of a green jade fish swimming against a blank white wall. He heard questions beating against his brain like waves against a seawall.

"Everybody has their own agenda in this game, but I'm telling you what *the* agenda is *this year*—put Ronny Reagan in the fuckin' White House. We'll worry about the rest of it after we do that. Money and meetings are what it's all about. Makin' plans and stickin' to 'em. We need friends. We need you right where you were, Joe."

"Or where you were," corrected Diane helpfully.

"Yeah," said the senator. "I think you're gonna be out of a job at the DNC on Monday morning."

"Who does Gold work for?" asked Joe.

"You're kinda single-minded, aren't you?" asked McCagg. "He's a fixer. He really is a free lance, only he does most of it for the Republican Party. Among other things, he controls the Conservative Party in New York City, which is no small thing in Queens and Brooklyn. Elections are still counted by votes. Big numbers are still a bunch of little numbers added up."

"He conveyed an offer to me," said Joe. "Who was he speaking for?"

"Himself, probably," offered the senator, glancing sideways at Diane, who nodded in approval. "I'll tell you what, Joe. You work for me, and I'll double Gold's offer. OK?"

Joe looked at Diane. She nodded. Joe said, "OK." Diane got an indefinable look of satisfaction in her face, somewhere far behind her eyes. Joe might not have noticed it if he hadn't been watching her eyes the night before when they were making love.

"But who the hell is Gold?" asked Joe.

"He's an independent bastard," said the senator. "Maybe he's after your loot."

"Everybody thinks I've got a big pile of loot."

"Not everybody," said McCagg, glancing at Diane again. "Just a few folks. There's no need for you to use hyperbole in this company." He pronounced the word, "hyper-bowl." McCagg chuckled. Joe wondered about the redneck act. In a man like McCagg, the habits of years were both deliberate and unconscious—they had once been deliberate, and now they were unconscious.

"Don't be upset, Joe-boy," said McCagg. "I'm gonna add to your loot, not take it away."

"What about Lazard?"

"He spends a lotta time with Gold, but I believe Diane here has got him by the short hairs. Isn't that right, Diane?"

She smiled and nodded. She was watching Joe.

"Gold and Lazard don't really give a shit about the campaign," said McCagg. "But I give a shit, I guarantee you. The RNC has worked since 1976 to take the Senate. We made good plans, we stuck to 'em, and we're in good shape. Damn good shape. We've got everything in position—good candidates against weak Democrats, plenty of money, hot issues. But it all hangs on Reagan. If he wins, we win. If he don't, we don't. You don't need a fifty-thousand-dollar poll to figure that out.

"Yeah-boy, I give a shit. And if you're working for me, you better give a shit too. I'm gonna be a committee chairman next year, by God, and then you're gonna see a few folks stand up and salute when I walk in the fuckin' room. Yeah-boy."

Joe wondered how there could be a conspiracy to elect a president. A conspiracy of millions of voters was not a conspiracy at all. It was impossible.

But a conspiracy to manipulate? Sure, but Joe knew enough about politics, or voting behavior, to know that political technicians didn't win elections, no matter what they told their friends in the captive press. It was the undercurrents in people's hearts and wallets that won or lost elections, which is why most politicians hated elections, no matter what they told *their* friends in the captive press.

These conspiracies were no more than a way of being able to say at the end of the election, to the winner, "Hey, old buddy, we did it for you." And taking the winner aside and whispering in his ear, "Hey, I did it all for you. These other guys, they sat on their hands."

It was a way of saying, "Hey, old buddy, you owe me." And of skimming a few bucks off the top along the way, just for the hell of it, even if you didn't really need the dough. Politics was still cash and carry, despite the illusory reforms of the seventies. It was hard not to grab cash when it was waved under your nose.

"Give me a week to straighten things out," said Joe.

"Sure," said McCagg. "But get 'em straight. No loose ends. I've got tough, messy jobs coming up. Can you handle 'em?"

"No problem," said Joe. "Can do, just like the old days."

"I like that," said McCagg.

"But since I'm gonna be out of a job Monday, I'd like a down payment. Fifty thou. In cash. By Monday at six PM. I'll call you to give you the drop."

"Can do," said McCagg. "No problem."

Diane stood up and smiled. Joe stood up, too. "We have to run along, Senator," she said. "Thanks for lunch."

"You goin' back to DC?" asked McCagg. "Both of you?" Diane smiled.

"Take the plane," said McCagg. "Send it back tonight. I'm goin' down in the mornin'."

McCagg sat motionless in his chair. He was a big man, gray, tan, lined and weathered, hard. He studied Joe, who in twenty more years would look the same. "Power, money, and sex, Joe. Get it? That's all you need to know. And don't pick your nose at the wrong time."

Joe nodded. He knew.

The plane dropped them at National Airport and turned right around and took off for Long Island.

"It's like the Toonerville Trolley," said Joe.

"What's that?" asked Diane.

"You're too young to remember trolley cars?"

"I know what they are."

"Were," said Joe. "Never mind. Let's find a telephone."

On the phone, Mike warned Joe to stay away from his house. "It'll take a few days to work out an agreement with the cops," said Mike. "Sooner or later, you'll have to turn yourself in. You better stay over here meanwhile."

They took a cab to Mike's Place, and walked through the unused dining room to the kitchen avoiding the bar. Mike was waiting. The kitchen was hot, full of smells. Mary was working too hard to talk to them.

Mike said, "There's a full house out front. You don't need to be seen here. Why don't you sit out on the back porch and have a beer? I'll be back in a little while. If you want some food, tell Mary. Joe, we have to talk."

"Tell me now: Do the cops know who I am? Or was?"

"They know who you used to work for, if that's what you mean, but they don't know what you're doing now. They don't know about Joe Ball Associates and they don't know about the DNC, but somebody's bound to tell them. You're lucky this happened on a holiday weekend. There was a small story in the back of the *Post*, but no TV. The cops agreed to kill the story for the time being. But they want to talk to you soon."

"OK," said Joe. "Soon, but not now."

Mike nodded. He said, "I put the phone in your room like you asked."

Joe said to Diane, "I have to make some calls. Get us some drinks. I'll be back down in a few minutes."

"Don't go in the bar, miss," said Mike. "Tell me what you want and I'll bring it back."

It was two hours before Mike could sit down with them on the back porch behind the kitchen. Mary came out to join them. It was an unusually clear night for Washington in the summer. The smog had dissipated during the long weekend. Traffic into the airport was light. A few sport fishing boats headed upstream in the dark river behind the building. Mosquitoes buzzed against the screens around the porch.

"It's lovely out here," said Diane. "This is a wonderful place."

"It depends on the wind," said Mary. "And the tide. And the time of day."

"Mary works so hard that she only spends five minutes a day out here," said Mike. "She doesn't know if it's nice or not. But she made me put the screens up."

"Authentic Oriental cooking does not include bugs," said Mary.

"That's not what my mother told me," said Mike.

"Where's Billy?" asked Joe.

"Not at the priest's house," said Mike. "He told me Billy stayed there last night and disappeared sometime before noon today."

"Did he have anything with him?"

"The priest told me, 'Just an orange backpack with some stuff in it.'"

"Did he have any money?"

"The priest said, 'Some money.'"

"A gun?"

"The priest said, 'I didn't search the boy's pack.'"

"Was the stuff in the house?"

"No."

"There could have been another person in the break-in, right?" asked Joe. "Who ripped off his colleagues after they found the stuff. And Billy walked in later, saw the mess, and split."

"No, Joe," said Diane. "You're not thinking straight. The cops answered a call from a neighbor reporting a shooting in progress. Billy wouldn't have had time to walk in, gather up his stuff, and leave."

"You're right," said Joe, with the effect of a jail door closing.

After a long silence, he said, "I went upstairs and called my bank. Offshore. Someone using my code called them this afternoon and transferred some assets to an account in another offshore bank. They won't tell me where, which is, of course, the way they work, and why people use them in the first place. Perfect secrecy."

"Was it a lot?" asked Diane.

Joe shrugged. "It doesn't matter what it was. All it is now is a clue to a puzzle. Somebody who knows how those banks work was in my house last night, and got away. It sure as hell wasn't Billy, because he doesn't know anything about offshore banks." He added bitterly, "At least he didn't the last time I talked to him."

"Where could he be, Joe?" asked Mike.

"I know where he is."

"Where?" asked Diane and Mary together.

"I once gave him Paul Lazard's card, way back at the beginning of this thing, and told him to call Lazard if anything happened to me. It was the biggest mistake of my life."

"They'll kill him," said Diane. Her voice was sharp and accusatory, as if she was blaming Joe for negligence.

"He's in New York," said Mary. "No one that young should go there."

"That boy," said Mike, "seems to know how to take care of himself all right."

"We have to find him," said Joe. "What if he shot those

two in the house? What if this third party kidnapped him?"

"Joe, Joe," said Mike. "Where would he have gotten a .22?"

Joe looked at Mike and shrugged. "He could have boot-legged it home the day we used your boat."

"This is very bad," said Mike. "I'll send two guys to New York tonight. If they need help, I'll send two more on Monday."

"I owe you, Mike."

"No, Joe. Not yet."

Later, in the dark kitchen, Mike stood talking to a man wearing khaki pants and a golf shirt with an alligator on it. The man was medium height, dark-haired, olive-skinned, and stocky. He wore a thick mustache. He spoke with an Eastern European accent.

Mike said, "Here's a thousand in cash. You and Harry take the first plane up there in the morning. *Find that kid.*"

"OK, Mike."

"And watch out for Lazard's boys, Volko. He's a very bad guy."

"I know him, Mike. Remember?"

"I remember."

"I owe him one."

"I remember. But the kid, Volko. Find the kid first."

Around dawn Sunday, it rained. The noise on the tin roof over his head woke Joe. He looked over at the woman sleeping beside him. This is permanent, he thought. I don't know how it happened. I didn't want it, but I want it now.

"Are you awake?" he asked.

"Yes. The rain woke me, and I felt you wake up. I was afraid you were going to get up and leave."

"I'm going to New York this morning."

"I thought you would. I'll go with you."

"No, I want to go alone. I'm taking the bus. I want to put myself in Billy's shoes, how he would go, where he would stay."

"OK. I understand. I'll fly. Call me when you get there. You can stay with me."

"I'll call when I find him."

She rolled over and sat up. Looking at her face and body excited him more than anything he had felt for a long time.

"Don't do it this way, Joe. Trust me. Let me help you."

"You can't help me. How can you? Who are you working for?"

"Trust me, Joe."

"You say that all the time," said Joe. That's what I told Billy, he thought.

PART 3

"People say we're destroying the political system. What system are people defending? No one gives a damn about it. His [John Anderson's] campaign serves as a real warning to the system: that either you do better than Jimmy Carter and Ronald Reagan or you can't bask in the security of the two-party system—that when fifty per cent of the people in this country don't give a damn about politics, you are on the very edge of instability."

David Garth, Anderson's media advisor, quoted by Elizabeth Drew in *The New Yorker*, October 13, 1980

ELEVEN ═══════════════

BILLY'S JOURNEY WAS a photocopy of a journey taken by thousands of kids every year, runaways heading for New York City, pushed by cruelty or loss at home, and pulled by a myth of excitement and opportunity. Detonated by little explosions in families and half-families in an arc from Duluth to Key West, the kids are set loose on a thousand and one roads to New York. The myth is a lie, but kids Billy's age are the last true believers in America. They *believe*.

They believe New York City holds the promise of more excitement and opportunity than wherever they come from. Who can say they're wrong? Most of the places they come from aren't very exciting, and are dry of opportunity. And in an odd way, most of these kids are more realistic about their chances than most of the adults they leave behind. Half a chance is better than none, and half a chance at fifteen or sixteen on the road to the big city looks better than a dead-end road to a county seat in western Ohio, or upstate New York, or North Georgia. It's just that, for some, the price is so high in New York City.

Most of them travel by bus. Billy was no exception. But

few are so well provided. Billy had $10,000 in worn hundreds; two excellent forged passports; two large, valuable diamonds; and an emerald that was nearly priceless because of its flawless color and quality.

And few teenage refugees are as well protected as Billy was, with a .22 automatic that he knew to be reliable and effective, and silent, too. Billy was also armed with the self-assurance that comes from experience. This set him apart from most others on the roads to the city. But at the end of the road, at the hub, in the hostile and predatory environment of New York's streets, it was not unusual to be armed.

In that arena, a .22 was a light weapon, favored mostly by the most elite of professional killers—mob hit men. The ordinary street kids hanging around Eighth Avenue and 42nd Street—a block or two north of the Port Authority Bus Terminal, or doing a little business in the city's open-air drug bazaars in Harlem or north Brooklyn or on Union Square, preferred heavier artillery. The guns of choice were 9-mm Browning or Beretta automatics, because they were compact and easy to carry. They were *fire-power*. They had *style*. They were *bad*.

And, of course, in the hostile, predatory life of New York's streets, Billy's baggage made him a target, a mark. This had not yet occurred to Billy.

Leaving Washington on Saturday, he was surprised by the crowd in the Washington Greyhound Terminal on New York Avenue, and pleased by the perfect anonymity of the place. He thought it would be deserted in the middle of a holiday weekend, but there were long lines at the ticket counter and the departure gates. The waiting room was full of people waiting—sleeping, talking, wandering around, staring into space. Buses came and went. The loudspeaker hummed and crackled.

He passed ten feet from a bored DC cop standing with his arms folded by a wall of lockers. The cop looked right through him. That pleased Billy. The travelers here dressed as they liked, came and went as they wished, and bought tickets for whatever destination they chose. With the gun, an airport would have been impossible. Billy had traveled by plane and had seen the X-ray machines and watchful guards. A train would have been all right, but train stations were open and somehow easier to watch, thought Billy; and the trains themselves were full of *officials*—taking your ticket, looking you over, asking you for your stub every time you went to get a Coke in the café car.

But a bus station was an extension of the city streets. People wandered in and out on all sorts of errands. Buses were comfortable and bus people were generally friendly, even when they were busy and harried. Airline people were brusque and officious, and railroad people were rude and distant. It had not taken much thought for Billy to pick Greyhound over the Eastern shuttle or Amtrak's Metroliner. He had traveled enough to know what he wanted.

People paying for bus tickets tended to pay with cash. While he stood in line waiting his turn, Billy watched closely and was relieved to see that few people used plastic. His hundred-dollar bill was not scrutinized by the clerk for more than a second, and the clerk never raised his eyes to Billy's face.

"One-way to New York," said Billy, sliding the folded bill out of his jeans pocket and onto the counter with one smooth motion.

"Next bus at one-thirty," said the clerk, sliding the ticket back, followed by the change. Billy stuffed the coins and bills into his pocket without counting them. He glanced at the clock, decided in that moment to buy a watch when he got to New York, and headed quickly for the newsstand and cafeteria.

He bought a paper, a copy of *Mad*, two Conan comic books, a ham and cheese sandwich, a Snickers bar, and a can of Pepsi. He hurried to the gate. He was first in line. He leaned against the wall and waited. He wanted to be first on the bus so he could get the front seat opposite the driver. The view was best, he could watch the driver drive, he was farthest from the smokers and the suitcase radios in the back of the bus, and he would be first off when the bus got to New York. He had it all figured out.

The pack had not left his back for a moment. As he leaned against the wall, the gun dug into his shoulder blade. He wondered if it showed an outline. He decided the thick Cordura nylon and the leather bottom of the climber's pack were stiff enough to disguise the contents.

The passports and gun were wrapped in one of Father Kelly's Fordham sweat shirts. The money was in a Baggie adhesive-taped to his abdomen under his underpants. The jewels were wrapped in pieces of paper towel inside a Baggie stuck down in his left front jeans pocket.

He wasn't sure why he'd brought the three jewels, but they were beautiful to look at and substantial to hold. They had seemed his rightful share of the loot. He wanted more than a wad of dirty, used money. And the jewels, he believed, were a legacy of his mother.

The line behind him lengthened rapidly. The bus was going to be crowded. The loudspeaker snapped and rasped, and announced his bus. He looked up above the door to double-check his gate. A porter opened the door and kicked a wedge under it to hold it open.

"Go on," he said to Billy. To the crowd-at-large he shouted, "One-thirty to New York City. Express Hound to New York City."

Billy stepped out to the ramp. The driver was a pleasant-looking man in shirt-sleeves, wearing dark aviator sunglasses and a cap crushed and shaped to look like a pilot's cap from a World War II movie.

"OK, kid," he said, punching Billy's ticket. "Smoking in the back but no pot on my bus."

"I'm sitting in the front."

"Good kid. Keep your nose clean."

Billy took the front seat by the door. There wasn't much room for his long legs, but once the bus started he could prop them on the railing. He sat by the window and put all his junk on the aisle seat. He hoped no one would sit next to him. He kept the pack in his lap, the straps wrapped through and around his big hands. The plastic bag taped to his belly was uncomfortable. The skin beneath was sweaty. It began to itch. He scratched it and waited for the bus to fill up and go.

It looked as though every seat would be taken. The line of passengers stretched from the bus door into the terminal. It was hot and humid. Diesel fumes gave the air a rank, dead smell. Passengers patiently filed up the steps past Billy and into the seats, struggling with shopping bags and suitcases, guitar cases, and cardboard boxes wrapped in string and tape. A woman carried a crying baby in her arms and shoved a small, reluctant child along the aisle in front of her. An argument broke out between three or four people in the back over the division between smoking and non-smoking seats. The driver intervened.

Finally, the last rider found a seat. The driver stepped up into the bus and stood by Billy counting the passengers. He wrote the number on a slip of paper and dropped it in an envelope with the ticket stubs. The seat next to Billy was the only empty seat on the bus. The driver looked down at Billy and winked. "You're lucky, kid. It's gonna be a long four hours."

The driver threw his hat onto the dashboard and climbed into his seat like a man climbing onto a horse. He started the engine, listened through the open door for a minute, then reached over and pulled the lever to close the door. The loud engine noise dropped to a heavy vibration from the rear. Billy watched the driver, fascinated. He wished he could see all the lights and dials on the panel.

There was a knock on the door and a loud yell, "Hey, let me on."

A girl stood at the door, pounding angrily. "Hey, let me on. It's not one-thirty."

The driver had already released the parking brakes with a hiss of air and had shifted into reverse. He turned to Billy, winked again, and said, "Whaddya think? Should we let her on?"

"Sure, why not."

"OK, kid, move your stuff." The driver shifted back to neutral, put the brakes on, and opened the door. "C'mon, honey, get on. You're holdin' up the train."

The driver took her ticket. She stood on the step below Billy. He could smell her. She was sweaty and fresh at the same time. Her hair was the color of dark honey. She wore it in two thick braids. Her skin was a light, even, pale golden tan.

"Sit there, honey," said the driver. "He won't bite." He closed the door again, jerked the bus into reverse, released the brakes, and began to back out of the dock into the yard. The girl had to grab the railing to keep from falling.

"Hey, take it easy," she said, and dropped into the seat.

She wore a blue and white striped T-shirt with a V neck and short sleeves, white painter's pants, and old tennis sneakers. She carried an old leather suitcase that had once been elegant and expensive, the sort of bag businessmen used to call an overnighter.

Billy's father had such a bag. Joe said they were too heavy for air travel. They were the sort of bag men carried on overnight business trips when they traveled by train and slept in Pullmans. Billy had thought that sounded like a wonderful way to travel. Joe had laughed and said, "It was, but you don't understand modern economics, kid. We looted the railroads and destroyed them. We like to do things the hard way in this country."

The girl sat with the bag on her lap until the bus stopped at a red light on New York Avenue. "That has to go up in the rack, miss," said the driver. She stood and hoisted the bag over her head. She did it easily, but the light changed and the driver stepped hard on the gas. She lost her balance. Billy leapt up and grabbed the bag. It was so heavy that he almost fell, taking them both down, but they managed to heave it into the rack.

"Hey," Billy said. "That thing weighs a ton. What's in it?"

"My weights," she said. "Can I sit by the window? You'll have more room for your legs on the aisle."

"I guess so." He grabbed his backpack before she could pick it up.

"What's in *that?*"

"Nothing. Just some books."

They sat down. The driver was watching Billy in the mirror. He winked and turned his attention back to the road.

"Weights?" asked Billy. He looked at her closely out of the corner of his eye. She had an open, pretty face with dark eyebrows and dark eyes, a broad mouth, and even teeth. Her nose was broad and straight. She had large ears, partly covered by her thick hair, but they fit her other features. She was about the prettiest girl Billy had ever seen, and about the first girl he had ever looked at closely, except his sister.

"I lift weights," she said. She grinned and flexed her left arm in front of his face. Her biceps bulged. Her triceps was as hard as a rock. The muscles of her forearm were like wires. Each muscle stood out in low relief as though modeled in clay or carved from stone.

"Good definition," he said. He knew some guys who lifted weights and he had picked up some of their jargon.

"*Good?*" she said. "It's *great.*"

"OK. Great."

"I just won a contest."

"In Washington?"

"No, over in Virginia. Some place called Vienna."

"Yeah, I know where it is."

"It's not far. The wife of one of the judges put us up last night, two of us, and drove us in here to the bus station today. The other girl had to go back to St. Louis. That's a long way."

"Yeah. How old are you?"

"Seventeen."

"I'm eighteen," lied Billy.

"Are you in college?"

"Yeah," he lied again.

"Where?"

"Ah, New York."

"Oh," she said. "That's where I'm going. I'm going to get a job."

"Where do you live?"

"Oh, in a little town up near Albany, in upstate New York."

"What's it called?"

"Oh, you never heard of it. No one ever has."

"Maybe I have."

"Watervliet. It's north of Albany on the Hudson River."

"No," said Billy. "I never have."

"That's what everyone says." She grinned again. She had a grin like a kid, a happy grin that filled her whole face. Billy was entranced. He grinned back.

"Good," she said. "I'm glad you're going to New York. I don't know anybody there. You must know all about it. I don't even know where I'm going to stay."

"I don't think that's such a simple problem."

"No, I guess not."

"Where are your parents?"

"Watervliet. I mean, my father. My mother's dead. She's buried in another little town, where we used to live."

"Why don't you go home?"

"My father threw me out. I mean, he wouldn't let me go to Vienna for the contest. I won a state contest in Syracuse last month, and somebody from this other contest wrote me and said I should enter it. This was like a regional contest."

"Contest? You lift weights? Like the Olympics?"

"No, stupid. Body building. Like a beauty contest, only they judge you on definition, proportion, grace, poses, speed, skin, that sort of thing."

"Speed?"

"How fast and how well you move from one pose to another. You do a routine. It's like the free routine in ice skating. It's sort of like dancing. It's all movement."

"Yeah, I see."

"I'll show you sometime," she said. "You'll see what I mean."

"Sure," he said. Holy cow, he thought. What am I gonna do with her? I've gotta find my dad.

"My father thinks I'm a freak," she said. "He got mad at me and threw me out. I mean, he said if I went to Vienna, I shouldn't come home again. So I took some clothes and my weights and my money, and I left. I won the contest in Vienna. Now they want me to go to the nationals."

"Who's 'they'?"

"Some people I met there."

"Have you told anybody else about this? Besides me?"

"No."

"Good," said Billy. "That's your first lesson in New York City. Don't tell anybody anything."

"I see what you mean," she said. She nodded and grinned. "You have to be careful."

He nodded.

"Do you have anything to eat?" she asked. "I'm starving."

He gave her half his sandwich. Holy smokes, he thought. He glanced at the driver. The driver looked into the mirror and winked again. The bus was just leaving the outskirts of Washington, where New York Avenue turns onto the Baltimore-Washington Expressway. "We're going the old way today," said the driver. "It's an ICC rule."

Billy nodded. He had no idea what the ICC was or why it should have such a rule.

As if reading his thoughts, the driver said, "The ICC is the Interstate Commerce Commission. It regulates interstate public transportation. This is the way we used to go to Baltimore before Interstate 95 was built. If we don't go this way at least once a week, we have to forfeit this route. We don't really want it anymore, but we don't want anybody else to have it either. Some local bus company could come in here and provide local service along this route and take away some of our business. See?"

Billy nodded again. For every rule, there was someone who knew what it was and others who didn't know. Billy decided it was important to learn all the rules. Maybe he should be a lawyer when he grew up. They knew the rules.

He thought about that for a while, watching the road roll beneath him, feeling the wheel under his seat go bumpeta-bumpeta, while the girl ate half his candy bar and drank most of his Pepsi. Then he decided it was more important to be one of the people who made the rules. He wasn't sure who they were, or how they did it, but he knew they were more important than lawyers. Joe could tell him who they were. He had to find Joe.

The Lincoln Tunnel spirals down the Palisades bluff in Weehawken on the Jersey side and runs under the river in a long, long slope down to the center and a long climb up to the other side. The lighting in the tunnel has been borrowed from a hospital emergency room. The tunnels—there are three tubes, not one—are never silent. There is a perpetual light smog in the tunnel distance that makes a nearsighted blur out of the receding taillights ahead.

It is like crossing over Jordan. When a long-distance bus emerges into the confusion of the exit ramps that give onto Tenth and Ninth avenues, the passengers have been baptized and made new, if they have never been to New York before. Many haven't. What they see looks and smells and sounds new. It *feels* new.

Coming up out of the Lincoln Tunnel into the streets of the West Side of Manhattan—the remnants of the brick tenements of the old Hell's Kitchen dock district—was for Billy and the girl like landing on a mysteriously inhabited planet after a space journey of light years. The bus stopped at a red light at the end of the ramp curving up out of the tunnel. The streets had the odd quiet of Saturday evening in the middle of a long summer weekend. There were few cars and fewer pedestrians. The vegetable stands and meat markets that characterize the district were closed. West 40th Street was empty. The driver drove slowly toward the Port Authority terminal. "Don't wanna be early," he muttered. "They'll yell at me."

The girl had slept with her head on Billy's shoulder all the way from Baltimore. The smell of her hair would stay in Billy's nose for the rest of his life, he thought.

She woke up when the bus rose out of the tunnel into the daylight. It was the end of a bright, hot day. Blue sky hung over the rooftops of grimy buildings jammed together in every shape and size. The sun, still high in the west behind them, fell on the bricks and stone and glass, turning the windows golden.

"Oh," she said in a quiet voice. "We're here." She didn't say: We're in New York, or We're there, or Where are we? But, "We're *here*," as if everywhere else in the world were now no more than somewhere else.

Billy's response to this moment of wonder was to ask her name.

"Annie," she said, with her wide grin.

"Annie what?"

"Annie Dmitri."

"I like your name."

"What's yours."

"Billy Ball." He had meant to give himself another name, a cover name, but he hadn't thought of one, and he didn't want to lie to her more than he had to.

She slipped her hand into his in the narrow space between them. Her skin was warm and dry, and her hand felt firm and strong. There was nothing more they needed to say. They were joined by their journey, made new and whole, no matter what they had done before. They were as innocent as lambs.

The driver steered his bus through the dim, cavernous horse-shoe garage under the Port Authority terminal where interstate buses are docked. He nosed the bus into his appointed slot and stopped. Before he turned the engine off, he turned and looked at the two kids. They looked back at him.

In a low voice no one else could hear, he said, "You're a coupla nice kids. I see a lotta kids, but none as nice as you. You kids take care of yourselves. This is a tough town. You watch each other's backs, you know? You look out for each other, you hear?"

They nodded. They could not help smiling at this message

of grim affection. He winked. In a moment, he had turned off
the engine, set the brakes, grabbed his hat and ticket envelope,
opened the door, and bounded out of the bus. Billy and Annie
leapt up, grabbed their bags, and followed him out. He turned
away to talk to a baggage man.

"Good-bye," sang Annie to his back. "Thanks for the nice
ride."

The two kids disappeared through the door into the lower
level of the terminal. It was crowded, hot, and noisy. It smelled.
They were in New York.

Upstairs in the main concourse of the terminal, lined with
shops, lunch counters, and the ticket counters of half a dozen
bus companies, Billy's sense of anonymity left him. In the half-
crowds of the slow holiday, Billy had the sense that everyone
was watching everyone else. The watching was direct, or out
of the corners of a score of eyes, and it was hostile and defensive
at the same time. Billy had never seen so many derelicts and
dudes in one place at the same time.

"Smoke?" asked a dude as they rode the escalator up to the
concourse. The dude was walking rapidly up the escalator. He
bumped Billy hard as he brushed by.

"Hey!" said Annie.

Billy squeezed her hand. She looked chagrined and angry.

"Let's not look for trouble," whispered Billy. He felt like a
small animal searching for cover.

The guy waited for them at the top of the escalator, leering
down at them, staring at Annie. "Smoke?" he said again, as
they stepped off. "Good smoke, pretty lady?"

"No, thanks," murmured Annie, now blushing from her
anger.

The dude's hand lashed out and grabbed Billy by the arm.
"Good smoke, white boy." This was a hard sell.

There was a sharp clang behind them. A Port Authority cop
rapped his night-stick on the railing around the escalator well.
"Keep moving," he ordered.

The dude strutted slowly away. Billy and Annie hurried
toward the Eighth Avenue exits. The small crowd of concourse
dwellers that had begun to close in on the little confrontation
just as quickly scattered.

"I have to make a call," said Billy. He stopped at a pay phone. He dialed the number on the business card his father had given him. The line was busy. Billy was surprised. At six o'clock Saturday night? A holiday weekend?

For the first time, Billy was struck by the absurdity of what he was doing, and a faint sense of threat. Why had he come here? *New York City?* On the most minutely surveyed and mapped terrain in the world, he was completely lost. He had no idea what he would see when he walked out of the doors marked EIGHTH AVENUE. He had no idea where Two World Trade Center might be. He had the strong sense that there were people out there at this very moment of this dead Saturday who were looking for his father, and looking for him.

It wasn't the police in their blue uniforms who worried him. It was the men and women who looked like all the other men and women. They were invisible. They were everywhere. They walked in and out of people's houses and lives at will and did what they wanted. Billy leaned against the side of the phone booth. He felt the gun in the pack against his back.

He had money. He had the passports. He had the jewels that reminded him of his mother. He had a phone number, a name, and an address. He had a father he couldn't find. And he had this girl. He had to start somewhere. What did Joe always say? *Do it by the numbers. When you don't know what to do, begin at the beginning and do it by the numbers. Do it right the first time and do it all. If you make a mistake, forget it and keep moving.*

His first mistake had been lying to Annie. He corrected the mistake immediately. "I lied to you," he said. "I don't go to college. I'm on my own, like you. I'm looking for my father. He's here somewhere, I think. I've never been here before in my life. I don't even know what's outside that door."

She looked a little scared for a moment. The color of her eyes darkened and her face flushed. Her mouth thinned and pouted. Then she grinned. "I'll help you," she said, "if you'll help me. I'll help you find your dad if you help me find a job and a place to stay. Then I'm going to learn dancing and acting. That's why I'm here."

Billy grinned back at her.

"Now we're like tourists," she said. "The first thing tourists do is buy a map." She took his hand and pulled him toward a newsstand. "Then they get something to eat. Tourists are always hungry. Then they find a place to sleep so they can go sight-seeing in the morning. And have a place to leave their bags."

Billy tugged her back. "First, we buy a map. Then find a place to stay. Then eat."

She grinned back at him and, inexplicably, blushed.

"What?" he asked.

"I don't have much money."

"I'll pay," he said. "Oh. Well. We'll get one room and two beds. We'll be brother and sister. Our parents are coming back from a vacation in Europe and their plane was delayed." He thought for a second. "We need time. Their charter flight was delayed a couple days. . . . Until Wednesday. OK?"

"That's good," she said. "That's perfect. What about names?"

"Do you have any ID?" he asked.

"My driver's license?"

"I'll be Billy Dmitri."

"Oh, that's perfect." She was grinning from ear to ear. "Let's go. I'm starving."

"We can't hold hands," said Billy. "We're related now."

Outside the terminal, they told their story to a cop. It worked like a charm.

"You want a safe hotel," he said. "But not too dear. Right?"

They nodded. They jammed their hands in their pockets to keep from reaching for each other in their excitement.

"Walk up here to West 47th Street. Five blocks. Walk smartly. Don't accept any offers of assistance, you understand? This is a bad area. Turn right. Go into the Hotel Edison in the middle of the block. That'll be about right. Mind your own business on the streets, you understand. Don't be stupid."

They thanked him.

"Where're you from?" he asked.

"Upstate," said Billy. "Waterford."

"Near Watervliet," said Annie quickly.

"Waterford," said the cop. "That's where my folks were from back in the old country."

They nodded and smiled in unison. Billy was almost ready to bolt.

He looked at them curiously. "Are ya Catholic?" he asked.

"Yes," said Billy. Annie nodded.

"Never been in New York before?"

"No," they both said.

"Then ye can go to St. Paddy's tomorrow for mass. It's a great cathedral. Right across town from the Edison. On Fifth Avenue and up a few blocks on Fiftieth. Do ya have a map?"

"Yes," said Annie.

"St. Patrick's?" asked Billy.

"A great saint," said the cop. "Ask him to protect ya while you're here. And me, too."

TWELVE ══════════════════════

ANNIE BOUNCED ON one bed, then the other. "I'll take this one by the window. It's softer." She heaved her bag onto the bed and snapped it open. Wrapped in a set of sweat clothes were the plates and collars and bars of a set of dumbbells. She began to fit them together. She was excited. "See? You put the plates on, with the sleeve in the middle and the collars on the outside, and you tighten the collars with the Allen wrench."

She held the assembled dumbbell out to Billy, who sat on the edge of his bed. He had to grab it with both hands to keep from dropping it.

"Seventeen pounds," she said. "The plates are fourteen and the rest is three."

"You carried this around? No wonder your bag is so heavy."

The bellboy had barked when he picked up her bag, "Christ, kid, what's in this?"

"There's more," she said, reaching into the bag. She pulled out a pair of leg weights—vinyl pouches about six inches wide and long enough to wrap around a foot or ankle. They were filled with lead shot. They had Velcro fasteners.

"See?" She kicked her shoes off and wrapped one of the pouches around her ankle. "You should try it."

"I've never lifted weights. I play basketball."

"I love basketball. We'll find a place to play and I'll play with you. I'm almost as tall as you. I'll bet I can beat you at O-U-T and P-I-G.

"But not at H-O-R-S-E."

"Oh yes I can. At everything." She was excited and happy. On the way up in the elevator, she had leaned over and whispered, "This is better than playing house."

He was afraid the bellhop had heard, but the little old man gave no indication. The desk clerk had swallowed their little story easily. He gave them a room through Tuesday night. Billy paid in advance with two of the used hundreds. The small change in return dismayed him. New York was amazingly expensive, and he'd gotten his first lesson in tipping from the bellhop. "A buck a bag," said the little man with his hand out. "And a buck for the key." Billy paid two dollars. He had refused to hand over the backpack. "But anything you want," added the bellhop. "I'll get if for ya."

While Annie unpacked, Billy tried the number for Paul Perrieux again. It rang. A man with a bored voice answered.

"Service."

It took Billy a moment to realize he'd gotten an answering service. He hung up. he didn't like the sound of the man's voice.

Annie came out of the bathroom and sat down on her bed opposite him. The phone was on a table between them. "Are you through?" she asked.

"Yes. It's an answering service."

"It's Saturday night," she explained. "It's a business phone." He had showed her the card.

She picked up the phone and dialed room service. "Room service?" She had the manner of an experienced traveler. "Can you bring me up a box of Tampax Regular?"

My God, he thought. It *is* like playing house.

To Billy, she said, "I've got my period. It's a couple days early. Otherwise, I would have had what I needed. It's not very heavy. It never is. I think it's from all the exercise. They say a lot of exercise slows women's periods. A lot of women runners don't menstruate at all. I wonder what exercise does to men?"

"I don't know," said Billy. It had been a serious question. She was exuberant and matter-of-fact at the same time, all the time. He shrugged. He got up and turned on the TV. "I never thought about it."

He stood by the window and looked down at the street, ten floors below. The gold of the setting sun lay on the windows of an office building in the next block, over the rooftops of lower buildings. The red glow of the big neon sign on the roof of the Edison was reflected with the glow of the sun in the windows. He stared across a landscape of black-tarred rooftops, great wooden water tanks, building façades in every conceivable period and style of architecture from the past hundred years. He had never seen anything like it.

"It's beautiful," he said.

"What's beautiful?"

"This city."

They went out and wandered around Times Square in the dusk like tourists, hand in hand. He took his backpack.

"Why do you carry that all the time?" she asked.

"Oh, I don't know. I don't want to lose it. It's a habit." There were things he couldn't tell her yet, couldn't ever tell her, but he felt the inner disorder of lies growing in him like a tumor. He wanted to tell her everything.

They ate in an Argentine restaurant on Broadway. For the first time in his life, Billy ate blood sausage. He liked it. Annie said her grandfather used to make it. She didn't talk much about her family, but there might have been a lot to talk about, Billy thought. What she did say made it sound as though her family had once been close and happy.

Billy paid with one of the hundreds. She watched quizzically but asked nothing. It was uncharacterisitc of her.

He wanted to break as many of the hundreds as he could. He figured he could break them in places like this one but not at lunch counters or newsstands. He needed a pocket full of smaller bills.

In one of the junky electronics stores that line Broadway he bought himself a digital wristwatch, a runner's watch with a black plastic case and band. He bought Annie one just like it. He paid with a hundred. The clerk gave him a hard look but counted out the change.

They walked across 45th Street to Fifth Avenue, past a row of electronics stores closed for the weekend. Billy decided to buy a radio on Monday when they opened. He didn't like TV much and he missed listening to music. He missed reading, too. The newsstands here had more magazines and paperback books than some of the bookstores in Washington and its suburbs. He would buy some books on Monday too.

On the way back, he realized that this was *Broadway*. This was where all the theaters and plays and musicals were, and movies. He said this to Annie.

"I know," she said. "I've been looking at every one we passed. This is where I'm going to be for the rest of my life."

Back in their room, they undressed in the dark and went to bed in their underwear. After a few minutes Annie said, "Billy?"

He reached out and took her hand. They fell asleep holding hands across the three-foot gap between their beds.

The phone rang at six in the morning. Billy's heart stopped. Annie answered.

"Thank you," she said into the phone, and hung up. "My wake-up call," she said to Billy. "After you fell asleep, I realized I don't have an alarm clock. This is when I get up every morning. I work out for an hour before breakfast. You can go back to sleep."

He tried. She slipped out of bed and into the bathroom. He caught a glimpse of white panties and bra against her golden skin. The fleeting picture stayed in his mind like a retinal afterimage. He heard her peeing and flushing the toilet and washing her face. This was an intimacy he had never imagined. He had never tried to imagine it.

When she came out, she wore a T-shirt and sweat pants. Billy watched her for the full hour, never taking his eyes off her. He was mesmerized. She went from one routine to another—a mixture of stretching, yoga, and weight sets. She worked hard and fast. By the time she was five minutes into the workout, she was sweating hard.

As hard as she worked, there was an ease to her movements, something effortless that was unlike anything Billy had ever seen. He had gotten the idea from his father that exercise was no good unless it hurt; and basketball was a rough, jerky game—much less graceful than the sportswriters said. She was pretty and graceful and strong. Billy knew, as he lay propped up in bed watching her, that he was completely taken with her, but he also knew he was watching something unusual. Annie had the inner grace of a great athlete. Or, if Billy had known about such things, a dancer or an actress.

She talked the whole time. It was nice to have someone watching her. It was nice to have *Billy* watching her. She explained every movement. She counted out loud. She thanked him for the watch for the hundredth time. She waved it at him from her wrist. She was using the stopwatch to time her workout. She could use it to check her pulse. And so on, and so on.

He wondered where she had learned it all. Not in school, certainly. She loved to read, she had said the night before, but she had gone to a lousy school. She had taught herself, he guessed. When she moved and stretched and turned, he saw the muscles of her back in the gap between the T-shirt and sweat pants. Her skin was smooth, glistening with sweat.

There was fine hair in the hollow of her back where the column of her spine rose from the double curve of her hips. There was the same fine hair on her forearms and wrists. When she raised her arms, he could see a light fuzz in her armpits. Her arms and shoulders were beautifully muscled. When she stretched and bent backwards, the muscles in her stomach rippled like sand under clear water. Every muscle and tendon stood out but moved and joined with every other.

By the end of the hour her clothes were soaked with sweat. Her T-shirt clung to her back and chest. Her hair was dark with sweat. The waistband and cuffs of her white sweat pants were wet. Sweat stains darkened the crotch. The whole room smelled of her sweat—a dense, living smell. She wasn't wearing a bra. Her breasts were small and hard, nothing but two points of muscle lifting and falling under the T-shirt. Every time she turned to face him she grinned at him, her braids flying as she moved.

In her matter-of-fact voice, breathing hard, she said, "I usually just wear my bikini bottoms when I work out. When it's hot like this. But I can't in front of you."

She stopped as suddenly as she had started and went into the bathroom to take a shower. He lay in bed listening to the water running and splashing. She was singing. He quickened with feelings he had never dreamed, and confusion and happiness.

Sunday was hot and bright. The streets were empty. The sky above the buildings was blue with a few high windswept clouds. Billy's confusion lifted, but his happiness was so sharp it ached in him as he walked hand in hand with Annie across 47th Street toward Fifth Avenue.

She wouldn't let him eat breakfast before mass. "It's not right," she said. "Even if they don't care anymore." So they ate afterwards in a coffee shop near the cathedral. Billy broke another hundred to pay for the meal. In this Fifth Avenue neighborhood, the cashier didn't seem to think a kid his age with a hundred-dollar bill was anything special.

Outside, Annie asked, "Where did you get all this money, Billy? Is it yours?"

He shrugged. "It's mine," he said.

"I'll never be able to pay you back."

"I don't care. It doesn't bother me."

"It bothers me, I think."

"You'd do the same."

"Yes."

"Then don't worry about it."

"OK." She grinned. She was six inches shorter than him, but he was several inches over six feet. Tall, slender, straight, with the good looks that come from both bone structure and personality, she was strikingly attractive even by New York standards. People turned to look at her.

Billy was stunned by her, but her open affection for him and her matter-of-fact honesty protected him from the consequences of his sudden vulnerability; his own common sense and single-mindedness found a match in hers. As innocent as they were, they were both survivors, and more. Each of them was somehow well equipped for what they had set out to do for themselves. Together, their chances for success were multiplied, or so their instincts told them. They both sensed that they could each trust the other to stand fast.

"I have a lot of money," said Billy, "but it may have to last us a long time, and it's very expensive where we're staying. And besides, I don't like to spend it for no reason, you know?"

She agreed.

"So unless I make contact with my father, we'll look for a cheaper place to live."

"Monday," she said. "And I'll start looking for a job."

"What about your age?"

"It might be a problem," she acknowledged. "But they might not care in a restaurant."

"I think they might," he said. "We'll have to think about that."

"What happens if you find your father?"

"I don't know. Sometimes I'm not sure I want to find him."

"Why not?"

"Because of something he did to me, and because of you."

She grinned. "That's the way I feel too. About going home. And about you."

He looked around. "There's a pay phone over there. I'm going to try that number again. If there's no answer, I'm going to call a couple of numbers in Washington. Then we can go sightseeing like tourists."

Annie giggled. "OK. Hurry up. I always wanted to do this, since I was a little girl."

"You still are."

She looked hurt for a moment, then giggled again. "Around you, I am."

The phone rang seven or eight times, then there was a faint double click and the phone rang a little louder than before. Billy wondered if the phone had been switched to another line, like the night line at Joe's answering service.

A woman answered. "Four two two three," she said.

"That's the number I'm calling," said Billy, never having heard someone answer a telephone this way.

"Yes, I know. And you've reached it. Can I help you?"

"I want to speak to Mr. Perr-us, please."

"Who?"

Shit, thought Billy. I can't pronounce his name right.

"Mr. Pear-ux?"

"You're asking me?"

"Just a minute." Billy held the card out to Annie, covering the receiver of the phone with his hand. "How do you say this name?"

"Perry-you," she said. "I took a year of French."

"Perry-you," said Billy into the phone.

"Oh, Mr. Perrieux," said the woman. "And who's calling, please?"

"Billy Ball." He took a deep breath.

"One moment please." There was more clicking. A man came on the line.

"Billy?"

"Yessir."

"We're very glad to hear from you. We were very worried."

"Where's my father?"

"He's with us. In fact, he's out of touch at the moment because he's out looking for you. You sound close. Are you in New York City?"

"Yes."

"Very good. Tell me where you are, and I'll send someone to pick you up right away."

There was something about this man's voice that Billy didn't like. "Who is this?" Billy asked.

"Paul Perrieux. I work with your dad." It was the voice of someone trying to put someone else at ease. Billy remembered hearing Mike make a remark about someone named Paul the day they went out in the boat. It was a remark Billy wasn't supposed to hear. Billy couldn't remember the remark, but it was clear Mike didn't like whoever it was. And Joe had listened to Mike that day, and trusted him.

"Billy? Are you there?"

"Yessir. I'm in a phone booth on the corner of Fifth Avenue and Fiftieth Street."

There was a moment's silence. "Can you see the buildings in Rockefeller Center?"

"Yes."

"In the block between Fiftieth and Forty-ninth on Fifth, there are a pair of buildings, twins, about five or six stories high, separated by a wide promenade that runs back in from Fifth Avenue to a sunken café. Over the café is a huge gilded statue of Prometheus. Can you see it?"

"No, but I know what you mean. I walked by there."

"Good. Right inside that promenade in the building on your left as you face the statue is a French bookstore."

"I saw it."

"Very good. Go right now and wait there."

"OK."

"My man will be there in twenty minutes. What are you wearing?"

"Jeans and a sweat shirt." Billy left out the pack.

"Are you alone?"

"Ah, yes."

"Good. How did you get to New York?"

"Ah, by train."

"Where did you stay?"

"With a friend."

"Good. We can talk about all that when we meet. I'm very glad you called, dear boy. We'll be right there."

Billy hung up and turned to Annie. "I don't like this, but come on." He took her hand and pulled her around the corner. He saw the French bookstore. They ran across Fifth Avenue through a break in traffic.

As soon as he got to the entrance of the store, which was closed, Billy's instincts took over. The promenade was wide, with low marble planters down the center filled with lovely flowers, and benches around them. At the edge of the planters were small bronze statues of muscular male and female figures riding the backs of fish. The nude bodies of the nymphs made Billy think of Annie's body.

People sat on the benches. Tourists took pictures of each other. The promenade sloped slightly down away from Fifth to the café, which was a level below the promenade in a kind of well in the center of the circle formed by the original buildings of Rockefeller Center. The café was an ice rink in winter. It was a pleasant and peaceful urban scene.

It was a trap. They were inside the promenade. People could block both ends.

"C'mon," said Billy, pulling Annie away from the window full of books about French wine and maps of the French wine country.

"What's wrong?"

"Hurry. But walk fast, don't run."

They hurried across Fifth Avenue again, in front of Saks Fifth Avenue.

"Faster." Billy broke into a trot. They crossed Fiftieth and ran up the broad stairs to St. Patrick's. There was a crowd of mass-goers and tourists on the upper plaza before the huge doors. He pulled her into their midst.

"Now wait," he said, and turned to watch the promenade.

Four men in dark suits stood in a group at the entrance of the promenade. A large van pulled up to the curb and two more men got out. The van's windows were smoked glass. The men gesticulated and looked around. Another man, tall and rangy, wearing Levi jeans and jacket, cowboy boots and dark sunglasses, ran up out of the promenade to join them. He pointed at the cathedral. The men began running toward the cathedral in a loose phalanx. People on the street began to stop and watch.

"Oh, God," said Billy. "Cowboy. Get inside."

He led her back into the immense cathedral and down the side aisle on the north side, past the side altars. They broke through a small knot of Japanese tourists listening to a guide talking quietly in precise, careful English. Billy moved as fast as he dared, his hand clamped on Annie's. At the transept, he turned left and led her out the side door on the north, and down the steps to the sidewalk on 51st Street.

"Now run," he said. "As fast as you can."

They ran to Madison and up a block, then across 52nd. They ran full tilt across Park Avenue and over to Lexington. This was a deserted neighborhood of office skyscrapers. Billy looked back.

"I think we lost them. I don't know where we are. Let's go down this street."

They ran hard, loping covering ground fast. At 51st Street, Annie shouted, "Subway." They darted down the steps, jumping three at a time, holding hands, having fun now like kids in a game.

At the token booth, Billy said, "How much?" He was breathing hard, less from exertion than excitement.

"Sixty cents." The clerk was a middle-aged black woman in Sunday clothes.

"Gimme eight, please." Billy pushed a five-dollar bill through the hole under the glass.

She pushed six tokens back and two dimes.

"Where does this subway go?" asked Billy.

"Where do you want to go?"

"The Staten Island ferry," said Annie.

"The World Trade Center," said Billy.

"Which one?"

"The ferry," said Billy.

The clerk pushed a folded map under the window. "Take this train to Brooklyn Bridge and change for a number six. Take that train one, two, three stops to Bowling Green and get off. That's the ferry. You can walk to the Trade Center from there. Hurry. Here comes the train." She smiled at them.

They smiled back at her and ran through the turnstiles to the train. It roared and rattled into the station, stopped with an ear-splitting screech, then rattled away down the tunnel. Billy and Annie held their ears at the noise, until they realized there was less noise inside the train than out. Then they pulled out their maps and bent their heads together to figure out where they were, and where they were going.

As the train left the station, a large man in a dark suit ran down the stairs from the street. He was sweating and puffing. He flashed a badge at the token clerk.

"Police. Did two kids come in here? A boy and a girl?"

The woman looked carefully at the badge and at the man. Impatient, he said, "Well, did they?"

"No," she said slowly, her face absolutely expressionless. "I ain't seen no two kids, officer."

"Shit." He spun and ran back up the stairs to the street.

She picked up the phone in her booth and dialed a number. "Lieutenant McArthur? A white man in a dark blue suit just left my booth. He flashed a badge at me and asked about two kids, but he didn't look like any police officer to me, and he sure wasn't one of yours. He was too polite."

"No. No kids," she said. "Just a couple of tourists, didn't even know where the Staten Island ferry is." She laughed, gave a description of the phony cop, and hung up. She turned up her radio and went back to her *Daily News*. It was a very slow Sunday, but she didn't mind filling in on holidays. It was overtime.

• • •

On the ferry, in the incredibly beautiful windblown bay, Annie asked, "Aren't you going to call Washington?"

"No. Not now. I can't. I don't know who's who anymore, or who might be listening."

"You mean bugs?"

"I guess that's what I mean."

She turned away from him and leaned over the rail, facing the skyline of lower Manhattan. The twin towers of the World Trade Center stuck up high over the jumbled heap of skyscrapers around Wall Street. The two towers looked like up-ended children's building blocks.

Billy said, "You're going to have to trust me, Annie. It's safer for you. Believe me."

She spoke into the wind. "I believe you, and I trust you. But I don't think I like all this running and not knowing. I just don't like it."

Billy shrugged. There was nothing else he could say.

They walked to the World Trade Center from the south, from Battery Park. The first tower leaned over them like a cliff. Looking up made them dizzy. High clouds blowing from the west made the tower seem to be falling.

"Wow," said Annie. "I think this is the weirdest building I've ever seen."

"I like it," said Billy. "I like this whole place."

Inside, they asked a guard about Perrieux's company. "I have an appointment here in the morning," said Billy. The guard gave them the floor number and added, a bit suspiciously, that it was closed now.

"Do you want to go up to the observation deck instead?" asked the guard.

"Sure," said Billy.

"No, thanks," said Annie. "I've seen enough big buildings. I want to see some people. Where's Greenwich Village?"

They walked up Broadway, past City Hall, and through the deserted court district—somehow the most desolate part of the city they'd seen. They found Chinatown. They ate a late lunch in a Chinese restaurant, ordering one familiar dish—pork lo mein, and one strange dish—chicken with walnuts. It was spicy, but they liked it. Annie drank water, Coke, and tea as though they had walked through a desert to get there. Billy ordered a beer.

"What kind?" asked the waiter.

"Bud," said Billy, as if he'd been ordering beer in restaurants in New York City all his life.

"The age is eighteen in New York State," whispered Annie when the waiter left.

"Oh," said Billy, remembering his little uncorrected lie. "I'm legal here." Then he remembered something else, something he had looked at once, one of those things that doesn't register at the time. He pulled the two passports out of his pack. In both his father's and his own, the dates and places of birth had been changed: Joe was shown as born in Massachusetts, not Wisconsin, and shown as older by two years than he really was. Billy was shown as born in a small town in Ohio, not DC, and his age was given as nineteen.

If he had known how it was done, he would have realized that someone had done considerable work to obtain birth certificates for people who had died not long after they were born, and whose living relatives would be difficult or impossible to trace. If Billy had known, he would have realized these two passports were airtight forgeries, as good as gold.

Then Billy realized that he and Annie were home free. The beer had given him a little buzz. He was very excited.

"We've got it made," he said. He gave her his passport and put Joe's back in the pack. "We can do anything," he said.

When she looked at the passport, her eyes widened and her face darkened. She opened her mouth to speak, but Billy said, *"Shh."*

"Gimme your driver's license," he said.

She pulled it out of her purse and gave it to him.

"We can do it," he said, holding the license in the light.

"Do what?"

"Make you older."

"How?"

"With a razor blade, a magnifying glass, and some rubber cement. And a toothpick."

She stared at him as if he'd gone mad.

"You were born in 1963, but I can make it 1960."

"I don't want to be older than you."

"Then I'll make it 1962."

"How?"

"I'll slice out a two from this long ID number here and replace it with the three from your birth date. I'll glue the two into the date. It'll be impossible to tell. I'll need tweezers, too."

"I have some."

"Good. We'll buy the rest today. And we'll laminate the card in plastic so the little numbers won't fall out."

"Billy, what's going on?"

"You'll be eighteen and you'll be able to get a job."

"But what's going on, Billy?" She was getting angry.

"I'll tell you," he said. "Let's go."

On the way out, he broke another hundred. The cashier turned it over in his hands twice, looked at Billy, and counted out the change. Billy was learning that he could carry almost any act off as long as he didn't stand out too much from the surroundings. In New York, it was hard to stand out. Nobody was surprised by anything.

Walking up Mulberry Street out of Chinatown and into Little Italy, he told her more, enough to dampen her anger and slow the growth of the tumor of lies in his own guts. He told her who Cowboy was, but he didn't tell her about the killings or the loot. He only said that he thought Cowboy was after his father, and had beaten him up as a warning to his father.

"Why didn't you stay home and wait for your father to come back?"

"The others came back again and I ran away."

She said, "You're still not telling me everything. I know you think you're protecting me, but you don't have to do that. I can take care of myself."

"It was my idea to fix your license. You couldn't get a job!"

She turned to him. "Bullshit, Billy. There are a hundred jobs waiting for me in this city right now." She grinned. "A thousand."

Billy shrugged and grinned back. She believed it, and he guessed he did too. If you believed something hard enough, and worked hard enough, you could make it come true. She could find a job, and he could find his father.

But he wasn't sure how hard he believed in finding his father. And he realized that the years of anger and confusion he felt about his father had finally come to the surface, as Father Kelly had always warned. Billy guessed he was really on his own, and knew he hadn't decided just how hard to look for Joe. He knew, too, that he had to decide soon, because the dead bodies and the guns and the loot were going to catch up with him sooner or later. Sooner, he guessed.

"C'mon," she said. She pulled him away up Mulberry Street. "Let's keep walking. I wanna look at more people. This city is a fantastic place."

They wandered all over SoHo and the West Village, up one street and down the other, in and out of galleries and shops. They bought new clothes, from underwear out, and put their old clothes in a shopping bag. They looked like different people in their new clothes. Annie wore a skirt and blouse with a lilac sweat shirt over her shoulders, the arms tied around her neck. Billy wore new Levi's and a white Mexican shirt. He had a new Levi jacket folded into his pack. She had new blue running shoes and he wore new white low-cut Pro-Keds. They both had dark aviator sunglasses. Billy had a dark blue Yankees baseball cap. In a used clothing store, Annie had found a man's straw hat that fit her. It had a wide red and yellow silk band. The two of them looked like a pair from the fashions pages of the Sunday *Times Magazine*.

"One more stop," said Billy. He led her up a flight of stairs into a sporting goods store in a small loft building on Spring Street. He bought a sturdy green climber's pack and stuffed his dirty orange pack inside.

Back down on the street, he said, "You know, if I saw us from a distance now, I might not know who I was. At least, I feel different."

"I think that's like the story about the emperor's new clothes," said Annie. "But you look nice. You look like that man you called Cowboy."

Late in the afternoon, they found themselves at the corner of Sixth Avenue and West 4th Street in the middle of Greenwich Village. It was a busy corner. The sidewalks were crowded, and the avenue was thick with traffic. The Sunday evening

homeward rush from the holiday had begun. Down the avenue
a little bit, on the east side, were several playgrounds—asphalt
basketball courts enclosed by high chain-link fences. There
were a few benches inside the fence along the sidelines by the
sidewalk.

On one court, some young white kids were fooling around
and shooting hoops. On the other court, there was a furious
game of full-court three-on-three. All the players were black.
These were older guys, in their late teens and early twenties.
A handful of others sat on the benches, their backs against the
fence along the street. A huge suitcase radio blared from the
bench into the court.

Billy stopped to watch. The black teams were fairly evenly
matched, except for the tallest player on the team defending
the uptown basket. He played very rough, in a game already
as physical as football. His team kept a steady advantage of
three or four points as the ball went back and forth from one
end of the court to the other. They did it, Billy observed,
because the big man took most of the rebounds. It wasn't his
height; it was his speed and strength. When he planted himself,
he was immovable.

Time after time, play after play, one of the other team,
trying to drive by him, would stagger out of control as the big
guy slammed into them. He cleared his zone with his elbows
and hands the way a hockey goalie clears the crease with his
stick.

Finally, one of the others went down. He bounced up with
blood streaming from his nose. He was hopping and prancing
in fury.

"Muthafucka," he screamed. "I ain't playin' with you no
mo."

The big man said, "Aw, shit, Jimmy. Shut your mouth and
play."

The other threw a ten-dollar bill down on the asphalt and
walked to the benches. He picked up a towel and headed for
the water fountain, talking to himself, muttering. No one else
said or did anything.

"Git in here, Soda Pop," said one of the players, motioning
to one of the bench sitters. Soda Pop shook his head.

No one moved. The big man turned and began shooting
foul shots.

Billy said, "Here, Annie." He handed her his pack. "Put it on your back and pull the straps tight. Fasten the waist belt tight too." He handed her his sunglasses. "Now you're gonna see what I like to do. Come inside the fence but stay by the gate."

He walked through the fence and onto the court. "My name's Billy. Can I play?"

"Shee-it," said one of the players, turning away in disgust.

"That's the white boy's court, over there," thumbed one of the others.

"*Can* you play?" said the big man. "That's the question."

"Ten bucks says I can," said Billy.

"You're skins," said the big man.

There were a few mutters from the others but no more discussion. Billy handed his shirt to Annie. She looked dubious.

The other two skins gave ten-dollar bills to the other team.

"Start over. New game. Your out," said the big man. He flipped the ball to Billy and backpedaled down the court.

Billy stepped out. One of the shirts rushed him. Billy flipped the ball in a short arc over the man's head. A skin grabbed it, bounced twice, and flipped the ball fast up-court into the corner. Billy cut through the slot behind the big man, took a hard pass, and laid the ball into the net.

"Shee-it," said one of the skins. "You play inside on defense. Don't let that big muthafucka shoot."

There was a braying laugh from the sideline, audible over the noise of the huge radio. "Gonna *have* his white ass," screamed someone.

The big man took a pass from the side and drove down on Billy like a bulldozer. Billy stepped to the side and slapped the ball loose. A hand whizzed past his ear like a stone. Annie squealed. Billy tipped the ball to one of his men. "Yo!" screamed the other skin. "Yo, yo, yo!" The man with the ball shot it up-court to the screamer, and the screamer drove past a shirt for an easy lay-up.

"Shee-it," said two voices from the bench.

The game went back and forth. Billy had never played rougher ball. The first time he tried a jump shot near the big man, the man slammed an elbow into Billy's gut as Billy went up and the man pivoted for the rebound. Billy almost puked.

There were few called fouls. The game was pure intimidation. A foul was sometimes called when all six players were breathing so hard they could barely move. The foul shot would go up in a slow arc. There would be a vicious fight under the basket for position, or for the rebound. The game was all fast-break, cut, pick, shoot, and rebound. It was all elbows, hands, shoulders, hips, and feet.

Billy couldn't move the big man out of the way, but Billy's reach was a little longer, and he found he could go up over the man from behind or the right. The man was right-handed and tended to reach for the ball with his right, allowing Billy to get in a little closer while the hand was occupied. Billy managed to take the ball away from the man enough to cut the other team's advantage in rebounds.

Billy shot less and began to feed the other two skins. One of them was the screamer: "Yo, yo, yo, yo!" But he only screamed when he was open. The other was a skinny guy with a big Afro and fast hands. He looked to be about Billy's age, and looked like he was going to get a lot taller and bigger.

The skinny kid scored. "Nineteen-eighteen!" he shouted. *"Get* that ball."

The big man drove down on Billy again. Billy stepped aside, but the man straightened up right under him to jump and shoot. Billy slapped the ball from the bottom. It hit the man in the face. His forearm slammed into Billy's head like a piece of board. Off balance, Billy swung as hard as he could. His fist caught the man behind the ear and the man went down.

There was a whoop from the bench, then total silence on the court. All that could be heard were the radio and the cars in the street.

Looking down at the man, breathing as hard as a racehorse, Billy said, "There are limits." He set himself for what he knew was coming.

"Shee-it," said the skinny kid from close behind. "The last dude that put him down was a big nigger played second string for the Knicks, used to play down here last summer."

The big man put his hand out to be pulled up. Billy pulled him up. The man stood very close to him, holding Billy's hand like a vise. "You got more balls than brains, white Billy-boy." He turned and walked away. The bench began to jabber. Billy turned and glanced at Annie, and rolled his eyes. His knees were shaking.

"You had the last foul," said the big man. "Our ball."

They passed in, there was a jump shot, and that was the game.

"I don't mind losin' that one," said the skinny guy. "That was worth a dime."

"Again," said the big man.

They played two more games. The skins won one and lost one. Billy was down ten dollars. Annie was sitting on the bench next to the guy named Soda Pop. The radio was his. She had the shopping bag between her feet and the pack snug on her back.

"No more," said Billy, wiping himself with a towel. "We gotta go."

"I'm Bro," said the big man.

"I'm Yo," said the screamer.

"I'm Bobby," said the skinny kid.

"I'm Annie," said Annie.

"We're down here every day," said Bro. "This is where we play."

"You wanna game," said Yo, "you come downtown."

"Where your from?" asked Bro.

"Washington," said Billy.

"Dee-Cee," said Yo, "My mama's from Dee-Cee. Too hot for me in the summer."

"You?" said Bro to Annie.

"Watervliet."

They all shook their heads.

"Upstate," she said.

"Too cold," said Yo. "Sixth Avenue and West Fourth Street's just right for me."

That night in the hotel, Billy altered Annie's driver's license. Around ten o'clock, they walked down through Times Square to one of the storefront arcades and had the license laminated. It was a perfect job.

"Now you're all set," said Billy.

"I was all set before," said Annie. "But thanks anyway."

"In the morning," said Billy, "I wanna buy us two cheap wedding rings, so we look married. Nobody's gonna believe that brother and sister story anymore. Then we have to find a cheaper room in one of those small hotels around here. And you can start looking for a job."

"I'll look in those little restaurants downtown," she said.

"And I'm gonna look for that guy Perry-you," said Billy. "I need to know more about him."

"What about your father?"

"He'll find me," said Billy. "If he wants to."

They walked back to the hotel through the late-night crowds. Times Square was always crowded, and it got more crowded the later the hour.

In their room, they fell asleep holding hands again, as they had the night before.

THIRTEEN

JOE STOOD IN the middle of the lobby of the Edison Hotel. He stared out the front entrance toward the street, frustrated and angry at missing Billy and the girl by half an hour. Now the trail was broken and he had no idea where to pick it up. He did know one thing—he was looking for the boy for reasons of his own that had nothing to do with the boy's safety or welfare.

Looking for Billy had helped Joe forget that he himself was on the run, although Joe nagged himself with the thought that his son would be better off without him. Joe had dragged the boy into a swamp. On his own, Billy might be able to get himself out. And Father Kelly, thought Joe, could help the kid—the priest has already helped Billy far more than I ever did.

I'm like a drunk, thought Joe, trapped in my own needs and addictions. Raw love is like a craving for booze—it's a need. It takes, it doesn't give. What have I given Billy? A collection of my needs—money and violence. But I need help now, and where else can I turn? Billy was the only person on earth who could help him.

Joe walked to a bank of phones at one side of the lobby.
There was one place where he might pick up Billy's tracks.

He dialed Lazard's number and asked for Diane. He knew
he was probing too hard. He was unsure of Diane's motives,
which were obscure, and which he had been content to leave
unexplored up to now. The reaction might be violent, but Lazard
was the only remaining lead to Billy, and the reaction of Diane
and Lazard might tell Joe some of what he needed to know.

"I almost had them," said Joe, when she came on the line.
"They left a trail as wide as the highway, right into the Edison
Hotel."

"Are they there now?"

"They checked out at eight-thirty this morning."

"They?"

"Billy and a girl he met on the bus from DC."

"Did they leave an address?"

"No. That's why I called. Did Billy call Perrieux and
Company this weekend looking for me?"

"I don't know."

"Check and call me back."

"Where are you?"

"On second thought, I'll call you."

"Where are you?" she insisted.

"Ah, the corner of Forty-second and Eighth."

"The Port Authority?"

"I came back down here to look around."

"Give me the number of your pay phone."

"I'll call you. I wanna keep moving."

She hung up. Joe bolted out of the phone booth and across
the hotel lobby. A few moments later he was standing in the
shadows of the deep-set stage door of a theater down the street,
from where he could watch the hotel entrance.

In another bank of pay phones across the Edison lobby, Volko
was reporting to Mike: "We picked Joe up at the bus station
here this morning. Harry spotted him showing photos to a cop
on Eighth Avenue, a guy on a fixed post. We think Joe tracked
Billy to this hotel, but we haven't checked at the desk ourselves.
Joe came straight here from the cop at the bus terminal."

"Stay with Joe," said Mike. "Kurt and Philly took the first

train this morning. They should be at Penn Station soon. They've got some hardware and tools you're gonna need, and more money. When they call in, I'll send them to the hotel to try to pick up the boy's trail."

"The boy might be here now."

"Joe would have gone up to his room."

"Maybe."

"What's Joe doing now?"

"Talking to a pay phone across the lobby from me."

"It's him I'm interested in. Stay with him. Has he made you yet?"

"No."

"You and Harry stick with Joe. I'll worry about the kid. I'm trying to do Joe a favor, and I can't help him if I don't know where he is, right?"

"He's going, Mike. Gotta go." Volko hung up. Joe was already out on the street. Harry stood in a coffee-shop window across the street. Volko pointed at Joe's back and motioned for Harry to follow. Volko and Harry changed sides of the street, crisscrossing. This was going to be tough, thought Volko. Two on one was never enough, and Joe knew both of them. But they were very good.

Joe didn't spot them. He was watching a van with smoked glass windows drive into the far end of the block off Broadway. It stopped at the curb. The side door opened, and a man in a business suit got out, followed by a man who looked like a ranchhand. They hurried into the Edison. A few minutes later, they emerged and ran back to the van.

Joe knew his probe had worked. An empty taxi came down the street from the direction of Broadway. Joe dove at it. "When that van passes you, follow it," he said. "Not too close, but don't lose it at a light."

"*Sí,*" said the driver, a grin on his face. "That weel be twenty dollars up front, plees, meester."

Joe scowled and dropped the money over the back of the seat. New York was worse than the Middle East.

• • •

Shit, thought Volko. This is worse than Tokyo. He stepped back into a doorway and watched the van pull away from the curb and speed down the street. He tried to pull an empty cab down the block for him and Harry by mental telepathy. It was even easier to get a cab in Tokyo.

In a phone booth next to St. Patrick's, on East 50th Street, just off Fifth, Joe called Diane again.

"Any luck?" he asked.

"He called Sunday morning. He was asked to come to a meeting, but, ah, left the site quickly before the meeting started. He may have tried to call Saturday night, but hung up without saying anything."

"Who did he talk to?"

"Mr. Perrieux."

"Where are you in all this?"

"Right where I've always been."

"Where's that?"

"This is not the time or place for an explanation."

"I may come to see you tonight."

"I'm not sure I'll be home. Call me later."

Joe hung up. A little flame of the old anger burned steadily in his stomach like a pilot light. It felt good. It wouldn't take much more to set off an explosion.

The van had disappeared down into a garage on West 50th Street under the Associated Press Building in Rockefeller Center. This mystified Joe, or rather, he reflected, completed his mystification.

He crossed the street and went up the steps into the cathedral. Inside, he sat in a pew in the back and tried to sort out his next step. He had lost his wife and daughter. He had lost his job. He had lost his sense of the way the world worked. Now he had lost his son.

In the perpetual dusk of the cathedral, Joe slid to his knees and hid his face with his hands. He could hear a low murmur from somewhere nearby, someone praying, or someone talking. Joe tried to say a prayer for Billy. He gave up. He had lost his faith long before he lost all the rest. Then he remembered a saying attributed to St. Alphonsus Liguori: "The man who prays is surely saved." Joe managed to pray for Billy to pray for him.

That was the best he could do. He went down the steps to the bright street. He looked for an unused pay phone. He had figured out his next step. It would be his last. Like an old fox, he would lead the hunters and the hounds away from the den where the kits where hiding.

Early Monday morning had been difficult for Billy—difficult and wonderful. Annie leapt out of bed in her white underwear and returned from the bathroom in T-shirt and sweat pants. Billy watched her work out with avid attention. He was in an agony of feelings.

As she sang in the shower afterward, he diagnosed his feelings as love and physical desire. The physical part was easy to figure out—he had an erection. He had to draw his knees up to make a tent of the sheet.

The other part was harder to figure out, but he did it by a process of elimination. His feelings for Annie were strong and pleasant. He had never had such feelings for anyone else. They were unlike his feelings for his mother, or sister, or Joe.

These feelings had an object. The object was Annie—not only her body, but her presence, her whole person, her companionship. Her face. Her grin. It must be *love*. It couldn't be anything else. It made him very happy.

He jumped out of bed and dressed quickly while she was in the bathroom. When she came out, she wore only a towel wrapped around under her armpits. His knees nearly buckled. She gave him a strange look, picked up her clothes, and went back in to dress.

They checked out, found a cab, and went to Grand Central Station, where they stowed their stuff in a coin locker. It was the morning rush hour, and the station was jammed with a swirling mass of people. They agreed to meet by the locker at five-thirty. Then they would find a cheap hotel in midtown, if there was such a thing. Billy was sure there was.

Annie kept the locker key. Armed with maps, a notebook, and her altered driver's license, she intended to spend the day in the Village looking for a job, and inspecting dancing and acting studios. As if she were a commuter herself, she kissed Billy good-bye and marched purposefully toward the Lexington Avenue subway, to go to Astor Place.

High as a kite, Billy headed through the mob in the main concourse of the huge station. He found the shuttle and took it to Times Square. He changed to the Seventh Avenue Local and took it down to the World Trade Center. He got out at Cortlandt Street. He and Annie were both learning their way around. They were fast learners.

Joe had to walk down to 46th Street before he found a vacant pay phone. They were all full of salesmen making appointments. He called Lazard at the Perrieux number in the World Trade Center.

"Why are you still in New York, Joe?" asked Lazard.

"You know damn well why."

"You have a lot to straighten out, Joe. At the moment, you're badly damaged goods."

"Want me to go public?"

"With what, Joe?"

"You."

"I don't have time to see you this morning."

Joe hung up. He called Diane.

When she answered, he said, "Tell him I'm serious."

"About what?"

"Just tell him that."

In a moment, Lazard came back on the line. "Eleven o'clock," he said. "Room 2500 in the RCA Building."

Lazard hung up. I should have guessed, thought Joe. I've got time for breakfast and some reconnaissance.

Wearing his new clothes, Billy walked into Perrieux's offices at nine-thirty. In his hand he carried a number ten business envelope addressed to Perrieux. It was inscribed, "Hand Deliver Only.'"

The receptionist said, "Oh, you can leave it here. We'll take it to him."

"Can't," said Billy. "It says right here, 'Hand Deliver Only.'"

"Well, you don't expect him to come out here to get it himself?" She was annoyed.

"That's what they told me." Billy had felt cool and nerveless, but suddenly remembered the menace in Perrieux's voice on the telephone. Billy began to sweat.

"You're a pain in the ass," said the young woman. "He's up at Rockefeller Center this morning. Twenty-five hundred RCA Building. Our midtown offices. Take it up there yourself."

"I will," said Billy. He felt reprieved.

Rockefeller Center, he thought. That explains how Cowboy showed up so fast at the French bookstore. He was coming from a hundred yards away. For the first time, Billy had a sense of the power of his adversary's team, and the strength of their bench.

For the first time, he admitted to himself that he was (1) completely out of his depth, (2) a little bit intimidated, and (3) in danger of losing his nerve. He began to think seriously about going into hiding with Annie for a while, finding a job or finding a school he could go to, living off his money. When he got down to the lobby of the World Trade Center, he decided to eat some breakfast before he took the subway back uptown. He needed some time to think about his next move.

Joe walked into the RCA Building under a red canopy marked 30 ROCKEFELLER PLAZA. Inside, he faced a long black marble reception desk. Behind the desk sat a loud woman in a blue suit. It wasn't a uniform, but she wore it like one. She had brittle, dyed blond hair. She was about fifty. She shouted into a phone. Then she shouted rude instructions at a messenger. She ignored as long as possible a well-dressed older man carrying a thin, expensive briefcase in one hand and his hat in the other.

Above the desk and the woman was a huge mural of bizarre titans and grotesquely muscled slaves and workers raising gigantic statues with primitive machines of wooden tripods, pulleys, and ropes. The mural was all tans, ochers, and grays. A behatted Abe Lincoln and a balding man in a modern business suit gave a hand. Joe wondered if the muralist had meant the old man to be an ikon of John D. Rockefeller. It was a mean trick.

Directly over Joe's head, another huge titan was painted on the ceiling, with its feet planted trompe-l'oeil style on two pillars that flanked the doors to the street. The titan's featureless crotch hung directly over the entrance. He and two titan helpers were using a great crude beam to set two painted hourglasses on the pillars. Time was apparently running out. Around and over the titans were flights of 1930s airplanes in a spiraling vortex of contrails and clouds.

If there was a specific message here, Joe didn't get it, but in general it was an ominous, cryptic, unsettling message about power from some dead muralist. A plainclothes security man walked to the desk. He reached over the chest-high top and took the phone from the woman without asking. She gave him a resentful look. The man wore a beeper on his belt. A gun bulged over his right hip under his suit jacket. As the man talked on the phone, he turned and looked at Joe, then hung up and walked out of sight.

Joe walked slowly around the banks of elevators to the right. There were guard desks at the entrances to the elevator banks for floors two to twelve and fourteen to twenty-seven. There was no thirteenth floor. There were no guards blocking access to the three banks for floors twenty-eight to sixty-nine, but a few guards watched the area.

There were more murals over the elevator banks. An immense steam engine hurtled over a trestle, while below it, enslaved workers harnessed into wooden traces with horses pulled a huge racheted machine of indeterminate purpose. Perhaps it was a crane. Huddled lines of broken people on some sort of exodus struggled over the elevator bank for fourteen to twenty-seven. In a village of desert forts and pillboxes, slaves were being whipped and unshackled. A naked man in a felt hat stirred an iron pot of food or medicine. A man standing on the end of a long gun tube was about to heave a small, naked child down a precipice into confused masses of people who looked like immigrants.

Joe thought about Diane. He had no idea who she was working for, or what her motives were regarding himself. Probably confused, like his own. His best guess was that she was working for the Agency in the most sensitive area the Agency touched—domestic politics, where the Agency was not supposed to tread, ever. He guessed her job was a kind of Nantucket sleigh ride—trying to manipulate, control, infiltrate, report on, analyze, or whatever she could manage of any and all of the above. In her job there would be no rules except deniability. People like Senator McCagg would "know" who she worked for, but would be unable to "prove" it. And presumably she would have enough on them to keep them in line. She would be expected not to make mistakes, not even one.

The point would not be the preservation of the Republic, but the preservation of the Agency. It worked both ways. For people like McCagg, Gold, and Lazard, she would be their line into the Agency if they acquired enough power to tip the scales in their own favor. For them, too, the only rule was deniability. The Agency was an organization of great potential power in domestic politics. It had always been so. Joe had stumbled like a sleepwalker into one of the battles for influence that were constantly fought on the fringes, like the nightly firefights on the perimeter of a base camp in Vietnam.

Joe wanted out, but he had to protect Billy, and protect himself as he withdrew. He had to trade up—to free himself as much as possible from Lazard, then see what McCagg really wanted, and find out what Diane was after in the long run. He felt a tenderness in her, odd under the armor of manipulation and power plays. She understood him. He wanted that. He wanted understanding. For him, understanding was all the forgiveness he would ever find.

Joe walked under the huddled lines of broken men and women, gave his name to the guard, and took the elevator to the twenty-fifth floor. It was exactly eleven o'clock.

This was a law office, paneled in dark wood. Dark oil paintings of dead partners hung on the walls. The receptionist was a middle-aged French woman. The firm was McCarry, Lazard, Thomas & Hammer. Joe was forced to wait fifteen minutes. He amused himself by reading *Forbes* and *Elle*. *Forbes* was somewhat better written and more interesting.

Lazard himself came out to escort him in. "Your boy," said Lazard when they got to his office, "is a chip off the old block. He showed up at my downtown office at nine-thirty this morning, dressed like a cowboy. He had a letter for me, marked 'Hand Deliver Only.' He must have learned a few things from you, Joe. He was wearing a backpack. I don't doubt that is where he carries the silenced .22 automatic with which he shot George Stewart and the wife of the man you shot.

"Oh, Joe," said Lazard. "You're in way over your head,

and you're pulling your boy down with you. What are you
going to do?"

"That's why I'm here," said Joe, feeling the touch of the
old rage in his guts.

"Well," said Lazard. "We'll talk until noon, then have another little lunch with Julius."

"What about Diane?"

"She has a prior engagement," said Lazard.

Lazard's midtown office was furnished like the one in the
World Trade Center, with antiques from eighteenth-century
France. He perched his fingers together in the shape of a steeple
before his triple chin. He peered over his Directoire desk at
Joe.

Joe began to speak, but Lazard held his hand up. "I know
what you're going to say, Joe. You're going to say, 'Leave my
boy out of this.' But it wasn't me who dragged him in."

Joe's angry guilt bubbled in his guts like napalm.

"Joe, it's time we came to a final understanding about who
you work for. Or rather, *why* you're working for who you work
for."

"Tell me," said Joe. His vocal cords felt like cast iron.

"The senator and Julius and I work together. Not perma-
nently, you understand, but at the moment we have a common
cause. Diane has her own loyalties. I believe it's accurate to
say we all use each other when we can."

Lazard is a genius, thought Joe. He's so good at reading
people and situations that he can almost read minds.

Lazard continued. "The senator put you to a little test on
Saturday. On the face of it, you failed, but in fact, you passed
it. You proved that you are for sale to the highest bidder.
Fortunately for us, *and for you,* dear fellow, we are the highest
bidder."

"Then you can drop the fifty thou on me right now," said
Joe. "And tell me what you want done next."

"Admirable, Joe. Admirable."

Lazard poured tea for Joe. They chatted and gossiped. Joe
drank his tea. Lazard fell silent.

After a long time, Lazard's voice came to Joe from a long
distance. It sounded clear and strong, but gave the impression
that Lazard was transmitting from another galaxy. Joe sat qui-

etly in the uncomfortable antique chair and listened to what
Lazard had to say.

"We're going to put you on ice for a while, Joe. You're too
hot. We have to cool you down. And we need time to find
your boy. We want to remove him from harm's way, so you
can do a few jobs for us without worrying who he's running
around with late at night. You know? I wouldn't be surprised
if he comes here today, looking for me. You gave him that
card, remember? And he used it. But he ran away from us
yesterday. He had a little girl with him. We'll find her, too."

Joe couldn't move.

"It's something like Thorazine, Joe. The sort of thing they
use to cool out the thousands of mental patients who wander
around the streets of this insane city. But it's not in the *Physician's
Desk Reference,* if you know what I mean, Joe. It hasn't been
tested by the FDA."

Joe couldn't even nod his head. He wanted to agree with
Lazard. Joe knew that if the drug ever wore off, he would have
a ball of rage in his stomach like a nuclear fireball. He wasn't
sure he wanted the drug to wear off.

"But it *has* been tested, Joe. I assure you, there's no danger."

Danger of what? thought Joe, slowly, slowly. There was a
long, almost endless silence. The receptionist brought in a
contract for Joe to sign. He signed it. Slowly, slowly.

"No need to read it," said Lazard. "Just do as you're told—
a new experience for you, I'm sure—and everything will turn
out all right."

There was another long silence. Lazard did some paperwork
and talked on the telephone. Then Lazard said, "Now we're
going downstairs to meet Julius in his car. Then we're going
to meet an old friend of yours for lunch. Kavenaugh. You
remember him. Now get up and come along with me."

Joe got up and went along.

The point of this, Joe," said Lazard as they waited for the
elevator to take them down, "is that some private agendas are
more equal than others. We would like our private agendas to
be the public agenda someday, and we want you to help us."

Joe stared at the light in the elevator button.

"OK, Joe?"

"OK," said Joe with enormous effort.

At eleven o'clock, Billy stood in a corner of the lobby of the
RCA Building, knowing there was no way he could get past
the guards at the elevators—and knowing he didn't want to
try. He looked at the weird murals. They made him uncomfortable. He walked through the lobby toward the back of the
building and down some stairs into the underground concourse
under Rockefeller Center.

He came up through the next building north—the Associated Press Building. He jaywalked across Rockefeller Plaza
past the parked limousines and the motorcycles of the NBC
couriers. A kid on a bike, with a big canvas bag flapping over
his shoulder, nearly ran him down.

"D'fuck outta d'way," cursed the kid, pumping hard to make
the turn onto 50th Street ahead of a pedestrian.

There were messengers like him all over midtown, pedaling
madly on their bikes through the heavy traffic, or loafing along
near the curb. They cursed at pedestrians, or ignored them, or
shrieked at them with whistles gripped between their teeth.
They locked their bikes to signposts or bike racks in front of
midtown office buildings. They went in and out of every building in town delivering messages and packages.

Billy knew he'd had the right idea to get to Lazard, but a
fake message wouldn't hold up under the tight scrutiny of a
serious guard, like these at Rockefeller Center. The guards at
the World Trade Center had barely looked at him as he walked
by waving the envelope. Here, Billy would have to send a
message, then deliver it himself under the guise of a legitimate
messenger. And what then?

Billy decided to find himself a job as a messenger. That
was perfect logic. Then he could look for Joe, or wait for Joe
to find him. And stay with Annie. Billy decided to hang around
Rockefeller Center for a while and watch the messengers at
work.

They had a style of their own. Most of them were black,
but there were a fair number of whites and Hispanics. A few
Orientals. Some young women. All on bikes. Every kind of
bike—fancy ten-speeds, beat-up old three-speeds, and delivery
tricycles with big bins in front for heavy packages. There were
classes of messengers. The trikes were at the bottom. The fast

ten-speeds with black or orange canvas bags were at the top.

Some of the messengers wore costumes. A black man in a black jumpsuit wore pink and white nylon kneesocks like puttees over his calves. A young black kid rode by on an old but sparkling-clean English three-speed, a Royce restored to perfect condition with original parts. It was like the work of an antique-car buff. The rider wore the summer uniform of the wartime British army—tan shirt, shorts, kneesocks, brown oxfords—but on his head he wore a cheap plastic mesh baseball cap in the square shape and black and yellow stripes of the Pittsburgh Pirates. The cap's bill stuck out over his right ear.

But costumes weren't mandatory. Most of the messengers wore the ordinary clothing of summer street life—baseball caps, T-shirts, cutoffs or jeans, and sneakers. There was probably a complicated underlying sociology of messengers, but Billy didn't see it and wasn't interested. He saw that he would fit in perfectly. Maybe that was all the sociology there was to see.

Rockefeller Plaza was more shadow than light, but as the morning drew toward noon the patches of hot sun grew larger. Billy sat on a low retaining wall around a planter full of red flowers at the corner of the International Building at 50th and Rockefeller Plaza. He watched the crowd thicken into a lunch-hour mob. The flags fluttered around the sunken café. People sat near him, eating their lunch. The three short blocks of Rockefeller Plaza, from 48th to 51st, were reserved for the limos and couriers, and the few taxis delivering riders to the canopied doors of the great gray-stone buildings of the Center. Little white signs on stanchions along the curb said PRIVATE STREET. NO PARKING.

A limousine pulled up to the red canopy of the RCA Building. Billy watched the car with interest. It was a white Rolls-Royce, pristine and beautiful. Two men walked out of the building in the deep shadow under the canopy. One of the brown-uniformed doormen hurried forward to open the car door for them. The taller man bent forward and stepped into the back seat of the car. He was helped by the other man. The other man hesitated a moment. He was heavy, dressed in a dark suit that hung on him perfectly, neither emphasizing nor hiding his considerable weight. He gestured up the sidewalk toward the AP Building.

It was like a movie. Billy was paralyzed with fear and anger. It was Joe getting into the white car. The heavy man's gesture was directed at Cowboy, who stood almost directly across the plaza from Billy, but whose attention was focused entirely on the white car. Cowboy held a black motorcycle helmet under his arm—the kind worn by cops, with leather earpieces and a visor over the eyes. At the gesture, he put it on and straddled a heavy Harley-Davidson motorcycle parked by the curb. It started with a roar that echoed in the narrow street. He looked like one of the NBC couriers.

"Dad," screamed a voice in Billy's brain. *"Dad. DAD."* But nothing came out. It was a silent movie. The big man got in the car. The car pulled away from the curb in perfect silence. Through the smoked glass of the side windows of the car, Billy saw the dim shapes of three men in the back seat. Joe was in the middle.

The car turned the corner onto 50th street and moved east with the stately elegance of a ship. Cowboy made a fast U-turn on the motorcycle, passing only six feet from Billy. He looked at Billy. Billy saw a look of surprise and recognition on Cowboy's face. With deafening noise, the cycle sped after the car and disappeared across Fifth Avenue past St. Patrick's Cathedral.

Billy leapt up and screamed *"DAD!"* so loud that hundreds of heads whipped around to look at him. Two men running for a waiting cab on 50th street stopped and gawked at Billy, then jumped into the cab. It took off, running a red light on Fifth and scattering pedestrians like chickens. Billy looked around him. The plaza was full of men in suits on their lunch hour. Half of them were staring at him. Some of them seemed to be moving toward him. He ran.

He didn't run far. He had already learned that running pell-mell down a crowded sidewalk in midtown New York was a sure way to attract attention. Even in Washington, a city of uniforms, there were not so many uniformed guards and police as there were in Manhattan.

When he stopped, he was at the corner of Sixth Avenue and 47th Street, at the edge of the diamond district. He and Annie had walked past some of these shops and arcades during the weekend, but they were closed then and their windows were empty. Now the windows were full of glittering rings and stones on velvet cloth under brilliant lights. The sidewalks and shops were full of people, all talking or looking.

He stepped into one of the larger shops. It was brightly lit. There wasn't a shadow in the place. If a tiny diamond chip dropped into the dust in a corner on the floor behind the counter, it would sparkle in the light and be found in an instant.

There were trays of rings, necklaces, and pins of every possible design. Most of the stones were diamonds, but there were rubies, emeralds, sapphires, opals; the settings were gold and platinum. A young man in a white shirt and dark pants, wearing a knitted yarmulke on his head, walked along behind the counter toward Billy. He spoke English in an accent Billy didn't know.

"Can I help you?"

"Just looking, thank you."

"For something special?"

"A ring, maybe."

"What kind of ring?"

"Engagement."

"How much you have to spend?"

"I want a large stone."

The man went to a counter, unlocked it, and pulled out a tray. He set it on the counter.

"This one," said Billy, pointing to the largest diamond.

"Five thousand dollars. One carat, very fine stone."

"That's not a large stone."

"You're not a serious buyer."

"Thank you," said Billy, and left the shop.

He went into four more shops. He finally convinced a salesman to show him a very good four-carat stone in a gold setting and quote him a price. In the setting, it was worth a hundred and twenty thousand dollars.

Billy walked out to the sidewalk. He went into a deli and bought a hot dog and a can of cream soda. He stood on the sidewalk watching people go by. Many of the men wore ill-fitting black suits and white shirts without ties. Most wore black felt hats. A few wore hats with round flat brims, like Amish hats, made of dark fur that looked to Billy like the fur of a beaver coat his mother once owned.

He guessed, without really knowing, that these men were Jewish and that they were speaking Yiddish or Hebrew. He did not know he was standing in the middle of the most important diamond market in the Western Hemisphere. He did know what he was going to do.

After another thirty minutes of scouting, he returned to a small shop inside one of the arcades that ran through several of the buildings. The shop was not much more than a window over a small counter, with enough space for a work table and two chairs behind it. Two old men in black suits and beaver hats sat talking quietly. When Billy stopped at the window, they stopped talking.

"Yes?" asked one of the men. "You're back? You want to buy?"

"I'd like to sell."

"I thought so," said the man. The other got up and left, saying nothing. "Come in," said the man. The man leaving held the door for Billy. It closed behind him. An electric lock snapped in the door.

"Sit down."

Billy sat.

"Show me, please."

Billy unwrapped one of the diamonds and set it carefully on the table. The old man held a loupe to his eye and held the stone under a jeweler's lamp. He turned the stone in his fingers. His fingers and beard were stained with nicotine.

"This is a very good stone. Is it yours to sell?" He looked at Billy. There was none of the anonymity of the confession box here, but there was the same sense of searching examination.

"Yes."

"You are not Jewish?"

"No."

"But it is wrong to steal no matter who you are."

"Yes."

The old man turned to the stone again. "Where did this come from?"

"My mother gave it to me. She told me to sell it when I needed money for college."

"Where is she now?"

"Dead."

The old man looked at Billy again. "Your father?"

"Gone."

"Do you have identification?"

Billy gave him the passport. The old man looked at it for a moment and handed it back.

"How much do you want?" he asked.

"I don't know what it's worth," said Billy, "except that it's in the ballpark of a quarter of a million dollars."

"No," said the old man. "The ballpark is smaller."

"Why?"

"This stone is very good, but not the very best. To your eye, the difference is invisible. But my eye sees more. This stone was cut in Asia, maybe ten or twelve years ago, in Bangkok, and I can tell you the name of the Chinese man who cut it, but you would not recognize him. Do you believe me?"

"Yes."

"Good, because it is the truth. This cutter was a good technician—he is dead now—but not an artist, and he damaged this stone. He cut it into the wrong shape—square instead of round. The form does not show the stone to its best advantage." He looked at Billy, and said, "Do you understand?"

"I don't know much about diamonds."

"You know nothing, but at least you are honest about it."

Billy shrugged.

The old man said, "I may cut this into smaller stones to sell it. Does that bother you?"

"A little."

"That is the right answer. It should bother you a little, because this stone has a history for you. It has none for me. I will pay you one hundred thousand dollars."

"Not more?"

"That is a good price. Diamond prices are falling fast."

"Cash," said Billy.

"Wait here," said the man, handing the stone back to Billy.

In an hour, the old man had resold the stone in one piece to one of the other old men in the arcade, for a profit of 12 percent, and the stone lay in a small case to be sent to Antwerp that night.

Billy had opened an interest-bearing checking account at the Amalgamated Bank on Broadway in his passport name and Annie's name, promising to return in the morning with Annie's signature on a card, and her social security number. He put $10,000 in the account. He decided not to tell Annie how much money was in the account. He rented a safe deposit box. In it, he put the balance of the money from the diamond—$90,000 in wrapped thousands, plus $5,000 of the worn hundreds, plus Joe's passport and the other diamond. He kept the emerald. Now he felt lighter and less vulnerable. His transaction with the old man had taught him a useful lesson in locating the fine line between honesty and expediency. Billy was getting older faster. He was a natural-born high roller.

Mike's guys were empty-handed and furious at themselves. Harry was talking to Mike on the phone. Volko was too mad to talk.

Mike was not disturbed. "You're shorthanded," he said. "You did the best you could."

Harry, tall and black, sat on the edge of his bed in a room in the Edison. Kurt and Philly slouched in chairs, drinking beer out of cans. There was an open briefcase on the bed. Guns and holsters were scattered on the bed cover. A set of burglar tools in a canvas roll-up lay in the briefcase.

Harry said, "It must be the only white Rolls in the city. We'll find it this afternoon through the dealer here." He held the gold shield and leather case of a New York City detective in his hand. "Joe is another problem."

"It sounds like a snatch," said Mike.

"It looked like one," said Harry. "But we can't figure it. Why would Joe walk into it? He's a smart guy."

"Smart in Laos," said Mike. "Not smart here."

"Yeah, we're not so smart here either. The rules have changed. And there are players we don't know. This guy on the motorcycle."

"He's new to me," said Mike. "Give the badge to Philly. He'll go to the Rolls agency. He and Kurt can look for Joe. You two can do something else."

Harry tossed the badge across the room at Philly, who snapped it out of the air like a second baseman.

Mike said, "I put Pete on this priest, this Father Kelly. They just got on a train for New York. You two meet the train. Stay with this guy. Maybe he'll lead you to Billy."

"Mike, what's in this for you?"

"Nothing special, Harry. I just wanna pull Joe's feet outta the fire, find his kid, do a favor. You know? You know."

"Yeah, I know. See you," said Harry, and hung up. To the room, he said, "Yeah, Mike, I know. Do a favor. Everybody's doin' favors all the time. Everybody's doin' a gum job on everybody else. Doin' favors. Doin' the old circle jerk."

"That Lazard," said Volko to the window. "I'm gonna jerk him."

Father Kelly went straight from Penn Station to an old brick building on West 41st Street. It was a refuge for runaway kids, operated by a Franciscan priest.

Father Kelly went inside and introduced himself. "Father Richter? I'm Father Thomas Kelly from Washington. I'm look-ing for a boy named Billy Ball. He's in real trouble and he needs help. I don't know where to start."

"Don't know him, Thomas," said the other priest. "But stick around and help with dinner. I've got forty-five kids tonight and I'm shorthanded in the kitchen. Then we'll talk."

"I found a job!" Annie was grinning and hopping up and down. "I start tomorrow for lunch. It's the nicest place."

Her thrill was infectious. Billy laughed and held out his arms. They hugged and danced around in a little circle, ignored by the commuters pouring through Grand Central toward their trains.

"I did too," said Billy. "And you won't believe how."

They took her suitcase out of the locker and walked out to 42nd Street. There, locked to a sign pole, was a battered silver ten-speed bike.

"It's mine," said Billy proudly. "I'm a messenger for Bro's Pros."

"Bro?"

"I got my job by playing basketball all afternoon. That guy Bro owns a messenger service. Most of those guys down there work for him."

"That's what he does? I don't believe it."

"Yeah, I didn't either. I asked him about it. He said, 'Hey, babe. That is what I like to do: play ball, drink beer, bet money, work, and get laid.' He said, 'Need money to do all those things. Need money *not* to work, you dig?' He said, 'You ever be black and try to find a job?' I said, 'No.' He said, 'I did. No fuckin' good.' So he set his company up. They were all messengers already. They worked out of a phone booth for six months, then rented a little storefront on West 24th Street. It's full of Spiderman posters. That's it. He said, 'You the first white boy we ever hired. But if you got the legs for this *game,* you got the legs for this *job.* We *hustle.'"*

Billy's imitation of Bro was perfect. Annie giggled. He tied her suitcase to the rack on the back of his bike with rubber stretch cords and they walked slowly west along 42nd Street, laughing and talking, telling each other the stories of their day. They walked up into the West Forties, looking for a cheap hotel.

"*First* we find a place to stay," said Billy. "*Then* we find a place to eat."

"I'm starving," said Annie. "But I agree. Tell me more about seeing your father and that man."

Joe lay on his side, his arms tied behind him around the back of a chair. His ankles were tied to the legs of the chair. He lay where he had fallen when the man finally hauled off and struck the final blow—a roundhouse backhand smash to the side of the head. He had been hurt worse, when the rocket fragments took half the skin off his side in the jungle, but he had never been beaten worse. It went on too long, thought Joe. It wore off the drug. It was supposed to soften me up, but this guy just loves to punch.

There was a strong smell of gas and diesel fuel and oil. POL, thought Joe. I'm in a basement. This is where they store the POL for the vehicles. It must be a subbasement. It was pitch black, at least one level below the street, too far down for a window. He had no idea what time it was, but he didn't think he'd been out too long.

He had probed too far, probed the wrong guy, misunderstood the rules. This wasn't the jungle, where stealth was sometimes a mistake and the bold move often won the battle. He had marched with his men into local warlords' camps and cowed them with threats, gifts, and promises. But his experience wasn't useful here, wasn't *transferable*. that's what they said when they fired him. They were right and he was wrong.

And his ambitions were foolish. He should have spent his loot. Then no one could take it away from him. He should have bought a fishing boat with the gold and taken Billy and gone to Shreveport or Biloxi or the Bahamas or some goddamn place and gone fishing. Period. End of joke.

That's what all the Special Forces team leaders and NCOs had done—the guys he'd fought with. He'd bump into them in a bar in Okinawa and they'd open their black Samsonite PX briefcases full of gemstones. None as good as his own. They went for quantity. His were special. But they got what they wanted—lifetime pensions and medical care after twenty years of Army shit, jungle wars, and MAG missions to Brazil and Chile and other piss-ant places. For their troubles, they paid themselves a nice bonus—their loot bought boats and little ranches, big cars, bars, motels, whatever turned them on.

Joe knew this was outright, open remorse. He was lying on his side in some godforsaken subbasement, hurting like hell, hurting all over, and he was goddamn *sorry*. He had made a terrible mistake, and he was paying for it, and he was *sorry*. He thought about Mike with his bar and his boat, and his Mary, and Joe was *sorry*. He thought about Diane, and he was *sorry* about that, too. He thought about Billy, and he was so sorry he began to weep. Then he thought about Billy some more, and he began to wait. Lazard was right. Billy was a chip off the old block.

In a little residence hotel called the Madrid, on West 48th Street in the block between Ninth and Tenth avenues, Billy stood staring down at the dark street from a window in a room in the front of the fourth floor. The harsh metallic silver glow of the streetlights only darkened the doorways and alleys along the street. Few cars passed. The night glow of the city cast red and bronze light on the underside of the scudding clouds overhead. It was hot and humid. It looked like rain.

The ancient, noisy air conditioner in the other window barely took the edge off the atmosphere. He wondered what the room was like during the day, being on the floor just under the roof.

They were lucky the room faced north. In a south-facing room, the daytime heat would be unbearable.

It was well past midnight. It must have been two or three, no later. The bars were still open.

"Billy?"

She startled him. He had thought she was asleep.

"Are you thinking about your father?"

"Yes."

"He's in trouble, isn't he?"

"I guess so."

"What are you going to do?"

"I don't know. Maybe I'll call someone in Washington in the morning. I don't know."

"Come over here."

Billy sat on the edge of the bed. He put his hand on hers.

She threw the sheet back and pulled him down next to her. She wrapped her arms around him and held him. He held her. Her skin was smooth and warm and damp with sweat. After a long time of slow, gentle, small movements, they began to touch each other and kiss.

They pulled their underwear off. The feelings in Billy were unutterable.

Annie whispered, "I'm not a virgin. Do you care?"

"No."

"Are you?" she asked in his ear.

"Yes."

"Well, that's OK. It doesn't matter. There's nothing to learn. There's only one way to do it anyway, I think."

After a while, she whispered, "I'm safe, I think. I just finished my period this afternoon. But you should wear a rubber."

"I don't have any."

"I bought some this afternoon."

A little while later, they curled up together and fell asleep, still as innocent as lambs.

FOURTEEN ══════════

FATHER RICHTER PUSHED his coffee mug away and lit a cigarette. He blew the smoke out into the empty room. It was a battered, scarred room with posters on the walls for brightness; grimy windows with heavy protective mesh over the outsides; long eating tables and benches. The tables glistened with a film of water from the cleanup the two priests had just finished.

The noise of television and Ping-Pong came from another room. The noise of cars and the heated smell of the street came through the windows, open to the heavy evening breeze from the Hudson River a few blocks west.

Richter said, "He'll be living somewhere in midtown. On the West Side. The trains and buses come into midtown. I'll bet he took the bus. The kids stay around here. They could find cheaper, safer places to live in other neighborhoods, or in the outer boroughs, but all those places are like the places they left. And the people, too."

He waved his hand in a small circle, trailing a little cloud of smoke. "*This* is New York City. *This* is what they came looking for. And *this* is what they find."

"You mean they stay here because they *like* it?"

"You got it, Thomas. They like it."

227

"Lord."

"Yeah." Richter held his hand up to a kid standing in the door. "Five minutes, Joseph. OK?"

The boy nodded and stepped back into the hall.

Richter said, "I don't think anyone likes being beaten, abused, sexually terrorized, pimped, sold, bought, filled with semen like an old Kleenex. No. It's the kind of liking that comes from the deepest sort of passivity, down in the bottom of the mind. It's an awful inner voice that tells these kids, '*This* is what you are. *This* is what you deserve. *This* is what you wanted. *This* is what you found. And *this* is what you're always gonna get. *This* is all there is.'"

"*This, this, this.*"

"Yeah," said Richter. "We live in a *this* culture, not a *me* culture. We'd be better off with the *me,* because there would be some worth assigned to the self, and you'd have half of the I-Thou, at least. But the *This*-thing has nothing to do with the self. It assigns a null to the self. It says the self is worthless, nothing but *this*ness. If I was a Jesuit like you, Thomas, I'd say *This* is the Enemy, is Satan, and that the awful passive voice is the voice of the Enemy. The voice isn't really a voice. It's an echo. It's the empty sound of all the ugly *this*ness out there."

Kelly leaned forward, his arms on the table. "That's good, John. You just made something clear to me for the first time."

Richter laughed. "It's a pleasure, Thomas. I can't talk like this to the kids, I promise you. I get about five minutes of talk like this a month. It's a real pleasure. Now, your problem."

Richter listened in silence for a couple of minutes as Kelly described Billy—his appearance, his habits.

"Basketball. I *know* I'm right," said Richter. "I used to play a lot of basketball with the kids. I know every playground game in town. You know what he'll do? This is a responsible kid, right? He'll find a place to stay, he'll get everything in place, right? Maybe he'll start looking for a job. He's mad at his father, right? Maybe he'll put off looking for his father for a while. Maybe he'll forget about it. And he'll be walking down the street one afternoon, and he'll pass a playground. And he'll look through the chain-link fence. And he'll see a *game!* Right?"

Kelly smiled at the scene and nodded. Yes. That's what Billy would do. He could see it.

"The thing is that here the game is a black game. How good is he?"

"Very good. He could play anywhere—North Carolina, Commonwealth, Maryland, out on the Coast—if he'd get his act together in school. Even if he doesn't. He's the kind of kid someone would fake a transcript for."

"Then he can play here. You say he's strong?"

"Wiry, fast, a lot tougher than he knows. This kid is ready to grow up fast."

"The kind of game we're talking about is like shooting craps. There are games, and games. The big time is up in Harlem— permanent games, you know what I mean? There're some good games in Brooklyn. But he's not gonna go to those places. There's a hot permanent game in some projects up behind Lincoln Center, but he's probably not gonna get up there, either. No reason to."

Richter got up and poured himself another cup of coffee.

"Thomas, you say this kid has some money?"

"A lot, I'm afraid."

"These games are for money. Blood and money. It's rough stuff. It's not the same game you play on a wooden floor with a ref in a striped shirt."

Richter whirled toward Kelly. "I know *exactly* where he'll go. Some courts down in the Village. Fourth Street and Sixth Avenue. One of the oldest permanent games around. Very tough. Start there. If he doesn't show up there after a couple of days, I'll give you a list of other places. And meantime, I'll ask around. Some of my kids might know something.

"Let me talk to Joseph now. You can bunk with me, but I'd appreciate a hand at mealtimes and after dinner, like now. Go in and talk to these kids. Get a sense of them. I promise you'll hear the voice of the Enemy in the mouths of some of the sweetest kids you ever saw."

"Eight-thirty, babe, is when we start, not a quarter to nine." Bro loomed out of the door of the storefront at Billy, filling the door from frame to frame. "One strike is a warning. Strike two, you owe me a free run. Strike three, I fire your ass."

"Sorry," said Billy. "I had a flat on this hot bike you sold me yesterday."

"Fix it. Tools and parts in the back. You sign out the parts and tools. You pay me cost for parts if they're new, cost less half if they're used."

The street was already in the dark shadow of a city canyon. Trucks, delivery vans, and cars jammed the curb lanes. It was where the edges of the garment, toy, lighting, and furniture districts intersected, but the old manufacturing lofts were retreating in the face of the new demand for residential space. Most of the buildings had storefronts or display windows at street level, and floors of manufacturing lofts above, but here and there in the block a smaller building had been converted to residential lofts.

Bro stood in the door drinking coffee out of a container. He watched Billy fix the flat. "Use a smaller patch," said Bro. "Don't waste that shit."

Inside, the phones rang continuously. The day's business was already in high gear. Bobby was on the phones. He made up runs for two messengers and they left, pumping hard across 24th Street toward Madison Square.

Billy finished and turned in the tools. He stood for a minute on the sidewalk with Bro. They watched workmen from a residential loft building dump boxes of broken lath and plaster into a huge dumpster on the street at the curb. Clouds of plaster dust drifted up the street.

"There's the real money in this town," observed Bro. "Real estate. This building's for sale." He shrugged his head back at the building behind them. "I'm gonna buy it, convert it to lofts with my own construction company. You wanna come in with me?"

"Not at the moment," said Billy. "I've gotta find my dad."

"You can do two things at the same time, like walkin' and talkin'."

"Maybe after, Bro."

"You think about it, Billy-boy. You got balls *and* brains, and I know you got a little money. You smell like it. Be a good thing in this town, a white front man. You wear the suits. I kick the ass."

"I can kick ass," said Billy.

Bro laughed. "Not like me, boy."

• • •

Bro's Pros did a lot of business with the big insurance companies. Billy's first run was from Metropolitan Life on Madison Square. He went in a side entrance to a mailroom where a bored clerk shoved a handful of large manila envelopes at him with a voucher. Billy signed for the envelopes and stuffed them in his big canvas sack. He put his copies of the voucher in his pocket. The smell of pot was strong in the room.

Bro had warned him. "All the clerks and jerks in New York smoke. *You* ain't no clerk and jerk. You don't smoke on the job. And don't carry."

Billy hadn't smoked a joint since he arrived in New York. The first night, when he tried to buy one on the street, Annie said, "Not around me," and that was the end of the discussion.

Billy headed uptown on Madison Avenue. "Use Madison or Park going uptown and Fifth or Park coming down," said Bobby. "And watch your ass. They're all killers out there. Jaywalkers and taxicabs the worst. They hate us. We hate them."

By noon, Billy was sweaty, dirty, and tired. He wondered what the insides of his nose and lungs looked like. He had never seen a dirtier city, never seen more frantic and free-floating hostility. A thin soot covered everything. He guessed it was from the buses and cars and trucks.

After his first stop, he bought a red bandanna from a sidewalk vender and wore it around his nose and mouth like an outlaw. In mid-morning, he ran across Soda Pop at the corner of Third Avenue and 47th. Soda Pop screeched and pointed his finger. "Billy the Kid. Billy the Kid."

They were all calling in for runs all the time ("Carry ten or twenty dimes," warned Bobby. "No one likes to give you change. I buy rolls in banks."), and by noon the nickname had stuck to Billy forever. It wasn't Billy-boy anymore, it was Billy the Kid. Billy liked it.

He straddled his bike by a pay phone at Fifth and 47th, talking to Bro.

"Lunch?" yelled Bro. "This is the hottest time of the day. Everybody in the city does a whole morning's work between eleven and twelve. They send it all around before they go to lunch. Then they call up after lunch and say, 'You get that shit yet?' That's when you eat your lunch—one-thirty, two o'clock. You eat fast, 'cause by two-thirty, three, it's picking up again, gets wild by four, dies at five. We go play a few games. Here's Bobby, give you a run."

"Billy the Kid?" yelled Bobby. "You got that red bandanna on your skinny nose? Soda Pop, he was shitten in his pants when he told me. Now, write this down. You go to Five-fifty-one Fifth, pick up a package for Five-nine-seven Fifth, pick up for Eighteenth and Fifth, come back here. Bro wants to see you."

When Billy showed up, Bro took him by the arm and walked him down the street. "Lunchtime," said Bro. They got a couple of slices of pizza each, and Cokes, and went to stand by the curb. They set their Cokes on the hood of a car and talked while they ate.

Bro spoke in undertones. "Took my machine"—Bro had a huge Honda motorcycle—"went down to play a few games about ten-thirty. Some white priest was there asking about you. Nobody said nuthin', but you gotta level with me. I don't want people nosin' around, you know? I got nuthin' to hide. I just don't like it, you know?"

"I understand," said Billy. "I know the priest. He's from Washington. I knew he'd come after me sooner or later."

"Looks like sooner," said Bro. "You in trouble?"

"Some," said Billy.

"I don't wanna know," said Bro. He dropped his pizza crust in the gutter and picked up his other piece.

Billy asked, "How much money you need?"

"Building's on the market for a million and a half. I been talkin' to 'em. I can get it for a million-two. I need a quarter mill or three hundred thou for a down payment. They'll hold the mortgage for the rest at seventeen. No bank. No points. No bullshit. Then I need maybe two or three hundred thou for the rehab. I'm gonna co-op it, sell the units before we even start gutting it. Keep the ground floor and one unit for myself. Got an architect. He'll come in for a piece, maybe a third. I need the other third."

"That's a hundred sixty-six, maybe seventy, apiece. Where'd you get the money?"

Bro's eyes widened in genuine amazement. "Did I ask you?"

"No," said Billy hastily. "I'm sorry. I really am."

"You interested?"

"Yes, but first I gotta find my dad."

"He holdin' your money?"

"Hey." Billy shrugged.

"Sorry."

"You help me find my dad. Then we'll do real estate deals."

"I'll think about it." said Bro. "I used to be a bad guy. Now I'm clean. I don't want to get dirty again. You understand?"

"I understand," said Billy. "I really do."

Billy wished he was clean again too. From something he had read, an image flashed at him—of an escaped convict in an old-fashioned striped prison suit running up a long hill, struggling through tangled underbrush and low trees. It was a cold November day with a sky as gray as steel. Bare branches whipped at the man's face. Dogs bayed in the hollow behind him, and the shouts of men from far away. The dogs drew closer, and the running man began to hope the men caught him before the dogs did.

Every year, thousands of kids arrived in New York City. They left behind in their hometowns thousands of adults who had, for one bad reason or another, averted their eyes from the lives of the kids. Many of the refugees found terrible fear, violence, and exploitation. Some found death. For a few, death was a merciful release.

Others found jobs, kindness, and opportunities. Their success wasn't by force or luck, or timing, or superior personality. In the unpredictable ecology of success and failure, it was all of these. Billy and Annie found their niches quickly, helped by knowing what they wanted. In just a few days, they settled into a comfortable routine together.

Annie, single-minded in pursuit of her own clear purposes, sensed Billy's attachment to Joe, and amplified it. If Joe was in trouble, and Billy was sure he was, then Joe had been in trouble for a long time. Joe's troubles were the end point of a long game. Annie made Billy understand this.

Billy fled Washington out of fear, but also out of anger at Joe. Billy wasn't looking for Joe as much as punishing him. Finding Annie, however, gave Billy a chance to recover his feelings for his father. Billy's feelings for Annie evoked his feelings for Joe. And in the fantastic complexities of daily life in New York City, Billy found a mirror of the complexities of Joe's life.

What Joe told Billy on the boat in Chesapeake Bay had not made much sense to Billy then, because it no longer made sense to Joe. But Billy began to understand now that people got where they were going because they had been on their chosen path for a long time. In New York, Billy could see more clearly why Joe had done what he did. Billy had a growing sense of the appalling choices people face in their lives. He now faced some of those choices himself.

In the myriad faces of the people of the city, Billy saw the smiles of success; and the awful grimaces of failure and loss; and something he had never recognized before—the grinning leer of what could only be called evil. In this larger world, with its fantastic landscape of accidental purposes, Billy knew that Joe could tell him more than anyone else. He knew now that Joe had been trying to do that all along, but was prevented by the character of his past. Billy knew now that Joe had struggled to break the grip of the past, and had failed.

Under Annie's influence and in the light of his own needs, Billy's fear at Joe's betrayals changed rapidly from childlike rejection to adult acceptance and concern. At first, Billy was afraid to disrupt the idyll of his new life with Annie, but Annie was the cause of the change, and she led him to embrace it. She was a risk-taker by nature. Some kids collapse when they're confronted with responsibility. Others grow up fast, when they are able and free.

Joe had been out there in the hostile world Billy now saw more clearly. Joe had been further out than most, and now he was trying to get back. Billy wanted to help him.

Billy needed his father, it was true, but that alone was not enough to make Billy act. In the end, Billy began to look for Joe because Billy wanted to. Joe was in trouble, Billy was sure. Joe needed help. Billy loved his father. Billy helped him. In the end, it was that simple.

"In your face," yelled Yo. The metal backboard shuddered and rattled from the force of his slam-dunk. The losers paid the winners. Billy's team had just beaten Bro's team three in a

row. It was a first. Both teams walked to the sidelines, exhausted. They were replaced by six more players from other teams.

It was a dusky, hot evening in high summer, nearing mid-July. It was about nine o'clock and getting dark. An airplane crossed the western skyline, flying north up the Hudson River. The brilliant strobe lights on the plane flashed on and off. The early stars were blurred by the shine of the city against the lower air but Billy noted that the sky over New York was clearer, less dense than over Washington.

The low buildings across Sixth Avenue were backed by rising tiers of higher buildings—apartments, warehouses, lofts. There were lights in some of the windows. The sky in the west behind the uneven horizon of buildings was red-orange-purple, fading to velvet black overhead. The lights of the airplane flashed in the blackness like a coded, monotone message.

There wasn't much about New York that Billy didn't like. The hardest thing was the amazing hostility in the midtown streets, but every day was easier and better. He adjusted quickly. Annie did more than help him. She pushed him and forced him.

He toweled his chest and arms off, and put his T-shirt on. Someone handed him an open beer. He leaned back against the chain-link fence and drank the cold beer slowly. He wasn't tired. He felt good, better than ever. Soon he'd meet Annie at her restaurant, a chic Italian place in the maze of Greenwich Village streets west of Seventh Avenue. She worked lunch, had the afternoon off, then worked dinner. She had already begun dance and acting classes in the morning and afternoon.

That morning, Billy had taken the first steps to look for his father. He cornered Bro and asked him to ask the others to watch for the white Rolls-Royce.

Bro demanded an explanation. "I wanna know what we're gettin' into," he said. "No bullshit, Billy-boy."

Billy said simply, "The guy who owns it might know something about my father. I think they're hiding him somewhere. If we find the car, and track it around the city, then we can look for my father in the places it goes."

"We, white boy?"

"Yeah, *we*. I can't do this alone, Bro. You help me, and I'll help you."

There was a long silence. Some of the others in the 24th Street storefront edged in closer to the two of them.

"What'd your daddy do?" asked Bro.

"He's a spy," said Billy quietly. But it was out. It was the first time he'd ever said it out loud. This was more than he'd told anyone except Father Kelly. This was more than Annie knew. This was how you made a deal, Billy guessed. You had to give some to get some.

"Shee-it," whispered Bro. "Bad stuff."

"Your daddy a good guy or a bad guy?" asked Yo suddenly from close in. He had edged his way right into the talk as though he was under the boards working his way in for a rebound. Bro scowled at him but said nothing.

"A good guy," said Billy. He looked at Bro. "But I don't think he always was. I think he was kind of dirty once."

The others looked at Bro. Bro looked around the circle. He looked at the Spiderman posters. He looked out the door. He walked out to the sidewalk and walked back in. He nodded.

"*El Jefe* has spoken," said Bobby. They were all excited.

Billy described the car, and where he last saw it. He described his father, the fat man he had seen with his father, and the owner of the car, who he had not seen clearly. He described Cowboy and his big Harley. Bro had seen him on the street several times. Bro said he looked like a bad dude.

At three-thirty, Yo spotted the car leaving the curb in front of the 21 Club on West 52nd Street, just off Fifth Avenue. He was on a run and couldn't follow it, but he stopped at the first empty phone booth and called the sighting in. Now Soda Pop, tall and skinny, with a two-foot seat post on his ten-speed, was cruising around midtown looking for the car while the others played ball.

The messengers had an amazing, encyclopedic knowledge of the minute details of midtown Manhattan—architecture, traffic, people, behavior. At one time or another, most of them had been in and out of nearly every building, restaurant, bar, movie theater, and storefront. Midtown was full of characters and oddities. The messengers knew every one of them.

The white Rolls-Royce was familiar to the messengers. They had seen it in the East Sixties, or on Fifth Avenue, or on Park

Avenue, or on Sutton Place, or in front of UN Plaza, or downtown in Foley Square—in the area of the courthouses, Federal
Building, City Hall, and police headquarters. This afternoon,
after Yo's sighting, Bobby gave the car a name. The name
stuck. They called it *The Ghost*. They figured it was just a
matter of hours, or a day at most, before they spotted it again.
This time, they said they'd stick to it like glue.

Billy tossed his empty beer can into a trash can and walked
over to the bench to get another. He listened to the chatter for
a few minutes, looking out at the traffic on Sixth Avenue,
watching the people on the sidewalks. It was a hot, comfortable,
pleasant evening. He felt at ease here, at home.

Most of the people on the street were in couples—men and
women, men and men, women and women. They were comfortable here, and Billy was, too. He had never been anywhere
that allowed its citizens such relaxed, live-and-let-live freedom.
New York was a very public place. Very little was hidden here.
Yet there was a common respect for privacy.

Billy watched two men walk slowly up the sidewalk on the
other side of the street. They dawdled, window-shopping, chatting. They were middle-aged. One was tall and black. The
other was short and stocky, vaguely European. They seemed
closely familiar with each other. Billy guessed they were a
homosexual couple. Here, no one was startled or offended.
Even in Washington, Billy knew, homosexuals had to be careful
about being seen in public with other homosexuals.

Billy turned away from the street and walked back to his
spot by the fence. He leaned back against it and sipped his
beer. He thought about Annie.

"Billy?"

The familiar voice was soft, no more than a foot behind
Billy's ear. Billy jumped. He wouldn't have been more startled
if someone had snuck up behind him and hit him in the ear
with a baseball bat.

Billy whirled. "Father Kelly?"

"How are you, Billy? I had a hard time finding you."

Billy said nothing.

"I've been down here every day for four days," said the
priest. "Nobody would talk to me. I almost gave up."

"I wish you had," said Billy.

"This morning some little white kid from the neighborhood, an Italian kid, probably afraid to lie to a priest, told me there was a big white kid playing basketball down here with the big black guys at night. I figured it had to be you, Billy. Who else could it be?"

The priest, Billy's closest friend, the only adult Billy trusted completely, loomed at Billy like a figure in a bad dream.

"Why'd you come here?" asked Billy. "I'm sorry you found me."

"I want to help you. You're in worse trouble than any kid I ever knew."

"I don't need any help."

"That's not true and you know it."

Billy shrugged.

"The cops are looking for you and your father in Washington. Where is he?"

"I don't know. I came here to find him."

"You came here because you were running away from something terrible."

"I have to find him before I go back," said Billy.

"They'll put out an interstate bulletin soon."

"So what? How can they find me here? You could hide here forever."

"You're wrong, Billy. It took me only four days."

"OK, Father, I need help." Billy hissed in an angry stage whisper at the priest through the fence. "But you gave me all the help you can. Just keep that stuff I gave you, OK? That's all I want from you. Now I need another kind of help you can't give."

The others had moved away from Billy, and Father Kelly, giving them room and privacy but watching closely.

"Where are you staying?" asked the priest.

"I have a place."

"Do you need money?"

Billy smirked. "That's a dumb question. Are you telling me you didn't look at what I left with you?"

"No."

"I have a job. I'm a messenger with these guys. They have their own company."

"These guys play good ball," said the priest.

"That's not all they can do," said Billy. There was a low note of hostility in his voice.

"I need help," said Father Kelly.

"You need help?"

"You left a big problem behind you, and you left it in my lap. Now you have an obligation to help me solve it. You made your problem my problem. You can't take a walk on me now." The priest was getting angry. "And you damn well know it," he added.

Billy shrugged.

"Well, Billy? Am I right?"

"Sure, you're right, Father. You're always right, goddammit. You're never, ever wrong, are you?" Billy felt a sense of defeat, somehow, and it made him more angry. He said loudly, "There's always a condition on your help."

Father Kelly looked surprised.

"Yeah," said Billy, his voice louder, seeing an opening, driving hard for the basket. "The condition is that the other guy always has to admit that you were right. You're *never* wrong. Well, you're good and goddamned wrong this time."

Billy was nearly shouting now. "I want help without strings. *Fuck* your problem. Fuck *your* problem. You wanna give me help with mine, that's fine. First, we solve mine, then we worry about yours, OK?"

A clear look of chagrin and embarrassment replaced the look of surprise on the priest's face. "OK," he said quietly.

"That's good," shouted Billy loud and clear. "That's good, because I need all the help I can get, and all the troops I can get. I need a fuckin' army. These guys"—he waved his hand around the playground—"are givin' me help with no strings, and you can do the same. None of your priest's bullshit. Just help. OK?"

"OK." Father Kelly was red.

"In your *face,*" said someone on the bench. "All *right.* Billy the *Kid.*"

Bro's heavy voice said, *"Billy's Army."* He was laughing. They all started laughing and slapping high fives.

Billy went out to the sidewalk to talk to Father Kelly. Bro walked up the street to a pay phone to call in to the storefront

on 24th Street where Bobby was waiting at the phones in case
Soda Pop found the Ghost. Talking to the priest, staring out
over the cars rushing up the avenue, Billy noticed the odd
couple again. They were still window-shopping. A little warning light lit up in the back of Billy's mind. He wondered if the
priest had led the police here. In a split second of blind rage,
he could have picked the priest up and thrown him into the
traffic.

Then he rejected the idea that the priest had led someone
here deliberately. Billy apologized silently, not taking his eyes
off the two men. There *was* something about them. They didn't
look like cops, but they looked like they ought to be.

Bro came back in a hurry. He motioned to Billy. Billy made
a snap decision. He said, "You can talk in front of Father Kelly."

Bro said, "Soda Pop found the Ghost."

Billy was electrified. "Where?"

"In front of a restaurant called the Italian Pavilion on West
Fifty-fifth Street. There's two men and a woman from the car
eating inside the place."

The others were suddenly in a half-circle around them.

"What else?" asked Billy.

"He said the woman was wearing a long white gown. He
said she was too high-class to be a pross. He said a big white
dude on a big Harley hog was hangin' round outside."

"He's a bad guy," said Billy.

"Soda Pop can take care of himself," said Bro. "Let's go."

"All *right*," yelled Yo. "Air*borne!*"

Bro picked two motorcycle helmets out from under one of
the benches. The others stuffed their things into their messenger
bags and unlocked their bikes.

Billy said to the priest, "Father, go over to the Fiorello
Restaurant on Carmine Street. Ask for Annie and tell her I told
you to take her home. Tell her who you are. She'll take you."

"Who's Annie?" The preist now looked completely bewil-
dered and defeated by his surroundings, by events, by what he
had seen and heard, by Billy's transformation.

"Just do it, Father. Wait for me with Annie if you want to,
or leave a phone number with her. OK?" Billy unsnapped his
green pack from the leg of one of the benches and started to
unlock his bike.

Bro threw a helmet at him and said, "Leave the bike here, kid. You come with me."

Bro shouted instructions to the others. They took off in a pack, then headed off in different directions, but all heading uptown, pumping like championship racers in the Tour de France. In a moment, they were gone.

In another moment, Bro and Billy were gone. The big Honda roared off and disappeared up Sixth Avenue into the night blur of red taillights and loud traffic noise. The odd couple across the street was sprinting up Sixth Avenue toward a blue sedan parked by a fire hydrant. Father Kelly stood paralyzed with amazement by the curb.

FIFTEEN

THE WHITE CAR was gone from 55th Street when Bro and Billy got there, cruising slowly down the block from the direction of Fifth Avenue. Soda Pop was gone too, and Cowboy on his big Harley. Bro pulled to the curb at an empty space in front of the MGM Building at the end of the block. A parking sign said GOVERNOR'S OFFICE ONLY.

The street was deserted. The uptown traffic on Sixth Avenue was light. Bro sat still and silent in the saddle of the motorcycle, waiting. A small crowd of young people came out of the MGM Building, leaving a movie screening in the small, private theater on the ground floor of the building. They were dressed in chic, trendy clothes. They surrounded Bro and Billy like butterflies, laughing and chattering, then drifted out to Sixth Avenue and disappeared, some in taxis, some walking uptown toward the bars and sidewalk cafés along Central Park South.

Yo whipped around the corner from Sixth Avenue. He skidded his bike in a half-turn to a stop next to the motorcycle.

"Gone," he said.

Bro said, "Wait for the others. Fan out over there and above here." His arm marked an arc east and north. "Don't go north of Ninety-sixth Street."

Yo said, "That's a lotta streets for three ten-speeds and one cycle."

"We'll find him," said Bro. "Call in to Bobby every fifteen minutes."

"Air*borne*," said Yo, and headed off the wrong way across 55th Street toward Fifth Avenue. The others were pumping wildly down the street toward him. He waved his arm at them to stop. In a moment, they were headed back like birds off a wire. At Fifth Avenue, they split up and disappeared.

When the light turned green, Bro eased away from the curb and turned uptown on Sixth. In a few moments they entered the curving roads of Central Park, going uptown, past the statues of a couple of Latin American heroes. The park was dark except for pools of light under the streetlights. There were few cars on the Drive. A solitary runner ran in the runner's lane. He wore only red nylon shorts, red running shoes without socks, and a blue bandanna around his forehead. A thick sheen of sweat glistened on his torso and arms. He was running fast.

Bro pulled up even with him and slowed down. He downshifted to second gear. The runner glanced at them, then ignored them.

"Twelve miles an hour," shouted Bro.

The runner smiled. He was in his late thirties, thin, with the scrawny chicken neck that older long-distance runners get. He held up his right and opened it quickly three times.

"Fifteen miles," shouted Billy.

The runner smiled again and made a gesture with his hand. They were breaking his concentration. Bro accelerated away.

"That's five-minute miles," shouted Billy into Bro's ear. "That's fast!"

Bro nodded. He drove out of the park at 72nd Street, stopping at the first phone booth. The streets in this part of the East Side were as deserted as the park. Billy called in. Nothing. He told Bobby where they were. Soda Pop hadn't checked in for half an hour. Billy reported this to Bro.

"Let's go," said Bro. "Won't find him sittin' here."

They headed across 72nd Street toward York Avenue.

The next half hour was like a dream, growing slowly more urgent. They cruised back and forth across the streets of the

East Side, each turn taking them another block downtown. They crossed the paths of Yo and the others, who were coursing up and down the avenues. Minute by minute, Bro drove faster and faster, until he was ripping through the streets like a motocross racer, bouncing over bumps and skidding at intersections.

Finally, Billy pounded him on the shoulder and shouted, "Bro, that's enough. Let me call in."

Bro wheeled over to a phone and stopped the bike. Billy jumped off, then Bro. Bro lifted his helmet off and threw it at a metal gate over a store window. The grate crashed and rattled. He sat down on a car fender and waited.

The message from Bobby was ominous. Billy repeated it word for word to Bro. "Soda Pop called in from Ninety-sixth and First. The Ghost saw him and chased him. The dude on the big Harley chased him but he got away. Then Soda Pop shouted real loud, *'Here he come again!'* Then he shouted one word. *'Armory!'* Then he dropped the phone. Bobby heard the motorcycle. That's all."

"Shit," said Bro.

It took two hours to find Soda Pop. His smashed bicycle lay in the rubble of a vacant lot in East Harlem. The body was a few yards away. The body and the bike lay in the bricks and broken glass like two pieces of useless junk.

"It's a fucking war," said Bro. "You brought some bad shit with you." Bro stood staring down at Soda Pop for a moment. "Fucking rats be around soon." He looked around. Housing projects rose behind them against the East River. Before them, a hill of tenements and vacant lots rose sharply west and south toward higher ground and the Upper East Side. "He got six blocks from where Bobby said he called. He was flying."

Billy bent over and picked up a large piece of broken plastic. He handed it to Bro.

"Motorcycle," said Bro. "Turn signal. Chased him right in here over all this shit. Look at the wheels on Soda Pop's bike."

The rubber tires and tubes were shredded and torn. The metal wheels and spokes were bent and broken. Soda Pop had ridden as hard as he could into the rubble, in terror, hoping the motorcycle would not follow.

Billy fished a small notebook out of Soda Pop's shirt pocket.

Bro said, "Let's go. We'll call in a tip to the police, then send his mama to the morgue to claim his body. He was all she ever had."

They stopped at a phone booth near Metropolitan Hospital at the corner of 96th and First Avenue. Billy called the police with an anonymous tip. He climbed back on the big Honda Gold Wing behind Bro, and they waited.

"See what's in that notebook," said Bro over his shoulder.

The notebook was new. The only entries were on the first page in dull, soft pencil. There were half a dozen entries, beginning with *Ital. rest. W. 55,* and ending with *amry.* Billy read them to Bro, who held his hand out for the notebook. He tore the first page into tiny scraps and dropped them to the gutter. He put the notebook in his jacket pocket.

Traffic lights cycled from red to green and back again. A few gypsy cabs sped uptown on First. A city bus cruised slowly by, its muffler broken, making an unearthly noise in the quiet night. After a few minutes, they could still hear it many blocks uptown.

Bro just sat. He snapped off the lights but left the motor idling evenly. The exhaust burbled and rapped quietly. The heavy machine vibrated steadily between their legs. Billy sat on a post seat, higher than Bro. He could see over Bro's head. He could feel Bro breathing in and out. The machine and the man had different rhythms, but now and then their rhythms intersected and ran in synch for a few moments, then ran ragged again. It was contemplative and peaceful, like sitting in the tree house.

Bro wore a black leather jacket over a white T-shirt. In the dull light of the city at night, his hands on the handlebar grips looked as dark as the leather sleeves of the jacket. The skin on the backs of his hands was worn and black and wrinkled, like the worn leather.

Billy wondered how old Bro really was. Billy looked at his own hands. They were unworn and smooth compared to the dark blue denim of his jacket. He put his hand on Bro's shoulder. He tried to describe to himself the color of his own skin in the warm glow from the sodium-vapor streetlights.

Orange-pink, a pale rose color at the roughened knuckles. The color was tangerine. He imagined someone saying, "Look at that black dude on that mean black motorcycle. And look at that tangerine motherfucker."

A police car swooped by on its way uptown, lights flashing, siren bleeping and whooping. Billy's heart bumped a few times, then settled down.

"Took the fuckers long enough," said Bro. He kicked the stand down. "Get off," he said. He left the engine idling and went to the pay phone. When he came back, he said, "They're gonna meet us."

They climbed back on the machine and sat in silence for a few more moments, then Bro slapped Billy hard on the knee. "I'm gonna find that car and that white dude on that motorcycle." He laughed. "You too young to be in the Army, right?"

Billy grunted.

Bro said over his shoulder, "I served my time in the old Hundred-and-First Airborne, before it was all choppers and airmobile. We had to *jump*. Me and the other brothers used to call it the Hundred-and-*Worst*. That's how I know Yo. In that outfit, when you salute, you see some officer comin', and you salute first, you know, and he'd salute, and he say, 'Air*borne*,' and you say, you shout, 'All the *way, sir.*'"

Bro snapped the lights on and pulled on his helmet. He tapped the cycle into first with his foot and turned out into the traffic lane. When the light changed, he slipped the clutch with his left hand and twisted the throttle with his right. The mufflers roared and cracked. He popped the clutch. The machine leapt up the street, across First Avenue and up the hill on 96th Street, ignoring red lights and traffic.

At Lexington Avenue they turned south, going faster. The hill peaked at 92nd Street. They could see a long way downtown. This was a quiet neighborhood, much the same as it had been fifty years before. They roared through it, shattering the silence. The Honda hit a big bump and bounced high in the air.

"*Airborne,*" shouted Bro at the top of his lungs. The cry rang over the noise of the motorcycle. "All the *way, sir,*" shouted Billy. The Honda bounced and flew down Lexington. They roared through the busy intersection at 86th Street on a yellow light.

At 67th, Bro hit the brakes and skidded to a stop at the right-hand curb. They looked up at a dark, unlit brick wall rising four or five stories to a crenelated roof like the top of a castle wall.

Bro shut off the machine. "Get off," he said.

"What is this?"

"The Armory. This is what he meant. This is a famous place. This is a high-society armory. This is a ghost armory. This is a white Rolls-Royce armory."

Billy snugged his pack against his back. "Yeah," he said. "I get it. Let's look around."

A block behind them, a dark blue Mercury Zephyr slowed and stopped on the other side of the street. The car looked like what it was—a rental car. Harry drove. Volko sat on the passenger side, picking his teeth with his fingernails and a paper clip.

He sucked the spaces between his front teeth and said, "We hit the jackpot. There is no such thing as coincidence in this work. There is only what Arthur Koestler calls circularity. You know Koestler, Harry?"

"Never met him."

"The white Rolls is at this very moment parked at the curb of the other side of this building on Park Avenue, waiting for its owner to depart from a testimonial dinner for two ex-FBI agents who were accused of bothering the poor little Weatherpeople during the sixties and early seventies."

"I know who the Weatherpeople were," said Harry, pulling a bottle of beer from between his thighs under the steering wheel and taking a long swallow.

"Inside at the dinner are Mr. Perrieux, aka Lazard. Also Mr. Julie Gold, who appears to be a close associate of our friend Lazard. And in their charming company is the lovely Miss Diane Kennedy, Joe Ball's erstwhile friend. Aka fnu mnu LNU."

"Also known as first name unknown middle name unknown last name unknown," said Harry to the windshield.

"Harry, I think I'll just slip out and take a walk around the block. Wait right here."

Harry took another suck on his beer. "That priest," he said. "He did us a favor."

Joe was tied to the same chair, with the same ropes, in the same clothes. He had not been out of the chair for days. He wasn't sure how many days. It felt like three or four. There had been an attempt to confuse him. He was moved from the garage where he first found himself to a small windowless room. He didn't know how he had gotten there—they had drugged him. He didn't know where he was.

But he knew night from day because there was a subway nearby. He could feel the vibration and rumble of the trains. He marked his day by the frequency of the trains—morning and evening rush hours, and the long silences at night.

Kavenaugh had tried to feed him soup and give him water at first, but Joe spit out the liquids on Kavenaugh's shoes. His fast and the beatings had left him as limp as a rag doll. He slumped in the chair, held up by the tight ropes.

His aches and pains turned on and off, and appeared and disappeared in various parts of his body—now the left ankle, now the back of his head, now his shoulder. It was as though his nervous system had become nothing but a switching network for shunting pain around from part to part; but there was no pattern to it. There was no director. Whatever it was that controlled the autonomic nervous system—the unconscious, automatic system that works on its own inside the body all the time—was broken or shut down. Pain flickered back and forth like heat lightning under his skin.

He had not been untied from the chair for a single moment. He had shit and peed in his pants. The feces and urine had hardened and crusted. There was nothing now but an occasional acidic discharge. At first, this had been the worst pain—the raw skin like massive bedsores on his thighs, in his crotch, on his buttocks. It made every move agonizing. He had held himself as still as a mouse when he was not being beaten. Then he got used to it. Now he squirmed during the beatings and interrogations, because the pain kept him alert—it was the only thing in the whole universe he could control.

Kavenaugh ran him through his entire personal history in

the CIA, back and forth, around and around. It was like the debriefing of an important factor, but there was no apparent object beyond the re-establishment of his biography. They knew nearly everything—the jewels, the passports, the cash. They knew about his politics—his stubborn Jeffersonian faith and his half-forgotten sense of a universal community of believers from his childhood Catholicism. They knew, *Kavenaugh* knew, every detail of his battle to keep the defoliators out of Laos, to keep the air war out of the secret war. Kavenaugh found that particularly significant.

That morning, Kavenaugh had arrived early, according to the distant vibrations of the morning rush hour transmitted to Joe through Manhattan bedrock and concrete. The customary beating took place at the hands of the man whom Joe had taken to calling Cowboy. The man enjoyed his work. He got an erection every time—the thick bulge like a Chiquita banana under the faded front of the Levi's. Then the man left, high-strung and excited, and Kavenaugh began talking.

"You're the first, Joe, you know? Of course, you don't know. You're the very first."

Since the beginning, Joe had not voluntarily looked Kavenaugh in the face. Joe had not asked or volunteered anything, but now he asked, "First what?" His voice was reedy and thin like an old man's.

"The first one to disappear."

"I don't understand," said Joe.

"Desaparado."

"Like Buenos Aires?" Joe could not keep the curiosity out of his voice. He knew Kavenaugh had him completely now. "I understand," said Joe slowly. "Brazil, Chile, Argentina, El Salvador."

"Yes."

"Why?" asked Joe.

"The polls here show that only about half the voters in the country are going to vote in a contest between Reagan and Carter. As voting declines, the country becomes more unstable. Do you understand?"

"Better than you, Kavenaugh. You've got it backward."

"Of course, you're right. The decline in voting is a symptom of underlying instability."

Joe's voice rasped and whistled like cattails in a sea breeze. "And you're going to stabilize it."

"We don't make extravagant claims. We are going to experiment with a method for stabilizing it. We are going to make people disappear. Journalists, union leaders, teachers, people like you who know their way around too well, who know too much, who can't be relied on to do the job they were hired to do."

"There are two hundred and twenty million people in this country," wheezed Joe. "it's not some fucking little banana republic."

"Well," said Kavenaugh in the tone of a theoretician in a think tank, "we're not sure that's true. We think this country is on the verge of becoming a kind of loose federation of banana republics."

"Political fragmentation," murmured Joe. "You've been reading the polls carefully. How clever."

"Yes, Joe, but as you observed, this is a very large country. If it fragments, as it is in the process of doing, the fragments won't be tiny little shards in the dust. They will be big chunks, like building rubble. And if one can control some of the important chunks, move them around, and neutralize or terrorize other blocs, then the importance of mass consensus will be considerably diminished. Voting will cease to have much significance except as just another form of opinion poll."

"This is bullshit."

"Perhaps. But we are going to test our theory. It has, after all, worked very well elsewhere. What the Balkans were to Europe before the war in 1939, Latin America will be to us during the coming two decades. We exported a great deal of political technology, as it were, to Latin America during the past twenty years. Now we are going to re-import it, and use it here."

"The politics of electrodes," said Joe.

"Oh, yes," said Kavenaugh. "The torture, the disappearances, the women beating pots and pans in the streets. All of it."

"Brazil, Inc."

"Yes," said Kavenaugh patiently. "Exactly."

"I still don't understand," said Joe. "What about 1984? What was your interest in the elections, if voting doesn't count?" Joe looked up at Kavenaugh for the first time in days. He caught Kavenaugh with a benign smile on his face.

"We have to be adaptable. The two-party system is breaking up. What Anderson is doing this year will be done by others in 1984. There will be several independent candidates. One of them will be ours."

Joe knew he was as good as dead now. They would kill him in this perfectly barren place—four gray concrete walls, concrete floor with dust balls in the corners, a steel door painted gray, and a gray concrete ceiling with a bare light bulb hanging down. Still, he was curious.

"Who?" he asked. "McCagg?"

"Yes."

"I guess I would have figured all this out sooner or later."

"Yes, I guess you would have."

"Who comes after me?"

"Billy."

"Where is he?"

"We have him."

It was the oldest trick in the world, Joe knew. But Billy was just a kid. If they didn't have him, they soon would. Joe had sent Billy straight to them. Joe gave up. He dropped his chin to his chest.

"One more thing, Joe. We have the jewels, the money, the passports. But we want the gold. We know you have quite a bit. We want the exact amount, and we want access."

"New Union Bank. A01777. You'll need a truck."

"Thank you, Joe. These operations always cost a lot of money. We can use your contribution."

"Send a receipt to my tax guy."

"Ha, ha, Joe." Kavenaugh walked to the door. He opened it and stepped outside. He turned off the light with a switch outside the door.

"Let my kid go," said Joe.

"Good-bye, Joe," said Kavenaugh, closing and locking the door.

Joe sat in the dark, feeling the distant noise of the trains through the chair and his feet on the floor. He felt cold and tired, but the pain in his heart burned like unquenchable white phosphorus.

SIXTEEN

BILLY WATCHED THROUGH the glass doors of the Armory like a kid with his nose pressed against the glass of a Christmas window. He had watched a few diplomatic receptions in Washington from a distance, but they were commonplace and discreet. What he saw here was a raw display of status and power, accented by being contained within the heavy walls of a Victorian mock fort. It was a glimpse into another world.

Men in dinner jackets and women in gowns stood in small groups in the brightly lit lobby, surrounded by glass cases of military memorabilia. There were a few men in the garish dress uniforms of the Army, and a few others in the more subdued dress uniforms of the New York City Police Department. The men and women in the lobby watched each other and talked to each other with the peculiar combination of boredom, fatigue, and social animation that follows a long testimonial dinner.

Oil paintings of officers in the uniforms of old wars hung on the walls. The men in the paintings wore dress swords and sashes or heavy shoulder cords. They looked stern and resolute. Billy wondered who they were. He wished he could get inside the building. He had a strong sense that Joe was here.

Billy felt exposed out on the stoop above the sidewalk on Park Avenue. It was lit by floodlights mounted on the Armory, as well as the streetlights. Limousines lined the curb at his back. Private security guards glared at him from inside the first set of glass doors. The Ghost was double-parked down the block. Cowboy was nowhere to be seen, but Billy knew he must be around.

Bro stood at the uptown corner, his Honda parked at a fire hydrant nearby. Yo stood at the downtown corner. They had decided on these positions after a quick reconnaissance of the block. The entire block between Park and Lexington was filled by the dark bulk of the Armory. The sides and back were dark. The only possible entrance was through the main doors at the front on Park. Billy had decided to get up close for a look.

He was rewarded. He saw the two men from Rockefeller Center. They stood talking between themselves at the foot of a broad staircase of heavy oak at the back of the lobby. The fat man was calm. The smaller man with the high forehead and bulbous nose was agitated. They were joined by a pretty woman in a long white dress. She appeared to be angry. The little group turned and started slowly up the stairs. A man of medium height, with pale skin and dark hair, wearing an ordinary business suit, caught up with them. Now they all hurried up the staircase out of sight.

At this moment, a guard drove Billy off the stoop down to the sidewalk. People were leaving. Shaking with excitement and frustration, Billy retreated slowly down the block toward Yo's corner, not wanting to stand directly in the path of the people leaving the Armory, hunting for their limousines or cabs.

Watching this from the shadows on the corner across Park Avenue, Volko raised a small walkie-talkie to his mouth and said, "Bring the car slowly down the side street and double-park about thirty yards from the corner. Keep an eye on the big dude." He didn't need to add "so we can go either way on Park, or across town." Harry would understand. He and Harry had worked together for years.

• • •

Yo and Bro were as jumpy as cats. They felt suspicious as hell, and conspicuous, too. This was not a neighborhood where suspicious, conspicuous blacks were made welcome. But they were committed. Yo looked up the block at Bro and made the motion of hooking up—snapping the rip cord of a parachute onto the static line inside a C-130.

In a private room on the second floor of the Armory, with a heavy oak door closed behind them, Diane's anger exploded at the three men.

"Four days," she shouted. "You had him for four days and you still don't have what we want. And *need*. Now we're out of time. We have to move him *tonight*."

There was no trace of hysteria or screeching in her voice. This was the powerful, focused anger of someone for whom something crucial has gone terribly wrong.

"I led him right to you. I held your hands every step of the way. And you still don't have the money. *Where the hell is it?*"

She stood alone at the head of a heavy oak conference table. It was polished like a mirror. Regimental battle flags stood at the end of the room, flanking a portrait of some long-dead officer. A US flag stood in one corner. In the other corner was a brass cross on a wood pole—the kind carried before the priest by the crucifer in an Episcopal church. Diane wondered what Victorian ceremonies were held in this place. The Armory and everything in it were anachronisms. She was sure the Armory officials were unaware what Gold and Lazard were doing, but it was the ideal place for this cabal of phonies.

The others stood grouped together opposite her, Kavenaugh a few yards apart. Diane's skin was flushed a deep rose above the low neckline of her dress, and redder still on her neck and face. She waited for an answer.

"We are terribly exposed, dear girl," said Lazard.

She despised him the most. She blew up. "Don't 'dear girl' me, goddammit. I'm the one who's exposed, far more than any of you." She slapped the flat of her hand on the table with a sharp noise. "You assholes are both lawyers. Maybe you should reread the US Code."

There was another silence, then Gold murmured, "We know

the law, Diane. You are right, of course."

"Damn right I'm right," she shot back. "But that doesn't solve the problem, does it?"

She paced to a window overlooking Park Avenue and paced back. The red blush on her skin subsided lightly. "Big-time conspirators," she said contemptuously. "High rollers. A pair of pathetic small-time fuck-ups is what you are." She threw her little purse on the table and ran her hands impatiently back through her hair. She looked at Kavenaugh.

He said quietly, "It is my best judgment that he told me all he knew. He exhibits the classic behavior of the subject who has given up and told the truth."

"Not just what he thought you wanted to hear?" she asked.

"No. The whole truth, as he understands it. He is completely disoriented. For example, he thinks it is now late morning. He senses the time from the distant vibrations of the subways and trains that pass beneath Lexington and Park avenues, but he doesn't realize how much time he has been sleeping or unconscious. He has eaten nothing. He took some terrible beatings from Mr. Lazard's violent friend."

Kavenaugh turned slightly and nodded at Lazard. A flicker of discomposure passed across Lazard's face.

Kavenaugh continued, "Ball is very tough, but quite vulnerable, too. The boy is his weakness. I'm sure Joe knows, in part at least, that I tricked him by telling him we had the boy. But I'm also sure Joe believes we will absolutely find the boy and kill him."

"What about a polygraph?" asked Gold.

Kavenaugh fixed Gold with the impassive, contemptuous stare of the total professional. "He's too battered. His physiological responses are completely erratic now. And besides, it didn't work before. You were there. You heard the questions. You saw the tape. He is unusually good at controlling his responses, even for someone in his rather practiced profession."

Gold nodded absently. He was sweating. He wiped his face with a linen handkerchief from his sleeve.

Kavenaugh added, "You, Julie. You would be fun to put on the box. It would be like shooting fish in a barrel."

Kavenaugh turned his gaze to Lazard. "Did the Bahamian bank say when the account was closed?"

"It isn't closed," said Lazard. "It's empty."

"As of?" asked Kavenaugh.

"They don't say, naturally," said Lazard. "That's not how they work. You should know that."

"I do," said Kavenaugh evenly. He gave the impression of a man puffing his evening pipe in front of a fireplace. "But I thought you might have some unofficial sources. I thought unofficial sources were your specialty."

Lazard looked away. Kavenaugh looked at Diane.

"Move him," she ordered Kavenaugh. "Clean him up. We have very little time."

She looked at Lazard and Gold with a gaze like Medusa's. They could not hold her eyes. She said, "The others are already in motion. Football is a man's game. Surely you understand that once the backfield is in motion it's too late to stop the play. *And find that boy.*"

"Why bother now?" asked Lazard.

She gave him a look that made him flinch visibly. "Because he knows too much. *I want him out of the way.*"

She picked up her purse and marched out of the room. Gold ran after her and caught her in the hall.

"Let me give you a ride home," he asked.

"I can manage," she said. She shook her arm free of his pleading hand. "Do what I told you," she whispered into his face. "And no mistakes. This is a no-prisoners operation."

She ran down to the lobby and out to the street. A doorman offered her a cab, but she ignored him and crossed to the other side of Park. She flagged a cab going downtown. She got in, gave her address, and sat back as the cab rolled slowly down the block, stopping for a red light.

Her sudden appearance galvanized Billy, who stood watching with Yo from the corner below the Armory, wondering what he should do. As Diane crossed Park at 67th, Billy decided. He crossed parallel with her at 66th.

As she got into the cab, he made another decision. When the cab stopped at the light, he jerked open the door on the street side and got in beside her.

"Hey," shouted the cab driver. "Get the hell out."

In that instant, Billy would have gladly jumped back out, but the driver panicked and hit the electric lock switch, locking him in. Billy fumbled frantically, trying to get his hand inside his backpack.

"Who are those men?" he shouted at Diane. He was at that moment the perfect image of a bumbling fledgling terrorist.

"Who are *you?*" asked Diane with cold outrage, knowing in that instant who he was.

"Billy Ball." He didn't know what else to say.

She smiled and held out her hand. "I'm Diane. I'm a friend of your father."

"Do you know where he is?" Billy's voice yodeled and cracked with excitement. He withdrew his hand from the pack and took hers.

She held it gently for a moment. "Yes, I do. And if you'll ride downtown with me, I'll tell you how we can get him back."

The driver threw up his hands in the New Yorker's gesture of unsurprised exasperation, slammed the taxi into gear, and sped down Park Avenue toward the looming, ugly barricade of the Pan Am Building.

Watching from the window, Gold said, "That bitch."

Lazard stood next to him, talking into a walkie-talkie no larger than a beeper of the kind worn by doctors. "The kid jumped right in the goddamn cab with her. Stay on them *tight.*"

They both watched the cab speed down the avenue. Cowboy roared out of 66th Street on his heavy Harley from the direction of Madison Avenue, tailing the cab half a block behind.

Kavenaugh murmured, "What about Ball?"

"Put him in a wheelchair," said Lazard. "Take him out the service entrance and put him in the van. Keep him quiet."

Kavenaugh nodded, like a consulting doctor who had offered his clients several options and been given a decision. He left the room.

"Come on," said Lazard. "I'll buy you a drink at the Carlyle. We've both been in hotter water than this before. There's always a way."

"Yes," hissed Gold, "but I wanted a way in, not a way out."

Bro hung back. He watched the big Harley go after the taxi. He went after the Harley. In his mirror, he saw a nondescript sedan turn out of 67th, stop quickly to pick up a man from the downtown sidewalk, and proceed to bring up the rear. Bro took

the first left and rode fast over to Lexington. The sedan stayed
on Park. He fell into line behind the sedan, smiling happily to
himself. This promised to get better and better. Yo followed
two blocks behind on his bike, going as fast as a car down the
long slope toward midtown.

"Who's your friend on the Harley-Davidson?" asked Diane,
turning to watch the man on the motorcycle behind them.

"He beat me up once," said Billy. "I don't know his name.
I call him Cowboy."

Diane told the driver to drop them off at the west entrance
to the Pan Am Building, on the Vanderbilt Avenue ramp that
rose through the older, small Helmsley Building at the foot of
Park. The ramp then circled around the Pan Am Building and
Grand Central Terminal one level above the street, and dropped
back down to Park at 40th Street. She pushed a bill through
the divider behind the driver and told him to keep the change.

"Move fast when we get out," she said to Billy.

"Where's my father?"

"We'll get to that," she said. "First things first."

When the cab stopped, she pulled him out the door and
across the sidewalk. A guard opened a heavy glass door for
them. She flashed a card at him.

"Law firms," she said, smiling. "It's worse than being a
doctor. They pulled me right out of a party to read a lousy
five-page brief."

The guard asked her to sign a night visitor's book. "Who's
this, miss?"

"A messenger," she said. "I'll be sending him back down
in a few minutes. That guy on the big Harley's been harassing
me. If he hangs around out there, call the cops."

"Yes, miss."

They got into an elevator. She punched 8. The cab rose fast.

"How'd you know I was a messenger?"

"I didn't." She looked at him. "Are you?"

"Yes." Billy had the sickening sense that he was trapped,
that the adults had taken over again. He had to get away. He
had to find his father. But she said she knew where he was.
Billy casually shrugged the backpack off his back.

Her hand clamped down over his wrist. She was surprisingly

strong. "Don't, Billy. You're in the big leagues now."

The door opened right into the reception area of an office. A hard-looking middle-aged woman in a guard's blue serge uniform sat behind a reception desk. Diane walked straight toward a door in the back wall. The guard buzzed the door open.

"Tell Jerry we've got a visitor," said Diane. "I'm putting him in Room Four."

Diane marched Billy through the door with her hand gripping his upper arm. He was unresisting. She shoved him firmly into a small room. "Give me the pack," she said. He complied. She left him there, closing the door behind her.

A moment later, the door opened again. A young man in a tan suit walked in and closed the door quietly. He smiled and held his hand out in greeting. He had an alert, friendly face, half hidden under a full, black beard.

"I'm Jerry," he said. "You're Billy Ball. Sit down, Billy. We've got a lot to talk about. Are you old enough to smoke? Do you want a Coke?"

They stood on opposite sides of a bare metal desk. Two chairs were the only other furniture in the room. The man was treating him like a kid. He reacted in blind fury, with the desperation of a prisoner.

Billy took the man's proffered hand, clamped his other hand over the man's wrist, and pulled him over the desk. There was a brief, vicious struggle—a street fight. The man butted Billy in the groin with his head and grabbed Billy behind the knee with his free hand to take him down. But Billy pulled the man all the way onto the floor, stomped on his back, and kicked him in the side of the head. He kicked him again and again. The man jerked and gasped. He fell unconscious.

In great pain, breathing as though he had run a fast mile, Billy cracked the door open. To the left was a short hall and the door to the reception area. He couldn't go that way. To the right were three more doors, then the hall opened into a large open room full of desks and file cabinets. Most of the desks had typewriters and telephones on them. It was like a newspaper city room, but there wasn't a scrap of paper in sight. All the file cabinets were made of heavy metal. They had large combination locks built into the top drawers. The room was deserted. He could hear Diane talking on a telephone somewhere around the corner in the big room, out of sight.

He closed the door again and searched the man on the floor. He found a snub-nosed .38 in a holster on the man's right hip. Billy stuck the gun in the waistband of his jeans. In the inside left pocket of the man's suit jacket, Billy found a set of heavy laminated plastic credentials in a leather case. They identified the man as a special agent of the FBI.

Billy's breathing came faster. He was a fugitive. He had shot two people. He had crossed state lines. Now this. They would put him away forever. But they would never find him.

He stepped out into the hall. He couldn't pass the receptionist again. He crept to the edge of the big room. It was big and brightly lit by banks of flourescent lights in the ceiling. There was a row of windows in the far wall, covered by venetian blinds. The woman was in an office to his left. He could hear her but couldn't see her.

He stooped and scurried up the aisle between the nearest rows of desks. There was a fire exit in the far corner. On his hands and knees, he crawled as fast as he could to the far wall with the windows, and along the wall to the fire door. He was now in line with the woman's office. She was still on the phone.

He tried to calm his breathing. He studied the door. It was an ordinary heavy steel fire door with a slam bar on it. Thin wires led to a switch at the joint of the door and the door frame. He was sure this was an alarm. He peeked over the desk. The woman stood at a desk with her back to him. He would do what he was best at. He would run.

He went through the door as quietly as he could, but as he took the first jump down the fire stairs, he heard a loud beeping in the room behind him, and he heard the woman yell. He went down the stairs four and five at a time, swinging on the banister at each landing. There was a shout down the stairwell but no footsteps followed.

When he reached a door marked LOBBY—UPPER LEVEL, he stopped. The stairs continued down, but he had no idea where they went. The lobby sounded quiet. He pushed through the door and walked out. The guard looked up from his podium near the door, surprised.

"Elevator was stuck," said Billy. "She sent me out with a message."

"Workin' now," observed the guard. The floor indicator showed the elevator dropping fast.

Billy headed for the door.

"Whoa," said the guard. "Gotta sign out."

Billy scribbled in the book the guard pushed at him. He signed his own name. He couldn't think of another. He walked out the door, out of sight of the guard, and ran. He ran down the roadway toward Park Avenue. He had ridden his bike up here the day before on his way back to West 24th Street from a delivery. He knew where he was. He ran around the corner of Grand Central and began down the long ramp to East 40th Street. He picked up his pace.

He heard a car behind him. He ran faster. The car passed him. It was a dark sedan. It was harmless. Then the sedan swerved right in front of him. He tried to dodge it but he couldn't stop. The passenger door opened and a heavyset man lunged out. Billy twisted and jumped, trying to go over the hood of the car, but the man tackled him in midair with the force and agility of a pro linebacker. It knocked the wind out of Billy. He felt a sickening pain under his ribs, and he passed out.

The man threw Billy into the back seat and jumped in after him. "Go!" he shouted. The car ran the light at 40th Street and sped down into the tunnel under Park Avenue that comes out at 33rd Street.

At 33rd Street, Harry turned west across Madison and Fifth, past the Empire State Building, and into the deserted garment district.

"Anybody behind us?"

"Uh, uh," grunted Harry. "Where we going?"

"Take the kid home to his hotel, Harry. We're gonna meet Kurt and Philly there, and go up and have a nice meeting with this kid and his girl friend, and that priest."

A moment later, Volko cursed in his own language, in surprise. "You won't believe this," he said.

"Uh."

"This kid has a set of boxtops from some FBI agent named Jerry Frame, and a goddamn snub-nose .38!"

"I believe it," said Harry. "This kid is for real. He'd be an asset on any team. All he needs is more experience. He's already had his on-the-job training."

Volko laughed. "I'll bet this guy Frame is on the bus to Boise right now."

"Naw," said Harry. "They don't do that anymore. They

assign 'em to the civil rights squad."

"Stop at a pay phone," said Volko. "Mike is gonna be very interested in this. We ought to touch base."

When they drove away from the pay phone, heading west into the garment district, Yo came wildly down the dark sidewalk on his bike. He skidded to a stop beside the phone. He pushed a dime in and stabbed madly at the buttons on the face of the phone. He was breathing so hard he could hardly talk.

"Bobby," he gasped. "Yo. Thirty-third an' Eighth. Muthas inna blue car got Billy an' goin' toward Tenth."

He moved off as he said the last words. The phone dropped and swung like a pendulum at the end of its steel-wrapped cord. Before it came to rest, Yo was two blocks away and out of sight.

There was another chase going on at the same time, but this one was slow and deliberate, a game of cat and mouse. Bro was cruising slowly up Third Avenue in the East Fifties. He was following Cowboy, or perhaps Cowboy was leading Bro. Bro stayed about a block behind. The blocks were short, not even a hundred yards long.

It was like a children's game of follow-the-leader. When Cowboy changed lanes to pass a slow bus, Bro moved over too. When Bro accelerated slightly, Cowboy matched his speed. The distance between them stayed the same. Their speed matched the cycle of the traffic lights. They moved steadily uptown past the darkened, ugly office towers at a little less than thirty miles per hour. It was a dignified procession.

When Diane had pulled Billy out of the cab and pushed him into the Pan Am Building, the chain of pursuers came to a screeching halt. For one crazy moment, it was like a scene out of an old slapstick movie, then it resolved itself in a blur of high speed motion.

Cowboy shot up out of the curving tunnel through the Helmsley Building. The tunnel lifted the roadway in a short, steep S-curve from the level of Park Avenue to the level of the Vanderbilt Avenue ramp. The cab had stopped by the side entrance to the Pan Am Building, and Diane and Billy were running across the narrow sidewalk into the doorway. Cowboy slammed on his brakes. The Harley slid and fishtailed on the roadway.

Behind it, the blue sedan shot up out of the tunnel, coming too fast. Harry slammed on his brakes with a screech. The car began to slide. Harry's beer spilled in his lap. Volko said quietly, "Shit."

Yo heard the screaming tires, up around the bend in the tunnel ahead of him, out of sight, and saw Bro's brake light flash on. Instead of slowing down, Yo poured it on, thinking Billy was in real trouble.

As Yo rose up the curve in the tunnel, standing up on his pedals and pumping with everything he had, he heard the roar of the Harley accelerating away, hard and fast. He heard the more muted but still very loud roar of Bro's Honda. He heard the scrape of metal against concrete and the angry blast of an auto horn.

As he came out of the tunnel, he saw the cabbie standing on the curb by the open door of his cab, screaming and gesturing after the blue sedan, which had sideswiped the pasenger side of the cab and skidded back across the two-lane roadway into the concrete wall at the edge of the ramp over the street below. The blue car righted itself and disappeared around the edge of Grand Central at the far end of the ramp.

Yo stopped and jumped off his bike. He ducked back into a narrow architectural recess of the building, pulling his bike in after him. It was shadowed here. He would be invisible to anyone driving by in a car. The two motorcycles were gone, but he could hear them racing down Park Avenue. Billy and the woman were obviously in the building. Yo decided to wait for them to come out.

The cab drove off. A few minutes later, the blue sedan with the two men in it came slowly back up the ramp, having circled around. The driver pulled over and parked next to the building. The driver, a tall black man, got out and urinated on the wall. Yo was well concealed, but the car was only fifteen yards away.

Yo held his breath. The man had the look of a cop. Yo did not want to be asked why he was hiding in the recess with his bike. Yo held his breath a long time. The man finally finished peeing. He reached into the car, took out a bottle of beer, unscrewed the cap, and took a long drink. That explained it, thought Yo.

Now Yo had to pee, but he didn't dare. He waited. He leaned back into the corner of the recess. He began to daydream and nod off. He had learned to sleep on his feet in the Army.

He was jerked awake by the sound of the beer bottle shattering against the wall. There was a shout from the entrance of the building. The car shot forward, wheels peeling.

Billy was running down the roadway. It was a hundred yards to the far corner. The building guard was running out the door, lifting a gun out of its holster. The woman was running after the guard, shouting, "Don't shoot!"

The blue car roared past them. Billy was nearly at the far corner of the ramp. Yo leapt on his bike and rode after. The guard was out in the roadway, raising the gun in a two-handed stance. The woman was screaming, "Don't shoot, don't shoot!" She was too far from the guard to stop him.

Yo rode the guard down. He planted his foot in the small of the guard's back. There was a sickening groan from the man as he went down. The gun flew off into the air. The bike lurched and wobbled, but Yo righted it and rode on as hard as he could pedal. Now the woman was screaming, "Stop, stop!" but Yo ignored her and kept on. He saw the stocky man tackle Billy and throw him in the back of his car like a sack of potatoes. Yo didn't even slow down. He went after the car as if he was tied to it by a long rope.

At 58th Street, the Harley turned right, ran a red light at Second Avenue, and went up the ramp to the Queensboro Bridge. On the bridge, the Harley turned on the gas. The gap between the two bikes opened up. Bro had trouble holding the Honda steady on the open metal grating of the bridge roadway. The Harley's fatter, softer tires gave it a better grip on the slick, studded surface.

At the bridge plaza in Queens, the Harley wheeled around in a tight U-turn and headed back to Manhattan. Cowboy gave Bro the finger.

By the time, just a few moments later, that Bro started back up the long slope of the high bridge, the Harley was at the peak. Bro turned on the power on the asphalt surface, but when his wheels hit the grating, the bike began to fishtail and he had to slow down. As he rose over the peak, he saw the Harley crossing Second Avenue. Bro twisted the throttle and flew, momentum and mass keeping him upright, but the light changed fifty yards in front of him. He skidded to a stop at Second Avenue. There was too much traffic heading downtown for him to run the light. The Harley was out of sight.

For fifteen minutes, Bro drove back and forth across the East Side in a box pattern—over a few blocks, up a few, then back, edging progressively uptown. He stayed east of Park Avenue.

Nothing. There was a pay phone on the deserted corner of 66th and York, across from the dark, enclosed lawns and big buildings of Rockefeller University. Bro stopped by the phone and pulled his helmet off. He was sweating and angry with himself. He turned the engine off. As he stepped toward the phone, fishing in his pocket for a dime, he heard it—the distant blast of the Harley's pipes echoing off the high, silent buildings across the street.

Bro yanked on his helmet, jumped on the bike, and began the pursuit again. The noise was somewhere uptown, not more than a couple blocks away. The guy must have been cruising around to make sure he'd lost Bro, or else he was looking for Bro. Either way, it was OK with Bro.

Bro drove slowly up York, looking down the side streets at each intersection. This was an odd neighborhood, very quiet, more like Queens than Manhattan. Bro turned west on 72nd Street, a narrow, two-lane street here. He saw nothing. He stopped and listened. Nothing. He drove fast over to Third and stopped. He shut off his engine and pulled off his helmet. He heard nothing. Traffic was light. The city was still.

He drove over to Park and listened. There it was again— the distinctive heavy *rap-rap* of the Harley's exhaust at cruising speed, faint but not too far away. It was west. It was a block west, on Madison Avenue, and moving uptown.

Bro drove up Park, parallel to the sound of the Harley, stopping at each block to listen. He stayed with it up to 82nd, then he lost it. He drove fast over to Madison. It was gone.

Bro stopped and thought for a moment. He shut the bike off and got off and stretched. He was stiff and tense. It would take him an hour to cruise the grid of streets in the East Seventies and Eighties. No good.

He got on the bike and went back to the intersection at 79th and Park, where he last heard the sound of the Harley. He retraced his route back up to 82nd at the same speed as before, counting out loud, "One thousand one, one thousand two. . . ."

It took him about thirty seconds to cover the distance between the two points—where he had last heard the Harley and where he lost it. He drove back down to 79th, then over to Madison. He guessed the Harley had been a little less than a block ahead of him. Bro drove up to a point just short of 80th and stopped.

He looked around. If any cops were watching him, they would be wondering what the *hell* he was doing. He was always nervous about cops in this neighborhood. It was a nervousness that derived from his younger days. But there were no cops watching him now.

He started up Madison at a moderate speed, counting out loud. He got to "One thousand twenty-five" at 83rd Street, which was westbound toward Fifth. He could see the northern wing of the Metropolitan Museum at the end of the block. He drove slowly down the block toward Fifth, still counting.

When he said, "One thousand thirty," he stopped. Directly to his right was an underground parking garage. The ramp spiraled down under a large apartment building that fronted on Fifth. The garage door was up. A black man in green cotton work clothes sat on a battered metal folding chair by the entrance. He was eating a sandwich and drinking something out of a Thermos.

Bro wheeled his bike across the curb and up near the man. He shut off the engine and took off his helmet.

"Say, bro," said Bro. "My man come in yet? Big white dude on a big Harley?"

The man looked up at Bro for a second. "Yeah, 'bout five minutes ago. He come in with the van and a man in a wheelchair. Pushed him up the street to the house. You must missed 'em."

Bro hung his helmet on the handlebar and walked quickly back along the street. He couldn't have missed them entering the house by more than a minute or two. There was a large apartment building fronting on 83rd, then a short row of five-story houses like brownstones. Only the first one had lights on, and as Bro watched from the edge of the apartment building, the outside entrance lights were extinguished, then the interior lights, one by one and floor by floor, until only one window was lit, on the fourth floor.

Bro walked back to his bike. "Shit," he said. "See 'em in the mornin'. Thanks, bro."

He backed into the street and drove away down Fifth past the floodlit façade of the big museum. There was no point in hanging around, he knew. Sooner or later he would meet a couple of white cops in a patrol car. He might even meet one who remembered him.

At 55th Street he headed west, across Sixth, Seventh, Broadway, and Eighth. Now he relaxed. In this neighborhood he was considerably less conspicuous. And he had found Joe, and the dude who killed Soda Pop.

When Bro walked into the hotel room, a hard-looking black dude stepped out from behind the door. He had an automatic in his hand. He held it on Bro's middle as he closed and locked the door.

Billy and Annie were not alone. The priest sat in one chair, and Yo in another. Three hard-looking white men faced the door. Annie and Billy sat on a bed.

"You the dude on the big Honda?" asked the dude.

Bro nodded. "Unless you wanna eat that thing in your hand," he said, "point it somewhere else."

"Bang," said the man. "You're dead."

Billy said, "These are friends of a friend of mine, Bro. They're OK."

"If you say so," said Bro.

"We are having a little council of war," said one of the white men. He was stocky and swarthy, with a heavy black mustache. "Join us."

Annie said, "These men are going to help find Billy's father."

Bro said, "I just found him, but I don't think it's gonna be easy to get our hands on him. Those dudes have him in a wheelchair."

Billy said, "We'll do it. These men and Bro's Pros together."

"And me and Father Kelly," said Annie.

Bro looked around the room and smiled. "Yeah."

There was a knock on the door. At the second rap, five guns were pointing at the door. Bro was in the line of fire. He stepped quickly out of the way. Harry stood back behind the door.

"Who is it?" called Billy.

"Diane. Mike sent me."

Harry pulled the door open. Diane stood in the doorway, wearing slacks and running shoes, with a light golf jacket over a polo shirt. A sardonic smile spread across her face. "Well, well," she said. "Billy's Army."

SEVENTEEN

SHE STEPPED INSIDE and closed the door. "You're in a lot of trouble, young man," she said to Billy. "But not as much as I'll be in with Mike if we don't find your father."

She looked around. "You must be Volko. And Kurt, and Philly." They all nodded politely. "And Harry's behind the door."

"Yes, ma'am," said Harry.

"And who's this?" She looked at Bro.

"Bro," said Billy.

"Ah, yes. Bro's Pros, the messenger service."

Bro nodded.

"Yes, Bro," she said. "Your reputation precedes you. You are very well known in certain circles, I believe. How interesting that you should be involved in this fiasco."

She looked at the priest. "Father Kelly?" He nodded. "Your collar may come in handy before the end of the day."

"I'm just a fifth wheel here," he said.

"And who's this?" She looked at Annie. "The lovely Annie Dmitri?"

"How did you know?" asked Annie.

"The desk clerk downstairs is very responsive. Now, if you'll all relax, I have a message from Mike, and then we can make our plans for the morning."

She sat cross-legged on the bed.

"How do you know Mike?" said Volko.

"Let's say that he knows me."

"There's something heavy in your jacket," observed Harry.

"Oh, it's nothing," said Diane. "Practically harmless. It's just a lady's gun."

"What is it?" asked Annie.

"Just a little .32 Beretta."

"Like the French *flics* use," said Harry.

"Yes," said Diane. "They don't go in for the macho artillery we like to carry over here."

"What's the message from Mike?" asked Volko.

"Find Joe."

"What's the big rush now?" asked Billy. "No one was in any hurry before."

"Your father," said Diane, "is about to receive the post-humous E. Howard Hunt Award for the 1980 presidential campaign."

"I don't understand."

"Neither did I until tonight. Gold and Lazard are playing Brazil. It's ingenious. They are going to destabilize the 1980 elections. They've laid a paper trail that leads from your father back to Langley, Virginia. They're going to dump him in a midtown hotel room tomorrow. Dead. Some forged papers in the room will lead the New York cops and the FBI to the Democratic National Committee *and* to a prominent Republican fund-raiser in this city. Joe's past employment will soon be uncovered. A *Times* reporter will get a tip. The Democrats will blame the Republicans. The Republicans will say the Democrats are setting them up. The *Times* will be burrowing toward Langley. Soon someone will stumble across a new Deep Throat."

"Watergate Two," said Harry.

"Very good point," said Diane.

"I don't understand," said Billy. "What's the point?"

"Destabilization and restabilization," said Diane patiently. "There *is* a strong right wing in this country. They're not going to be happy with Reagan and they know it already. But he's the only game in town right now. They're not stupid, but they usually do things one step at a time. This time, however, unlike 1964, 1968, and 1976, they're planning ahead. Their year is 1984. They can't win by themselves. They don't have the numbers. But if the two major parties are weak in '84, and there are several independent candidates in the race besides the Democrat and the Republican, they think they can split the vote and carry the contest. It's a pretty good scheme. They think it's worth a shot. The ripple effect of their little nuke tomorrow will be devastating. I wish I'd thought of it myself. I might be the first in line to run on their ticket."

"How do you know all this?" asked Billy.

"It was sort of my idea, but they ran away with it."

"Jesus," said Billy. He looked at Volko.

Volko had a tired expression on his face, an expression of disgust. "They do this all the time," he said. *"Agents provocateurs.* It's been done in Eastern Europe since the Huns. You find a group, speed them along to their climax, and smash it, or turn it to your own purposes. It is a classic technique in a filthy business. Jungle warfare is cleaner than this, Billy. You should understand that, for what it's worth to you."

Diane said, "Thank you, professor. Are you done?"

Volko nodded and turned away.

"Unfortunately," she said, "there is a great deal at stake here. The original conspirators were willing but not able. It is no good having loose cannons rolling around the deck in a battle. We simply had to establish control over this group. We don't like being blind-sided. So I helped them along. They had the right instinct but they couldn't get it up. I was finally forced to loan them a theoretician."

"Kavenaugh," said Volko.

"How did you guess?"

"I got a glimpse of him earlier tonight."

"The guy in the Armory?" asked Billy.

Volko nodded.

"He's a mean bastard," said Harry.

Volko, Kurt, and Philly all nodded. Diane said, "Yes, but he's the very best."

There was a long silence. Father Kelly watched Billy. Billy and Annie looked at each other. Everyone else watched everyone else. Volko pulled an edge of the blind aside and looked down at the street.

"You bring any troops?" he asked Diane.

She shook her head. "My end of this is very closely held. Jerry Frame was my only troop, and Billy put him in the hospital tonight."

"All *right,*" said Yo.

She looked at Billy. "Do you have Frame's boxtops and gun? I think if you return them, we can paper over your stupid assault on a federal agent."

"You can have the boxtops," said Billy. "But I'll keep the gun for the time being."

"Billy the *Kid,*" said Yo.

"It's like Frankenstein," said Annie.

They all looked at her.

"Yes," said Diane. "Now we have to eliminate my monstrous creation." She looked around. "Who's in charge here?" She looked expectantly at Volko.

Billy said, "I am."

"Well, now you're the executive officer," she said. "And I'm the boss. Any problems with that?"

Bro looked at Billy over her head and winked. No one said anything.

She looked around again. "Does anyone know where Joe is?"

"You said you did," said Billy, cutting off a comment from Bro.

"I ordered him moved, but now they won't tell me where he is." She looked at Volko, who watched her with glittering intensity. "I can read your mind," she said. "No. I don't think they caught on. But I know Gold is very pissed off at me and thinks he can use Joe as a blue chip."

Billy stepped forward. "Let's get started."

"Billy the *Kid,*" said Bro. "Let me get my dudes together."

"Where is this place, Bro?" asked Volko.

"Looks like East Eighty-third, off Fifth."

"My God," said Diane. "How did you find out? It's Gold's house. It's a fortress."

"Have you been in it?" asked Volko.

"Yes."

"Good," he said. "First, you draw us a map. Then, since you're our leader, you can lead the charge."

• • •

Kurt and Philly left the room, taking a few tools with them. They returned an hour later with a florist's delivery van. They brought a large take-out breakfast, too.

At the first light, Volko, Philly, Bro, and Billy drove slowly past the house on East 83rd. It was a substantial brick row house with the entrance a few steps below street level.

"Four floors and a garret," said Volko. "She says there's an elevator in the back. It doesn't go up to the garret. Gold has a gym in the fourth floor rear. What do you bet they put him in there?"

"Yeah," said Philly. "It's possible. But we'll have to go through the whole place. She says they're gonna plant him this afternoon?"

"Yeah," said Volko. "The press'll figure out a little bit today, and a little more tomorrow, just in time for the front page of the Sunday papers. Gold is looking for big coverage. The conventions are only a month away."

Looking at the building, Bro said, "There's no way."

"All the glass in the front windows has a blue-green tint," said Billy.

"Armored," said Volko. "She was right about the fortress part."

"Go around the block again," said Philly. "I want another look at the entrance."

The entrance was a shuttered metal door. The ground-floor windows were barred and shuttered. Blinds and curtains covered every window in the façade.

After the second time around, Philly said, "I've done a lotta bag jobs, kid, but I gotta tell you, this looks tough. Impossible, maybe."

"You guys have enough tools for a bank," said Billy.

"Yeah, sure. We can get in. But it'll be noisy, too public, you know? The whole point is to get out, you know what I mean?"

"Now what?" Billy was discouraged. They had discarded one plan after another.

"Nice house," said Bro. "Must be worth a couple million."

They stopped at Fifth and 81st. Bobby walked out of the

shadows under the trees in the museum plaza. He was pushing his bike.

Volko said, "Keep an eye on the house. If anybody moves in or out, use the walkie-talkie. If you can't raise us, go to a pay phone and call Billy's room. Somebody'll be there, probably Annie and the priest. Got it?"

Bobby gave a thumbs-up to Billy. The van moved off, down Fifth Avenue past the early-morning runners and dog walkers. Billy was in despair, but in the end, they found a plan. They decided on a mugging. It was Yo's idea.

Harry and Yo and the others were waiting in the hotel room.

"Tell 'em," said Harry. "We figured it out. It took a brother to figure it out. Tell 'em, Yo."

"A mugging."

"A mugging?" asked Billy. "What kind of bullshit is this?"

"Yo is gonna mug the lady here," said Harry.

"A push-in," said Yo.

"You'll have to explain," said Billy. "I don't live up here in this city."

"You push 'em in the door," said Yo. He was excited at the prospect of a legal mugging. "You know. The old lady walks up to her apartment door, fumbles for her keys, puts down her groceries, puts the key in the lock, opens the door, bends down to pick up the grocery bag, and you come outta the stairwell and push her in the door."

"Jesus," said Philly, taking a step forward. "You do these things, guy?"

"No, no, not me," said Yo, holding up his hands in mock horror. "I just heard about it from some guy on my block."

Philly said, "Somebody did that to an old lady in South Philly, he'd be dead."

Harry laughed and said, "Don't get hot, Philly. You don't understand. Yo here understands the theory of the thing. It's just a theory. It's harmless, like political theory, like that harmless little .32 Diane carries in her pocket."

"I understand," said Philly, looking down at Diane sitting cross-legged on the bed, drinking coffee.

She was cold and distant. She gave no reaction to the taunts. Harry said, "Diane is gonna call Gold at his house, tell

him it's an emergency, tell him they hafta meet at his place.
She's not gonna take no for an answer. She's gonna show up
at the door five minutes later, before they have time to move.
When she goes to the door, and they open it, Yo is gonna push
her in and go in with her. Then the rest of the assault team
goes in. Easy, huh? Simple, huh?"

Volko said, "I like it."

Billy turned to Philly. "It's kamikaze."

Philly said, "It's the only way, kid."

"Let's go," said Volko. "I want to do it around eight o'clock,
when the cops are changing shifts. I want to be in and out in
five minutes."

Billy said to Annie, "You and Father Kelly stay here. Stay
by the telephone."

"I don't like any of this," said Father Kelly.

"You're not any part of it, Father. You're just a chaperone
for Annie here."

"That's good thinking, kid," said Philly. "You should be a
Jesuit when you grow up."

Volko drove the van, with Diane in the passenger seat and the
rest in the back with half a load of potted palms. Bro followed
on his Honda. At Madison and 79th, Volko pulled to the curb
by a phone booth. Philly slid the side door open, and Yo got
out, dragging his bike.

"Just get up there and loiter," said Philly. "You know?"

"Yeah, I think I know," said Yo. He climbed on his bike
and pedaled slowly up the street toward 83rd.

"Go to the phone," said Volko.

Diane got out, followed by Billy. She looked sharply at him
but said nothing.

"A good deputy should know everything his boss knows,
right?" said Philly loudly.

Volko sat calmly, smoking a pipe, watching the street ahead
and the rearview mirrors.

Diane called. The phone rang once and was snatched up.
"Get me Gold," she said to someone. "This is Diane."

She waited a moment, then said, "This is Diane. You were
expecting me? Your hood answered fast enough."

"No," she said. "I haven't been in my office or apartment.

"I've been working. . . . Telling you assholes what to do isn't my only job. . . . Yes, assholes. . . . And a few other things, too. . . .

"I have some bad news from someone. We have to meet. . . . Now. . . . Hold everything right where it is. . . . Don't move the package.

"I'll be there in fifteen minutes. . . . No. Wait for me there." She hung up.

Billy held his thumb up.

Volko looked at his watch.

Billy and Diane got back in the truck. Volko got out and walked back to talk to Bro for a minute. When he returned, he tapped his pipe out on the side of the truck, put the pipe in his pocket, and got in. He looked at his watch again and eased the truck away from the curb into a break in the heavy morning traffic. Bro followed on his motorcycle.

Bobby was waiting on the southwest corner of Madison and 83rd. Volko pulled in by the curb in the crosswalk. Bobby held his thumb up.

Volko said to Diane, "Go. Make it fast."

She got out and dog-trotted down the street toward Gold's house. Volko turned the corner slowly. Bobby followed on his bike, a whistle in his mouth. Bro hung back.

Diane crossed the street to the north sidewalk. Volko picked up a little speed.

Yo closed in from the other end of the block.

"Remember, Billy," said Volko. "You're the doorman. Don't go upstairs no matter what happens. Get that front door closed after us as soon as we're all in. Keep the noise in the house. You're the last in and the last out. Got it? Hold that door for us on the way out. And no shooting with that cannon of yours. You're the only one without a silencer."

"What about her?" asked Billy. He nodded at Diane's back.

Philly held up the little Beretta. "She's a few ounces lighter than she was before."

She was almost at the door. Volko drifted along the line of parked cars on the north side of the street. Bro stalled his motorcycle in front of a taxi trying to turn into 83rd and Madison. The driver yelled at Bro. With great deliberation, Bro got off his motorcycle, put the kickstand down, and walked back toward the cabbie.

Diane rang the buzzer. Volko stopped the van. Bobby stopped forty yards ahead at the corner of Fifth. The door of the house opened. A man wearing a dark suit and sunglasses peered out. He opened the door wider to let Diane in. Yo whipped around the edge of the building and slammed into Diane from the back like a free safety going up for the football. With one hand, Yo held the door open. With the other, he grabbed the man by the throat. It was a perfect, silent mugging.

Philly slammed back the side door of the van. Philly, Kurt, Harry, and Billy piled out onto the sidewalk, each carrying a potted palm. Volko trotted around from his side of the van, his pipe back in his mouth, his hand in his jacket pocket. He was the first into the house, then the others. Billy was last. He heaved his palm into the entry hall and slammed the door, jamming a piece of plastic into the latch in case the lock was electric.

There was no shooting. There was no one in the house but Gold, Lazard, and the hood who lay on the tiled floor of the entry hall, his neck under Yo's white leather Puma basketball shoe. Philly and Kurt went upstairs and came back down again.

"Nobody," said Kurt.

Harry came up from the basement. "Nobody," he said.

Volko looked at Gold. "Where's Joe?"

Gold tried to speak but gagged with fear. His voice squeaked. He was running with sweat as though he was in a Turkish bath.

"Where?" said Volko to Lazard.

"Fuck you, Bulgarian pig," said Lazard.

Harry smiled.

Volko slammed Lazard in the stomach, spun him around, and frog-marched him into the next room. Volko closed the door.

There was a long silence, then a high-pitched, endless scream. Gold puked into the broken palms.

Volko came out of the room, holding a bloody switchblade. He wiped it on Gold's jacket, and closed it. He dropped it in his pocket and pulled out his pipe.

"What did you do?" asked Diane.

"Carved a word on his chest and threatened to give him a higher voice. He did something to me once, years ago."

"What was the word?"

"Fascist."

"Where's Joe?" she asked.

Volko didn't answer at first. Then he said, "I was going to leave you here with these animals, but I don't think I will. Kurt can watch them. You come with us. The Hotel Van Gogh on West Forty-fourth Street. Let's go."

"Wait," cried Billy. "How long ago?"

"Fifteen minutes. They must have slipped past Bobby when he left the museum steps to meet us."

"How did they know we were coming?"

"They didn't, I don't think," said Volko. He looked at Diane.

She looked back with hot anger. She was scuffed and bruised from the mugging. "No," she said. "They sure as hell didn't."

"Let's go," said Volko.

Billy picked up a telephone and called Annie.

"I want my gun back," said Diane.

Volko nodded. Philly handed it to her. She checked it and put it in her jacket pocket. She brushed herself off.

"Let's go," she said, recovering her sense of command.

They filed out to the van. Bobby gave a shrill blast on his whistle. Bro walked slowly away from the screaming cabbie and got on his motorcycle. Bobby and Yo headed down Fifth on their bikes. Volko drove the van slowly around the corner onto Fifth, through a red light, and picked up speed. Bro followed.

"What's the fastest way?" he asked Diane.

"Just stay on Fifth. This is the worst time of the morning, but there's no other way."

Volko looked at his watch. "Six minutes in the house. That was slow."

Annie slammed down the phone. "Wait here," she said to the priest. "I gotta go help Billy."

She pulled a sweat shirt on over her head. Billy's bike leaned against one wall. There was no other place to keep it. She lifted it easily over the bed near the door.

"Where are you going?" asked the priest.

"Van Gogh Hotel. That's where they took his dad. He thinks I can beat them there and spot the room."

She jerked the door open and pulled the bike out into the hall. The door stayed open behind her.

Father Kelly sat for a few moments, listening to the noises of the old hotel, the old men shuffling to the bathroom at the end of the hallway, a loud TV nearby. The thought came to him from somewhere that politics was by its nature violent, no less violent here than in many other countries, but the violence here was oddly sublimated and displaced. Hitler, he remembered, had been elected. Hitler, he remembered reading somewhere, was the bad conscience of democracy.

He looked around the little room where two kids had lived together for less than a week. They were nice kids. He hoped nothing happened to them. He hoped nothing happened to their friends. He hoped nothing happened to Joe. He bowed his head and made a short prayer for the safety of Billy and Annie and their friends. He was a priest. He was a pacifist. Praying was all he could do. But it was something, he reminded himself dully.

He left the little room. He locked the door behind him. He decided to go to the Van Gogh to pick up the pieces.

The Van Gogh was a good hotel, small by midtown standards, a bit old and seedy, but clean and quiet. It was a mixture of residents and transients, the sort of place whose employees respected privacy, and protected it. Occasional groups of Latin American or Japanese tourists booked there. Business people whose work took them to New York for extended trips rented suites for a week, or a month or two.

Such a suite had been rented for June and July by a man calling himself Joe Ball, and a man calling himself Joe Ball had spent about half the nights of June there. He let it be known that he was a public relations and political consultant, but he kept to himself. He was joined by a good-looking, dark-haired woman of about thirty nearly every night he spent there. He was a heavy tipper. Several times, the desk clerk and the elevator operator heard Mr. Ball call the woman Diane. He had asked about having a private phone installed in his room, then changed his mind. The switchboard placed all his calls, and kept a record for his bill.

A week before this Friday, on the day before the beginning of the long holiday weekend, two men who looked like cops or bodyguards came to the desk and asked to speak to the

assistant manager. They inquired about renting the best available suite on a long-term basis for a reclusive and senile old
industrialist named Fritz, who had lived in the Southwest for
many years and now wanted to return to the city of his birth
and youth. A monthly rental was agreed on and paid in advance.
A suite was readied. The staff was warned to expect Mr. Fritz
on short notice within a week or two. The staff was amused
and curious, remembering the stories of the eccentric Howard
Hughes.

This Friday morning, the switchboard got a call, saying Mr.
Fritz would arrive in a wheelchair at eight or shortly after.
Please to have the room ready. The switchboard operator alerted
everyone.

At eight-fifteen, a van pulled up outside the hotel. The two
bodyguards in dark suits got out and slid open the side door.
A tall, rangy man in Levi's got out, followed by a pale man
in a suit who looked like a doctor. The tall man lifted a skinny
old man in a wheelchair to the sidewalk from the inside of the
van. The move seemed effortless. The man in the wheelchair
was wrapped in a heavy blanket pulled up around his head and
down around his face.

"Mr. Fritz," announced the man who looked like a doctor.

The doorman tried to help with the wheelchair, but the
bodyguards, who had taken flanking positions on the sidewalk,
swept him out of the way. One of them opened the front door.
The tall man carried the chair up the few steps and set it down
inside the lobby. The other bodyguard drove the van away.

The tall man pushed the old man in the wheelchair through
the small lobby toward the elevators in the back. The doctor
preceded and the bodyguard followed.

"Where's the elevator?" asked the doctor. "It's not here."

The desk clerk came around to the front of the desk and
looked at the indicator. "It'll be down in a moment, sir."

"This the freight elevator?" asked the tall man, nodding at
a second elevator door.

"Yes, sir."

"Take us up."

The clerk hesitated for a moment.

"Now," said the tall man.

"Yes, sir."

They all stepped into the freight elevator and went up. It was slow and noisy, but it seemed to satisfy.

A moment later, Annie darted into the lobby and up to the desk. There was no one there but the telephone operator in a little alcove.

"Yes, dear?" she called.

Annie was breathless. "My grandfather," she said. "My grandfather. Was that him?"

"How should I know, dear?"

"I haven't seen him for years. I was just going by." Annie was hopping up and down with excitement.

"Ten-oh-eight?"

Annie shrugged.

"Mr. Fritz?"

"Fritz?" said Annie. "No, no. Not Fritz. Kaplan. Mr. Herbert Kaplan. From Albany."

"No, dear. I'm sorry."

"Oh, I'm sorry too," said Annie. "Are you sure?"

"Yes, dear. Oops, there they are now. Gotta go." She punched a button on her switchboard.

Annie waved thanks with her fingertips and ran out to the sidewalk. The bodyguard who had driven the van away brushed past her as he went inside. She looked after him. He sat down on a couch in the lobby and opened a *Daily News*.

Annie headed east up the street in the direction the others would come from.

Upstairs in 1008, the bodyguard put the phone down. "No answer at the house."

"Odd," said Kavenaugh. "Wait a few minutes and try again."

The bodyguard went to the window and stood peering down at 43rd Street from the back of the hotel. He could see the barren, litter-strewn plaza behind the Grace Building, near the corner of Sixth Avenue. The tall man shoved the wheelchair into the corner and flopped down on the bed. Kavenaugh sat in a chair.

"Grungy goddamn place," said Cowboy.

"No one's gonna live in it," said the bodyguard.

Joe stared into the dark corner of the room where Cowboy had shoved him. He was awake and conscious. The drug they'd given him had had no effect. He supposed his body was so badly short-circuited that the chemical reactions were all funny and wrong. He hadn't struggled or fought because he didn't want another beating or another injection. He would just hang on as long as he could and see what happened. He knew something had gone wrong with their plans, but he didn't know what. Under the hooded blanket, his eyes peered out of his emaciated, bruised face at the faded flowers of the wallpaper a yard away.

The phone rang. Kavenaugh answered.

The operator said, "Mr. Gold coming up, sir."

Kavenaugh set the phone down. "Something's wrong," he said. "Gold's here."

The scene in the lobby was a frozen tableau. Harry stood behind the desk next to the switchboard operator. He held the gold shield of a New York detective in one hand and a cop's .38 in the other. The desk clerk stood in terrified immobility. On the floor behind the desk lay the bodyguard, his feet tied with his tie, his hands cuffed behind his back, a wad of newsprint stuffed in his mouth.

The switchboard buzzed. "Don't touch it," growled Harry.

"But it's old Mrs. Espy, wanting her breakfast. She'll come down to see what's wrong."

"We'll be gone."

"She'll have a heart attack," said the operator helplessly.

Diane stood by the front door. Bro stood next to the doorman on the sidewalk, about an inch away from him.

Billy, Philly, and Volko rose slowly in the freight elevator to the tenth floor.

"This is police business, old man," said Philly roughly.

"This kid ain't no cop," said the elevator operator with querulous insistence.

"This kid is cop enough to give you a hard time," said Philly. "And he's gonna stand right here with you while you wait for us."

"Which way is the room?" asked Volko.

"Left," said the old man. "There's an alcove down at the end. It's the first door on the left in there."

The elevator quivered to a stop. The old man opened the door.

"Fast and hard," said Volko. He ran down the hall, Philly on his heels.

On West 44th Street, Father Kelly turned the corner from Sixth Avenue and walked slowly up the block. He saw Bro standing next to the doorman. Bro was looking into the lobby. He held the doorman by the arm. Father Kelly saw Bro press something into the doorman's hand. The doorman smiled and nodded his head in agreement with something Bro said.

The Algonquin, thought the priest. Here it is. I never knew where it was. He was standing across the street from the Van Gogh. Annie stepped out of a nearby doorway and joined him on the sidewalk in front of the famous hotel at their backs. They stood in silence, waiting.

The door of 1008 burst open as though a grenade had hit it.

"Freeze," shouted Philly.

Cowboy came up off the bed like a vicious dog. Volko's gun butt came down like a hammer. Cowboy fell back and came up at him again.

Philly's gun went *"pffutt, pffutt"* and Cowboy fell back down on the bed, bleeding from the chest. Another *"pffutt"* produced a small black hole in the middle of Cowboy's forehead.

The bodyguard was reaching for a gun. *"Pffutt, pffutt, pffutt"* went Volko's gun. The bodyguard slumped into the corner. The gun dropped out of his hand.

"Pffutt" went Philly's gun again, and made a hole in the bodyguard's forehead.

"Bring Joe," said Volko. "Let's go, Kavenaugh."

Kavenaugh rose meekly out of his chair. The smell of shit followed him. There was a wet puddle on the chair seat.

Billy said nothing when he saw his father in the wheelchair. Volko had told him not to speak in the hotel. But there were tears in Joe's eyes. That was enough for Billy.

Harry was the last one out of the lobby.

"But what about him?" cried the switchboard operator, pointing at the hood handcuffed on the floor behind the desk.

"Call the cops," shouted Harry over his shoulders.

Father Kelly watched in stupefied amazement as the procession emerged from the hotel. Annie ran across the street. She rode off toward Sixth on Billy's bike. The others lifted the wheelchair into the florist's van and drove away. Bro walked quickly back to Sixth, where he had parked his motorcycle on the sidewalk around the corner. The doorman ran inside the hotel.

No one on the street seemed to notice anything unusual, or if they did, they ignored it. A police siren rose and fell somewhere in the middle distance. The Algonquin doorman offered Father Kelly a cab, which the priest politely refused. The priest walked away toward Sixth Avenue. The noise and heat of the morning rush hour rose from the streets, enfolding him. There was nothing for him to do.

EPILOGUE ═══════════════

IT WAS THE Sunday of Labor Day weekend. A sign on the front door of Mike's Place said CLOSED, but inside there was a re-union in progress.

Volko, Harry, Philly, Kurt, and Pete stood at the bar drinking beer in their accustomed places, in their customary clothes. Annie and Billy sat at one end of the bar. Joe stood next to them. Mike stood behind the bar.

Annie was drinking Perrier and lime. When she ordered it, Mike's eyebrows rose slightly. "New York chic," he said. When Billy ordered a beer, Mike served it but admonished, "Nurse it."

Of those present, only Joe was changed. He looked rested and he had his tan back. He wore a snappy lightweight suit with a proper shirt and bow tie, but he was thin and his face was marked by some ugly new scars. He sipped a vodka martini on the rocks with a Salonika pepper in the bottom. "My first," he said, "since the troubles. I've been running a lot. I've switched to beer. You can't drink anything but beer and run a lot."

Mary came out of the kitchen and set trays of egg rolls and Sicilian pizza on the bar. "There's more," she said. "Joe, stay away from the hot mustard."

"It's OK," he said. "The doc says I'm all in one piece again."

A taxi drew up outside and drove quickly away. Heavy footsteps crossed the wooden porch. A heavy fist hammered on the door. Mike went to open it. In strode Bro, followed by Bobby and Yo.

"Air*borne!*" shouted Bro.

"Billy the *Kid,*" yelled Bobby, waving a red bandanna.

Yo was laughing. "Shee-it. That cab driver thought we were gonna mug his white ass."

"Not you," said Philly. "It's all theory where you come from."

"Where's that priest?" asked Bro, when he had a tall Scotch and water in his hand.

"He's coming," said Billy.

"Then there's only one missing," said Annie.

"She's been missing since July," said Joe.

They told the story over and over, laughing and teasing. How as they drove away from the Van Gogh, Volko had looked at his watch and said, "Six minutes. Not good enough." How they abandoned the van and wheelchair in front of the Public Library and scattered.

How Billy and Diane took Joe to a doctor she had alerted, then put Joe on a private plane to Washington, Diane with him. She took him to a private clinic in the Virginia countryside, where Joe spent six weeks recovering and resting.

How Billy and Annie found an apartment in the West Village, where Billy spent the summer and Annie was to remain, working and going to her dance and acting classes.

"I wish I'd seen you doing your number in that hotel lobby," said Joe to Annie. "You must be great."

"Hey," said Philly. "We weren't so bad either."

How Bro and Billy and Bro's architect bought the building on 24th Street, set up a real estate company, formed a corporation for construction, and started making money with their money.

"No sense in letting it sit idle," said Bro in a polished boardroom accent.

"That money," said Harry, "was *never* idle."

"Hey, bro," said Bro. "Do I jive *you?*"

Left unsaid was how Mike, Mary, Volko, and the other hoods each got an investment-grade diamond in the mail one day in August; and how a messenger arrived at the storefront on 24th Street that same day with packages for Yo and Bobby and Soda Pop's mom—when opened, the packages contained substantial sums of cash equal to the value of the diamonds sent to the others.

Billy had quietly queried Bro about the arrangement. Bro had confirmed that it would be dangerous for dudes like Bobby and Yo, and a poor old lady like Soda Pop's mom, to try to sell high-grade stones in the diamond district.

"They'll slap 'em in jail if they don't cheat 'em or shoot 'em," Bro had said.

They talked about basketball and schools, and told old war stories about the photos on the wall. Mike took a camera out from behind the bar and took a picture of the group. He promised to frame it and add it to the gallery. Bro and Yo and Bobby were as thrilled as kids.

"There goes your cover," said Philly.

"Seen one, you seen 'em all," said Harry.

At one point, Annie looked at the shattered glass over the photo of JFK, and asked, "How did that happen?"

Mike shrugged and pointed to Volko. "Ask him."

Volko looked at Annie over the rim of his beer glass and said, "Better a dead lion than a live dog."

Annie looked surprised, then she understood.

They talked on. It grew late. Still, Father Kelly did not show up.

Mary came out and announced dinner. They all drifted into the back room except Joe. He stayed at the bar. He was thinking about Diane. He knew she had known about the torture, condoned it, maybe ordered it. But the torture had freed him from the game. His anger and guilt were burned out. Now he could go fishing with Billy.

Joe looked at his scarred face in the mirror. He was secretly glad it had happened. He had talked to Father Kelly about it, and the priest had understood. So in his mind, Joe thanked Diane for what she had done—entirely unintended by her, he knew. He raised his glass to her image in his mind. He re-

membered the peculiar cryptic murals in the RCA Building,
and the cold concrete floor in the Armory, and he forgave her.
He hoped he would be forgiven his own long, long list of
trespasses.

He lit one of his cheap Filipino cigars and blew the smoke
at the mirror. This was another old habit that had become no
more than an occasional indulgence. He got himself a beer and
joined the others.

Three tables were pulled together and set with tablecloths
and napkins. There were chopsticks next to the flatware. Mary
had promised a feast. The others were already sitting. Mike
had found some nice music on the bar radio and switched it to
the speakers in the back room. Everyone was mellow and
happy. Mike and Mary began to bring out the food.

There was a light, tentative knock at the front door. "I'll
get it," said Joe. He walked up front. At the door were Father
Kelly and Diane.

"Was this arranged?" asked Joe.

"No," said Diane quickly. "I really wasn't going to come.
We just happened to drive up together."

Joe snorted. The priest smiled.

Joe got Father Kelly a beer from the bar. The priest walked
back to the others. The greetings were loud.

"Couldn't figure out what the hell you were doing all night,
just sitting there," said Philly. "Then it came to me. I thought
to myself, He's a priest. He must be praying."

"Good guess," said Father Kelly. "You should be a Jesuit
when you grow up."

"Make me a martini, Joe. Straight up." Diane sat on a bar
stool. She ran her fingers over the scarred surface of the zinc-
topped bar and watched him mix the drink. "You look good,
Joe. How do you feel?"

"OK. Where've you been?" He looked up at her.

"Cleaning up the mess. It was a real mess, Joe. And there
were a couple of older messes that you didn't know about.
Lazard and Gold are in up to their noses, Joe, and they've got
some very, very powerful friends. But you guessed all that."

Joe nodded. He set the drink in front of her. He stayed
behind the bar.

She sipped the drink. "This thing turned out to be much
rougher than anyone anticipated. But I got it all straight. Today

was the last loose end. I just got off the plane from a visit with
Dan McCagg in East Hampton. That's why I'm late. I put the
hammer on him."

"Did he stand up and salute?"

"You bet. And he asked about you too."

"What'd you tell him?"

"That you were off-limits."

Joe looked at her face. She had tears in her eyes. She patted
the stool next to her. "Sit next to me, Joe."

Joe reached across the bar and took her hands. "I've missed
you," he said. "Six weeks ago I would have killed you. But I
never stopped missing you. Then the anger burned out and I
still missed you."

"Me too," she said. Her voice was a whisper. Tears streamed
down her face but she couldn't take her eyes away from his.

"You paid your dues with this one," he said.

"You paid them for me."

"Stay with me tonight," he said.

"No, you stay with me. Give the kids a little privacy."

"A deal." He leaned close to her. "Now tell me your real
name."

She laughed, but the laugh was a whisper. "You always had
everything figured out."

"No, I didn't. I didn't ask for what I got from Kavenaugh."

She dropped her gaze. "Oh, God. Neither did I. He's like
a machine. You wind him up and point him and he goes. I
never worked with him before."

"That's always the way," said Joe. "It was easier in the
jungle. You could look on a map and see where you were."

"Maria," she said. "My name is Maria Rivera Kennedy. My
mother was Mexican and my father was Irish."

"Marry me," he said, "and go fishing."

"I won't quit my job. But I'll marry you, and you can go
fishing all you want."

At the table, Billy asked Diane what happened to Gold and
Lazard and McCagg.

There was a brief silence. The instincts of the insiders around
the table ran toward secrecy, even when the secrets were known.

But Diane said, "It's all in the family, I guess. We just keep them in the bank. We'll use them sometime for one thing or another. They're on a very short leash now. Gold has close ties to the lunatic fringe of the Republican Party. Lazard knows all of Rocky's old buddies. McCagg is a powerful senator. It looks like Reagan's going to win. Who knows? They'll be quite useful. McCagg can help at budget time, for one thing, and we need his approval for certain operations. It's all politics, pure and simple."

"It's not pure, and it's not simple," said Annie.

No one asked about Kavenaugh.

After dinner, Joe took Father Kelly aside. "You've got something that belongs to me, Father."

"I transferred it back to your account weeks ago, Joe."

"I'm kidding, Father. Actually, you do have it."

As the priest opened his mouth to protest, Joe raised his hand for silence. "I owe you, Father. That move of yours saved my life. I don't think you realize that. They would have killed me the instant they got their hands on the gold. I didn't fully realize it myself until I unraveled the whole thing one sleepless night in the clinic."

The priest said, "I certainly didn't know what I was doing, but I'm glad it had the effect it seems to have had. It certainly affected me. Priests like to pretend they're incorruptible. Now I know I'm not."

Joe said, "I opened an account for you. I know you can't take the stuff for yourself, but the Church can use it. And I know the Church knows how to launder money."

The priest shook his head. Politics and money went hand in glove with violence. The Church in history was no stranger to any of it, but the priest wanted no part of it.

He thought of the odd parallels between Joe's colonial armies in the jungles of Southeast Asia, and Billy's army on the streets of New York City. He thought of Joe's astonishing forgiveness of Diane. He thought of Billy's powerful love for his father.

Joe pressed a slip of paper into Father Kelly's hand. "Here's the bank name and the account code. It's all in there now. What's left is quite a lot. I don't want the damn stuff anymore.

I bought a new house on the beach and a new boat. I've got Billy. I've got Diane. I've got everything I need. So give it to the Pope."

"Can we really do this?" asked the priest.

"Is the Pope Catholic?"

That night, when they got to her place, Diane took Joe's hand and guided it between the buttons of her blouse. Stuck firmly in her navel was the emerald.

"I stuck it in this morning when I got up. I knew today was the day."

Joe began to sing. It was the last stanza of the song.

> *If any girl'll have me,*
> *She'll only have to say.*
> *I'll hang my halo on a hook*
> *Until another day.*
>
> *For the leaves are getting greener,*
> *And spring is on the way,*
> *And girls are gettin' prettier,*
> *And younger every day.*

At one in the morning, Billy led Annie up into the tree house. They were both as naked as the day they were born. Billy slipped a ring onto Annie's right hand. It was a large, flawless emerald set in gold.

"It's the most beautiful thing I've ever seen," she said. "But we're just kids."

"That's OK," said Billy. "No matter what happens to us, this part of us is going to be kids forever."

POSTSCRIPT

"The bar silver and the arms still lie, for all that I know, where Flint buried them; and certainly they shall lie there for me. Oxen and wain-ropes would not bring me back again to that accursed island; and the worst dreams that ever I have are when I hear the surf booming about its coasts, or start upright in my bed, with the sharp voice of Captain Flint still ringing in my ears: 'Pieces of eight! pieces of eight!'"

   —Robert Louis Stevenson, *Treasure Island*

Bestselling Thrillers —
action-packed for a great read

*Riveting novels of intrigue
and adventure from one of
the great masters of suspense*

JACK HIGGINS
WRITING AS
JAMES GRAHAM

"Slambang action...hairbreadth escapades
and rescues." — *The New York Times*
Three novels of death-defying bravado, mind-boggling
deception and heart-pounding adventure.

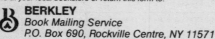